A Riddle in the Lonesome October

A Rae Riley Mystery

JPC Allen

M✟ Zion Ridge Press
Books Off the Beaten Path

www.MtZionRidgePress.com

Mt Zion Ridge Press LLC
295 Gum Springs Rd, NW
Georgetown, TN 37366

https://www.mtzionridgepress.com

ISBN 13: 978-1-962862-85-1
Published in the United States of America
Publication Date: October 1, 2025

Editor-In-Chief: Michelle Levigne
Executive Editor: Tamera Lynn Kraft
Cover art design by Tamera Lynn Kraft
Cover Art Copyright by Mt Zion Ridge Press LLC © 2025

Rae Riley Mysteries

"A Rose from the Ashes" in *Christmas Fiction Off the Beaten Path*
A Shadow on the Snow
A Storm of Doubts
"Bovine" in *Ohio Trail Mix: Adventures and Inspiration Along the Ohio Literary Trail*

Find most of the titles above at this code.

To Ellyn, Anna, and Cole —

Who like their mysteries with cobwebs, cemeteries, and shrieks in the night.

The House of Reuel and Lydia Malinowski

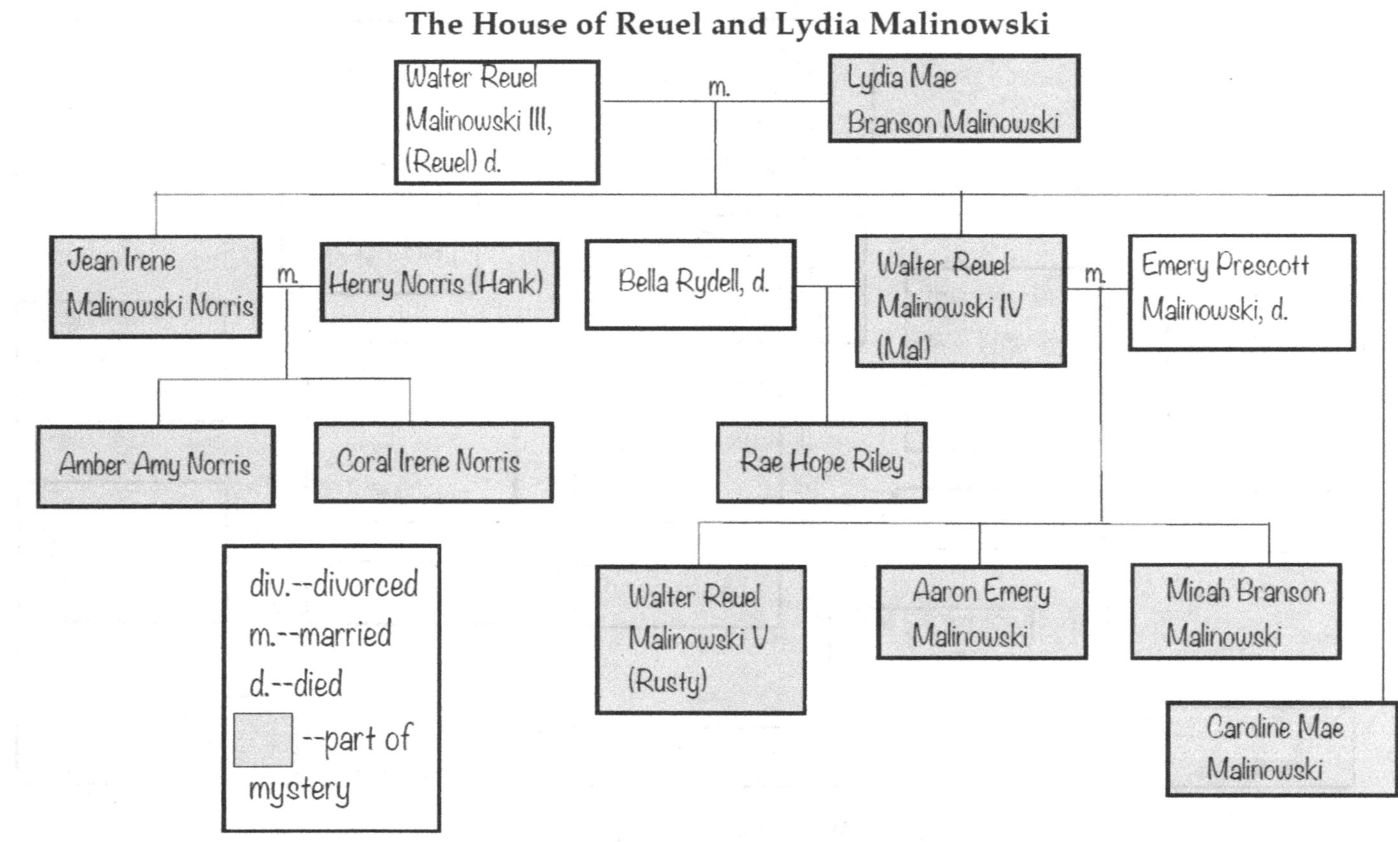

The House of Walter Malinowski Jr.

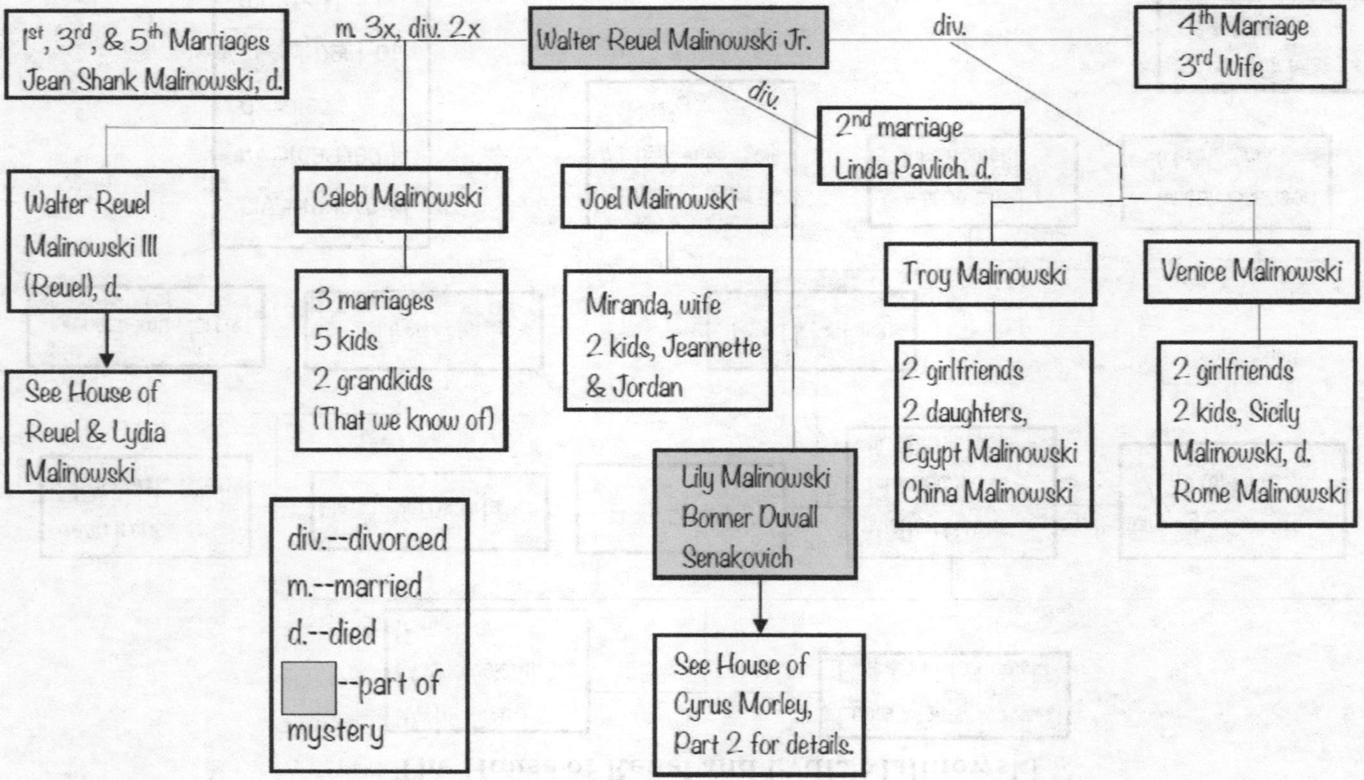

The House of Cyrus Morley, Part 1

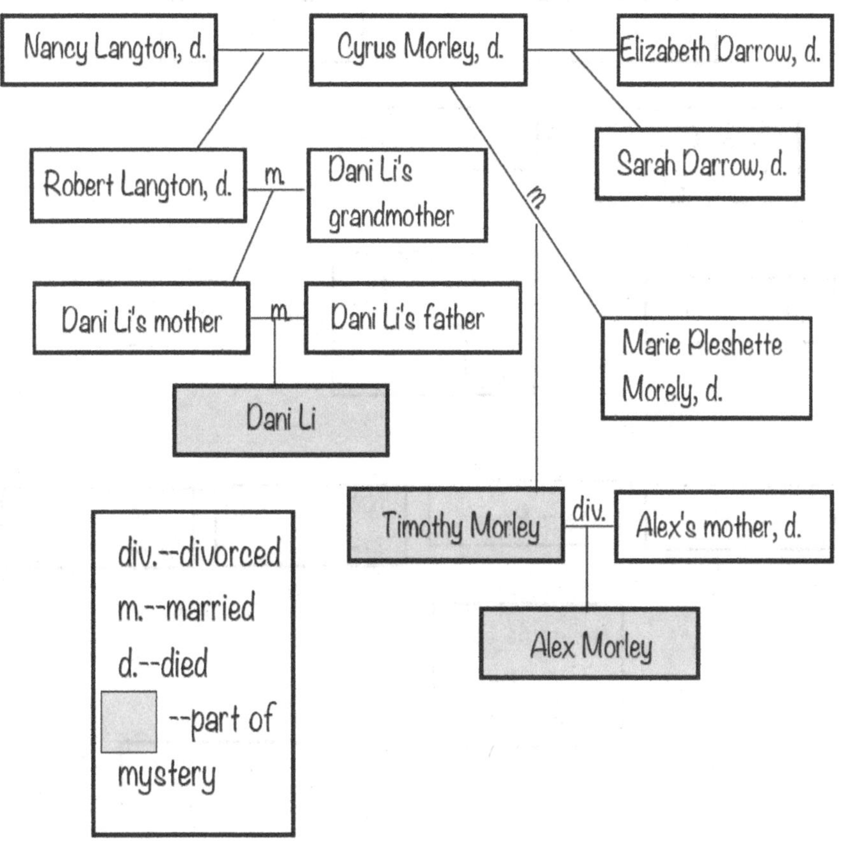

The House of Cyrus Morley, Part 2

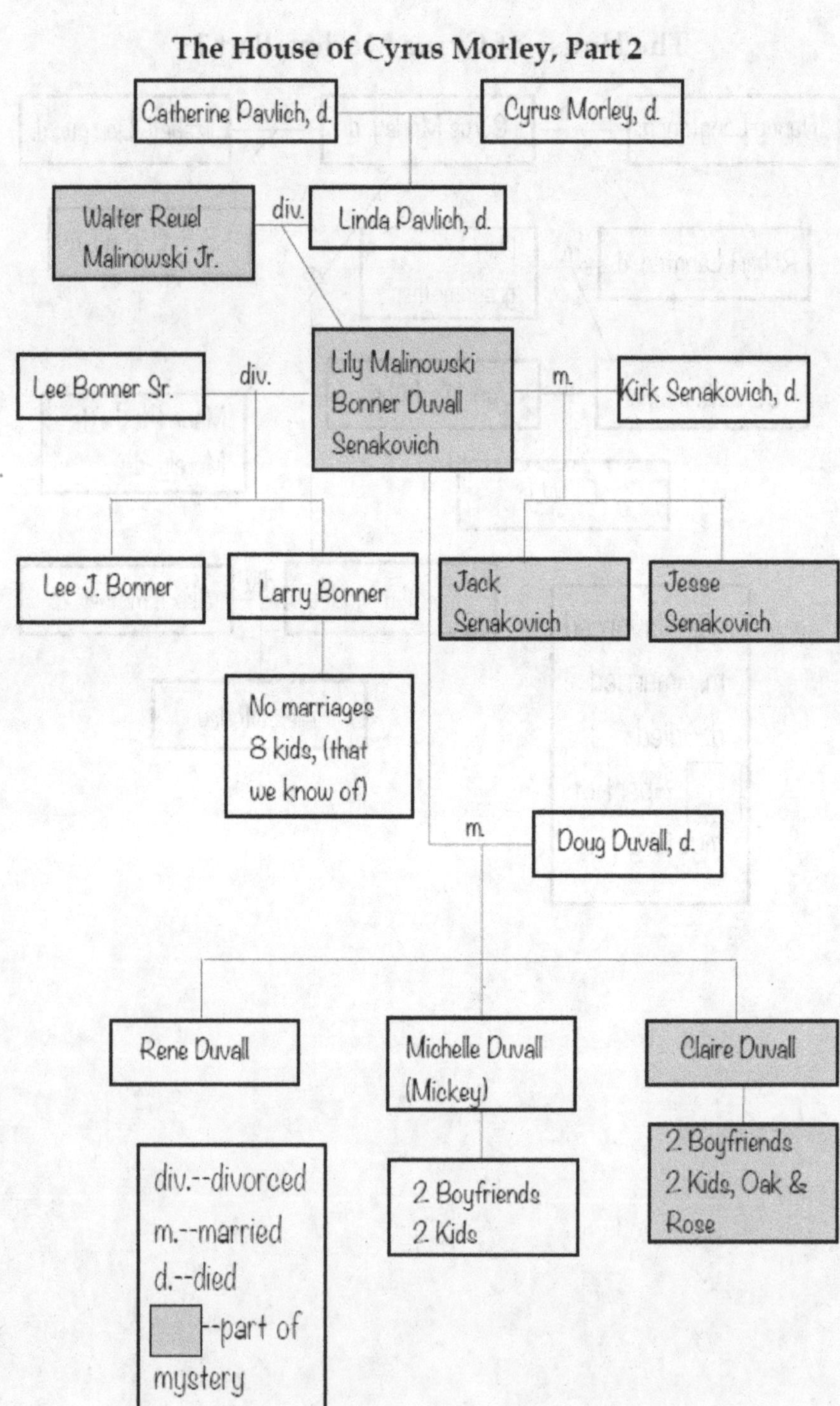

Citizens and Visitors of Marlin County, Ohio

Timothy Morley: only legitimate son of Cyrus Morley

Alex Morley: only child of Timothy Morley

Danielle Li: great-granddaughter of Cyrus Morley and owner of The Haunting in the Hollow

Luke Norris: father of Rae's Uncle Hank

Chris Kincaid: Marlin County deputy and Rae's friend

Kyle Garrison: bigfoot hunter

Lyra Vex: medium and possible grifter

Rick Carlisle: owner and editor of *The Marlin County Recorder*

Jason Carlisle: Rick's younger brother and family friend of the Malinowskis

Devon Majors: Rae's best friend and clerk at the library

Liberty Stone: Devon's ten-year-old daughter

Serenity Stone: Devon's six-year-old daughter

Barb Hanson: library director and Rae's boss

Eric Simcox: Chief of Police of Wellesville

The skies they were ashen and sober;
The leaves they were crisped and sere —
The leaves they were withering and sere;
It was night in the lonesome October
Of my most immemorial year

From "Ulalume" by Edgar Allan Poe

Chapter One

"We've got a bit of a situation here at the children's home, Mal." Aunt Carrie's voice came over the phone. "Or maybe I should call it The Haunting in the Hollow. The signs for it are up now."

"It's Rae," I said. "Dad's driving us home. I'll put you on speaker."

The situation couldn't have been too bad. Carrie sounded annoyed, not concerned. But then as a former deputy marshal and current private detective, my aunt could stay chill during events that would panic most people.

I propped the phone on the computer between me and Dad in his patrol SUV.

Carrie said, "We've got a trespasser. Danielle Li and I told him to leave, but he says he won't go until he speaks to the sheriff. He's Timothy Morley—he showed me his driver's license. He says he's the son of Cyrus Morley, the guy who built the house the county turned into the children's home."

As he pulled the wheel to round a tight bend, Dad's boyish face turned thoughtful. "I remember him. He was trespassing there three years ago."

The phone skidded off the computer. I grabbed it and held it since it wouldn't stay propped.

Dad said, "We'll be there in ... twelve minutes."

As usual, Dad knew exactly how long it would take him to drive between any two points in the county.

"Good deal." Carrie clicked off.

I placed the phone in the pocket on the door, and Dad adjusted his seat so his impressive, 6'6" frame might be a little more comfortable in the patrol vehicle. "Call Ma, Rae. Tell her to have supper without us. I don't know how long we'll be." He glanced at me. "Hope you don't mind."

"Nope." I scrolled to the number of the landline at our farmhouse. "I'm in no rush." I had an empty evening ahead of me, something I'd had too much of recently.

As I swiped off after talking to Gram, Dad muttered, "As if October isn't bad enough." He guided the SUV through a narrow cleft in the rolling hills that made a contour map of Marlin County, Ohio, look like a stormy sea. "That article from a few years ago had to claim Marlin County is one of the weirdest spots in the state. So we get the weirdos—mediums trespassing in cemeteries, ghost hunters trespassing just about anywhere. This Haunting in the Hollow will attract mobs of high school and college kids who may start partying before they get to the county line."

I'd only known Dad was my dad since Christmas, but I'd already heard his October rant too many times. And we were only in the first week. But I was pretty sure he wasn't really exasperated about all the extra work. His father and wife had died in October, and tomorrow was the anniversary of his wife's death. Those facts could make anybody hate it.

"With Morley back in the county—" Dad turned off the windshield wipers "—I may also have to deal with a treasure hunting nut."

My eyebrows bunched. "What treasure is he hunting for?"

"You don't know about Cyrus Morley and the inheritance he hid?"

I tugged on my earlobe. "I've read a little bit about it."

Last year at this time, I was trying to figure out who my dad was. The abandoned children's home had been my late mother's unofficial headquarters for parties and secret meetings with boyfriends when she'd lived in Marlin County before I was born. So I'd dug into its history. But I hadn't looked back much before 2000. All I knew about Cyrus Morley was that he built the house as his private residence in the 1930s. The county bought the house after his death and converted it into a home for orphans. It had stood empty for over fifty years now.

"Cyrus Morley lived off and on in the county for about ten years, using his house as a rustic getaway." Dad veered onto a road so skinny that goldenrod scraped the SUV's side. "When he died, his wife found he had taken most of his money, and all her jewels, and hidden them. In his will, he listed three or four heirs, gave them a clue to the whereabouts of the money in a book of Edgar Allan Poe poems or stories, and stated that whoever of those heirs and—I think—their descendants touched the money first, they got to keep it all."

"How long ago was that?" I said.

"Around 1950."

"And nobody's figured out where he hid the treasure in Marlin County in—in—in seventy years?"

"Well, the clues didn't point only to Marlin County. The man owned other properties. Or he could have hidden it anywhere. Timothy Morley's his son. He got it into his head three years ago that the treasure had to be at the children's home. I found him trespassing there. He went to the county commissioners, and they gave him one weekend to look as long as an officer accompanied him. I was assigned that duty for most of Saturday. He found nothing and decided he had the wrong location."

"So why would he be back?"

The wheels protested around another sharp turn.

"We'll find out," said Dad.

We wound our way through hills and narrow passes. In the first few days of October, the weather had put on a dress rehearsal for Halloween. All day, a marbled gray sky, perfect for witches to take joyrides on their brooms, had loomed over the county while chilly rain spat in fits, and a stiff wind tore at the faded green leaves of oaks, maples, sycamores, and tulip trees.

The roads grew thinner and rougher until we emerged from between two steeply sloped hills into a valley with hunched hills that curved around more than half of it. At the open end of the valley, woods of oaks and maples, flinging arms thick with leaves, covered gently rippled land. Fields punctuated the woods, and at the top of one of them stood the old children's home, originally the Morley Mansion, which looked as eerie as it always did, except trailers and tents ringed it now.

"They did what they promised." I pointed to the line of temporary shelters. "With all the activity of actors and staff working around the home, nobody will think it's cool to sneak in there."

"I hope not." Dad turned onto a drive that was a patchwork of mowed weeds and crumbling asphalt. "It should discourage some, but I never underestimate people's stupidity."

Dad's main objection to the county commissioners allowing Danielle Li to stage her Halloween attraction here was that someone would get hurt in the crumbling, old home as they tried to give themselves a good scare.

We drove under the banner that bellied taut as a gust of wind fattened it. Against a black background, letters printed in fiery red and orange issued the question, "Do You Dare Defy The Haunting in the Hollow?"

Aunt Carrie jogged down the drive to us, and Dad stopped.

She got in the backseat. "Follow the drive up to the house." Taking off a black baseball hat that had "Security" printed on it, she ran her hand through her long, white-blonde hair. "We may have trouble brewing. No danger. Just a family feud they've moved to Marlin County."

Taking his foot off the brake, Dad growled. "Oh, goody. A treasure hunter and a family feud. October's going to be exciting."

Carrie said, "Timothy Morley's complaining that his son, Alex, has only financed The Haunting to gain unrestricted access to the land here so he can hunt for the treasure and prevent Timothy from doing so."

We passed a small, metal shed that would be the ticket booth and a towering banner displaying a man in a black cloak that swirled around him. He stared down at us with a thin eyebrow arched mockingly and a contemptuous smile beneath a black slit of a moustache. "Cyrus Morley" appeared in the same fiery letters as the banner above the entrance.

Had the guy really looked that nasty or was that an artist's invention for the attraction?

Dad parked several yards from a white trailer where an elderly man and the attraction owner, Dani Li, faced each other. As the three of us got out, the wind pushed at our backs, hurling long strands of my mass of hair past my face. Days like these made me wish for a crewcut like Dad's. At least the rain had stopped.

In a few strides, Dad shifted into cop mode—his face grew blank, he straightened to his full height, and his strides picked up speed. Carrie matched his pace and posture. With their athletic builds and serious expressions, they looked like Thor and Valkyrie preparing to battle a supervillain.

Glancing over the tents and trailers situated around the home, I was glad the old ruin wasn't a scene in The Haunting. Last year in October, I'd laid roses in the grate of the enormous fireplace to get people talking about the fire that had supposedly killed my mom and me as I tried to uncover who my dad was. At a meeting at the home on Christmas morning, Dad and I figured out it could only be him. So the dilapidated mansion was special to me. Using it as a stage for a fake bloodbath felt wrong.

Dani Li said in a sharp tone, "Why do you keep saying this event is a fraud, Timothy?" She was about thirty, the ends of her black hair sneaking from the hood she'd pulled up on her rain jacket. "I'm not hunting for any treasure. I'm putting on a five-star entertainment."

"If that's true, then Alex has duped you as well as the county commissioners." The elderly man—he had to be over seventy—spoke in a high, clipped voice and clutched a thick book in one hand, looking down on Dani like she gave off an unpleasant odor.

Not that he had far to look down. He was probably half a foot shorter than my 5'11" and appeared withered. His dark eyes and cheeks were sunk, his coarse gray and white hair looked dry enough to work as tinder, and his moustache appeared shriveled to his lip.

He turned to Dad. "Sheriff, if my son and this woman—" The old man peered at him. "I know you, don't I?"

"Yes, Mr. Morley." Dad used his cop voice, putting more volume and authority into his already strong baritone. "W.R. Malinowski. Three years ago, I escorted you when I was a deputy and you had permission to search the property. You didn't find the treasure then. Why are you back?"

"I've uncovered new information that I want to test."

"Then you should go to the county commissioners and get their permission."

"This young woman—" he snapped a nod at Dani "—has no authority to tell me to leave. Neither has your sister. I am my father's only—" He stared at me. "Another sister?"

"No," Dad said. "My daughter, Rae Riley."

Mr. Morley drew back like he suspected a lie, while Dani raised her eyebrows above her thick-rimmed glasses.

Their reactions weren't unexpected. Being only eighteen years apart, Dad and I were often mistaken for a couple or brother and sister, although the only features we shared were dark gold hair and way above average height.

Mr. Morley said, "If you tell me I'm trespassing, Sheriff, then of course, I'll obey an officer of the law. But I see no reason to listen to Ms. Li or her head of security because she happens to be renting my father's land."

"It's the county's land." Dad rested his hand on the butt of his gun. "They both have the authority to bounce anyone they wish while the land is leased to Ms. Li."

"Look, Timothy." Dani's tone turned friendly as she touched him on the arm.

Mr. Morley's expression of displeasure froze.

Dani snatched her hand back. "Personally, I have no problem with you searching for the treasure, but my insurance won't cover you if you have an accident. And Alex specifically stated he didn't want you on the grounds. He's the money man."

"I suppose the fact that your grandfather is one of my father's illegitimate children and is mentioned in his will had no bearing on your decision to go into business with Alex."

She shrugged. "No. I go where the money is. I didn't even know I was related to Cyrus or an heir to his fortune until I met Alex."

Mr. Morley looked in the direction of the banner of his father. "You're certainly exploiting your connection."

"Exploiting? The guy was a 24/7 Halloween party." A grin rounded her cheeks as she looked to us. "Cyrus Morley was an occult geek. Every Halloween, he'd throw a party here for his high society friends. He was an Edgar Allan Poe geek too, so he actually called his party — get this — The Masque of the Red Death. My whole storyline for the attraction is based on Cyrus and Poe. He'd love this!" She waved at the woods and house. "Timothy, talk to Alex. If he says it's okay for you to search here, then I can come up with some rules that will be compatible with my insurance."

The little man stiffened. "I am not a fool, Ms. Li." He wheeled and marched down the drive.

"FYI, Dani." Carrie watched Mr. Morley head toward a sedan parked along the road, "Alex can't prevent his father from paying admission to attend. That'd be discrimination. But if Mr. Morley doesn't stick with his group, I can remove him."

"I hope it doesn't come to that." Dani thrust out her hand to Dad. "Nice to see you again, Sheriff. I remember you from the commissioners' meeting."

Dad's hand enveloped hers. "Call me Mal."

Shifting her attention to me, she cocked her head to one side, like a curious warbler. That was what she reminded me of when she interviewed me for a job at The Haunting—a little bird that had twice as much energy as bigger creatures because it had so much less to fuel. She said, "We've met, haven't we?"

"Yes. Rae Riley. You hired me to work in the ticket booth."

Dad frowned, like he always did when the topic of my temporary job came up. But since I was twenty, all he could do was frown. And object. A lot.

"That's right." Dani's head cocked a fraction more, tilting her black bangs. "Your dad is Malinowski, and you're Riley?"

I opened my mouth, but words didn't form. It'd take an hour to explain the whole thing properly, and my mind wrestled with a succinct reply.

"Long story," Dad said. "You also hired Amber Norris, Carrie's and my niece."

She fired quick glances at both of us. "Is this county entirely populated with your relatives?"

"At times, it seems like that," Dad said, heaving a sigh. "Ms. Li, don't hesitate to call my agency if there's any trouble." He looked to Carrie. "You can have supper with Rae and me if you want to."

"Thanks, but I'm working here as long as I can since we're opening in two days." Turning her back to a gust of wind, Carrie disappeared between two trailers.

Dani rubbed her hands together. "Online tickets are almost sold out for this weekend. It's the best opening of any of my attractions, and this is my fifth year doing them." She gave us a friendly nod and then climbed the steps to the white trailer.

As Dad and I walked back to the SUV, he said, "I need to talk to Jeanine about this whole Morley treasure-inheritance mess. About five years ago, she researched it for a mystery she was writing, and I know she'd file all that material away in case she could use it in another—holy smoke!" He stopped dead next to his vehicle.

Raising my hand to block hair being blown into my face, I said, "What?"

"I just remembered a part of that stupid will. Aunt Lily is a granddaughter of Cyrus Morley."

My eyebrows rose. "Does that mean we're related too?"

"No. Thank You, Lord," Dad said to the sky. "Aunt Lily's mother was Linda Pavlich. She was one of the illegitimate children Cyrus listed as an heir. Linda was Walter's second wife. Since we're descended through

Grandma Jean, we're no relation to the Morleys."

"Mr. Morley said Dani's descended from an illegitimate child too. Sounds like Cyrus was a colossal jerk."

"Based on her research, Jeanine said ol' Cyrus built the house here, not to look after the coal mines in the county he owned, but so he could engage in all kinds of immoral activities that were harder to get away with in New York or Boston or wherever he was from." Dad scratched an eyebrow. "I'll have to refresh my memory, but I'm pretty sure Aunt Lily and all her descendants have a legal right to that treasure."

I brought up in my mind the family trees I'd drawn when I discovered I had a horde of new relatives to learn about, all descended from my great-grandfather, Walter Malinowski Jr. "Aunt Lily has seven kids and — and —"

"Twelve grandkids, that she knows of." Dad flung open his door. "Just what I need — another headache in October."

I wiped grass clippings from my shoes as best I could before I got in the SUV.

Great-Aunt Lily's family belonged to the outlaw branch of the Malinowski clan, and if they bought the possibility that they could find the treasure, they might try to live up to the outlaw part even more.

Chapter Two

The thickening gloom of the overcast evening was nothing compared to the gloom that radiated from Dad as he turned onto the dead-end road that led to our farm. He hadn't spoken since we'd left The Haunting, and I'd sensed he didn't want me to break the silence.

Maples and tulip trees lined the rough road while honeysuckle strung with blood red fruit filled in every space between the trunks. Stalks of faded blue chicory bent in the wind.

Dad finally said in a quiet voice, so unlike his usual booming one, "The family's laying flowers on Em's grave tomorrow. We can meet you at the church after you get off work. If you want to come. You don't have to. You didn't know Em."

"She was your wife and my brothers' mom. I'd like to come." I put my hand on his right one as it turned the wheel.

He threw me a grateful smile.

The SUV swung onto our drive and followed it down past the alpaca barn. My uncle's black stallion Knight and my cousins' two bays nibbled wet grass in a pasture the alpacas weren't occupying.

"Gram must have invited Uncle Hank and Amber and Coral for supper," I said as we rolled past the horses and then up the drive to our pale yellow farmhouse with the half-moon window overlooking the front porch.

"I bet Jeanine's got a story or editing deadline," Dad said.

The door to the double garage was open as we pulled up to it, the light inside as inviting as a crackling fire on a winter's night. And the night was feeling more like winter every minute.

Uncle Hank had the hood up on my truck, his hands fiddling with the innards.

Dad turned around the SUV so it pointed down the drive, and we got out.

Pushing back his worn, brown cowboy hat over his dark, wiry hair, Hank stepped back from the hood. Anyone wearing a cowboy hat in Ohio stood out, but Hank's lanky build suited it. He looked to his younger daughter seated behind the steering wheel. "Try 'er now, Coral."

My cousin cranked the ignition The engine caught, and through the windshield, Coral's freckled face brightened.

Unfastening his duty belt, Dad said to his brother-in-law, "I suppose you didn't leave much supper for Rae and me."

"Couldn't help it. Okay, Coral, cut it." Hank picked up a rag from one of the shelves that lined that side of the garage and wiped his hands. "When Jeanine's got a deadline, nothing else matters. The girls and I were so starved, we could barely ride here."

Dad hung his belt over his shoulder. "Too bad Jeanine didn't marry someone literate. You could help her with her writing."

"Jeanine's too good a writer to need any help." An ornery glint lit up Hank's extra big brown eyes, and his usual good-humored grin stretched his extra wide mouth. "But I know you sympathize with me. Who reads for you at the office?"

Watching Dad and Uncle Hank, Coral climbed out of the cab and grinned too.

I was still getting used to their relationship of insults. It'd been just Mom and me growing up, so male behavior was as exotic to me as the habits of red-spotted newts. But since I'd moved in with Gram, Dad, and my three half-brothers in February, I'd taken an intensive course in guyness.

Letting my camera backpack hang from my hand, I said, "Thanks for fixing the Rust Bucket, Uncle Hank."

"Our pleasure," he said, and Coral nodded, her chin-length copper hair swishing against her cheeks. "But if you want to keep your truck on the road, you're gonna have to invest in a new timing chain."

"Since I'm working at The Haunting in the Hollow, I'll have some extra money."

"You can put that toward college tuition," said Dad.

My jaw clenched. Yet another missile launched in Dad's battle to persuade me to go to college. That was his main objection to me working at The Haunting. If I had enough free time for a second job, I had enough time for college.

"Oh, hey, Rae, Uncle Mal." My cousin Amber rode up to the garage on her bay, Shadowfax. "Wish I could stay and visit but I've got to study for a pre-calc test."

My cousin's powder blue rain jacket and leggings seemed all wrong for her fairytale princess beauty. Thick, red-gold hair grew to her waist, and her brown eyes had long lashes that appeared black against her pearly pale complexion. If she wore armor or a silk gown, she'd look perfect on her horse.

Shadowfax threw up his head with a loud whinny.

Dad started and took a big step backward into the garage.

Leaning over her horse's neck, Amber murmured in his twitching ear. Then she sat up and said in her breathless voice, "Sorry, Uncle Mal. You don't have to be afraid."

"Horses just make me nervous." Dad trotted out his usual explanation for his reaction to horses and took another step back.

In Dad's case, "nervous" was a synonym for "scared." Perfectly understandable since he'd fallen off a horse and broken his arm as a kid.

"Mal, you have any second thoughts about the girls working at that Halloween thing?" Hank returned the rag to the shelf. "I figure if any guy gets out of line, Carrie'll hammer him."

"Dad." Amber groaned. "Uncle Mal's taught us self-defense, and Rae and I are Malinowskis. We can take care of ourselves."

My cousin had a lot more confidence she could deal with any would-be drunks or creeps than I did. And I'd survived some pretty dangerous situations.

"Self-defense lessons don't mean you can take care of yourselves like Carrie," Dad said. "It'll be fine, Hank."

"It's great we'll be working together, Rae." Amber squealed the last word, her stunning face glowing.

My fanatical following of one. Amber considered me the coolest person on the planet. At first it was because I was four years older than she was, which automatically made me fascinating to her. Then the criminal cases I'd been involved in had only increased my coolness.

Hank placed a wrench in a toolbox. "Amber, tell Mom that me and Coral are going on a trail ride as long as the rain holds off."

Backing her horse a few steps, Amber looked down at her younger sister. "Coral, don't you have math homework?"

Folding her arms, Coral slouched against my truck. "That's none of your business."

Hank glanced at his younger daughter. "Do you, punkin?"

"I did." Coral spoke to the grimy concrete floor. "I got it done."

Amber rolled her eyes. "Then why didn't you say so?"

"Because it's none of your business." Coral shoved off the Rust Bucket. "I'm in seventh grade. I can keep track of my own homework. You're not Mom. You're not—"

"Amber, you'd better get home," Hank said in a tired voice.

I got why he sounded so weary. Any time I had to referee one of my cousins' fights, I felt exhausted.

"I was trying to help." Amber turned Shadowfax to head down the drive, her long hair swirling around her like a fiery cape.

Coral's big brown eyes attempted to drill holes in that cape.

As he resettled his cowboy hat on his head, Hank's ornery grin was back in place. "When it's harvest time, Mal, you should help us. You need some kind of exercise. Although after riding a desk for so long, I'm not sure you can handle real work."

Leaving the garage, Dad said over his shoulder, "Must not be real work if you can do it."

I followed Dad through the breezeway to the screened porch on the side of our house. We took off our shoes and left them on the porch before we entered the sunny yellow kitchen.

Gram twisted a knob on the stove. "Spaghetti will be ready in five minutes after the water boils." Her dark blue eyes held a calm that always welcomed me.

After Mom died, I didn't know if any place would ever feel like home. But seeing Gram, her slim figure sauntering between the stove and counter, working her culinary arts in a kitchen as cheerful as a May morning, had become a new sign of home for me.

As I hurried through the big living-dining room, thumps came from overhead. In the upstairs playroom, my three half-brothers were playing, or fighting, or possibly both.

I changed from my work clothes into jeans and a sweatshirt. The first week of October seemed too early in the fall for a sweatshirt, but I was chilled from standing out at the children's home. The Morley Mansion. The Haunting. Whatever.

Dad was already seated at the table. His worn plaid shirt and jeans transformed him instantly from upright, imposing cop to rumpled dad.

As we dug into our spaghetti, we chatted about his day at the sheriff's office and mine at the library. Dad was interested in what I had to say — he always was — but from his odd pauses, he acted preoccupied.

Helping himself to a third breadstick, he said, "Did you have a chance to look at those brochures I got from those colleges?"

A sigh escaped before I could intercept it.

"Rae, I wouldn't keep bringing up college if I didn't think you could do it or it would benefit you."

I spun the few remaining noodles I had on my fork, but they wouldn't catch. "I told you my grades."

"Just because your grades slipped while your mother was dying doesn't mean —"

"My grades didn't slip." I dropped my fork. "They sank without a trace. I'm sure I didn't pass half my classes, and the only reason I graduated was because some of my teachers took pity on me."

"That was two years ago. Now you're in a position to do school right."

I fell back against my rail chair. "Feels like it's been a hundred."

So much had happened since Mom had given me the clues to my dad's identity — her death, my move to Marlin County, my investigation for my father, discovering Dad, and getting to know him and all my new relatives, some of whom I'd rather forget. On top of all that, I'd been caught in mysteries — a stalker, a disappearance, and whether Chris Kincaid, after knowing me a year, wanted to be more than friends.

Dad speared lettuce from his salad bowl. "I know you're bored. That's why you took the second job."

I reached for a bottle of salad dressing. "Yeah, sometimes. But everybody is now and again."

But it had been a whole lot more of now than again over the past couple of months. I'd held my job as checkout clerk at the library for over a year now, so there was nothing new to learn. As much as I loved being a member of my new family, I sometimes stared at my days off like they were huge holes I was desperate to fill. Unless I'd planned to hike somewhere with Chris and take photos.

Dad ripped his breadstick in half. "You're too smart to settle for your job at the library for the next forty years. Adding whatever second jobs you can pick up won't help."

Wow. He hadn't used that argument before. Combined with my current attitude about my job, his statement made working as a library clerk seem like cruel and unusual punishment.

As the landline rang, I hooked a few strands of dark gold hair behind my ear. "I don't know what to major in, so I'd waste your money. I can't major in photography. Most jobs in that field don't pay enough to pay off college debts."

Dad swallowed a chunk of breadstick. "It depends on what degree you get. I've done some research, and photography could —"

"That was Jeanine." Gram placed the landline in its base, concern creasing her normal expression of quiet assurance. "Something's wrong. Coral's horse came back to their house without her."

Chapter Three

As I turned in my chair, Dad was on his feet. "Is Amber home?"

"Yes," said Gram. "She said Hank and Coral were trail riding as long as the rain didn't return."

Dad strode through the maze of toys, books, shoes, and socks in the living room, glancing out one of the front windows as the rain beat a steady rhythm on the roof of the porch. "Coral may have been thrown, and Hank's staying with her until help comes."

That catapulted me out of my seat, and Gram ran to join Dad at the coat closet.

Reaching for her broad-brimmed hat on the shelf, Gram said, "Jeanine and Amber are riding the trails from their farm toward us, and Luke's set out from his farm."

"Boys," Dad called up the steps, loud enough to make me jump as he handed me my rain jacket. "Come down."

My three brothers thundered down the stairs in opposite order of age: Micah, his strawberry blonde hair plastered to his forehead from sweat; Aaron, breathing hard; and Rusty, towering above his younger brothers from a growth spurt.

Dad explained the situation, his tone matter of fact, his words neutral. But Rusty's pipe cleaner body went stiff, and his bony hand clutched the railing.

"I'm sure it's not serious, boys." Dad looked straight at Rusty. "If Coral fell off and broke something, Hank won't leave her."

Aaron massaged his chin. "But why wouldn't he carry her out?"

I zipped my jacket. I'd been asking myself that question since Dad suggested our cousin had been thrown.

"Boys, stay here." Dad shrugged into his tan work coat. "We'll be back as —"

Micah yanked on a pocket of Dad's coat. "We can help you look."

"No." Dad gave his head a sharp shake. "I can't be trying to keep track of you all and —"

"Mal." Gram placed her hat over her smoke gray hair. "If you, Rae, and I split up, each of us can take one of the boys. They can be runners to guide the rest of the family to Hank and Coral when we find them."

Dad went still, his focus turning inward as he considered.

"It's a good idea." I put on a baseball hat, then pulled up the hood of my rain jacket.

At eight, ten and thirteen, my brothers were surefooted and moved faster through the woods than any of us adults could. And we had to have some substitute since our phones got no reception on the farm. But I knew Dad was afraid of the boys seeing what we'd find.

Father, please let this all be something silly or not serious.

"If you all can get ready in three minutes, you can come." Dad moved toward the kitchen.

We shoved on boots that we'd left in the screened porch, and in less than two minutes, the six of us shot out of the breezeway and down the hill to the woods.

The rain poured, but inside the woods, the still-thick canopy of maple, tulip, and sycamore leaves cut the waterfall to a shower.

Handing out flashlights, Dad said, "Micah and I will take the direct trail to the Norris's farm. Ma, you and Aaron head—"

"Dad." Micah tugged on the leg of his jeans. "Do you hear the yodel? Maybe it's Uncle Hank."

Dad hushed all of us, and we listened for the call Gram had learned from her father and taught us to use over long distances, like when she wanted the boys to come in for supper.

The leaves clattered under the drive of raindrops, but no human sound reached us.

"Must've been an animal." Dad clicked on his flashlight. "Ma, head east along—"

The Branson yodel slipped under the rhythm of the rain.

Dad shone his light along the riding trail that followed the creek west, dividing our property from the Norris's farm.

I said, "Could it be Aunt Jeanine or Amber?"

Dad shook his head. "They couldn't have gotten here so fast. Boys, you stay here. And I mean that." He broke into a run. "Ma, Rae, come on."

Gram and I switched on our flashlights and followed the trail as fast as we could, playing the light over the path to reveal half-buried roots and rocks, the creek churning with rainwater to our right. With the interlocking grips of overhead branches blocking what little light the evening still held, the woods became a cavern.

The Branson yodel, bouncing between two notes three times, pierced the twilight.

Dad spurted ahead, and I cranked my legs faster, honeysuckle and spice bush fingering me with their spindly twigs.

Please, Father, let Coral be all right.

Panic clawed my chest. The rain, the woods, our running were a little too much like a night I'd experienced back in June. At least there was no wind and lightning. And no nut job behind me.

Steep hills reared up black and featureless as the yodel rose above the boil of the creek.

My toe snagged a root. A desperate grab at a tree trunk kept me upright.

The hills loomed larger, like the blank wall of an evil fortress.

The closer we got, the more distinct the yodel grew, and it sounded too high-pitched for Hank. And another noise reached us — a squeal from an animal. It had to be Knight.

The beam of Dad's flashlight stopped bouncing and shone over the spot where the creek widened into a pool as skinny streams of water fell from the hills to form it.

Coral was standing in the middle of the pool.

Holding Hank's head and shoulders above the water.

As Knight, on his side in the pool, flailed his legs and his head.

Hank had to be pinned under his horse, and only Coral was keeping him from drowning.

Chapter Four

I crashed to a halt on the edge of the pool.

Her hands under Hank's armpits, Coral moved her head a millimeter toward us. "Dad's trapped," she said in a flat voice. "He's trapped under Knight."

That was what it sounded like, but Coral's teeth were chattering so much that it was hard to tell.

Knight held his head above the water as his legs thrashed, spraying the creek. His neck trembling, he released a terrified whinny.

Throwing off his jacket and plaid shirt, Dad dropped into the pool.

Gram ran out of the gloom and skidded to a stop.

Plowing through the water toward Coral and Hank, Dad said, "We gotta get Knight on his feet."

"You can't." Coral spoke in a monotone. "Knight broke his front left leg."

I aimed my beam at Knight as his legs pawed the air and ... I swung the beam away, swallowing.

Hank's head lolled against Coral's shoulder, the water streaming around his limp body. No sign he was conscious.

Dad waded in until the water swirled at his knees. "Ma, go tell Rusty to call 911. Tell him to tell them we've got a man who probably has a badly broken leg and may be hypothermic. He should call Doc Volmer too and explain Knight's injuries."

"Absolutely." Gram sprinted back down the trail.

Stripping down to my t-shirt, I sat on the bank and then slipped into the pool. The cold water sucked my breath away.

"Rae, hold your flashlight on Hank." Dad felt around his neck. "Coral, was your dad conscious after he landed in the water?"

"Yeah." Coral stared ahead.

Dad worked his hand under the back of Hank's jean jacket. "Was he moving his arms and legs?"

"Yeah."

I thought she might add some details, but she didn't, so I said, "Was he trying to free himself?"

She nodded.

"When did he become unconscious?" Dad continued his exam of Hank's back.

"He yelled." She didn't look at either one of us. "And his head went under the water."

"Knight probably moved, and he passed out from the pain." Dad straightened and waded to where Hank's leg was trapped under the horse. "Hold the light high, Rae."

As I lifted it, Dad plunged beneath the water.

Knight's head fell under the surface, then sprang free. He whinnied in a shriek. How long could he hold his head high enough to breathe?

I looked down at Hank. His lips appeared blue.

Father, bring help fast.

Dad emerged from the water. "Hank's right leg is smashed between Knight and the creek bed. His foot may be stuck in the stirrup."

"Oh, no." A raspy cry drew my attention to the bank opposite of the one Dad, Gram and I had followed.

Luke Norris slid off his appaloosa and down the bank, his baseball hat falling off, revealing his thick black and white hair. He thrashed through the flowing water and shoved Coral out of the way to hold his son's head out of the water.

"Get that horse up," Mr. Norris said in a croak.

"His leg's broken." Dad shivered, his black t-shirt dripping. "Can you get Knight to roll onto his chest, even a little? The rest of us can use branches to leverage Knight off Hank's leg even more. Then we can pull Hank free."

"You'll have to unbuckle the saddle first." Mr. Norris held Hank with one arm against his knees, pressing shaking fingers into his son's neck.

"I'll hold Uncle Hank, Mr. Norris, while you help Knight." I hugged myself as goose bumps rose under freezing droplets on my arms.

The old man stared at me, like he struggled to translate my offer, his drenched slicker making him look more like a scarecrow than usual. Then he let me slip my hands under Hank's shoulders.

Mr. Norris sloshed through the pool to Knight's head. "Hold the light, Walter, so I can grab the reins."

Stooping over Hank, I gritted my teeth. Even in an emergency, Mr. Norris couldn't call Dad by his preferred name, once again showing how much he disliked his daughter-in-law's family.

Dad pointed the beam at the stallion.

Making soothing noises, Mr. Norris fished in the running water and picked up one of the reins. Choking up on it, he approached Knight's head.

Coral stood behind me, every inch of her shaking.

"Get on the bank, Coral," I said, my back muscles sending out aching questions about the hunched posture I'd assumed. "Put on my jacket."

Reeling closer to Knight on the reins, Mr. Norris pulled the stallion's head against his chest.

"I'll get the saddle free." Dad waded around Knight's rump.

"Oh, my — " Amber clopped up beside her grandfather's appaloosa on Shadowfax. "Dad? Dad!" Her screech sent a shiver through me and set off more.

Knight jerked, rocking Mr. Norris.

"He'll drown!" Amber screamed.

Arching his neck, Knight pawed at the water.

Hank hadn't made a sound or move since I'd seen him. Tears wanted to mingle with rain on my icy cheeks.

Cradling the stallion's head, Mr. Norris said, "Walter, you can't unbuckle the saddle that way."

Stopping between Knight's legs, Dad stared at him across the injured horse. "What do — "

Knight's body convulsed in a frenzy of kicking.

Tumbling away from the flailing legs, Dad landed on his butt in the pool. He snatched his flashlight out of the water and scrambled to his feet.

"Whoa, easy." Mr. Norris hung onto the horse's head as it pulled him around.

"Please, God, please," Amber sobbed. "Don't let him die."

"Dad." I fought tremors in my voice. "The buckles are facing up. You might be able to reach over Knight's back and undo them."

Dad trudged toward the bank where Amber sat glued to her mount. "Amber, get down and hold the light so I can unfasten the buckles."

Amber said through sobs, "Please, God, save him. Save both of them."

"Amber!" Dad released his bellow at top volume.

Usually, that would have startled me, but my body was too busy shivering to react. Amber screamed but stopped praying, staring at Dad like she'd just realized he was standing in front of her.

"I'll hold the flashlight." Coral appeared by his side.

"Point it at the saddle." Dad waded back to us.

The rain increased, penetrating the leaf shield, but I only noticed because more water dripped from the bill of my cap. I was too wet to feel more wet.

Leaning over the horse's back, Dad fumbled around the buckles and jumped back when Knight kicked. The kicks weren't as high or frantic. Either Mr. Norris was soothing him or Knight was losing strength.

"The saddle's loose." Dad stepped back by me. "Amber and I will get some branches. Then Rae, Amber, and I will leverage Knight up long enough for Coral to pull Hank out. If she can." He turned to the bank where the two horses shifted on their hooves. "Amber. We need you. Now."

Amber swung her right leg out of her stirrup and fell between the horses. The appaloosa whinnied and trotted out of sight, up the trail.

Rolling to her knees, Amber burst into louder sobs.

Muttering a word I'd never heard him use, Dad splashed to the bank, picked up my cousin, and carried her into the pool.

He plunked her in the water and took her face in one hand. "Stand here."

She nodded, tears and rain coursing down her cheeks.

"What can I do?" Gram ran up to the pool, unbuttoning her duster.

Dad climbed up beside her. "Find the strongest branches you can. We've got to pry Knight off Hank's leg."

My spine sent out creaking protests as my toes lost feeling.

"Daddy?" Amber touched Uncle Hank's shoulder.

"He's unconscious." I had to say the obvious before she jumped to the worst conclusion.

"Are you—are you sure?" Her tears fell in a torrent.

Dad carried two thick branches that looked as tall as he was into the water while Gram dragged in a third.

His face stern, Dad glanced from Gram to Amber, weighing some kind of judgement. Then Dad grabbed Amber's hand. "Amber, hold your dad. Ma, you, Rae and I will hold Knight up with the branches." Bit by bit, I moved out of the way as Amber, her body convulsing with sobs, shoved her hands under her dad's shoulders.

Aiming the flashlight up between them, Dad gripped Amber's chin. "Keep your dad above the water. He'll die if you don't. When I say 'pull', you pull. Coral can help, but I doubt if she can do it on her own. You have to do this. Got it?"

Shivering from her head to where her legs disappeared into the gushing water, Amber nodded.

"Coral, help your sister." Dad handed me a branch.

Coral waded to Amber with slow steps, like she was hanging out in the creek with my brothers on a summer afternoon.

Dad and Gram stationed themselves by Knight's rump. I positioned myself by his withers. None of us could block the saddle. I planted one end of my branch into the bed and spaced my legs, left one forward. Dad and Gram did the same. My fingers felt thick as they numbed, and I gripped the branch until the rough wood bit into my palms.

"When you're ready, Mr. Norris," said Dad over the racing water.

Nodding, the old man wound the reins around one hand.

I tightened my grip on the branch.

Mr. Norris murmured to Knight, his soft voice coaxing, pulling on the reins and leading the horse's head forward.

Knight's back rolled up.

"Now." Dad pushed his branch forward. "Pull, Coral. Pull, Amber."

Grinding my frozen feet into the rocky bottom, I pressed the branch against Knight's withers, my arms expending every ounce of energy I could dredge up.

The saddle shifted and then slid off.

"He's free." Dad's deep voice went high. "Mr. Norris, you can let Knight down."

Still talking in soothing tones, Mr. Norris let the reins go slack, and Knight rolled toward us.

I jerked my branch out of the water.

Dad gathered Hank in his arms and carried him to the bank. "Ma, spread your duster, dry side up. And see if any of our clothes here on the bank are dry."

He laid Hank on it and pressed trembling fingers against Hank's throat

Amber and Coral kneeled on either side of their father.

I'd barely made it to the bank when Dad thrust his pen knife at me. "Cut Hank's clothes off him." He placed his hand on Hank's chest.

I unbuttoned my uncle's jean jacket, my fingers fumbling. "We can't pull his clothes off?"

"A hypothermic person is very fragile." Dad's fingers probed Hank's body, performing some kind of first-aid assessment. "Too much movement could trigger a heart attack."

"Oh, God, please," Amber screamed.

"Somebody take this horse." That was the loudest Mr. Norris had ever sounded in the months I'd known him.

"Mr. Norris, I'll take your place as soon as I immobilize Hank's leg." Dad peered at the bloody tear in Hank's jeans right below his knee. "Ma, press your hand above the wound." He grabbed his plaid shirt, tore off a sleeve, wadded it, and handed it to Gram.

I sawed on Hank's clothes, avoiding any glimpses of the unnatural way his right foot lay, while Gram applied pressure. Dad tore his plaid shirt into strips and tied the wad of cloth over the wound.

"Wh-what's wrong?" Riding a palomino, Aunt Jeanine reined in beside Shadowfax, who nibbled at something by the base of a tree.

"Hank broke his leg. And his ankle and foot." Dad placed two straight branches on either side of the injured leg. "He's hypothermic too. Cross the creek wherever you can stay dry. We need dry clothes."

As Dad used more strips of his shirt to fix Hank's leg to the branches, I tossed away most of his left pant leg. "That's all the clothes I can get rid of without moving him."

"Cover him with whatever clothes are dry."

In a couple minutes, Aunt Jeanine was beside me, draping her sweatshirt over her husband's bare, wet chest.

I tucked Dad's coat around Hank. "I'll take care of Knight, Dad."

Freezing in the water wasn't much different than freezing in the air.

"No, I can take the cold better than you." Dad tied the last knot on his rough splint, then dropped into the pool. "Go get more blankets and towels and dry clothes for everyone. And lead the paramedics if they've made it here already."

As Gram, Jeanine and I covered Hank with every dry garment available, Mr. Norris transferred Knight's head into Dad's arms. He said, "Someone has to call Dr. Volmer. She'll have to put Knight down."

My stomach turned as icy as the rest of me as Amber loosed a scream, "Not Knight!"

"I already told Rusty to call her." Gram had wrapped her arms around Coral.

Trembling, Mr. Norris pulled himself out of the pool and sank to his knees beside his son, his only child, and Jeanine removed a knit hat she was wearing and gently pulled it over Hank's head.

"Rae, get going." Dad's teeth clacked together. "Take Amber with you."

"Got it." I picked up a flashlight from the ground where someone had tossed it and pulled Amber to her feet.

"Watch out for the monster." Coral spoke in the same tone she'd have used if she was warning me about poison ivy.

The whole family stared at her, even Dad from his awkward position, holding Knight.

"What monster?" Gram wiped wet hair from the side of Coral's blank face.

"The one that spooked Knight. That's why Knight fell and Dad got trapped." Her big brown eyes were aimed at me, but I wasn't sure how much they were seeing. "The monster did it."

Rain pitter-pattered on the overhead leaves, and the water in the pool churned into the creek.

"We'll be careful." I towed Amber after me.

What monster was Coral talking about? Nobody knew the woods better than Coral. She wouldn't mistake a coyote or a hawk for a weird creature.

Amber stumbled behind me as if she'd forgotten how to do anything but cry. I couldn't even break into a jog, and she stopped moving completely if I let go of her hand.

The rain petered out to a drizzle. The wind made the only sound, scraping the leaves against each other at the tops of the trees, whispering through the —

What was that smell?

I stopped, swinging my light over a huge sycamore that had fallen beside the path, and sniffed.

It wasn't skunk. This stench was even more rank. It smelled a bit like the possums that got into our alpaca barn way too often.

I took another sniff and fought a gag. "Do you know what that is?"

"What is what?" Amber said, crying.

I played the beam over the woods, but it didn't even reveal animal eyes, let alone a whole animal. Or maybe monster eyes didn't reflect light.

I shook my head in a jerk.

I had to get home and leave monsters to nightmares.

Wishing we could run, I dragged Amber behind me as fast as I could.

Chapter Five

We'd left the woods and were climbing the hill to the house when we met Rusty, Aaron, and Micah trotting down it with two paramedics carrying a stretcher. Aaron and Micah wore big grins, caught up in the excitement of a rescue.

Thank You, Father, that they haven't seen Uncle Hank.

Walking with the paramedics was Chris Kincaid. Since he was wearing his deputy uniform, he must have learned about the call for the ambulance on the radio in his patrol SUV.

His intense, sculpted face distracted me from how miserable I felt. I'd known Chris long enough to know that in a crisis, I could rely on—really, anyone could rely on—his calm strength and practical outlook.

"Boys, I'll take the paramedics to Uncle Hank." I wiped a soaked clump of hair from my forehead. "Rusty, did you call Doc Volmer?"

"Yeah, she's on her way. I tried to get Aunt Carrie." Rusty held a small flashlight up between us. "But she doesn't answer."

"Keep trying. She's at The Haunting in the Hollow, and reception's spotty there. You wait here for Doc Volmer."

"She has to put Knight down," Amber said, her last word touching on a scream.

"She might," I said. "We don't know."

Chris slipped out of the rain jacket that went with his black uniform and held it out to me.

"You'll get wet." I hugged myself so hard that I was in danger of dislocating my shoulders.

"It'll be a while before my teeth are chattering so hard that I'm difficult to understand," he said.

Was I speaking that badly? I was shivering but ... pulling on his rain jacket, I felt instantly warmer.

Micah's cute face lost its grin. "We've been praying for Knight and Uncle Hank, like Gram told us to."

I zipped Chris's jacket. "You and Amber and Aaron should get together dry clothes and blankets and towels. People are freezing on the bank. I'll take it all to them when I get back."

The thrill of the rescue dulled in Aaron's light blue eyes. "What will Uncle Hank do without Knight?"

"I—I don't know." I headed down the hill.

Chris came alongside me as we entered the woods. "How bad is your uncle?"

"He's completely unresponsive." Over my shoulder, I said to the paramedics, "He's out of the water, and we're trying to warm him up." I described the first-aid Dad had administered.

"Got it," said the taller paramedic, slipping on the trail, allowing the stretcher to drop onto it.

I stepped closer to Chris. "I'm glad you took the call."

"Actually, I'm off duty. I was on my way home when the call came over Dispatch." His rich bass, which didn't match his average size, had a reassuring steadiness. "Houston and Corliss were on a domestic violence call, so I told Dispatch I'd see if I could help."

My hand bumped his. I left it there, touching, then squeezed it. "Things are better now that you're here."

His white teeth flashed beneath his trim, black moustache in what might have been a smile. But Chris's smiles were like shooting stars — hard to spot, brief, but dazzling if you caught one.

"I'm glad I could come." He pressed my fingers.

Rays of warmth shot through me. If that didn't take off the chill, nothing would.

We followed the creek through the drizzle. As soon as I saw a speck of light ahead, I shrugged off his coat. "Follow the creek to the light. I'm going back to help Amber and the boys get towels and clothes."

"Don't forget to dry yourself." Chris peered at the pinprick of light along the creek. "You can keep my jacket."

I shook my head. "I'll be dry in ten minutes. You'll be out in the weather longer."

Reluctantly, he took the jacket from me, and reluctantly, I turned away from him and ran back along the trail.

Chapter Six

"You should call Aunt Carrie for the latest details on Uncle Hank, Walter," I told my great-grandfather, more than an hour later, on the landline. "She's driving to the trauma center in Columbus to meet Aunt Jeanine and Mr. Norris. The paramedics drove Hank to meet a life flight." My throat tightened again, like it had when the paramedics told us that Hank needed a medical helicopter. "Gram took Coral to the hospital in Zanesville because Coral said her back and shoulders were hurting. Amber went with her."

By the time Gram had helped Coral dry off, Amber had calmed into a zombie-like state of exhaustion, but Gram had taken Amber to the hospital, in case she got hysterical again, so I would only have the boys and Dad to focus on.

"What's Mal doing?" Walter's deep, rocky voice grated over the landline.

"Getting dried off and warmed up." I explained what had happened to Knight. "After Chris took the horses back to the Norris's farm—Chris Kincaid's a deputy—he took over holding Knight's head out of the water. So Dad came back to our house. The vet's with Knight now."

"Your dad froze himself over a—a—a horse?"

I held the phone away from my ear.

Rusty ran into the kitchen. "Rae, Dad says he doesn't want to take a shower. He wants to lay down." He breathed like he'd run from the county seat and not around the foot of the stairs.

If he'd been concerned when he thought Coral was hurt, Rusty was panic-stricken now. He, Aaron, and Micah had watched the paramedics loading Hank into the ambulance, an oxygen mask strapped to his face, without a sign of life, and then saw Dad stagger into the kitchen.

"Gotta go, Walter. Do you have Aunt Carrie's number? Okay. Talk to you later." I hung up and followed Rusty into the living-dining room.

Staring at nothing in particular, Dad hung on the post at the bottom of the stairs like it was the only reason he wasn't on the floor. He said in a thick voice, "I just need to lie down for a minute, boys."

"That's fine, Dad." I put his arm across my shoulders. "How about you crash on the couch?" No way could I guide him to his bedroom in the basement.

And he needed guiding. The cold seemed to have dulled his brain, and he'd strained his left knee that was weak from an old football injury, so he limped badly. From what I'd been able to look up online, fighting our satellite connection the whole time, he seemed to have mild hypothermia.

With Dad leaning on me, we made it to our worn, brown couch. He collapsed on it, swung his feet up, closed his eyes, and in half a minute, was breathing in the deep rhythm of sleep.

My brothers stared down at him.

"Are you sure Dad doesn't need to go to the hospital?" Rusty squeaked out.

"Yes, all he needs is rest." I projected a reassurance in my voice I wasn't sure I believed. "The paramedics weren't real concerned."

"Anything new about Uncle Hank?" Rusty's skinny fingers flexed over and over, either in a panic attack or on the edge of one.

All this drama was hardest on Rusty. Aaron was two and Micah was nine days old when their mom died in a car accident. They couldn't remember her, and I thought, deep down, they considered Gram their mom. But Rusty was five when his mom walked out the door to get diapers and never came home.

As I tried to remember the technique I'd seen Dad use when Rusty got panicky, Aaron said, "Uncle Hank didn't look very good." He bit the side of his lip.

My ten-year-old brother had enthusiasm for almost everything life threw at him. Reality had to turn seriously ugly to dampen his spirits.

"Uncle Hank's young and very healthy. He'll recover." I attempted an upbeat tone, rubbing the seashell locket that Dad had given me for my birthday and contained a photo of me and Mom.

Father, let him recover.

"He's not young." Micah picked up an afghan from the wood floor. "He's forty."

"Forty-one," said Aaron.

"Close enough." Micah shook out the afghan. "Rae, should we cover Dad up?"

"Yeah. Aaron, get the comforter off Dad's bed. You can get mine too, Rusty. Those will work better than an afghan."

As my brothers separated, Chris and Doc Volmer entered the kitchen from the screened porch, dripping from every piece of clothing. Since they kept a change of clothes in their vehicles, I directed Chris to the bathroom by the boys' bedroom and led Doc Volmer through Gram's room to the little bathroom built off the back of it.

Crossing to the linen closet on the back wall, I said to the vet, "Did you have to ..." I hated to put my fear into words.

"Yes." Doc took the towel I held out to her. "There was nothing else to do." She rubbed the towel over her white-tipped gray hair. "It would cost a fortune to repair a break like that. Even then Knight might not live. He'd also hurt himself internally from thrashing on his side for so long." Lowering the towel, she sighed. "A magnificent horse. It's always wonderful to see a horse and human connect deeply. Knight and Hank became one being when Hank rode him. I'm so sorry." She sighed again. "How's Hank?"

"Aunt Carrie, Aunt Jeanine, and Mr. Norris haven't gotten to the trauma center in Columbus yet, so no news. Would you like coffee or tea?"

She said she'd take decaf coffee, and I left her to change.

In the living room, Rusty spread the second comforter over Dad as Aaron and Micah shook out a sleeping bag.

Aaron smoothed his bag. "Rusty said we should sleep here to watch Dad."

"But y'all won't sleep well out here," I said, "and you have school—" School was the least of our worries. "Go ahead. I'll call you all off school tomorrow. I guess I should call Gram off too."

Even if Coral was fine and Gram drove home with her and Amber in a few hours, I couldn't imagine her being in shape to head the cafeteria at Barton Elementary School in the morning.

Aaron and Micah exchanged grins, but Rusty only nodded, breathing harshly through his mouth.

"Rusty, take some deep breaths. Slowly." I snapped a pod into the coffee maker.

He didn't even glance my way, as if he hadn't heard me.

Chris carried the plastic bag holding his wet uniform to the back door. He'd changed into jeans and a long-sleeved white t-shirt. His black hair, still wavy despite his crewcut, was damp.

I opened a cupboard. "Can I get you something hot to drink?"

Chris sat on a stool at the bar between the kitchen and dinner table. "Coffee is welcome."

Rusty darted to the bar. "Rae, do you think two comforters are enough for Dad?"

Chris looked past him to the couch. "I'm sure two are enough. You could put a winter hat on his head, but rest is the best medicine. Even mild hypothermia is exhausting."

"How do you know?" Rusty shifted from foot to foot, his fingers working.

"When I was in high school, I went hiking with some classmates in the Cascade Mountains. A freak snowstorm took us by surprise. We turned back, and by the time we returned to our cars, we were very cold. Some of us might have been hypothermic. But we grew warmer in the car and then drove home. I was tired for a couple of days, and then I was fine."

Rusty's feet stilled, his hands relaxed, and he took a normal breath.

As my brother turned back to the living-dining room, I mouthed "thank you" to Chris.

His shooting-star smile streaked by, the only clue I ever got to what Chris was thinking or feeling. His taut face might have been carved into fierce lines from any hardwood. Cop training hadn't made him mask his thoughts and emotions so well. Dad wasn't like that at all.

Chris picked up one of the brochures Dad had collected from the community colleges. "Have you applied yet?"

I removed Doc's steaming mug of coffee from the machine. "I don't know if I'm going."

One of his thick eyebrows rose half a millimeter. "No money?"

"That and no brains."

Both of Chris's eyebrows rose a full millimeter.

I hadn't thought I had the power to shock him. Pouring more water in the coffee maker, I explained the dismal path my grades took in high school.

"You were a victim of circumstances," said Chris. "Those have changed."

"Do you see a benefit in getting a degree?"

"Definitely. My associate's degree allows me to run for sheriff in Ohio. When I finish my bachelor's in criminology, I have options if I eventually dislike working as an officer. You should—"

The back door smacked open.

Chapter Seven

I screamed, Rusty yelped, Aaron jumped out of the recliner, and Doc Volmer dropped her satchel as she entered the kitchen. Only Micah and Chris reacted normally by glancing at the door.

"What's the matter with y'uns?" Walter stomped into the kitchen.

I held my forehead. "We're a little on edge, Walter."

"You know —" Doc said, her gaze fixed on my great-grandfather "— I'll take a raincheck on the coffee. Need to get home."

Actually, her need was to get away from Walter. His scary reputation had that effect on people, although he was eighty-one. And except for a stiff gait, you wouldn't guess he was that old. His massive frame wasn't stooped at all, and his deep-set eyes scoured everybody with a sharpness no senility had blunted.

"I have it ready for you." I picked up the mug.

"How's Mal?" Walter's craggy voice sounded like it came from the bottom of an empty well.

"He's sleeping on the couch," I said. "He's getting warm."

Walter stalked toward the couch as Doc scurried past, and Rusty and Aaron retreated to the dinner table.

Doc said, "Thanks all the same. Tell Jeanine how sorry I am. I'll call later about the details of Knight's injuries. She doesn't need to deal with that now. Please keep me posted about Hank."

I told her I would, and she left.

Walter said, "If Mal's gonna sleep here, you should start a fire." Grunting, he knelt on the hearth. "You boys — you know what I need to start one?"

"Sure." Micah spoke to Walter like any other guest.

Rusty and Aaron nodded, watching our great-grandfather like he was a strange dog they suspected was actually a wolf.

"Then get it for me."

My three brothers zipped through the kitchen and out the back door.

Walter eyed me. "You need anything for Mal? I can go get it before I drive to Zanesville."

I squinted. "You're going to the hospital tonight?"

"That surprise you? Why wouldn't I go see how my great-granddaughter's doin'?" Walter set his jaw at a belligerent angle.

My breath came short. He could instill fear quicker than any haunted house in the country.

The kitchen door took more abuse as Micah kicked it open, loaded down with newspapers and thin scraps of wood.

"Sorry, Walter," I said. "Dumb question."

"You got that right." Walter took the newspapers from Micah.

Rusty and Aaron brought in armloads of logs, and Walter had a fire going so quickly that you might suspect he'd zapped the kindling with a secret superpower.

Walter stomped to Chris and me at the bar. "Tell Mal to take it easy — don't go into work for a few days — or I'll bust him wide open."

"Mal has good sense, Mr. Malinowski," Chris said.

"I wasn't talkin' to you." Walter leaned in, probably trying to intimidate Chris with his juggernaut build. "If he had any sense, he wouldn't have made himself sick over a horse."

Chris's black coffee eyes held Walter's deep-set ones naturally. "I'm sorry, sir. I didn't mean to intrude."

"You're one of Mal's deputies, ain't ya? Don't you gotta go back on patrol?"

"My shift's over."

"Then go home."

The idea of being left alone with the boys and Dad cut my wind as easily as Walter's presence. If bad news came...

Chris looked to me. "It's up to you, Rae. Do you want me to leave?"

"No." My answer was too loud, making Chris's eyes widen a fraction, and my brothers turn toward me. "No, I could use the company. We all could. At least for a while."

Walter's x-ray gaze raked us, then landed on Chris. "I reckon Mal bein' your boss'll keep you in line."

My mouth dropped like on a rusty hinge. Did Walter seriously think that after seeing my uncle lying like he was dead and knowing his favorite horse had been put down and watching my dad limp around, sick, I'd be in the mood to make out with my boyfriend? When he wasn't my boyfriend?

I pressed my lips together. Better to keep those thoughts out of the air because I'd lose any argument with Walter.

"Call me if you hear anything, Rae." Walter stomped out.

Micah clambered onto a stool beside Chris. "So what do you want to do?"

I glanced at the clock on the microwave. "It's past 9. Y'all should go to bed." It hadn't even been three hours since Jeanine had called about Coral's horse coming home without her.

"But we don't have to go to school tomorrow." Aaron's beaming grin was almost at normal radiance.

Chris looked to Rusty, who hovered above Dad. "Are you the one writing a fantasy novel?"

"Rae told you that?" Rusty jerked around, his face deepening to a red that clashed with his hair.

I hadn't thought I'd violated a trust telling Chris, but Rusty was a shy kid, especially about his writing. I'd been private about my photography when I was his age. "Rusty, I'm sorry. I forgot that you might not want me to mention it. You've said your fight scenes were boring, so I asked Chris if he could come up with something different. He's studied several martial arts."

Chris got off his stool. "I can show you some moves."

"Y'all can go downstairs," I said. "There's more room."

Rusty hesitated, looking between Dad and the basement door.

"Rusty." I locked gazes with him. "We can all take turns coming up and checking on Dad."

He looked to Dad again. "Okay." He headed downstairs.

When my last brother had disappeared into the basement, I whispered to Chris, "Thank you."

"Glad I can help." He started toward the top step, then turned. "I'm glad—very glad—I can help you." He flashed his smile.

A surge of something welled in me, and I found myself beside him taking his hand. The surge clogged my throat and all I could say was "Thank you" again.

"You guys coming?" Micah called up the steps.

I dropped Chris's hand, and he glared down the stairs.

My voice shaking, I said, "I'll get my tea and come down. I'll bring your coffee." I raised my volume. "We're coming."

Chris nodded and descended to the basement.

I turned to the cupboard and pulled out a tea bag. What had just happened? Maybe I didn't feel like making out, but I found Chris seriously attractive tonight.

Chapter Eight

Carrie kept calling with updates, none of them good. The multiple breaks in Hank's lower leg, ankle, and foot were jagged, which meant he'd need surgery, maybe several. But the doctors couldn't do more than clean them up until he wasn't hypothermic. The delay could make recovery from the breaks more difficult and longer.

I kept most of that information to myself, telling my brothers that the doctors had fixed Hank's leg as best they could until he was warmer.

At 10, Aaron and Micah crawled into their sleeping bags on the living room floor and were out like somebody had flipped a switch. But Rusty was so tense I doubted he'd sleep at all. Chris asked Rusty and me if we knew how to play euchre, explaining that he knew a three-handed version. So we sat at the dinner table and played round after round.

By midnight, all the cards were swimming together in my view, and Rusty was still wound tight but exhausted.

"Rusty, lay down." I smothered a yawn, handing Chris my cards. "You don't have to sleep. Just rest."

"I guess I can do that." Rusty slid out of his chair and tumbled onto his sleeping bag. "You'll keep checking on Dad?"

"For sure."

Dad had rolled once onto his side, but that had been his only movement.

Chris shuffled the deck together. "Do you still want me to stay, Rae?"

"Yes." I didn't have to think. "But you have work tomorrow, don't you? I'm sorry I've kept you up."

"I told you. I like helping you." He reached across the table and gripped my knobby hand. "And, I think, you like me helping you."

"Very much." I was close enough to him to discern the black pupil from the rich, coffee brown iris. And to discern how inviting they were.

Chris leaned in. "Rae, we've done a lot together since January, and from your attitude tonight, I think you'd like to be more than—"

The back door swung open. Again.

I flopped back in my seat as Chris turned a grimace in its direction.

Was God trying to tell me something, or did I have too many relatives?

Amber slipped into the kitchen, shoulders humped, head bent. Walter tromped in like he owned the place. Could he ever walk quietly?

"You still here?" Walter aimed that at Chris.

My great-grandfather's hostility seemed out of place, but then, he'd had too many experiences with his children's and grandchildren's disastrous relationships. Not to mention his own.

Walter shrugged out of his corduroy work coat. "You can hang out with your girlfriend another time."

"Chris isn't my boyfriend." My heart skipped around. "Yet."

A smile sped beneath Chris's moustache, deflecting pleasure into his eyes.

"Walter said Doc Volmer euthanized Knight," Amber said in a ghost of a whisper.

"She had to." Chris's deep voice was quiet. "Knight was too badly injured."

Leaning against the honey-colored cabinets, Amber sniffed but not a tear fell from her red-rimmed eyes.

I got to my feet. "Amber, you can have Gram's bed. And a pair of my pajamas."

Sniffing again, she nodded. "Coral's okay. They'll release her tomorrow. Dad could die."

My stomach tightened so quickly I was afraid it would launch the tea up my throat.

Amber blundered to Gram's room like she was blind.

"You can leave, Deputy," Walter said. "I'll be here if Rae needs anything." He looked to me. "Lydia'll throw a fit, but I can stay if you say it's okay. Unless she lied about you being able to invite in whoever you want."

"Gram doesn't lie." I snapped the sentence.

The dislike between Gram and Walter had probably lowered the temperature in the waiting room at the hospital in Zanesville to hypothermic levels. Gram had never gotten along with her father-in-law, and my grandfather Reuel getting killed at a bar saving Walter's life had only made a bad relationship non-existent. Gram was polite when they met, but Walter never saw a need for manners.

"Do you want me to stay, Rae?' Chris's tone was mild.

Yes, because Chris seemed on the verge of taking our relationship to the next level. But I didn't want him to wear himself out when he had a twelve-hour shift the next day. Actually, today.

"You don't have to since I'm going to try to get some sleep. I'll walk out with you." I set the cards on the bar. "Walter, you're welcome to stay. You can have Dad's bed."

Although why Walter wanted to remain when he only lived fifteen minutes away puzzled me.

I tiptoed past my snoozing brothers and dad to the coat closet by the stairs and took out my jean jacket.

Walter stared down at Dad. "He wake up at all?"

"No. But he's warmed up."

"I'll sleep in the boy's room since they ain't in there. If Mal needs help, you get me."

"Uh—for sure." I watched him stalk into their room and then joined Chris at the front door.

Was Walter that worried about Dad? Even if I asked him, he'd never admit it.

We strolled onto the front porch, down the steps, and along the walk to the garage. Chris's hand touched mine, and our fingers interlaced. As we stopped at his SUV, the wind snatched at us.

"About what I was going to say earlier ..." He trailed off, as if gauging my response.

"If it's about being more than friends, then yes." I tightened my grip on his hand.

Even in the darkness, I glimpsed Chris's smile.

He lifted his face, and I lowered mine, compensating for our two-inch height difference.

Our first kiss delivered a jolt that stole my breath better than the cold water of the pool.

We parted, and I said, "Can you stop by tomorrow—or today—after work?" Why was I so hoarse?

"I was planning to. I thought I'd come back to pull Knight from the creek and bury him before your aunt and uncle come home. If your uncle has a tractor with a backhoe attachment, I can use that."

"That'd—that'd be great." I'd forgotten that someone would have to do that sad job. "Uncle Hank does have one of those. Where'd you learn to use a tractor and a backhoe?"

"At my high school." He put his hand on the door handle.

"Where'd you learn to handle horses?"

"My high school."

"You have a lot of hidden talents, Deputy."

"They keep me from being too boring."

A sudden gust made me turn up the collar of my jacket. "You could never be that."

"I'd better not be. You're a girl who always seems to find adventures." Chris got into his SUV.

A burn stole up my neck. I buttoned the top button of my jacket, glad for the darkness, but enjoying the tiny jolts it gave me at the same time.

Chris backed down the drive, leaving me way too wired to even think about sleep.

Chapter Nine

Something heavy hit the floor, and I jerked upright in the recliner, my great-grandmother's hunter green quilt sliding off my lap. In jeans and an undershirt that had been white a thousand washes ago, Walter walked past me to the kitchen where Micah poured milk into a cup on the bar.

Slipping out of the chair, I whispered, "What time is it?"

Micah pointed at the clock on the microwave. "9:17."

I stared out the windows behind the dinner table. Swollen dark clouds pressed against the woods and the fields behind our house, giving no sign it was late morning.

"What you got to eat?" Walter opened the fridge. "How come you slept in the recliner, Rae?" He made no attempt to soften his cellar voice.

"I was so wound up that I had to read to relax and fell asleep in it." I didn't add that I wanted to monitor Dad.

Micah screwed the lid on the milk jug. "There are muffins in the freezer." He didn't act at all surprised Walter was in our house for breakfast, but Micah took after Gram — only an earthquake could touch his mellow.

Rusty and Aaron stirred in their sleeping bags.

Walter took an orange from a drawer in the fridge. "Mal been awake yet?"

Just as I said no, Dad rolled onto his back and blinked at the ceiling.

I catapulted out of the recliner and knelt by the couch. "How're you feeling?"

Dad rose a little and then fell back on his pillow. "How's Hank?"

I told him the report I got from Carrie last night. "Nothing new this morning."

He stared at the ceiling, expressionless.

Walter towered above him. "You're an idiot."

Meeting Walter's glare, Dad placed his hand on the top of his head and pushed off the knit hat Rusty had put on. "Oh, hey, Walter. Staying long? Don't let me keep you."

Aaron sat up and yawned while Rusty stretched his arms out of his sleeping bag.

"What's the matter with you?" said Walter in a growl. "Makin' yourself sick over a horse when you got your mom and four kids dependin' on you. Jeanine and Amber and Coral need you too, since

Hank's bad off. I thought you had at least half a brain."

Dad closed his eyes. "It was Hank's horse, and he was going to drown, and Amber and Coral were right there, and ... it was Hank's horse. But I got bigger problems than your opinion of me."

"Like what?"

"Like how I'm going to get off this couch to go to the bathroom."

Walter snorted and held out a calloused hand. "Come on."

Rusty leaped to his feet. "Are you okay, Dad?"

Dad laid an arm over Walter's shoulders, then rubbed Rusty on the head. "I'm fine, bud. How about you go get my knee brace?" He put some weight on his left leg and sighed. "I'll probably have to wear it for a week."

As all three boys trundled downstairs to Dad's bedroom, he glanced about. "How's Ma? I think her back was bothering her last night. Some of the details ..." a yawn stretched his face "... they're a little hazy."

His memories might have been hazy, but Dad was back to being himself, not talking in the dull, stupefied way he had last night.

"Gram said she pulled something in her back leveraging Knight," I said. "She stayed at the hospital with Coral, and Walter brought Amber home."

Dad limped beside Walter as they made their way to the bathroom beside the boys' room. He'd just closed the door when the landline rang. It showed Aunt Carrie's number.

My heart contracted so hard that it must have squeezed all the blood out. I took the receiver from the base, afraid to ask but knowing I had to. "Hey, Aunt Carrie. How's Uncle Hank?"

"No change, but that's not unexpected," said Carrie.

She was texting me a list of clothes and necessities for Jeanine, Mr. Norris, and herself. "I'd already packed the things I needed for the weekend since The Haunting is opening tomorrow. My stuff's by the air mattress in Jeanine's basement." She also said that since Gram's sister and brother-in-law lived so close to the hospital, anyone who needed to stay overnight in Columbus could sleep there.

Amber bolted into the living room. "Is Dad still okay?"

I nodded and said to Carrie, "So you're staying at your apartment tonight?"

"No. At Aunt Marti's. My apartment's on the west side." Her voice dropped. "I don't want to be that far from the hospital."

My heart constricted again, and I winced. "I'll let you know when I'm coming to the hospital today with all the stuff."

As I hung up, Amber said, "I've got to get to the hospital now."

Still wearing my sweatpants and hooded sweatshirt, which she'd borrowed in exchange for her wet clothes, Amber was a mess — her waist-length hair fuzzed in all directions and her brown eyes appeared smaller from the puffiness surrounding them.

"Your dad isn't any worse," I said. "Aunt Carrie didn't say you needed to get there immediately."

"She told me last night it could take a couple days for Hank to improve much." Walter waited at the foot of the stairs. "Don't go buryin' him before he's even dead, Amber."

I groaned inside, pulling mugs from a cupboard. Walter had a too perfect way of putting things.

Dad limped out of the bathroom as the boys emerged from the basement with his heavy knee brace.

Leaning on Walter, Dad said, "Who called?"

I repeated what Carrie had told me as Walter helped him to the couch.

"No change isn't all bad." Dad blew out his cheeks. "Holy smoke, I haven't felt this lousy since I had the flu when Em was pregnant with Aaron."

"'Cause of a horse." Walter picked up his mug of coffee.

"You can drop that, Walter," Dad said in full cop voice. He took the brace from Rusty and then reached for Amber's hand, pulling her down beside him, and asked in a quiet voice, "How're you doing, kiddo?"

She hung her head. "I'm so sorry, Uncle Mal."

He stared. "About what? Oh, boy." He sat up straight. "I should apologize to you. I was too rough on you last night. I was scared, and I let that—"

"You weren't rough on me. I was acting like a baby. I'm sorry." She pulled in her lips, her chin quivering.

"You did nothing wrong. That was a horrible situation to confront. You can't expect to handle an emergency like that without training."

Amber stared at the brace propped against the couch like she'd just noticed it. "You hurt your knee? Because I was such a mess I couldn't pry Knight off Dad?"

"No, no." Dad's assurance was quick, too quick. "I think I hurt it standing in such a weird position in the creek for so long."

"You don't have to be nice to me." Her voice shook. "Gram hurt her back because she took my place leveraging Knight off Dad's leg. I'm so sorry." She hurried to Gram's room and slammed the door.

"What'd she do?" Walter wiped a crumb of blueberry muffin from the corner of his mouth with the back of his hand. "Or didn't do?"

"Yeah, what?" Aaron's nosiness had kicked in as he stared after our cousin.

"It's a very long story." Dad held the top of his head again.

I edged toward the bedroom. "Maybe I should ..."

"Give her some time alone," said Dad with a sigh.

Amber's crying seeped through the closed door.

Chapter Ten

After I'd fixed breakfast for all the guys, I tried to talk to Amber through the door, but the only response was sobs.

Then Gram called, sounding weary. All the tests showed Coral hadn't damaged anything. She was just sore and would be released soon.

Several friends and church families called, and two ladies from our church dropped off casseroles.

Finally, Amber shuffled into the living room, her pale face streaked red.

"You'd feel better if you ate something," I said.

She shook her head and whispered, "Let's get the things Aunt Carrie said everybody needs. I'll pack a bag for myself."

Taking the Rust Bucket, we drove around until my phone found a pocket of reception and got Carrie's text with the list. Along with about a million other texts. Then we drove to Mr. Norris's little white farmhouse and collected clothes and other items in a suitcase Amber pulled out of a closet. We also refilled several bowls with dog food for the various dogs that roamed freely across the road separating Uncle Hank's farm from his father's.

In the stable at Amber's farm, we turned out the horses, mucked out the stalls, fed the barn cats and refilled more bowls for the dogs. Since we'd left my house, Amber had said about six words.

While she showered, I thought to call my best friend Devon Majors. I punched in the library's number. I knew she was working at the checkout desk.

"I'm so glad you called." The relief was clear in Devon's voice. "I heard Hank had a riding accident, but that's the only fact people agree on. Nobody's posted anything. How is he?"

"Not good." I gave her Carrie's report while packing a small suitcase for Jeanine. "I'm sure Aunt Carrie will post something soon. She's the only one in the family who uses socials regularly because she doesn't have to worry about reception, living in Columbus."

Devon said in a subdued voice, "Let me know if there's anything I can do."

"Thanks."

I hung up the Norris's landline and went back to Jeanine and Hank's room, putting her laptop in its case. Then I went to the basement and gathered Carrie's clothes and items. As I set the cases beside the oval dinner table in the tiny eating area, I noticed a stack of books with manila folders under them. I picked up the top book, a spiral bound one with a photo of our church on the cover. A photo of an elderly woman was inset on the left. The book's title was *In His Service*.

I flipped through it. It seemed to be a memoir of a pastor's wife. Her husband led our church from the late 1930s into the '60s. The second book was thick, a selection of stories and poems by Edgar Allan Poe. It was the first volume of a two-volume set and looked old. I opened it to the copyright page. 1946. For being over seventy years old, the book was in good condition. The pages weren't even yellowing.

My gaze strayed to the folders. One was labeled "Cyrus Morley" and the other, "Morley Treasure."

My grip tightened on the Poe book. Hadn't Dad said the clue to the treasure was found in a book of Edgar Allan Poe's writings? Dad must have called Jeanine while I was changing for supper last night, and she'd set out all her research to give to him before ... everything happened.

I set down the book of Poe, and it fell open to reveal a piece of paper stuck between two pages. Printed in black ink, it said, "Beneath My Contempt."

I held up the note. Why would Jeanine write that, just that, and tuck it into a book? Was it a reminder for the story she was writing when she'd done her research? But Jeanine usually wrote in cursive.

A sound of tearing — paper tearing — reached me from the back of the house. I entered the hall that led to the bedrooms and followed it to Amber's room at the end.

In her lavender and pale gray bedroom, Amber tossed two halves of a poster onto other ripped sheets, which lay on the fuzzy charcoal rug beside her bed. Her wet hair hung in a thick rope over her shoulder.

The wall above her desk was empty.

"You tore up your poster of Wonder Woman?" I said. "And the poster of — of —"

"Eowyn." She opened a drawer in a bureau. "From *The Lord of the Rings*."

"Why? They're your heroes."

Her mouth gaped, her hand freezing in the drawer. "How can you ask that question? After last night, I can't pretend I have courage." She slumped onto her bed. "Last night, I saw my true self. Coral's right. She's always said I'm pathetic." She toed the ragged posters. "Do you remember when Eowyn saved her uncle from being eaten by an evil beast?"

I'd watched *The Lord of the Rings* trilogy a couple times with Dad and Amber because it was their favorite. Although I liked the action sequences, the characters blurred together when I wasn't watching the movies.

"Not exactly. And Coral's wrong."

"Eowyn's uncle, King Theoden, is badly injured by a Ringwraith." Amber spoke like she hadn't heard me. "She keeps the Ringwraith's foul beast from eating him." She wiped at her eyes. "My dad was badly injured, and I did nothing."

"Yes, you did. Once Dad told you what to do."

"Only after he dragged me into the water. Uncle Mal probably hurt his knee because of me. I know Gram hurt her back because she had to work the branch under Knight. Uncle Mal wanted me to do that, and I couldn't keep calm enough." She took a shaky breath. "Poor Knight."

"Amber, you shouldn't compare yourself to fictional characters. Of course they're brave. They have to be. That's how the writers wrote them."

"You and Coral didn't fall apart." She plucked at a raised flower on her lavender bedspread. "My brain froze. All I could think of was Dad was dead or dying and no one could help him." Her voice shrank. "Dad would be dead if I'd been riding with him."

"You don't know that." I tried to put conviction in my words.

"Yes, I do." A quivering sigh. "I'll get my stuff together." She brushed by me, into the hall, and went into the bathroom.

I returned to the dining area.

Father, what can I say to help?

Turning over my prayer in my mind, I leafed through the folders. Newspaper articles from the 1930s, probably printed from the microfilm machines we had at the library, filled them.

Cyrus Morley hadn't been shy about publicity. Year after year, in *The New York Times*, his name appeared in articles, most often in connection with a police call—a party someone complained about, drunken behavior in public, and at least two car wrecks in which the driver, who wasn't Cyrus, was drunk. Some articles were from *The Marlin County Recorder*, but Cyrus appeared much more respectable in these as the owner of several local coal mines. One was about a donation he made to the library. No mention of his Halloween party, The Masque of the Red Death.

A few of the articles had his photo accompanying them. They were grainy, and he appeared younger than the man printed on the banner at The Haunting, but that portrait was dead-on accurate. In every photo, he looked prepared to unleash a crushing comeback.

"Mom said Uncle Mal wanted all her research." Amber stepped out of the hall to the bedrooms, pulling a small, navy-blue suitcase and carrying a flowered bag over her shoulder.

I scooped up the stack, turning to my cousin. "Don't be so hard on yourself. Don't focus on what you could have done better. Your mom and dad and sister really need your support. Do whatever you can for them now."

"You're right." But she still stood like the flowered bag was full of lead.

I opened the Poe book and removed the note. "Is this the book with the clue to Cyrus Morley's treasure?"

Amber studied it. "Yes. Mom told me all about the will and the hidden treasure when she did her research about—it's been about five years ago. That book was left to Aunt Lily's mother. She was one of four children Cyrus Morley named as an heir in his will. I think all the kids were illegitimate."

"Not all of them. I met his legitimate son, Timothy Morley, yesterday at The Haunting."

"Oh." Amber shrugged. "When Aunt Lily's mom died, I guess she got the book, and she let Mom borrow it. She must not have asked for it back."

I held up the note. "Why did your mom write this?"

"She didn't. That's part of the clue."

My eyebrows lowered. "What do you mean?"

"When Cyrus Morley died, his lawyer gave each of the four heirs a copy of this book with that note inside, tucked between the same pages."

On the left page was the end of a longer poem and the beginning of the poem called "Eldorado," which finished at the top of the right page. Another poem started beneath it.

I read "Eldorado," the only complete poem between the two pages.

> Gaily bedight,
> A gallant knight,
> In sunshine and in shadow,
> Had journeyed long,
> Singing a song,
> In search of Eldorado.
>
> But he grew old--
> This knight so bold--
> And o'er his heart a shadow
> Fell as he found
> No spot of ground
> That looked like Eldorado.

And as his strength
Failed him at length
He met a pilgrim shadow--
"Shadow," said he
"Where can it be--
This land of Eldorado?"

"Over the Mountains
Of the Moon,
Down the Valley of the Shadow,
Ride, boldly, ride"
The shade replied,--
"If you seek for Eldorado?"

"Do you know what Eldorado was?" said Amber.

I tugged on my earlobe. "I think so. It was a golden treasure the conquistadors were looking for when they explored the New World."

"Eldorado was a city of gold the Spanish hunted for in the Amazon. Of course, it didn't exist. Since the note was placed by a poem about seeking a treasure, the note and the poem are the key to finding the inheritance."

"That's all the heirs got?" I stared at the note, then the poem. "Not much to work from."

"Mom thought the clues might be a code based on the code in the Edgar Allan Poe story, 'The Gold Bug'. That's in the book too. Mom and I tried to crack it, but we got nowhere."

"You'd think somebody would have cracked the code with a program. Three years ago, Timothy Morley hunted for the treasure at the home and couldn't find it. Now he's back with a new theory, I guess. He's afraid his son and Dani Li will find it first since they have access to the property that used to belong to his father."

"Dani Li? She has no right to the — " Amber's brown eyes widened. "Is she a descendent of one of the four heirs?"

"Yeah. If the Morleys, Dani Li, and Aunt Lily's kids all look for the treasure at The Haunting — " I snapped the book shut " — the actors will be the least entertaining thing there."

Chapter Eleven

When I guided the Rust Bucket up the drive, the Beast, Dad's big black truck, was parked in front of the garage, meaning Gram and Coral were home. Walter's heap was gone. That was for the best. I didn't want to witness another clash between Walter and Gram.

As Amber and I entered the kitchen, my brothers had Coral surrounded while she ate a muffin at the bar.

Rusty said, "Rae and Dad said Uncle Hank would've died if you hadn't held him out of the water." He patted her on the shoulder, and she winced.

"Boys," Gram called from the recliner, "give Coral some space. She can tell you all about it when she feels like it." For the first time since I'd met her, Gram acted old. Propping her head on her hand, she'd collapsed into the recliner instead of sitting in it.

Coral shrugged, wincing again. "There's nothing to tell. A monster made Knight spook, and he slipped on the trail 'cause it was—"

"Monster?" Aaron came to attention. "What monster? Nobody said anything about a monster."

"There was no monster," Gram said. "Coral saw a big, black animal in the bushes."

"Then it had to be a black bear," said Aaron with authority. "There was one hanging around Lake Sycamore last fall. It left a paw print, and Dad took us to see it." He leaned closer. "What else did you see, Coral?"

"Nothing. It just stunk. That's what bothered Knight first—the stink."

Aaron crossed his arms and raised one hand to hold his chin. "If we get Uncle Hank's trail cam, we can set it up where Knight fell. If the monster comes back, we can confirm it's a bear and then we can set a trap for—"

"You are not setting any traps!" Dad charged out of the basement. "You are not creating, designing, engineering, or constructing any kind of trap for any kind of monster. Or any kind of bear. Got it?"

As Amber placed her flowered satchel on the bar, I hid a smile.

Dad's panic was understandable. Aaron, the ten-year-old mad engineer, was always inventing something that somehow targeted Dad, regardless of its real purpose. Aaron and Micah had dug pits last spring to catch the person stalking me and caught Dad in one of them.

Dad's gaze swept over my brothers. "Am I clear?"

Rusty said, "Yes," as Aaron and Micah glanced at each other.

"I need verbal agreement from all three of you," Dad said.

Micah shrugged. "Sure."

Aaron frowned. "Okay."

"Coral," said Gram, "I know you didn't get any sleep in the hospital. Why don't you lie down in my room?"

My cousin inclined her head in a minimal nod and drained a glass of milk.

Dad kissed Gram on the top of her head. "You should take your own advice."

"I know, sweetie." Her usual placid face tensed. "I know I should rest my back, but I feel Jeanine needs me."

Dad said, "She'll still need you in a day or two. We can cover for you."

Amber stepped over to the recliner. "I'm really sorry, Gram."

"Now, Amber." Gram's tone was kind but firm. "I told you last night you didn't need to apologize to me. You did not hurt my back."

Amber pressed her lips out of sight. Then she squared herself to Coral, lifting her head. "Thank you, Coral. You saved Dad's life."

I held my breath. If she called Amber a coward or pathetic or ...

Leaving the stool, Coral made another miniscule nod and sat on the couch.

Amber's posture relaxed as puzzlement wrinkled her pretty princess features, reflecting my own feelings. Coral never ran her mouth, but her reaction was odd.

~~~~~

Throughout lunch, Coral didn't say a word. Even my brothers noticed. When Micah asked what was wrong, Gram said Coral was tired. Phone calls from friends asking how Hank was and how they could help interrupted our lunch, and two more church members dropped off casseroles.

After Rusty helped Amber and me load the dishwasher with lunch dishes, Dad heaved himself off the couch like he was attempting to lift a thousand pounds. "Boys, stay in the house while Rae and I take Amber to the hospital in Columbus. In case Ma needs anything."

I wiped my hands on a dish towel. "Dad, if you're still tired, I can take Amber by myself."

"I'm going." Dad gave me a severe glance. Not quite the male version of the mom look, but stern enough to prevent me from arguing.

"Then you should let Rae drive." Gram flinched, shifting in the recliner.

The left side of Dad's face contracted. That was a mannerism we shared. We used it when we were reluctant to do something we knew we should.
~~~~~

He sighed. "Rae can drive."

"Thank you, sweetie."

Dad, Amber, and I loaded all the suitcases and satchels in the backseat of the Beast, and then we rolled. Dad and I talked, trying to bring Amber into the conversation, but she only responded in monosyllables. When the skyline of the state capital came into view, we all grew quiet. In the rearview mirror, I saw Amber clutching at the strap to her mom's computer case, knuckles white.

My stomach churning, I wasn't doing stellar myself. I'd spent way, way too many hours in hospitals and clinics while Mom fought cancer for four years. All the surgeries and treatments hadn't saved her.

As I turned into the parking garage, Dad said, "We'll have to take turns visiting Hank. They only allow two people at a time in ICU."

I shifted into first. "I'm not going in."

I knew what I would see—Uncle Hank hooked up to tubes and sensors like a test subject in a mad scientist's laboratory.

I pressed my hand against my gut.

Dad said, "You don't have to come inside."

I met his kind eyes. He knew. He remembered how the hospital had sickened me last summer.

Withdrawing the key, I gulped and gave him a small smile. "I'll stay in the waiting room."

Amber shrank into herself as we made our way through the maze that all hospitals adopted as their floor plan. Even if the color scheme was different from the hospitals in North Carolina, the miles of dead white light made it look the same.

In the elevator, Dad put his arm around Amber, and she leaned into him, her breathing loud.

I swallowed for about the hundredth time, trying to ignore the antiseptic stench that permeated every inch of every hospital I'd ever been in.

As we left the elevator, Carrie met us, hugging Amber. She studied her big brother. "You've looked better."

"So have you," said Dad. "But I wasn't going to mention it."

Carrie's white-blonde hair hung limp over her shoulders, and her dark blue eyes seemed too bright, like she was channeling all remaining energy into keeping them open.

She said, "Mal, when you and Amber go back, I'll try to get Jeanine and Mr. Norris to go to the cafeteria. Mr. Norris hasn't eaten since yesterday, and Jeanine only ate a granola bar because I forced her."

"I'll go to the cafeteria with them," I said, "and make sure they get something to eat."

I'd have gone to the roof to escape the misery in the waiting room.

Relatives and friends sat in deflated knots, as sick from worry as the patients were from injury and illness.

Carrie called Jeanine, and after a few minutes, she and Mr. Norris entered the waiting room. Jeanine moved like a sleepwalker, her small face empty. Mr. Norris ... I never thought I'd feel sorry for him. He was always too ready to look down his nose at us "wild" Malinowskis. Although Dad and Carrie and the rest of us were members of the law-abiding branch, Mr. Norris acted like our inherent criminal tendencies could burst out at any moment. But now, a battle had ravaged his gaunt, deeply tanned face, laying waste to every emotion but one: fear.

Amber flung herself at her mom, and Jeanine stroked her daughter's red-gold hair that was a shade darker than her own.

We stood as if suspended. Amber didn't make a sound as she buried her face against her mom's shoulder.

Eventually, Carrie said, "Mr. Norris, Jeanine, give your stickers to Mal and Amber so they can go back to Hank. Rae's going to the cafeteria with you. I'll wait here."

Mr. Norris wiped a bony hand over his white-streaked black moustache. "I'll stay too." His soft voice barely registered as a whisper.

Since he looked like he existed on bread and water, skipping meals was not a wise choice. It wasn't wise for Jeanine either, who favored Gram's side of the family with her willowy build.

"We should eat something, I guess." Jeanine twisted the wedding band on her finger, then stared at it like she wondered how it got there.

Maybe Jeanine and Mr. Norris could use a distraction. I'd gotten bone-tired of people asking me how Mom was doing, how I was doing. When someone who didn't know about Mom's illness had talked to me about something normal, the relief was like a mini-vacation.

I strolled toward the elevator. "Aunt Jeanine, I found the stack of materials about Cyrus Morley and the hidden inheritance you set out for Dad."

"Oh — uh — good." She shambled behind me.

I pressed the button for the elevator, and the doors slid open. "Did Dad or Carrie tell you what happened at the children's home yesterday?"

I chattered away as we descended to the second floor. Neither Mr. Norris nor Jeanine responded or looked my way. I might as well have been sharing the ride with the living dead.

By the time Jeanine and Mr. Norris sat down with trays at the table where I was sipping tea, a glimmer of interest peeked from the depths of Jeanine's enormous, dark blue eyes. They seemed to take up half her face, so their lifeless appearance made her entire face look dead.

She stirred her tomato soup. "It sounds like Timothy and Alex Morley are in competition. Alex has come up with a creative way to thwart his father. If that's why he's invested in The Haunting."

"We don't know," I said. "Dani Li, who's running the attraction, is a descendant of an illegitimate child. Is Aunt Lily?"

"Yes. Cyrus only had one legitimate child. A son by a French woman, who was much younger than himself. I think her name was Marie."

I poured another packet of sugar in my tea. "Are the note and the poem the only clues?"

"That's it." Her voice sounded less vague.

"I can't believe no one in seventy years has solved it. Do you know how much the treasure is worth?"

"From what I pieced together from newspaper accounts," Jeanine said, "around $200,000 cash and about that amount in jewels. The jewels are likely worth a lot more now."

My eyebrows rose.

Jeanine swallowed a spoonful of soup with difficulty. "In 1951, Cyrus's wife Marie informed him that she wanted a divorce. A few days later, he accumulated the cash and took her jewels. Marie reported the jewels and her husband missing. For two months, the police searched for Cyrus. They finally found him in a hotel in Pittsburgh, dead from taking too much pain medication. It turned out he was dying of cancer."

I drank my tea. "So he wrote the weird will, left the copies of the Poe book with his lawyer, hid all the cash and jewels, and then committed suicide?"

"His death was ruled an accident, but from what I've learned about Cyrus Morley, I bet he did kill himself."

Mr. Norris bit into his chicken salad sandwich like it was a new skill he hadn't mastered yet. He had remained silent. Gram said he was a shy man, but he was never shy about expressing his disapproval of our family, although he'd finally accepted Jeanine as his daughter-in-law. Carrie said it'd only taken a decade.

I took another sip of tea. "Amber said you thought the key to the clues was a code found in another Edgar Allan Poe story."

Nodding, she wiped her mouth. "Poe used a simple substitution code in 'The Gold Bug.' For every letter, he substituted a number or symbol. The coded message was a hodge-podge. If Cyrus used a substitution code, it must be more complicated, and somehow, the note and the poem are part of it. Or he used a completely different code. Or he didn't use a code at all, and the clues are a riddle." Jeanine took a long drink of iced tea. "I think the key is 'beneath my contempt.' If someone figured that out, maybe the poem would make sense."

Mr. Norris dabbed a napkin at his moustache. "Take your time, Jeanine. I'm done." His bowl of soup looked untouched, and only a few bites were missing from his sandwich.

Jeanine pushed away from the table. "I'm done too."

When the three of us stepped onto the ICU floor, Amber was clinging to Dad in the hall outside the waiting room, her shoulders shaking. Dad had his arms around her, blinking a lot.

"He died," Mr. Norris said in a bleak whisper.

The bottom of my stomach hit the floor.

Jeanine's slim hand went to her throat, then dropped. "No, no. Carrie or Mal would have called us to come back up."

"Th-th-that's right." I held both hands against my stomach.

Covering half his thin face with a rough hand, Mr. Norris sank against a wall.

"Amber's just upset." Jeanine went over to Dad and her daughter.

Taking an enormous inhale, Mr. Norris lurched off the wall and trudged into the waiting room.

When I'd come to Marlin County to find my father, I thought I might get a stepmom or some half-siblings. I never expected a back-up dad as well as a dad. That's what Uncle Hank and Dad were to each other's kids. I'd only been in the family nine months and couldn't imagine how my brothers and I would function without our back-up dad.

Father, have mercy on us.

Amber hung onto her mom as Jeanine and Dad talked in lowered voices. Then Amber and Jeanine returned to the waiting room.

Releasing a long sigh, Dad said, "Rae, let's transfer all their stuff into their vehicle and head home."

Our conversation was restricted to essentials until I had the Beast back on the state highway. A light rain pattered on the windshield.

Dad said in a somber voice, "Do not mention Em to anyone today."

I took a quick breath as a car swished by me. "I—I forgot we were going to the cemetery today."

"We aren't now. We'll honor Em when ... when things are better." His last word was hoarse, and he cleared his throat. "She'd understand."

The rain streaked our side windows, and I cranked my wipers to a higher speed. I had a glimmer of why Dad loathed October.

Hands on his knees, Dad stared down. "You know, there's never been a time I didn't know Hank."

I moved my hand from the knob for the wipers and squeezed his fingers.

Chapter Twelve

Neither of us had a stomach for supper, so I drove straight home. A white sedan that could steal the title "Rust Bucket" from my truck was parked on the drive.

"Aunt Lily's here." Dad's statement held a note of surprise.

I trudged and Dad limped into the kitchen. A middle-aged woman with the comfortable figure of a grandma popped out of the easy chair.

"Hey, Aunt Lily." Dad covered a yawn. "Didn't mean to startle you."

"Oh, oh, you didn't." Aunt Lily's voice always had a hint of a tremor, and her gray eyes always looked ready to tear up. After surviving three husbands who abused her one way or another, no surprise she was a nervous wreck.

"Lily brought us dinner." Gram still occupied the recliner. "It was wonderful."

One dinner down. How many had been brought since Dad, Amber, and I left?

Aunt Lily's waxy cheeks reddened. "I'm glad you liked it, Lydia. But Claire made it. I worked all day."

Dad gave his aunt a one-armed hug. "How many days in a row have you worked?"

"Only nine," said Aunt Lily. "I have Saturday off this weekend." She picked up a fake leather purse with spots worn white.

"Don't let Diane take advantage of you," said Dad. "You're her best cashier, but you can't carry the IGA on your own."

She gave him a trembling smile. "That's something Reuel would say. You don't look a bit like your dad, but you're as nice as he was."

Dad gave her another hug. "That's one of the nicest things anyone has told me."

Her cheeks reddening even more, she fluttered her fingers before her smile. Then she looked down at the books and folders on the bar. "Is that my mother's book? The one with the clues for the treasure?"

"Aunt Jeanine had it," I said. "Dad wanted the research she'd done on the treasure."

She picked up The Book, the one with the poem. "That's right. I'd forgotten Jeanine borrowed it because she was writing a story. The other day, Jack asked me where it was, and I couldn't find it." She touched the clip holding back her hair that ran from buttery blonde to frosty white, her teeth gnawing her lower lip. "He didn't like that at all."

I could imagine. Jack was the same age I was, which I disliked because I wanted nothing in common with this first half-cousin once removed. He acted like his mother existed for one purpose — to supply his needs and/or wants, which usually meant money.

"How come you want the book, Mal?" Aunt Lily looked up to him.

"Some of Cyrus Morley's descendants are back in the county," he said, "and at least one is determined to find the treasure, so I thought I'd study up on the whole mess." His voice dropped a few decibels. "Why did Jack want your book?"

Jack was the only one of Aunt Lily's outlaw kids currently in the county who'd make trouble if he was looking for the treasure. But Dad had said Jack could talk his younger brother Jesse into anything and might bully his half-sister Claire into helping him with less than honest activities.

"I don't know." Aunt Lily's fingers fanned before her mouth again. "Maybe it's 'cause he got a job at that Halloween thing they're doing at the old children's home. Somebody said it's all about Cyrus Morley and some scary stuff he used to do when the children's home was his house."

Dad's drooping shoulders straightened, but he kept his voice casual. "What job does Jack have there?"

Aunt Lily twisted her mouth to the side. "I think he said ... tech crew. Something like that. It's the same job Jesse has."

Dad's eyes widened. "Both of them are working there?"

"And Claire. But she's taking tickets, and the boys have the same job."

"I'm glad Claire got a job." Dad's sentence sounded automatic as if his focus had turned inward. Maybe he was assessing the amount of trouble Jack could make in a hunt for the treasure.

I was glad for Claire too. After enduring two abusive relationships, Claire's self-worth was zero. Jeanine and Gram had encouraged her to get a job to help support her two kids and acquire some confidence in herself since her last boyfriend had overdosed several months ago.

Aunt Lily said, "Claire applied for a job at the lodge, like Jeanine told her to. But this is a good job for now. I work day shifts, and she can watch the kids. Then I can watch them at night." Catching her lip again, she touched the book. "Do you need this, Mal? Jack really wanted it."

A spasm of some potent emotion passed over Dad's face, then he smiled. "Tell Jack I need it for my job. When I'm done with it, I'll give it back to you." His voice took on an edge of steel. "If he'd like more details, he can come talk to me."

Her troubled expression cleared a little. "You said some of Cyrus Morley's family are in town." She dug in her purse. "Can you tell me their names? If they stop by the store, I want to let them know I'm family."

"Your half-uncle Timothy Morley, his son Alex, and a distant cousin

Dani Li. She's running The Haunting in the Hollow."

Aunt Lily jotted the names on a scrap of paper, and Dad walked her to her car.

The house was way too quiet.

Flopping onto the couch, I said to Gram, "Where are the boys and Coral? Getting the alpacas in for the night?"

"The boys are. Coral was falling asleep on the couch, so I made her move to your bed. Do you mind sleeping on the inflatable mattress?"

"Not at all."

"I knew you wouldn't." Gram leaned over the arm of the recliner. "How's Jeanine? And Luke? This has to be killing him."

I told Gram about our visit, and Dad returned to the kitchen with Chris coming in behind him.

So much had happened, and I was so worried about Hank that I'd forgotten Chris had said he would stop by after his shift.

He only wore old jeans and a jean jacket that revealed a black t-shirt, but my breath took a couple hops.

"Hey." I started toward him.

Chris crossed to me and took my hand.

Dad's eyes rounded like he'd been whacked on the back of the head with a bat.

Chris's quick glance caught his reaction. "If Rae hasn't had a chance to tell you, she and I are partners now. I know some people in town will think I'm trying to influence my boss."

Dad shook himself. "Uh—yeah. Some will. But that's on me. I have to show voters I'm impartial."

"So it's no ethics violation?" I said.

During the many times I'd wondered what it'd be like if Chris and I became partners, I'd also wondered if our relationship would put Dad and Chris in awkward positions. Dad had only won his office by two votes. Many people would have liked to prove that even if Dad wasn't a criminal like some of his relatives, he was at least dishonest.

"No. My job can't keep my daughter from dating who she wants."

Chris said, "I came to bury Knight. Rae said Hank has a backhoe attachment for a tractor. I know how to work that."

Dad still seemed fixated on our hands. Then he lifted his head. "I'll come with you. I don't think it's a two-person job."

My stomach twisted. "I wasn't planning on helping with the ... burial. I was going to show Chris where the machines were and then take care of the animals and clean up the house."

"That's fine. I can help Chris." He went to the basement door. "I'll get my work coat."

"Are you sure you aren't too tired?" I said. "What about your knee?"

"This needs done," Dad called up the stairs. "I think Chris and I can manage."

I wasn't so sure as I followed Dad's slow steps to the Beast, carrying Jeanine's research. If I had to wait on Dad and Chris, I needed something to do, and my conversation with Jeanine had stirred my interest in the lost inheritance.

At the Norris's farm, Dad and Chris disappeared into the woods to assess the problem while I brought in the horses and fed and watered them. As I refilled water and food bowls for the dogs and cats, a tractor roared to life and drove away.

I cleaned the kitchen, sorted laundry, and gathered clothes and other items Coral had asked for at lunch. Dad and Chris still hadn't come back. I spread the books and folders over the walnut dinner table.

Dad had remembered the terms of the will correctly. The four children named in it and any of their descendants had a right to the treasure. Whoever touched it first got to keep it all.

I tugged on my earlobe. If I cracked the riddle, I could take Aunt Lily or Claire with me so they could touch the treasure. Claire was the only one of Aunt Lily's seven kids who'd use the money to benefit their whole family. Except maybe Jesse, but he was only eighteen and couldn't stand up to his older brother Jack. Of course, Aunt Lily wouldn't waste any money she inherited. Unless someone like Jack scared her out of it.

Cyrus Morley had certainly shown contempt for his family with his will. Maybe the clue "beneath my contempt" pointed to the treasure being buried under something connected to the Morley family—an ancestral home or family cemetery?

Cyrus's widow Marie seemed to share my conclusion. A newspaper article from 1968 contained an interview with Marie Pleshette Morley when she donated a large sum of money to an art museum. Either Cyrus swiping all that cash and jewels hadn't depleted Marie's bank account or she'd recovered her wealth in the intervening seventeen years.

At the end of the interview, the reporter asked about the will.

Marie answered, "My husband designed a game to drive his family mad. It is a fool's game. And I am no fool."

She sounded like she hadn't bothered to solve the clues. Had Timothy worked on this for over fifty years and gotten nowhere? Or had the treasure bug only bitten him recently?

I'd pushed back my chair to get paper clips from Jeanine's writing desk in her bedroom when someone knocked at the front door.

Expecting more food from friends, I opened it to find a strange man, nearly as tall as Dad, grinning at me.

"Is Mr. Norris at home? I'm Kyle Garrison." He handed me a card.

He was about thirty with a furry, brown beard. Long clumps of hair fell from under a green camo baseball hat with the silhouette of an ape on it. "I want to interview him about his bigfoot encounter."

His card dropped to the floor of the porch along with my jaw.

He scooped it up, holding it out to me. "Yeah, most people are surprised bigfoots are active in Ohio, but I've found evidence of bigfoot activity in twenty-seven of eighty-eight counties."

I regained control of my jaw and said, "My uncle's in the hospital, and I don't know when he can give anyone an interview."

"The bigfoot actually attacked him?" Eagerness rang in his voice.

"No, his horse slipped and fell on his leg."

"Oh. That's the story I saw online--something spooked a horse and maybe injured a rider." He took one step too close. "Could you show me where the incident occurred? I want to set up cameras and see if I can get a photo of the bigfoot."

This guy couldn't be for real. I'd never heard of bigfoots--bigfeet?-- in Ohio. He hadn't expressed even a polite concern that Hank was hurt. And did he seriously think I'd walk into the woods, in the dark, with a strange man?

I was formulating how to tell him what he could do with his request when Dad and Chris walked onto the porch, carrying Hank's cowboy hat and other clothing we must have left by the creek.

Dad's slack expression seemed to indicate that he was working on his last drops of adrenaline. Then he saw the stranger. Cop mode took over, straightening his spine and fixing a level stare on the guy.

"Dad." I held out the card to him. "This man wants to set up cameras on the property."

"'Buckeye Bigfoot Investigations'?" Dad read the card out loud. "What bigfoot?" Despite his exhaustion, he released the question at full, deafening volume.

Garrison swayed back like the sound waves had pushed him but kept grinning. "That's what I'm trying to find out."

Dad said, "A black bear scared my brother-in-law's horse."

Garrison nodded. "Many bigfoots are mistaken for black bears."

"Only my brother-in-law or sister can give you permission to set up equipment on their property, and they're not here."

Slyness creeped into the grin. The guy took out his wallet and removed some bills. "Give this to your sister and keep some for yourself. I'll set up a few cameras. Won't bother anybody."

"You better believe you won't." Dad's bellow didn't touch the man's grin. "Let me make myself clear. I can't give you permission because it's not my property. I will advise my sister against granting permission, and she won't because she's got way too much to worry about right now. But I'll be checking this property regularly, and if I find a camera, I'll know exactly who to ask about it, Mr. Garrison."

The grin grew. "Are you threatening me?"

With deliberate slowness, Dad took out his own wallet from his back pocket and flipped it open to his badge. "I'm not threatening. I'm carrying out my duties as sheriff. If you want to conduct bigfoot investigations in my county, you will obtain verbal or written permission from the owner of each property where you plan to set up a camera, or I will do my best to see you are prosecuted for trespassing."

"Of course. I'm a professional." Garrison touched the bill of his cap in a casual salute and sauntered back to a mud-splattered, gray SUV parked on the drive.

As we watched him back down the drive, Dad shoved away his wallet. "All this county needs. Bigfoot hunters."

Chapter Thirteen

Back home, Chris and I said goodbye at his truck. My feet floated me to the front door.

As I sat on the bench inside the door and removed my boots, Aaron and Micah said good night and disappeared into their bedroom. Rusty lay on the couch with another epic sci-fi or fantasy novel.

I glanced about. "Did Gram go to bed already?"

Rusty turned a page and murmured, "Yeah."

Dad sat on the piano bench, his head lowered, his arms straight as he gripped his knees. Either he was thinking something over or propping himself up.

"You should go to bed too, Dad."

He staggered upright. "I will in a minute. Bed in fifteen, Rusty. Rae, come downstairs." He broke into a self-conscious smile. "I mean, would you please come downstairs?"

"For sure." What did Dad want to discuss in private?

In the basement, Dad turned on the bare bulb above the laundry area and sagged against an old table we used for sorting clothes. "I may have waited too long for this conversation, but, well ... " the self-conscious smile again "... I'm still figuring out my job as a parent of a young adult."

"You're doing a fantastic job."

"Thanks, kiddo." A sharp glance. "Why are you dating?"

"Dating Chris?" Wasn't it obvious? "I like him."

"No, I mean in general. What's your goal for dating?"

"I—uh—I guess to find a husband."

He nodded. "Good. That's why Christians are supposed to date. So you're hoping Chris might be the candidate?"

"Well—uh—yes. I—I guess." I rolled the hem of my t-shirt. "I mean, it's too soon to know."

"Right, right. You're just starting to know each other." He pressed the heels of his hands against his eyes. "You need to know what Chris believes about God." He lowered his hands. "Have you talked to him about your faith?"

I shrugged. "I've mentioned my faith a few times, like I only survived the stalker because God gave me inspiration. But ..." My jeans and t-shirt suddenly felt too tight or too big or something uncomfortable. "Chris is a very private person. It's hard to talk to him about personal stuff."

"Yeah, I figured that out when I interviewed him for his job. But if he wants a relationship with you, he has to loosen security. Since your relationship has turned serious, you have to discuss serious issues. Nothing is more serious than what you believe. As a Christian, you have to marry a Christian."

I stared at him. Mom had mentioned this, but since I'd never dated before, I hadn't thought much about it. "Is that what the Bible says?"

"Yes. I can give you chapter and verse."

"Chris doesn't seem opposed to my faith."

"I'm sure he isn't. That'd be fine if you were just friends. But marriage is a whole other ballgame. You can't play the game if the husband and wife are using two different playbooks."

I threw out my hands. "We've only been partners for twenty-four hours. I can't dump all that on him tomorrow."

"I know. So start small. Invite him to church." He blinked several times, like he was losing a battle with heavy eyelids. "Or have you invited him and he turned you down?"

Feeling more uncomfortable than ever, I said, "No, I've never invited him. I—I've never been very good at that." Not at all good, really. In my whole life, I'd only invited one person, Devon, and she'd said no thanks.

A frown fought to surface on my lips. Why did Dad have to bring up all this serious stuff now? Couldn't Chris and I enjoy the newness of our relationship first?

Dad's gaze had wandered to a spot past my shoulder.

I touched his arm. "Dad?"

He wrenched his focus back to me. "I thought it was my job to bring this up."

"Thanks." I kissed him on the cheek. Although I didn't like him sucking the joy from my new relationship, I knew he meant well, and I could thank him for that. "Better get some sleep. I don't want to drag you across the basement floor to your bedroom."

He kissed me on the forehead before limping to his finished bedroom on the other side of the stairs.

Upstairs, I told Rusty to go to bed and then went into Gram's bedroom.

Coral had moved to Gram's bed, curled in a ball beside her. She had to be scared about her dad and needed the comfort of being close to someone. Hopefully, her movements wouldn't aggravate Gram's bad back.

I went through the door that connected my newly built bedroom to Gram's and changed into pajamas.

Dad was right. I could start small. Inviting Chris to church was a good start.

My lungs cramped, and I sank onto my double bed.
If it was a good start, why did it make me feel bad?

Chapter Fourteen

"How's Hank?" Devon Majors rushed across the parking lot to the basement entrance of the library as I punched in the code to unlock the door. "There's still no posts on Jeanine's socials." A series of molasses brown braids were piled on her head. Another set swung across her back.

"Aunt Carrie called this morning." We entered, and I shut the door behind us. "Uncle Hank's still unconscious. I'm surprised she hasn't posted something."

In the employees' kitchen, Devon placed her lunch bag in the fridge. "I haven't told the girls. They love Hank. Every time Amber brought them to the farm this summer while she was babysitting, Hank always took time to tell the girls a few jokes, no matter how busy he was." She fingered one of the many studs lining her right ear. "Liberty is so sensitive and anxious that she'd make herself sick with worry if she knew how seriously he's injured."

We climbed the back stairs to the children's room, passed through it, and came into the two-story lobby of the main branch of the Marlin County Library System. Overcast skies lingered like a guest who didn't know when it was time to leave.

A hint of moisture glinted in Devon's forest-green eyes as she logged on a computer. "Hank's a truly nice guy. When you've been around as long as I have, you realize nice guys — kind men — are rare."

At thirty-three, Devon hadn't been around all that long. Although the death of her boyfriend, the father of her two daughters, before she was thirty had given her an experience usually reserved for people twice as old.

I bent over the drop box and collected materials that had been pushed through the slot beneath the window after closing. Devon would want to know about Chris and me, but her belief that only thugs and thieves became cops would prevent her from seeing our relationship as positive.

My arms loaded, I turned to the desk. "Chris Kincaid and I are partners now." My muscles braced themselves.

One thing I liked most about Devon was that she said what she thought, and she meant what she said. But the past thirty-six hours had made me allergic to any more stress.

Devon had been rummaging on a shelf under the desk. Now she jerked upright, her small mouth twisting in her thoughtful frown. "I suppose I should say it's about time. You two have gone on enough non-date dates. But"—her frown deepened—"I hope you know what you're letting yourself in for, Rae."

Squashing a harsh reply, I grabbed the keys to the lobby doors and hurried to unlock them.

Every single person who entered the library asked about Hank. No surprise. Except for a few years after he and Jeanine were first married, Hank had lived his whole life in Marlin County. Everybody knew him. And everybody liked him.

At noon, Chris texted to ask if he could treat me to lunch at Cervelli's Deli since it was his day off.

Me: For sure.

I waited for him outside the library, studying a new sign on a storefront that had been empty during the sixteen months I'd lived in the county.

When Chris joined me, I pointed across the street. "That sign for the medium says 'entertainment only.' Do you think she means that, or is she covering herself against a customer charging her with fraud?"

"Most likely the latter." Chris took my hand, and shivery prickles danced up my arm. "We already had a complaint about Lyra Vex. She was offering palm and tarot readings to customers outside the IGA. When I told her she couldn't do it in front of a business, she said she didn't understand all my English words but left without a hassle."

"Lyra Vex? That can't be her real name," I said as we strolled to the deli. "I think she was here last year. I remember a woman posting flyers for readings all over town. But she hadn't rented a storefront."

Chris held open the door to the shop. "The fortune telling business must be paying off."

We ordered at the counter and then took our soup and sandwiches to a table in the corner of the small storefront.

Slipping a straw in my soda, I said, "Was the backhoe at the farm the same as the one you used in high school?"

"Very similar." Chris bit into his Reuben sandwich.

"Why did you get to use one at your high school?"

Chris stopped in mid-chew. Then he continued, very slowly. He swallowed and took a long drink of soda, like he was buying time.

Why? Yes, he was private, but all I wanted to know was a fact from when he was in high school.

"I helped with maintenance," he said.

I nodded. Should I ask about the horses? Shoot fires, if I couldn't ask him something that harmless, how could I invite him to church?

Now I took a long drink of soda. "Why did your school have horses?"

More very thoughtful chewing. "Some students boarded their horses at the school. The school also owned some." He cleared his throat. "It was a Catholic school. About half the students boarded and half were day students."

I fought my eyes from bulging. Chris had mentioned his mom was an actress, but I didn't know she had that kind of money. He'd also said she was an addict.

His reply looked like a good opening for talking about faith. "So you're Catholic?"

He shrugged, brushing stray strands of sauerkraut to the side of his plate. "I take it no news on your uncle."

Beneath that statement seemed the clear message, "Subject closed."

"No. It's still a waiting game."

We cleared our table, dumped our garbage, and, holding hands again, returned to Main Street. The cast iron lid of gray had cracked enough to let a few brave shafts of sunlight touch the sandstone courthouse and buildings across the street.

Mayor Teague, Ms. Zollars, and a man who introduced himself as a farmer friend of Hank's stopped me to ask about him.

Outside the library, Chris lifted my hand, kissed my knuckles, and jogged down the street toward his truck.

I rested against the glass doors to the library. This was too good to mess up. I had to figure out a way to discuss what really mattered with Chris.

Chapter Fifteen

Later in the afternoon, at a brisk pace for seventy, Timothy Morley marched in. With a satchel over his shoulder, he held a thick book in his right hand. It had to be The Book, the volume of Poe he'd inherited. Without looking left or right, he went straight through the lobby to the local history room.

Devon whispered, "Do you know him? He's been in here several times this week."

Between waiting on Mr. Olsen and repairing books, I explained who Timothy Morley was and about the will, the inheritance, and the connection to The Haunting and my great-aunt's family.

Devon drew a bead of glue down a cracked binding. "Doesn't sound like you'll be bored working at The Haunting."

Devon's daughters, Liberty and Serenity Stone, bent under their backpacks, came through the front doors. Wellesville Elementary School was less than a half mile away, but being loaded down like army recruits when you're only ten and six years old transformed a pleasant walk into a marathon.

While they waited for closing time, Liberty hunkered down behind a middle grade novel at a table, and Serenity surveyed the lobby like a Viking deciding which part of a town to pillage first.

Five minutes later, Devon removed a phone from Serenity's grubby little hand.

"Why did you take his phone?" Devon handed it to a weedy, spluttering junior high boy.

"He said I was fat." Serenity stomped her foot, making her long hair, the same rich brown as her mother's, bounce.

She was definitely chubby, but not fat. And a lot of first graders were just as chubby.

"That was mean." Devon glared at the weedy boy's back. "But you still can't take his phone. You only have to wait twenty minutes until we close. I'll get you some crayons and coloring sheets from the children's room. But you stay in the lobby."

Pouting her lips, Serenity doubled her arms over her chest.

Devon walked under the balcony overlooking the lobby as a young woman with the most unusual dye job I'd seen entered from Main Street. The top layer of her long hair was bleached, the underlying layers were varying shades of brown, and the tips were jet black. The pattern created an animal appearance, perfectly matching her cat-like face and tilted, sly eyes.

"Who do I talk to about library program?" She had an accent but wasn't hard to understand. She might have been my age or ten years older. "I want to do program about history of tarot cards." She broke into a feline smile. "I am Lyra Vex. I have store across street."

"Our program schedule is already set for October," I said. "We plan months in advance."

The corners of her mouth dropped in a more sophisticated pout than Serenity's, but still a pout.

"You don't like mediums?"

"No." I scrubbed grime off a picture book cover. "We don't have room for additional programs this month."

Timothy Morley carried The Book and another large book to the table with office equipment beside the copier.

"I give free readings too," said Ms. Vex.

"Give me that!" Serenity yelled.

Looking up, I saw Weedy Boy standing near the copier, holding Serenity's water bottle just out of reach above her head.

"You don't like having something taken away from you, do you?" He jerked the bottle higher as Serenity jumped for it.

I raised my voice. "Hey, kid."

He snapped his head in my direction as Serenity, her face screwed up in a furious knot, glanced about and then grabbed one of Timothy's books from the table.

"Serenity!" Devon yelled, coming out of the hall under the balcony.

Holding the book by its cover, Serenity swung it at the boy.

Devon snatched it from her younger daughter before it made contact.

The junior high kid dropped the bottle and ran out the front doors.

"What's the matter with you, Serene?" Devon flipped the book open, front and back. "This isn't a library book. Where did you—"

Timothy ripped it out of Devon's hands with so much force that she staggered forward.

I dashed around the desk.

Clutching the book to his chest, Timothy trembled all over, and his withered cheeks flushed to a deep burgundy. "It's mine." His clenched teeth and the tremors obscured his words. "How dare you touch it? How dare this—this brat touch my—"

"This brat is my daughter." Devon moved Serenity behind her. "I'm very sorry she grabbed your book. It's not damaged."

"It better not be." Timothy marched, or tried to, back to the local history room. But his outrage gave him the unsteady steps of a drunk.

Devon escorted Serenity back to the table where Liberty hid behind her book like it was a shield of invisibility.

Ms. Vex aimed her cat eyes in Timothy's direction, then switched back to me. "You sure? No tarot program?"

"I'm sure." I looked back to the picture book I was cleaning.

Maintaining eye contact was hard. Ms. Vex's gaze was calculating, like a cat determining if you qualified as prey.

Timothy stormed into the lobby, one arm pressing The Book against his chest.

Ms. Vex stepped in front of him, fishing in a purse knitted in shades of purple and green and slung across her body. "You are very upset. Have trouble? I can help." She produced a business card.

He blinked, as if uncertain of what he saw, then glanced at the card. "No, thank you." The words barely escaped his dried-up lips.

He flung open a door to the vestibule and exited.

Ms. Vex watched him through the two sets of glass doors. Or maybe "scanned" was a better word. Then she gave me a sly glance and left, the black tips of her hair swaying.

Devon said in a low voice, "The book Serenity grabbed — was that *The Book*? The book of Edgar Allan Poe with the clues?"

"If it was an Edgar Allan Poe book, yes."

Devon shook her head. "That guy is wound way too tight. I thought he might attack me or Serenity or both of us."

"I thought that too, but I think you could've taken him."

Devon released a noise that came close to a snort. "I hope I can take an elderly man when he's that frail looking and only a couple inches taller than me."

~~~~~

After supper, I collected a few sheets of paper from the printer, Aunt Lily's copy of the Poe book, Jeanine's folders, and a children's book about codes I'd borrowed from the library. I had an hour before I needed to leave for the opening night of The Haunting in the Hollow.

Two minutes was all it took for my brothers to surround me.

"What're you doing?" Micah rested his elbows on the dinner table.

"Trying to crack this code and find the lost inheritance for Aunt Lily." I leafed through the code book.

Rusty sat down across from me, and Aaron knelt on a chair beside me. I showed the boys the poem and the note and explained Aunt Jeanine's theories about what the clues meant.

"Because Edgar Allan Poe wrote a short story with a code, and it's in this book, Aunt Jeanine thought Cyrus Morley might have used a similar code."

Aaron reached for The Book. "Which short story is it?"
~~~~~

"'The Gold Bug.' It was written almost two hundred years ago, so it's hard to read."

About impossible when I tried last night. I eventually skipped to the part with the code.

With Aaron still holding The Book, I flipped to those pages. "In the story, a pirate creates a code by randomly assigning numbers and symbols to the letters of the alphabet."

Rusty peered at the yellowed note. "But you don't have lines of symbols and numbers. You've got a note with three words and a poem."

"The Morley code has to be more complicated. If it is a code. It could be a riddle. Cyrus may have used the lines in the poem to describe a place." I pointed at the poem. "'Mountains of the Moon' could mean mountains or hills that resemble the moon in some way. Maybe made of bare rock. 'Valley of the Shadow' might be a valley beside the mountains or hills. It also means death, so it could be a valley associated with death in some way."

Aaron threw up his hands. "But there are a million places with hills and valleys."

I tapped the note. "But he hid the cash and jewels in a place that was 'beneath his contempt.' That should narrow the locations."

"What does that mean?" Micah picked up the note. "'Beneath my contempt'?"

From the couch where she and Coral watched TV, Gram said, "It means you have no respect at all for a person or thing. They're less than trash."

"So-o..." Rusty stared at the poem. "You have to research the guy to figure out what he had contempt for."

"According to what Jeanine told me years ago—" Dad shut the basement door and limped over to the table "—there's no shortage of those things."

"Maybe it is a code." Aaron took the note from Micah and placed it above the poem. "The note has three words and seventeen letters. Maybe the code is every third word of the poem. Or every third letter. Or every seventeenth word. Or—"

"If it was that easy," said Rusty, "somebody would've cracked the code years ago."

"We should eliminate all possibilities." I turned around in my chair. "Coral, do you want to help?"

"C'mon, Coral." Aaron waved her over.

She continued to stare at the TV. "I'm good." She'd been surfing the few channels we received since I'd come home from work.

Her head tilting to one side, Gram studied her granddaughter's profile.

Rusty got more paper, Dad took a seat, Micah squirmed onto his lap, and the five of us tried the different codes from the library book that might apply, but all our efforts produced the same result: nonsense. Some very intriguing nonsense, but still nonsense.

Aaron bounced the eraser end of the pencil on the table. "We need to code a program to do all the analysis."

Dad loosened a strap on his brace. "Timothy Morley would have solved it by now if a program could crack it."

Coral got off the couch. "It's after 7. We gotta get the horses in and feed the dogs and cats. Uncle Mal, will you drive me and Rusty over?"

Dad blinked a couple times, and I did too.

Coral always preferred to walk, any excuse to get outside. But the sun had set, and the windows behind the dinner table showed the eastern horizon had already turned a slate blue. Maybe Coral didn't want to risk meeting the big, black animal again.

Poring over the poem, Rusty said, "Why do you want me?"

Gram said, "It's already taken care of, sweetheart. I've had so many people offering to help that I asked if they could look after the animals. I made sure they had experience with horses. Enough people volunteered for both mornings and evenings that we're covered until next Friday."

"That's a relief," Dad said. "Nothing like good neighbors and church family."

"Absolutely." Gram's usual mellow smile grew. "And if they're taking care of the animals, they're not making casseroles."

Chapter Sixteen

A carnival atmosphere, like night on the midway at the county fair, hung over the field directly below the stone husk of the Morley Mansion as I drove past in the Rust Bucket. Subdued orange illumination from temporary streetlamps along the drive to the house mixed with the blaze of spotlights on top of the ticket booth. A long line wound through the gates that organized the crowd, and The Haunting in the Hollow didn't open for another hour. A couple of food trucks with their own bright lights and their own long lines were stationed at one end of that field.

I pulled into a field across the road from the event, driving between long rows of vehicles, to the far end, where employees were supposed to park. Maybe I'd have time to capture that atmosphere before we opened.

I slung on my camera backpack and was locking the Rust Bucket when an ancient, dark blue van, pockmarked with rust, lumbered into a spot. The doors opened and out spilled Aunt Lily's three youngest kids — Claire Duvall, Jack Senakovich, and Jesse Senakovich. Like me, they were all dressed in various shades of black, although some of their clothes were so old they'd faded to a grainy gray.

"You got a job here too?" Jack yelled at me. His hatchet face held a nasty leer, and the tips of his dirty blonde hair waved in the breeze like a messy shock of wheat.

"That's obvious." I walked up to Claire. "We're working the ticket booth together."

Her head bent, she smiled, but it flew away like a startled deer. Claire had Aunt Lily's thick, buttery blonde hair, and a smooth, round face that seemed better suited to an updo and a wide Victorian hat with plumes and flowers. Her old-fashioned beauty might have been the reason she looked older than twenty-three. But the main cause had to be the toll from enduring two abusive boyfriends.

"I was real sorry to hear about Hank." Claire's words scurried out, like they were afraid of being heard. "It'll be nice to work with someone I know."

"Amber's working Saturday nights, and maybe Sundays too," I said.

Jack draped an arm over his older half-sister's shoulders. "You know us, Claire. Don't we count?"

Dislike tensed her lowered face.

Jack laughed, a mocking, rattling noise.

We crossed the road to a gap in the barriers lining the bottom of the hill the home sat on. Carrie stood in the gap with a tablet.

She and Jack spotted each other and said, at about the same time, "You're working here?"

Carrie scrolled on the tablet while Jack and Jesse traded significant looks, as if Carrie's presence meant something. If Jack planned to hunt for the treasure, he might have thought that job had just gotten a whole lot harder.

"I hadn't seen the list of everybody on the crew." She looked up from the tablet.

You never would have guessed she'd spent the past two days living at ICU, worried sick. She was every inch the professional head of security from her black baseball cap and windbreaker to the taser on her black jeans and the glare she aimed at our cousins.

"Let's start off on the right foot, guys. You do your job, and you'll never have to see me do mine. Am I clear?"

Jesse overdid the nodding while Jack said in a hurt voice, "Aw, c'mon, Carrie. We ain't done a thing, and you're already threatening us." Then he broke into his leer, revealing long teeth.

"You all heard me." She stepped aside and aimed her stylus toward the old home and the tents and trailers near it. "Dani wants all staff to meet at the trailer she's using as her office."

The Haunting employed a lot more people than I expected as we gathered in front of the white trailer in loose arcs. Dani Li stood on the top step leading to the door of the trailer, a spotlight shining down on her.

She picked up a battery-powered megaphone. "This is it, people. I've put 200 percent into getting us ready, and I expect just as much from each of you. If we work hard, we'll give our guests an unforgettable Halloween experience. Any make-up or costume problems, see Adam Hardy. Any problems with guests, go to Carrie Malinowski or another security team member. There are three tonight."

Carrie raised a hand at the crowd, flanked by an officer who was new to the Wellesville town police and Deputy Miguel "Houston" Blank. Houston must have wanted some extra money from a temporary job on his days off from the sheriff's department.

"None of this could happen," Dani continued, "without the financial backing of Alex Morley. Yes, he's related to Cyrus Morley, the main character in our story and the man who built this house and owned the property eighty years ago. He's his grandson. C'mon up here, Alex."

A lean man, around forty, jogged up beside Dani. I never would have guessed Timothy was his father. Looking like he could advertise fitness equipment, he was bronzed all over—dark blonde hair brushed back and a tan he must have perfected years ago.

Dani handed him the mike of the megaphone. "I'm glad I can be part of something positive in Marlin County," Alex said in a nasal voice. "My grandfather wasn't a model citizen, and in many ways, he exploited the people of this county. So I'm glad to have the chance to give back to the community."

Was Alex referring to the illegitimate children Cyrus had left here? Or the safety record in the mines he owned? Jeanine had copies of several newspaper articles describing accidents in local coal mines. Curiously, none of those articles were from the local paper. They'd all appeared in *The Columbus Dispatch.*

We broke into polite applause.

"All right, people," Dani shouted in the mike. "It's showtime. Let's knock opening night into the record books."

Claire and I walked down the hill from the home to the ticket booth. The shed only had enough room to pivot from the ticket windows to a folding table snug against the back wall.

Dani bustled in with a third clerk, Nora Oller, and reviewed with us the app for collecting tickets and money. She pointed to a walkie-talkie on the table resting in its charger in a quick, distinct movement that reminded me again of a tiny bird. "Phone service is spotty, so we have walkie-talkies. I taped the list of frequencies for me, security, and costumes and make-up to the table."

She flew out the door on the back wall.

Squeezing past Claire to an open window, Nora muttered, "She didn't need to remind us of the bad cell service. We all live here."

The first hour rushed by with wave after wave of customers. Half wore everyday clothes, and the other half had gotten into the Halloween mood early, many of them wearing clothes that would have made Edgar Allan Poe think fashions hadn't changed since he'd died in 1850.

Each ticket had a timed entry, but no one seemed to mind waiting a half hour or more to get in. A fire-eater and a magician worked the crowd, while a storyteller spun wild tales about Cyrus Morley and his haunted land. Lyra Vex handed out cards and seemed to give free palm readings.

Screams echoed from the woods that extended back from the mansion, making us jump, but after about the twentieth one, Nora and I ignored them. Claire kept flinching.

When the waves quit hitting us, I said to Claire, "The last entry is at 1 a.m. Do your brothers have to stay until closing?"

She nodded. "That's 2, isn't it?"

"Yeah. Would you like me to drive you home so you don't have to wait?"

A piercing shriek spiked from behind the booth, and I didn't even blink.

When Claire's breathing returned to normal, she said, "That'd be nice. I'm not putting you out, am I?" Gratitude brought a little glow to her pale green eyes.

"Not at all." Although I was a little hazy on where the house she and her kids shared with Aunt Lily and Jesse was located.

Catching movement out of the corner of my eye, I turned to my window.

Timothy Morley held up his phone. "I have my ticket here."

I scanned it, and he joined the other customers waiting for the 10:45 entry.

Should I tell Carrie about Timothy? Nothing wrong with him taking a tour. But Dad always liked as much info as he could gather on a troublesome situation.

After Timothy was out of earshot, I picked up the walkie-talkie. "I need to call security."

Wiping springy cinnamon curls from her flushed forehead, Nora handed a customer change. "What's up?"

"Nothing, I hope." I stepped outside and twisted a knob to the correct frequency and pressed a button on the side. "This is Rae Riley at the ticket booth."

"What's the problem?" said Carrie.

I explained Timothy had purchased a ticket.

"Oh, joy. Thanks for the heads up."

Another swarm of customers kept us busy until 11, when Alex Morley slipped into the tiny building.

"Mademoiselles, how's business?"

"Booming." Giggling, Nora handed wrist bands to a couple.

"That's what I like to hear."

This close, I noticed lines etched into his tan, which gave his complexion a leathery look. His narrow eyes were hazel.

Dad might like a little intel on Alex Morley.

"It's nice you want to give back to people in the county, sir." I ripped a wristband along the perforated line. "Is this your first investment in a Halloween attraction?"

Claire shot a quick peek in Alex's direction and then scanned a paper ticket for a customer.

"Total first," he said, "and it couldn't be in better hands. Dani knows what she's doing. And call me Alex, please."

A pained smile started to form, but I stiffened my lips. My mostly Southern upbringing cringed at the idea of calling someone as old as my father by his first name. But if I was going to get information from him, I had to agree. "Okay. Alex. What's your usual business?"

"I make investments."

Was that code for independently wealthy, no need to hold a job?

Alex went on, "I may back more ventures like this." He beamed. "It's the most fun I've had in an invest—can I help you?" His question was sharp.

Claire had kept glancing at him. Now a blush flooded her smooth face, and she became fascinated with her tablet.

"Claire's your cousin." I assumed that was her interest in Alex. "Cyrus was her great-grandfather."

"Really?" His nasal voice lost its piercing quality. "I thought Cyrus only had four living descendants—Dani, her mother, my father, and me."

Interesting. Was he right? Besides Aunt Lily and her kids and grandkids, could only four other people inherit the treasure? It sounded like Alex had been doing some genealogy research and not accurately. Maybe Timothy was right—the attraction was a cover for Alex to hunt for the treasure.

I said, "Claire's grandmother was one of the heirs named in the will. Linda Pavlich."

Alex stroked his top lip. "I remember that name, but I didn't—"

"This is outrageous!"

I knew that clipped, superior voice.

I leaned out a ticket window as every head in line turned to watch Carrie escort Timothy Morley down the drive.

Carrie held Timothy's arm. "Both I and one of my team told you that if you didn't remain with your group, you'd be ejected. I am now doing my job."

"Any problem, Carrie?" Alex strode toward them.

Bright lights on the ticket booth caught his smirk.

"None at all, Alex," said Carrie.

Timothy jerked out of her grip and stalked up to his son. "You told them to do this. You have no moral right to the inheritance. I'm my father's only legitimate heir."

"Grandfather didn't seem worried about the legalities of his children's parentage," said Alex, "or he wouldn't have named them in his will." A gloating note fattened his voice. "I'm your son, completely legitimate, so I have as much moral right as you."

Shaking, Timothy glared up at him. "Not as long as I'm alive."

"You're seventy-three. Grand-mere living to eighty-nine doesn't mean you couldn't drop dead tomorrow."

Carrie said, "You need to leave now, Mr. Morley. Or you will be arrested. I have a deputy working with me tonight."

Timothy gave his son another blast of his glower and then stormed across the road, vanishing into the night.

Alex raised his voice. "A little extra entertainment, ladies and gentlemen. Hope you enjoy the rest of the show."

Laughter bounced around the crowd, and the line at our windows began moving again.

Alex sauntered through the narrow door of the booth. "Claire, about your grandmother ... by the way, what's your last name?"

"Duvall." It was a squeak as she took money from a customer. "Claire Duvall."

"Is your grandmother still with us?"

"No. She died ... it's been about twenty years ago."

"Are you the only descendent?"

Nora snorted so hard that she broke out coughing.

Since Claire seemed to find talking to Alex a chore, I said, "Linda Pavlich had one child, Lily. Aunt Lily's still alive. She has seven children and eleven or twelve grandchildren." I raised an eyebrow at Claire.

"Twelve," she said. "We know twelve for sure."

Alex's mouth worked for a moment, his hazel eyes glazing over.

I must have looked like that when I found out the sheer number of Malinowskis I was related to. "They don't all live here," I said. "Four of Aunt Lily's kids are out of the county right now. Larry's in prison, Rene's in the army, Mickey's in rehab, and no one's heard from Lee J. in a couple years."

His mouth worked again, but words were missing.

"Claire's half-brothers Jack and Jesse are on the crew."

"So three of you are work—are you another relative?" He spun to me. "You said Aunt Lily."

"I'm from another branch of Claire's family. No relation to you."

His eyes still glazed, he nodded at Claire. "Very nice to meet you." Then he stumbled out of the tiny building.

"Guess that's too much family for him." Nora took a swig from a bottle of water.

Possibly. Or too much family with access to a likely hiding place of the treasure.

~~~~~

At 1 a.m., while covering yawns, I checked in the last customers. Then Nora, Claire, and I locked the booth and took the tablets and cash box to Dani's trailer. Using our phones for light, the three of us walked back toward the parking area.

Screams echoed from the woods behind us.

Nora said, "I can't wait to bring my friends on a night off and use my free pass."

"You can have my pass for one of your friends," I said.

"You don't want it? The storyline and all the screams—don't you want to see what everybody is lining up for?"
~~~~~

"I'm hoping to work every night we're open." But more importantly, treating people like cuts of meat was not my idea of entertainment.

We passed the banner of Cyrus Morley curling his lips in a sneer.

Claire looked up at it. "He sort of looks like Jack."

"A bit," I said. "Jack has his bony nose." And the nasty expression.

A tall, thin figure came into the small cones of light aimed at the banner.

Houston Blank said in his Texas drawl, "Dani told me y'all were leaving. Thought you ladies might need an escort. Dark things are afoot tonight."

Nora giggled while Claire edged closer to me.

Houston fell in step beside us as we moved on. "So you and Chris finally decided to admit you actually like each other."

A tightening in my chest quickened my pulse. "Yeah. It took a while. We're both shy, I guess."

"Sorry the best man didn't win this time." He gave me his good ol' boy grin.

Was there sarcasm in his comment? I couldn't tell, and his passive-aggressive manner was one of the reasons I'd cooled my interest in him after being attracted to him last winter.

To alleviate the awkwardness, I said, "Have you met my cousin, Claire Duvall? Claire, this is Miguel Blank, one of Dad's deputies. Everybody calls him Houston."

"For the weird reason that's where I'm from." He nodded at her.

Claire returned it, then looked to her scuffed tennis shoes.

Houston studied her in the light thrown out by her phone, his sea-green eyes conducting an appraisal I wasn't sure I approved of.

"Oh, you're with security, aren't you?" said a man dressed in a black cape.

He walked through a gap in the barriers marked "exit" with a woman wearing a black corset and black and purple make-up.

"Yeah." Houston sounded irritated, shifting his attention away from Claire.

"Something died along one of the trails." The man tossed his head back. "You need to find it and — "

"It's a skunk." The woman removed her wide-brimmed hat. "The stink will be gone by tomorrow."

"It smelled nothing like a skunk."

Houston said, "I'll check it out and remove the source if I can. Where is it?"

A stench somewhat like skunk, but not really? A cold thread wound down my spine.

The woman waved at the exit with her hat.. "On the path between

The Premature Burial and The Pit and the Pendulum."

"No." The man unfastened his cape. "It was before The Premature Burial, near the Raven's Riddle Escape Room."

"I'll cover both." Houston started toward the entrance as the couple left us.

"Wait, Houston," I said.

He turned. "Having second thoughts about Chris?"

His joke wasn't funny, and I ignored it. "About the smell. It's not likely, but it could be a black bear."

"Here?" Nora squealed the question, whipping her head right and left.

"They come around every once in a while," said Claire in her soft voice.

I explained how Coral smelled something awful when Knight got spooked, and I had too while following the riding trail Wednesday night. Had it only been forty-eight hours ago?

"Thanks for the warning, Rae." He winked. "'Night, ladies." He strode into the night.

When Claire and I drove off in the Rust Bucket, Houston hadn't come tearing out of the woods with a bear on his tail.

Chapter Seventeen

At 10:30 the next morning, I crawled into the kitchen and met Dad hunched over a mug at the bar.

"Did you just get up?" I sounded like a bullfrog.

He nodded, rubbing a glassy eye.

"You shouldn't have worked yesterday. And you should have gone to bed at a decent time, instead of trying to wait up for me and falling asleep on the couch." I opened the door to the fridge. "That's why you built my room with an outside door to the porch. So I can come and go as I want."

"Yeah, but I'm new at this adult parenting." He lifted his mug like it took all his strength. "How was that Halloween thing? Carrie didn't call Dispatch about any trouble."

Placing a bag of scones and one filled with sausage on the counter, I told him about Timothy and Alex and the mysterious stench.

Dad looked grim. "If people post about that stench, Carrie could be battling bigfoot hunters as well as treasure hunters. Have you seen what people are posting on local sites?"

I nodded. "I didn't have much of a chance yesterday on my breaks, but people either posted how sorry they are about Uncle Hank and Knight or wondered where the bigfoot is now and then got in a fight with other people who say they're stupid for thinking it's bigfoot." I set a frozen scone on a plate. "I thought bigfoot was a legend from the Pacific Northwest."

Dad swigged coffee. "I did some research yesterday. People have claimed to see them all over the country. Salt Fork State Park in Guernsey County is a hotspot for sightings. They even host an annual conference. I found at least five bigfoot organizations in Ohio."

"If hunters sneak cameras onto Uncle Hank's farm ..."

"I've only met one bigfoot hunter, so I'm hoping he's an outlier. Most of the ghost hunters and mediums who turn up in Marlin County are polite, law-abiding citizens. But if a few of them are determined to find 'the Truth' at all costs, they give my whole agency a migraine for October."

Coral came up from the basement. "I'm ready when you are, Uncle Mal. Rusty said he'd go with us."

"Where are you going?" I put the plate with the scone in the microwave.

Dad said, "We're checking the riding trails over at the Norris's for cameras set up by that bigfoot hunter." He drained his mug. "Coral said she'd help me, and I guess Rusty is too."

"Aunt Carrie's over there," said Coral, "so she can help us."

"If she's up."

I turned on the water in the sink. "Aaron and Micah aren't going? They're always up for an adventure."

"There's no adventure." Coral almost shouted. "We're just walking along the trails and looking for cameras. I didn't ask them because they went fishing before I got up."

"And you didn't go with them?" The microwave was beeping, and I opened the door.

Before Wednesday, Coral would have been the first one outside since she was an early riser. And she wouldn't have waited on Dad to go over to her own farm. I was pretty sure she hadn't been alone one minute since she came to our house Thursday morning. Last night, she went to sleep in my bed, but at some point, migrated to Gram's again.

Coral shoved stray copper hairs under her baseball cap with the patch of a running horse on it. "I didn't feel like fishing. I want to check on the horses and cats and dogs and help Uncle Mal."

Dad said, "If you're worried about meeting the bear again, don't be. I'm sure it's miles from here by now."

I removed the scone from the microwave and put in a mug of water. Hopefully not miles away at The Haunting.

Coral blinked a few times. "I don't care if I meet the bear. If I did, I'd get a gun and shoot it. He's the reason Knight's dead and Dad's in the hospital."

"True, but the bear didn't attack, did it? It was just being a bear."

Coral crossed her arms. "I'll just be a hunter."

"For your information, you can't hunt bears in Ohio. I don't want to call the game warden on you." Dad looked stern and then grinned.

But Coral only returned a frown.

Dad swiveled on his stool to me. "After lunch, we're taking Jeanine's SUV to her. If you drive that, I'll drive the Beast. Ma's going to stay with Jeanine at Aunt Marti's until Monday night since her back's better. We'll bring Amber back with us. Jeanine thinks Amber's stayed long enough and needs something else to occupy her mind, like working at that Halloween thing tonight."

"Mom wants me to come," said Coral. "Even though they won't let me go back and see Dad since I'm not sixteen."

The landline rang.

The three of us riveted our attention on it like we'd suddenly noticed it was a bomb. My lungs revolted at the idea of working.

The left side of his face scrunching, Dad picked up the receiver.

"What's going on, Jeanine?" The question creeped from his lips. In a few seconds, Dad's whole body loosened as a grin spread over his boyish face.

My lungs decided they could work after all.

"That's great news. Wonderful ... Yes, we're still coming. We're bringing Coral. Yes, she's right here."

Handing Coral the phone, Dad said, "Hank needs the ventilator less and less. It's a good sign."

I placed both hands on the counter and hung my head.

Thank You, Father. Let this be a sign of a complete recovery.

"Kiddo?"

I looked up and found Dad watching me. "I'm fine. And very, very, grateful."

He gripped my right arm. "Me too."

Coral jammed the phone in its base. "Why does Mom keep asking me how I am? I didn't break my leg."

"She's worried about you," said Dad. "That's what moms do."

"How long will it take you to get ready, Uncle Mal?"

Studying her, Dad said, "If you're in a rush, you and Rusty can go over ahead of me."

Coral froze, except for her eyes leaping wide open. "No. I can wait." She went into the living room, dropped onto the couch, and picked up the remote.

"I'll be ready in five minutes." Dad pushed himself off the stool and turned his back to Coral, raising his eyebrows at me in a silent question.

I shook my head.

Her reaction had bordered on terror. Something besides getting comfort by staying near family was going on inside her.

After I showered, I sat on my bed and, with an old notebook and paperclips, rearranged Jeanine's research in a way that made sense for someone treasure-hunting.

On the first clean page of the notebook, I drew a line. Sorting through several sheets of copied newspaper articles and what looked like sections of books, I added events and dates to the line, charting Cyrus Morley's life.

About 1942, Cyrus bought a house in Hollywood, and articles mentioned him escorting this or that young actress to premieres and nightclubs and charity events. He put his house on the market in 1945.

The book excerpts were copied from biographies and autobiographies of people in the movie industry in the 1940s. Most of the authors commented that Cyrus's home became a magnet for anyone interested in occult practices, and several studio bosses forbade their biggest stars from attending Cyrus's parties for fear that association with him would tarnish their reputations. One director believed Cyrus only left Hollywood when several bosses bought him off. He had so much dirt on so many people in the movies that it was cheaper to pay him to leave.

I stacked the Hollywood papers together. I couldn't find any proof the Hollywood house sold before he died, so maybe he hid the treasure there. If he enjoyed blackmailing people, he certainly showed them contempt.

I was flipping through papers to make sure I hadn't missed anything concerning Cyrus's Hollywood period when my arm knocked the book written by the pastor's wife onto the floor.

I picked it up. Why was this with the Cyrus Morley files?

I opened it and scanned the pages. It was a straightforward autobiography. Rebecca Cutler was born in India to parents who were missionaries in 1908. She came to the United States to go to college and met her husband, Joseph Armstrong, who was studying to be a pastor. He came to lead our church in 1934. She had grown bored with the women's ministries she led and her duties as a wife and mother, longing to return to India and the mission field.

She wrote:

> "All the problems Joe and I handled at the church seemed petty compared to what I'd seen my parents battle in India. I wanted to feel I was accomplishing important work for the Lord and stupidly thought I couldn't do that in Marlin County, Ohio."

"Hey, Rae." Micah knocked on my door as he opened it. "Gram's fixing sandwiches for lunch. You want one?"

"Sure. I'll help." I skimmed the text to the end of the chapter.

Rebecca's dissatisfaction grew and grew. Then I read the last line and sat upright. I skipped back a few lines.

> "So I lost my enthusiasm for the work the Lord had set before me. My work was as fruitful as a dead branch on an apple tree. Of course, that led me to be even less enthusiastic. I was ready to suggest to Joe that we leave Marlin County when I had an encounter that changed my life.
>
> "God knew what I needed. You wouldn't think meeting the devil would make you obedient to the Lord, but that's what meeting Cyrus Morley did for me."

Chapter Eighteen

I chopped fruit while Gram made sandwiches, trying to hide my impatience to get back to Rebecca's story.

Dad, Rusty, and Coral entered through the back door as Gram, Aaron, Micah, and I sat down with the sandwiches, chips, and fruit salad.

"No cameras." Dad took his seat at the head of the table. "But the three of us couldn't cover every trail."

Dropping potato chips onto my plate, I said, "Gram, did you read the autobiography Rebecca Cutler Armstrong wrote? It was in Jeanine's research on Cyrus Morley."

"A long, long time ago." Gram spread mustard on her ham sandwich. "She was the kindest person."

"It's spiral bound, which is odd for a book."

"It was privately printed," said Gram. "It was Mrs. Armstrong's eightieth or eighty-fifth birthday, and somebody in the church—I can't remember who—thought it'd be a wonderful addition to local history if she wrote about her life, especially as the wife of a pastor of our church. So she wrote it—I'm pretty sure somebody helped her—and then they printed it cheaply and members could buy it. I'm sure they gave one to the library."

Dad scooped fruit salad into his bowl. "Why is that book with Jeanine's research?"

I swallowed a bite of turkey sandwich. "Because Cyrus Morley was evil incarnate, and that restored Mrs. Armstrong's desire to serve God here in Marlin County."

"What's evil incarnate?" said Micah around the chunk of pineapple he was chewing.

"A really, really bad person," Dad said. "Close your mouth when you chew. I'll have to read this book after you, Rae."

I hurried through cleaning up the lunch dishes and then lay on my bed, turning to where I'd left Rebecca's story.

Cyrus Morley inherited three coal mines in the county in 1935. He began to build his country mansion in the spring of 1936. That was when Rebecca first met him.

Louise Kendall, the wife of the pastor at First Baptist Church, and I were walking down Main Street when we saw the most outlandish character. The man dressed like he didn't know it was the twentieth century. He wore a black cavalier hat with a black feather, a black cloak, and boots that my grandfather would have owned.

He swept off his hat and introduced himself as Cyrus Morley.

Louise, a very timid creature, stared while I made the introductions, mentioning that our husbands were pastors.

His dark eyes glinted in an unsavory way. He said, "There should be a law against such attractive women marrying pastors. All that beauty wasted."

Louise gaped. I was about to walk right past him because I knew he was stirring up trouble. But Louise asked, 'Why?'

He bowed and then tilted up his head. "Because you could make so many men happy."

Louise gaped so much I feared her teeth would fall out. I grabbed her hand and turned into the nearest store.

Since this was 1936, his comments had to be beyond outrageous.

"Carrie's here to stay with the boys." Dad stood in the doorway. "We should get moving."

I swung my legs off my bed. "Gotcha."

But I wished I didn't have to drive to Columbus. I had to know what else happened when Cyrus lived in Marlin County.

Dad, Gram, Coral, and I went out to the Beast and the Norris's maroon SUV, damp wind driving mist into our faces.

Dad dug in his pocket for the keys. "Ma, why don't you ride with Rae and I'll drive Coral?"

Coral said, "I'll ride with Gram and Rae."

He stopped digging. "You don't want to ride with me?"

"Well, if you want me to." Coral dragged out the sentence. She looked hopefully at Gram. "Will you ride with us?"

Already behind the wheel of the SUV, I threw Dad a confused look that matched his own.

Why didn't Coral want to ride with Dad alone? She'd been fine going over to her farm with him this morning. Well, no, Rusty had been with them.

"I'll ride with you, if that's what you want," Gram said, her light tone conflicting with her concerned glance to Dad.

"Yeah, that's what I want." Coral pushed forward the passenger seat in the Beast and slipped into the cramped backseat.

She'd rather sit there than with me in the front seat of her own family's SUV? Coral didn't want to be alone, which was understandable, but what else was bothering her?

As if I didn't have enough puzzles to think about.

~~~~~

When Jeanine and Amber met us in the ICU waiting room, their teary eyes didn't fit with the morning's good news.

"We just spoke with the doctor." Jeanine sank into a seat in a corner of the room. "If everything goes well, and I mean no major setbacks, Hank will get home by Thanksgiving."

"Oh, dear." Gram put her arm around Jeanine's shoulders as Dad said, "What?"

"He'll have weeks of recovery from the surgeries, then weeks of rehab. And that's only if no complications develop. The longer the doctors wait for him to regain consciousness and strength for the operations on his leg, the more likely ..."

"Dad could lose his leg." Amber covered her face and bawled.

My gut crumpled like it'd been punched.

"That's better than dead." Coral leaned back on a taupe wall, one foot pressed against it.

Jeanine broke into hysterical giggles, pulled Coral down to her, and kissed her forehead. "Leave it to you to get to the heart of the matter."

Dad said, "It'd be a shock, but Hank can take it. He's annoyingly optimistic." He enveloped Jeanine's slender hand in his. "You're getting ahead of yourself, sis. Let's see how he's doing when he's finally conscious."

She nodded, then grabbed her younger brother in a hug.

Gram got to her feet. "Has Luke been eating?"

"Not much," said Jeanine.

"You and I will take Luke to the cafeteria and see that he eats something while Rae and Mal see Hank."

"I'll go with you." I pushed back my chair to the wall.

Dad and Amber stayed with Hank while the rest of us went with Mr. Norris to the cafeteria.

Gram lifted a tray from the stack by the utensils and cups. "Luke, Amy would scold you up one side and down the other for not eating."

A phantom of a smile at the mention of his late wife's name wavered on Mr. Norris's thin face. Then he swallowed. "I really don't think I can keep anything down."

Gram surveyed the counter ahead. "We'll find something. You girls go ahead."

Coral and I got drinks while Jeanine bought soup and salad, and we
~~~~~

found a table against the back wall. Gram led Mr. Norris to a two-person table several feet from us. Did she want to speak to him privately? Or maybe she thought he'd appreciate only dealing with one person during his meal.

I took a sip of soda. Did my aunt and cousin need a distraction now? Wouldn't hurt to try. "Aunt Jeanine, I know now why you included the book by Rebecca Cutler Armstrong with your research."

The tight lines clutching my aunt's small face lost a bit of their grip. "Have you read the entire book?"

"No. I read up to Mrs. Armstrong's first meeting with Cyrus."

"Then I won't spoil it for you. But you'll find information there you can't find any place else. Shortly after Cyrus moved here, he became pals with, or bribed, the owner of *The Marlin County Recorder.* The owner either ignored negative stories about Cyrus, or if a story was too well known to ignore, he'd spin it in Cyrus's favor."

"That's why I found some articles from a Columbus paper about safety violations in his mines, but nothing in *The Recorder.*" I took another drink. "Did a Carlisle own the paper then? I know it's been in the family for years."

"No. The next owner was a Carlisle—Roger Carlisle. That's an important development in the history of Cyrus Morley in Marlin County."

I angled my head. "How come?"

A tiny glint of mischief sparkled in Jeanine's enormous, tired eyes. "You'll have to read Rebecca's book to find out."

I fiddled with the paper from my straw, wishing I'd brought the book with me. "From what I've read so far, there's no shortage of people and places Cyrus had contempt for."

"That's a fact. He had contempt for people wherever he lived—New York City, Hollywood. Even in Paris, where he had an apartment, and I assume, he met his wife. But when you read more of Rebecca's book, you'll learn he had a special contempt for the people of Marlin County. I wouldn't be surprised if he buried the treasure here. The question is where."

"It's a spot revealed in the poem." I sat back in my chair, looking past my aunt and cousin. "Are you sure it couldn't be in Hollywood? He dumped woman after woman there, according to those biographies you copied from. If any actress dumped him first, he took revenge. One of your sources says he circulated nude photos he'd taken of an actress he'd dated after she announced her engagement to a director. Although no one had proof he did it."

"That's mean." Coral pushed and pulled on the straw in her drink. "But the lady shouldn't have let him take pictures of her naked."

Jeanine said, "But he might have taken the pictures when she thought she had privacy."

"That's mean and creepy."

I wadded up the paper from my straw. "I think you just summed up Cyrus Morley."

Chapter Nineteen

After sorting which luggage we had to take and which vehicle we were leaving, Dad drove Amber, Coral and me home in the Beast. I wolfed down a supper of casseroles, retrieved *In His Service* from my room, tucked my long legs under me in the recliner, and got lost in the Marlin County of the Depression and World War II.

Wow. When Alex said his grandfather took advantage of the people here, did he know all these details? Two girls in Rebecca's church came to her when they were pregnant by Cyrus. Whenever a young woman left the county to live with a relative — always out of state — people speculated that Cyrus had produced another illegitimate child. He fathered many more children than the four listed in his will.

Several outraged fathers objected to Cyrus's behavior and lost their jobs in the mines. One man took a shot at Cyrus. The court sentenced him to a long prison term. Cyrus shot and killed a young man who was the boyfriend of one of Cyrus's victims when he trespassed at his mansion.

As awful as that behavior was, it became even weirder as Halloween approached. Strange people would arrive a week or two before Cyrus's party, The Masque of the Red Death. The night of the party, citizens claimed they saw fires glowing in the woods near the abandoned church at the back of Cyrus's property. Churches and cemeteries suffered damage, like broken windows or toppled headstones. The Armstrongs' home was always a target — their garage caught fire one year. In 1939, three days after The Masque, the body of a young woman was found, wearing a toga, in a wooded valley a couple miles from the Morley Mansion. She was never identified and had died from a poison that was never identified either.

The local sheriff went through the motions of investigations, so Cyrus was never charged with any crime. Cyrus contributed heavily to his elections.

After the death of the young woman, Rebecca wrote that everyone steered clear of Cyrus as much as they could when he visited the county. No one complained about his behavior to the authorities since he had law enforcement and the press in his pocket.

"Shouldn't we leave soon?" Amber's voice sounded like she was calling up from the basement.

I lifted my gaze from the book and found her standing over me.

"It's after 8," she said.

"Uh—uh—yeah." I shut the book and hurried to my room.

"That must be a great book." Amber followed me. "You hadn't moved a muscle since you sat down to read."

"You'll have to read it when I'm through." I sorted through clothes in my closet for something dark.

Mean and creepy was what Coral had called him. A 24/7 Halloween party was the term Dani Li used. His hobbies were women and the occult. Cyrus Morley had many sides and not one was good.

~~~~~

In the cramped ticket booth, Amber and I powered up the tablets to get ready for opening.

Glancing out the ticket windows, she said, "Wow. You'd think Halloween was tonight."

Many of the customers had painted on skeleton faces, acquired black pseudo-Victorian clothes, or gone the vampire route.

The fire-eater, magician, storyteller, and Lyra Vex were all back working the crowd.

"Are there only two of us?" Amber studied the app on her tablet.

"I think Claire will be here."

I looked out a ticket window. Claire, Jack, and Jesse were coming up the drive. Claire broke into a jog, but Jack stopped dead, Jesse bumping into him, and stared at the waiting customers.

Even in the dim orange light, I could see a mask of pure fury mar Jack's hatchet face. He marched toward the crowd.

"Sorry I'm late." Claire rushed through the door. "The van died, so we had to jump it. Oh, hey, Amber. I'm sorry about your dad."

"Thanks." It came out choked, and she handed Claire a tablet.

"Never thought I'd see you again." Jack pressed into Lyra's personal space.

Holding a customer's hand for a reading, Lyra glanced over her shoulder. "Oh, hello. Good to see you ... John?"

Jack's angular body jerked like she'd slapped him. He grabbed Lyra's arm. "No games, Lyra." He yanked her away from the waiting customers.

Several people raised protests while Jesse touched Jack's shoulder.

You could tell they were brothers from their wiry builds. But Jesse's narrow face didn't have Jack's sharp edges, and his green eyes were large and liquid, not deep-set, like Jack's.

Jesse said, "Jack, we're late. We'd better—"

Jack shoved Jesse away and pulled Lyra closer to him.

"Leave her alone," Amber shouted through her window. Spinning, she opened the door and charged through it.

I stared into the twilight of the open door. What did Amber think she
~~~~~

was doing?

Claire said in a terrified whisper, "Amber shouldn't take on Jack."

I shook myself, grabbing the walkie-talkie, and raced outside.

As I caught up to Amber, Jack said to her, "This ain't none of your business."

"We'll make it our business," said a college-age guy as he and a friend detached themselves from the line.

"No need." I held up the walkie-talkie. "Jack, I'm calling security."

Despite Jack's rough treatment, Lyra didn't look the tiniest bit concerned. Her lips pursed, reflecting amusement on her cat-like face.

Jack gave me a scowl sharp enough to skin me and then threw Lyra's arm back at her, making her lose her footing for a moment. He stormed past the ticket booth, Jesse trailing behind.

I approached Lyra. "Are you all right?"

She flung back her head and launched a full-throated, mocking laugh.

A titter of laughter dribbled through the crowd, but Lyra wasn't laughing to reassure us she was okay. Her laughter was a missile that could reach Jack even though the night now hid him.

As we reentered the booth, I said, "Amber, what in the world did you think you were doing?"

"That woman needed help." Amber picked up a tablet. "Just because I was a coward at the creek doesn't mean I'll always be one."

My lips parted, words drying up.

"You should stay away from Jack." Claire's buttery blonde hair brushed her cheeks as she looked to her feet. "He's mean, real mean. He always has been, even when we were little."

I tore my attention from Amber. "Claire, do you know what happened between Jack and Lyra?"

She lifted her head a fraction. "When Lyra left the county after Halloween last year, Jack went with her. We never heard a word from him—he didn't even text Jesse." She gave a contented sigh. "The house was peaceful for three months. Then Jack came back in February. He never said what happened. If somebody asked him, he looked ready to murder you. He belted Jesse when he asked."

"I'll tell Carrie." I turned a knob on the walkie-talkie. "That's why, Amber, you don't get involved in a domestic situation."

She stared at me. "You sound like Uncle Mal."

Dad would be so proud. Not sure I was.

The door flew open and slapped me on the butt as Dani burst in. "What's going on in here? It's 9:02. Time is money." She vanished just as fast.

The customers poured at us like water from a busted dam, leaving me no time to contact Carrie.

I was tearing my thousandth wristband when I noticed Amber handing change to Timothy Morley.

Claire recognized him, pausing as she reached for some coins.

Something else Carrie needed to know.

When my aunt entered the tight space fifteen minutes later, I blew out a sigh of relief while counting bills into a customer's hand.

"Why didn't anybody tell me Timothy Morley was back on the property?" Carrie said.

I handed the woman her last bill. "We didn't have time. What did he do?"

"Nothing yet. I've got Franklin—he's a Wellesville cop—shadowing him. Dani could bar him because of his behavior last night, but she says as long as he follows the rules, she's happy to take his money."

I scanned a printed ticket. "I think she's happy to take anybody's money."

Carrie huffed a laugh. "That's no joke. She was going to charge bigfoot hunters for allowing them to put cameras on the property, but I told her she might scare off customers who are afraid of bigfoot and/or black bears."

"News gets around fast," I said. "Nora Oller or somebody else must have posted about the stench some customers reported last night."

"What stench?" said Amber. "Why are bigfoot hunters here?"

Between customers, I recounted the hunter's visit to her farm, the stench by the creek, and the customers' complaint last night. "Bigfoot hunters must have seen a post and interpreted it as proof that a bigfoot is at The Haunting."

Carrie said, "Mal told me about this hunter, Kyle Garrison." Her tone turned disgusted. "Garrison's one of the hunters who talked to Dani. He's certainly the most obnoxious. The others politely took no for an answer. He kept raising the price to get Dani to cave." She rubbed her temples. "So my team has to be on the lookout for Timothy Morley, Garrison, and Jack, along with the normal amount of drunks and troublemakers."

"Treasure hunting isn't the only way Jack can make trouble," said Amber.

She and I described what happened between him and Lyra.

Carrie gaped. "Is this a Halloween attraction or a reality show? No wonder Mal hates October." She jabbed a finger at Amber. "Rae's right. You should not have gone out there."

"That woman was in trouble." Amber took a credit card.

"Calling security would help her more than anything you could have done."

"I'm not scared of Jack." Amber sniffed.

Claire said so low that I almost missed it, "You should be."

After Carrie left, the crowd thinned. Lyra handed out cards and read palms until midnight without Jack making another appearance. Shortly after that, a gangly man with a fixed grin approached Amber's window and bought a ticket for the 1 a.m. entry.

Turning my back to him, I waited on a young couple. I didn't want him to start a conversation with me.

When he'd left, Amber said, "That's the bigfoot hunter who came to our farm, isn't it? His credit card said Kyle Garrison."

"That's him." I removed the walkie-talkie from its charger and pressed the talk button.

Chapter Twenty

When Amber, Claire, and I left at 1 we hadn't seen anyone from security escorting any of the "persons of interest" off the property, so everyone—treasure hunters, bigfoot hunters, and dumped boyfriends—appeared to have behaved tonight.

I fell straight to sleep in my own bed while Amber and Coral shared Gram's, but calls around 3 and 4 a.m. pulled all three of us to our feet.

Both times they were people who bypassed Dispatch and called Dad instead. One was sure a dangerous black bear was nosing around his garage, and the other was sure a dangerous bigfoot was nosing around her barn.

Dad answered on the phone in his room, then came upstairs to let us know the calls weren't about Hank.

Despite the late night and the interruptions, we all made it to church—Dad, Carrie, my cousins, my brothers, and me. With Gram, Jeanine, and Hank missing, our usual pew felt empty. Our church family overwhelmed us with questions and condolences for Hank. And more promises of casseroles. Coral got extra attention as people congratulated her for her heroics. She met the praise with a stony face. I hoped Amber hadn't heard.

But she had to hear Pastor Hopkins say during the congregational prayer, "Thank You for Hank's recovery so far. Please heal him, and thank You for giving Coral the courage and strength to save him."

After the service, we worked our way to the parking lot through a sea of comments and offers of help. The little white clapboard church on the ridge, warmed in fresh sunshine and surrounded by cornfields and wooded hills, looked ready to represent rural America in a graphic.

Coral was waiting by the Beast when I reached it, the noon sun making her copper hair glow. "Can we leave now?"

"Too many people?" I said.

She shrugged, her freckled face as blank as new drywall.

Dad, Carrie, Amber, Aaron, and Micah emerged from the departing congregation and joined us.

"Not bad." Dad unlocked the Beast. "Only short one person. Anybody know where Rusty is?"

Amber held back flying strands of her red-gold hair. "I think he went to Aunt Em's grave."

Dad handed me the keys before heading for the cemetery that spread over the slope to the left of the church.

Micah climbed onto the running board of the Beast. "We should be putting flowers on Mom's grave soon. We always do that after the fair and before Halloween."

"That was Thursday," Aaron said in a gasp. "I can't believe Dad forgot."

"He didn't forget." Carrie gazed after her brother. "With Hank in the hospital, he decided you boys could lay your flowers later."

Coral, Aaron, and Micah piled into the back of the Beast.

Untwisting her seat belt, Coral said, "Rae, ride with us. Rusty and Amber can ride with Aunt Carrie."

More of Coral's mystifying system for not being alone. As we got ready for church, the three younger kids were finished before Amber, Rusty, and me. Dad said he'd take them and those of us running late could ride with Carrie. Coral had asked him to wait for at least one of us older kids. She'd actually gotten out of the truck. So Dad had to wait.

"Coral." Carrie shielded her eyes, looking to her niece. "Why does Rae have to ride with you in the Beast?"

Coral's gaze locked on Carrie, her arms closing around herself as if she was cold.

Carrie's phone rang. Like everybody else in the family, she took her time swiping to answer.

My fingers tightened on the armrest of the open door of the truck.

In a few seconds, Carrie's round face cleared like the sun breaking through storm clouds. "Hank woke up." Her shout turned every head in the lot. "He's been off the ventilator since last night." She kept listening. "They backed off the sedatives, and he was conscious ... But he's in a lot of pain, so they sedated him again ... but they'll be adjusting his medication so he can be awake more ... maybe surgery for his leg on Tuesday or Wednesday."

Bursting into tears, Amber threw a chokehold around my neck. A cheer went up from behind the Beast, and then our church family mobbed us with congratulations and relief.

I sniffed back tears.

Father, thank You so much. We all need Uncle Hank.

"Hank's awake?" Dad said as he and Rusty swam through the crowd.

Carrie repeated the details, and Dad let out a sigh that would have extinguished a forest fire. "Thank You, Lord."

Amber hugged him and Rusty, whose relieved expression turned into a grimace.

Aaron whacked Coral on the shoulder. "I knew Uncle Hank would be okay. He's tough, like Dad."

Coral nodded. Her face, her posture, everything about her was exactly the same as it had been since she'd gotten up this morning.

Aaron tilted his head. "Aren't you glad about your dad?"

She nodded again. "Rae, you're riding with us, right?"

I'd started to text Chris and Devon the good news but studied my cousin. "If you want me to."

"Yeah, I do." She rested her hands in her lap, waiting as if behind a wall of glass that kept her from experiencing the joyful turmoil surrounding the rest of our family.

Chapter Twenty-One

After lunch, Chris and I hiked the trails between the farms, chatting, me taking photos, being close. Asking Chris about going to church with me never left my mind, but I didn't want to ruin our fun.

I lowered my camera as a hawk I'd been focusing on took off from a snag.

Why did I think an invitation to church would ruin our relationship? Because Chris never talked about any kind of faith? Because he was so private?

"We should leave now." Chris slipped his phone into the back pocket of his jeans, looking up to where I stood on the huge sandstone boulder I'd climbed onto to get a clear shot at the hawk. "Your aunt said supper was at 6. It'll take us about twenty-five minutes to get back."

"All right." I slithered down the steep boulder.

Chris caught my feet in his hands, braking my descent, then held me around the waist as I touched down.

His taut face ... sculpted and intense ...

He kissed me, and we might have been there until dark, but I broke off, sighing. I didn't want the whole family to grill me if we were late.

Holding hands, we tramped down a hill, the wind making the shadows of the maple and sycamore leaves dance on the ground like dim fish in a sea of light.

Would now be a good time to invite him?

I glanced at the severe lines of Chris's profile.

I couldn't just bring up my invitation out of nowhere, right? Too awkward.

When we came in the front door, my brothers surrounded Chris. His fighting lessons had won them over.

As Chris and I took seats at the opposite end of the dinner table from Dad and Carrie, Amber said in her breathless way, "Your hair looks great today, Rae. I mean, it always looks great, but it's even better today."

I brushed wild dark gold strands of my mop behind my ear, fighting a cringe.

My cousin was promoting me to my partner. Nice but not needed.

During our meal, Amber boosted my dark chocolate brown eyes, my bony build, and my brains.

I hoped Chris ate fast.

When we'd polished off most of the casseroles, Chris gathered his dishes. "I don't want to eat and run, but I have homework I should finish tonight."

Micah's fork hovered near his lips. "You have homework?" He looked to Dad. "You give your deputies homework?"

Dad chuckled. "I give them a lot of tough assignments, but not that. Chris is going part-time to college. You can work full-time and do college."

I frowned behind the glass of water I'd lifted. Another of Dad's unsubtle hints.

After accompanying Chris to his truck, I found Dad and the boys in a wrestling match behind the couch, and Amber speaking to someone on the landline.

I entered Gram's bedroom to reach mine. Sunday had been so busy that I hadn't read any of Rebecca's autobiography since yesterday. I stretched out on my bed, opened *In His Service*, and dove back into the battle of Marlin County vs. Cyrus Morley.

Cyrus disappeared from Marlin County from the time of his masque on Halloween in 1942 until the summer of 1946. Rebecca Armstrong couldn't have known it, but he was living in Hollywood then.

The passing years hadn't changed Cyrus, but it had Marlin County. The local pastors had banded together and helped elect an honest man for sheriff in 1944. The owner of *The Marlin County Recorder* sold the paper to Roger Carlisle. So when Cyrus returned in 1946 and totaled a car while driving drunk in Wellesville, he was charged and fined. Roger Carlisle not only reported it but printed an editorial about what a menace Cyrus was.

The resistance infuriated Cyrus. The sheriff's family found dead animals on their porch. Someone started fires in the newspaper office and several churches. When a couple more young women approached pastors, tearful that they were pregnant by Cyrus, the pastors and sheriff decided the time for a showdown had come. It was October, and Cyrus was gearing up for his latest masque.

One evening in the middle of October, Sheriff O'Brien, Pastor Joseph Armstrong, four other pastors, and the local Catholic priest drove to the Morley Mansion.

Rebecca wrote:

> The two cars entered the valley but stopped when they
> found a car with its headlights on blocking the road. It was
> Morley's roadster.
> Joe said they were shining their flashlights around
> when they heard the screams.
> The seven men ran into the woods. Joe and Sheriff
> O'Brien pushed through a patch of poison ivy, but they

didn't realize it until the next day. Poor Father Novak became entangled in scarletberry vines and twisted his ankle. But they finally made it to the source of the screams.

Beside the old lane that led to the Baptist church that a tornado had damaged, Cyrus Morley had been strung, spread eagle, between two oak trees, although the assailants hadn't had time to tie his left leg to the trunk of one of the trees.

While the men tried to untie Cyrus, they took turns, letting him place his left foot on their shoulders to take his weight off his arms. The entire time they were freeing him, Cyrus screamed that "imps of hell" and "shades from the pit" had come after him, that he'd never believed they were actually real, that he hadn't meant to conjure them.

The change in Cyrus shocked all the men. The sneering atheist now begged for the pastors to bless him as protection against the imps. He was so hysterical that even when they had lowered him to the ground, he couldn't do anything but sob and scream, so Joe, Pastor Kendall, and Pastor McElroy carried Cyrus to their car.

Joe had never seen anyone so terrified. He and Father Novak drove him to the hospital in Zanesville as Cyrus continued to plead for blessings and to never be left alone.

Sheriff O'Brien and the other men scoured the woods for the assailants, but the sheriff believed that when they heard his party in the woods, they escaped.

"Rae, shouldn't you be getting ready for work?"

I looked up from my book and started when I realized it was Dad talking to me and not Cyrus Morley.

Chapter Twenty-Two

I took *In His Service* with me to The Haunting. I had to know what happened, but if the crowd was as big as the other two nights, I wouldn't have the chance.

Claire and Nora hadn't arrived yet. I went to Dani's trailer to get the equipment, knocking on the door. She told me to come in.

Papers covered every horizontal surface, including the stove.

"Oh, it's you." Her fingers clicked away on her laptop. "Everything you need for admissions is in that bin." She waved toward the couch. "Once you set up, help pick up the garbage that some animals spread all over the food truck area."

I said, "I saw people cleaning up over there when I pulled in. It was probably raccoons." We'd all better hope it was raccoons.

"I've ordered employees to put all leftovers and garbage in trash containers, and those will be put in a trailer until someone can take them away." Her voice soured as the clicking on the keyboard increased. "I knew an outdoor event would have special issues, but I didn't expect that included raccoons."

Bending over to pick up the bin, I noticed a book with a familiar format lying open on the couch.

I paused, scrutinizing it.

Yep. It was The Book.

Hoisting the bin, I said, "So you got your family's copy of the Poe book."

"No, it's Alex's." Her brown eyes narrowed behind her thick-rimmed glasses. "How do you know that's the right book?"

"My great aunt has her mother's copy. I've seen it."

Her eyes reduced to threads. "So you're an heir."

"No. Just my great aunt and her kids and grandkids."

"Alex told me about them, and I told the heirs working here if they look for the treasure on my time, they're fired."

"Claire isn't looking for it. I don't know about the guys." Shifting the bin under one arm, I nodded at The Book. "I guess you are."

"Why not? Alex bought a copy of the book, and he remembered the clue on the note found by the poem, so we have all we need."

"I didn't know you could buy a copy. It's from 1946."

Dani puffed a derisive chuckle. "That book isn't rare or anything.

Alex bought the two-volume set off eBay for forty bucks." Her fingers flew over the keyboard. "You'd better get ready."

Claire, Nora, and I weren't as busy as the two previous nights, but I didn't get enough of a break to read *In His Service*. Unanswered questions made it hard for me to concentrate on my job.

Who were the attackers? What had Cyrus done to them to make them string him up? Did the sheriff catch them? Did Cyrus fully recover?

Near 10:30, Alex entered with a shrill scream following him from the woods. "Everything running smoothly, mademoiselles?"

"No probs whatever," Nora told him.

Since we had a lull, and Dad might like to know who was engaged in treasure hunting, I said, "Alex, do you think the inheritance is hidden in Marlin County?"

He rifled bills in our cash tray. "If you're asking me if I'm searching for the treasure, the answer is no. Dani can look for it all she wants, but helping my father solve the code for a year has inoculated me against treasure fever."

"Y'all worked together at one point?"

"Right after my grandmother died. She thought the will was some kind of sick game of Cyrus's. When my father persisted in trying to solve the clues, she told him, and later me, that if she discovered we were trying to find the lost money and jewels, she'd disinherit us. Grand-mere was very wealthy."

I waited on three college kids, then said, "So your father has only been looking since your grandmother's death?"

"I'm sure he worked on it very quietly while she was alive. But once her estate was settled — that was four years ago — he became obsessed. He invited me to help him, but after a year, he grew suspicious of me. His own son." His hands stilled in the drawer. "He was afraid I'd solve the clues and take the treasure for myself. So he cut me off. The only nice thing he's ever done for me."

Nora said, "How come?"

"Because Grand-mere was right. Cyrus left us nothing. He probably sunk the money and jewels in the ocean or something equally destructive. The terms of the will were his parting shot to his relations, meant to divide us and drive us crazy." He stroked his upper lip. "It has certainly driven a wedge between my father and me, although not by much. I'd hardly seen him from the time of my parents' divorce when I was five to when we tried treasure hunting together."

Alex looked at Claire. "By the way, I met your mother. She waited on me at the grocery store. I know now where you inherit your beauty."

An appreciative expression flickered across her Victorian face, then she spun to her window, although no customers were lined up there.

Alex frowned, then snapped, "Have I offended you?"

With her back to him, she shook her head.

His frown turning annoyed, Alex left.

Claire was too timid to explain her reaction, but I was pretty sure I could and darted outside after him. "Alex?"

He turned. "Yes ... it's Rae, isn't it?"

"You have a good memory."

Behind the ticket booth, the only light came from the open door, outlining half of Alex's lean body. But I had to shut it so Claire wouldn't overhear us. The light from the fat crescent moon made Alex a gray shadow against black land.

I said, "Claire wasn't offended by your comment, sir. She's uncomfortable around men. She's lived through two abusive boyfriends and watched her mother survive three abusive marriages. And some of her half-brothers are total jerks. Claire doesn't know how to react to a guy acting genuinely nice. She's not at ease with my dad, and she's known him her whole life."

Silence as his hand went to his chin. "She has children, doesn't she?"

"Two. This job is a big step for her after all she's been through."

He was quiet—he seemed to stare past me—and then without a word, he turned away, heading toward the trailers and tents.

I looked up to the banner of Cyrus Morley. It hung limp without a whisper of a breeze.

My hands closed into fists. I had to find the inheritance. Aunt Lily and Claire could seriously use the money, and Cyrus would have hated doing anything to benefit his family.

And I would love it.

Chapter Twenty-Three

Despite dragging into the house at 1:40, I poured a glass of milk and curled up in the recliner with *In His Service*, switching on the lamp on the nearest end table.

The pastors took turns staying with Cyrus Morley in the hospital until he'd recovered enough to give the sheriff his statement.

Cyrus said that as he was driving home the night of the attack, a skinny tree fell across the road. When he got out of his car to examine it, four people dressed in black grabbed him. Without a word, they carried him down the abandoned road that led to the wrecked church. But they stopped by the oak trees before they reached that building.

They hoisted him quickly, so they must have had the ropes ready. Cyrus shouted to attract attention, although he knew the chances of anyone passing on the road were slim.

Rebecca wrote:

> Cyrus gave Joe and the others that infuriating leer that made every woman in the county want to run.
>
> He said, "I never would have guessed carloads of Good Samaritans were bound for my home.' He chuckled in that horrible, mocking way of his. 'I thank you for cutting me down, but you holy types are so gullible. You bought my performance without question."
>
> This despicable cretin went on to say that his hysterics had been a sham, meant to fool the men into believing that Cyrus Morley had seen the error of his ways.
>
> Joe couldn't understand him. Here, the very people Cyrus had ridiculed and abused had set aside those sins against them to save him. It took weeks for the cases of poison ivy that Joe and the sheriff contracted to clear up. Father Novak actually broke his ankle in the scarletberry. And Cyrus's sincerest form of gratitude was scorn.
>
> However, I understood perfectly. Those four people who attacked him had exposed Cyrus Morley for who he really was: a sniveling coward. And they had exposed him to the last group of people he'd want to see his true self: Christians.

I believe, now as I believed then, that God gave Cyrus one last chance to repent. Those attackers did frighten him, he never had believed in any of the occult nonsense he played with, he dabbled in it to be outrageous or rebellious or both, and he was scared to death, almost literally, when he thought the nonsense was true.

Cyrus Morley was confronted with a choice once he had collected himself. Either he could express genuine gratitude to the men who deplored his conduct but rescued him anyway, or he could lie like a fiend.

I'd always known he was a fiend. Cyrus finally proved it.

The words on the last page blurred so badly that I read through it three times before I got the meaning. I couldn't read any more this exhausted, so I slunk to my bed.

Pulling the quilt up to my chin, I stared at the ceiling.

Cyrus couldn't have believed the pastors, sheriff, or priest bought his story, unless he was stupid as well as depraved. Rebecca was right. He'd humiliated himself and either had to admit the truth or concoct a lie.

A chill stole over my skin, and I snuggled deeper under my quilt and blanket.

How horrible did you have to be to laugh at people who saved your life?

~~~~~

The next morning, fighting eyelids that weighed a pound each, I opened the front doors to the library and found Lyra Vex waiting, dressed in skinny jeans, flat sandals, and a poncho.

I held open the door for her.

She pointed to the bulletin board in the little vestibule between the outer and inner double doors to the lobby. "You let me put this here?" She held out a flyer.

I took the full sheet of paper. "The director or assistant director has to approve all items for the board."

"Are they here?"

An enormous photo of Lyra dominated the flyer, and its font was the same as the one on the ads placed around town for The Haunting. It also had The Haunting's logo in the center at the top.

One Night Only!

Medium Lyra Vex will attempt to contact the ghost of Cyrus Morley and discover the location of the Lost Morley Inheritance.
~~~~~

The date was set for this coming Friday.

My eyelids flew back. "Dani approved this?"

Lyra broke into a sneaky cat smile. "Oh, yes. Dani a-proov. She says Timothy and I could try and contact his papa if we did it during time when customers come."

My eyelids attempted a deep dive into my skull. "T-T-Timothy Morley hired you?"

She tossed back the black tips of her hair and threw back her shoulders. "He gives me job. I tell him I go to Halloween thing and read palms and I feel someone wants to talk to me. I think it Cyrus. I tell him he can pay me to contact his papa. He says okay. Dani says she lets us so people pay more."

Timothy Morley was that desperate? Did Alex know? Did Dad?

I must have stood there like a statue because Lyra waved the flyer in my face. "You get a-proov?"

I took the paper. "I'll show it to my boss."

She nodded and strode outside, the fringe on her poncho rippling.

In the lobby, I laid the ad on the checkout desk and punched in the number for my boss, Barb Hanson.

Devon read the sheet. "Is she serious?"

"That she's a medium? No way. That she'll put on the performance of a lifetime? You got it."

When Barb answered, I reported what Lyra had told me, and she said she'd be down in a few minutes. I hung up, lifted my phone from a shelf under the desk, and pressed the button for Dad. Maybe it was early enough that he hadn't gotten too busy yet.

"How's my girl?" he said.

I smiled. No matter how bad I was feeling, hearing my dad ask me that always pulled up a smile from somewhere.

I repeated what I'd learned from Lyra.

"Oh, goody," Dad said. "This inheritance mess keeps getting messier. I'll see if Ms. Vex has priors. I'll try to talk to Morley Sr., but if he's willing for the world to watch a medium contact his father from beyond the grave, I doubt anything I say will change his mind."

As I swiped off, Barb Hanson descended the curved stairs from the balcony, looking taller and slimmer than usual in her deep plum suit.

I handed her the flyer.

She removed her cocoa brown glasses, biting one stem. "I guess it's okay." A plum-colored nail pointed to teeny tiny print in the left-hand corner. "It says 'entertainment only.'"

"That seems to be Lyra's motto," I said.

Barb put on her glasses. "Since we've already allowed the owner of

The Haunting in the Hollow to post flyers, I don't think I can refuse this request. Personally, I don't like it." She tapped her fingers on the counter. "Rick. I wonder if he knows about this."

"I'm sure Lyra will give him an interview or anything else he needs for the paper." Devon placed books on a cart behind the desk.

"I'll call him." Barb took the flyer as she climbed the stairs to the balcony.

Once she was out of sight, Devon said, "I think Barb and Rick are a couple again."

"They've only had a few lunches together that I know of." My mood sank a bit as I opened a DVD case and counted disks.

During the summer, Rick Carlisle had seemed interested in Carrie. And she seemed interested in him. If he was getting back with Barb after their breakup, I hoped Carrie hadn't been interested at all.

"Since the freak show is Friday night," Devon said, "I could ask Jason to host a sleepover with the girls and Alli." She snapped shut an audiobook case. "But Jason may want to go as his big brother's guest. I guess Rick could get them both in for free as the owner of the paper." She sighed. "I may end up hosting a sleepover."

At noon, I opened my lunch bag and *In His Service*. Twenty minutes later, I realized I'd eaten none of my lunch and bit into my pepperoni roll.

They never caught the four people who had strung up Cyrus, and he seriously wanted them caught. As soon as he was discharged from the hospital, he fled the state and put his mansion up for sale. But he called Sheriff O'Brien every week, demanding a progress report on the investigation. When O'Brien said he wasn't getting any leads, Cyrus accused him of negligence and hired private investigators, who got nowhere faster than the sheriff had.

If anyone besides the four people involved knew anything, they had kept that knowledge buried.

Rebecca wrote:

> Since Cyrus stated there were four attackers, I had some suspicions, but suspicions aren't proof.
>
> Cyrus Morley never returned. His mansion sat empty for years. After his death, his widow sold it to the county for a dollar, and the commissioners turned it into the children's home

I wished Rebecca had indulged in a little gossip. Now that over seventy years had passed, the identity of Cyrus's attackers was lost to history.

Chapter Twenty-Four

After school, Liberty Stone peered up at me with her shy, brown eyes, whispering, "What's Hank's birthday?" She always whispered in the library.

"July 6," I said. "Do you need the year?"

"No." She wrote on a sheet of graph paper. "I can work with two numbers. What's his favorite color?"

"I have no idea, but ... his wife and daughters all have red hair. Uncle Hank's always joking about living with a tribe of redheads."

Her black braid swaying, Liberty added another note and scurried back to the table where she and Serenity had dumped their school backpacks.

By keeping Serenity busy behind the checkout desk with book repairs, Devon prevented her younger daughter from disrupting the library. Again.

I left work at 5. As the Rust Bucket wheezed up the drive to our farmhouse, Aaron and Micah piled small logs and rocks near the entrance to the breezeway.

I parked and joined them. "What're y'all doing?"

Aaron plopped a flat rock on top of a pile. "We're testing bear alarms." He stepped back and studied his work as Micah assembled another pile. "Coral's gonna feel safer because we have a working bear alarm. Rusty said she got real upset when Amber and Aunt Carrie were going to go to the hospital, and Coral and Rusty would be the only two people here until me and Micah got home."

"Did Coral go with Aunt Carrie and Amber?"

"Yep," Micah said through a grunt, heaving a rock onto the pile.

When I entered the kitchen, Rusty looked up from a binder he was writing in at the dinner table.

I let my backpack slip from my shoulder. "What happened with Coral?"

Rusty rolled his pencil between his fingers. "We'd got home from school, and Aunt Carrie was waiting to take Amber to the hospital to visit Uncle Hank. When Coral found out it'd be just us guys and her until you got home, she got really upset and said she had to go with them. Aaron thinks she's scared of the black bear, even though she says she isn't. Or maybe she thinks it's bigfoot."

"Coral doesn't believe in bigfoot." Frowning, I shrugged out of my jean jacket.

After depositing my jacket and backpack in my room, I took vegetables from the fridge and sliced tomatoes and cucumbers. As I browned ground beef in a skillet, a cascading crash, followed by a bellow, sounded from the side of the house.

"Aaron!"

Rusty and I traded knowing looks and then bolted for the kitchen door.

In the breezeway, gloomy from the low cloud cover, Dad used the wall of the garage to get to his feet as Aaron reached out his hand. "Do you need help, Dad?"

Micah thrust his face into Dad's. "Is your face okay?"

"I told you, Aaron," Dad said through his teeth, "no bear traps. Or bigfoot traps." He flexed his knee with the brace.

"Are you all right?" I said.

"Of course. I tripped over a line of some kind, something fell, and my brace cushioned my fall." He put some weight on his knee and clenched his jaw.

"It's not a trap, Dad. It's an alarm." Aaron pointed to the logs and rocks scattered in the flower beds and grass. "Micah and I piled up debris and attached fishing line to a piece on the bottom. When the bear walks into the line, it pulls out the bottom piece, and the whole pile falls over. I think the noise will scare it off. The bear didn't bother Uncle Hank and Coral after Knight fell into the creek, and I think it's gotta be because of all the noise they were making."

Dad said, "If any of your experiments are operational, you're supposed to yell 'Fire in the hole!' before you set it off."

"But it isn't operational," said Aaron. "Micah and me are testing different kinds of alarms. We're making ..." His light blue eyes lit up. "Prototypes. We're making different prototypes."

"Okay. New rule: no making prototypes without warning us. Got it?"

"But you weren't here, Dad. How could I warn you?"

Dad opened his mouth, closed it, and then limped into the breezeway. "When's supper?"

His question reminded me of the meat I'd left browning in the skillet, and I raced ahead of him to check on it. The taco meat was a little crispy but still good enough to eat. In ten minutes, I was setting taco shells and a bowl with the ground meat on the table. Dad and the boys took seats.

Aaron placed a notepad beside his plate and clicked a pen. "Since I don't have a bear to test my prototypes on, I gotta ask you some questions, Dad. On a scale of one to ten, how scared were you?"

Dad's hand froze above the bowl of grated cheese. "You want my reaction as your accidental test subject?"

Aaron nodded. "I can't talk to a bear."

Dad wiped his hand over his lips. Either he hid a smile or blocked a shout. Then he took the bowl of cheese. "I'd put it at seven. But, bud, we have motion sensitive lights on the outside of the house, and we've never had any trouble with animals or people."

"I know, but I think Coral will feel better if I have a fool-proof bear alarm around the house. Then I can build one at her house when they move back there."

"Piling up all the stuff is a lot of work," said Micah, taking a shell.

Rusty stared ahead, pushing meat around his plate. "Could you use a motion sensor to trigger sound?"

The suggestion brought Aaron out of his chair, his small face glowing with the thrill of a new idea. "Like trigger music on an old phone. Aunt Carrie gave us one of her old phones last summer."

He, Rusty, and Micah discussed possibilities through supper until Aaron remembered he hadn't finished questioning Dad about his experience as a bear.

After we cleaned up, all five of us went to the alpaca barn.

I lifted a hose off a hook. "Dad, did you talk to Old Mr. Morley?"

"Couldn't track him down." He placed the end of the hose in the bucket wired to the stall for the males. "I'll still try to contact him, but I might have more luck scaring off Lyra."

"She has a record?"

"No. In fact, I can't find any documents for a Lyra Vex, so it must be an assumed name. Her socials only run back two years." Dad carried the hose to the bucket for the females. "If Lyra knows I'm waiting to catch her in a fraud, she might clear out. But she's got hold of a good thing in Morley Sr. She won't let go easily."

"Won't she have to find something at the ... séance, I guess you'd call it? I mean, she's not stupid. With all the publicity, she's going to have to — to fake something."

"Like a second clue? Because she can't fake a fortune in cash and jewels. If her hooks are in Morley Sr. good and deep, she can lead him around, 'discovering' all the fake clues she can create until she drains him of money. Or he catches on."

I grimaced. I didn't like Timothy Morley, but I also didn't like the idea of an old man getting ripped off.

Once we returned to the house, I went to the desk in my room, got the timeline of Cyrus Morley's life, and worked on it at the dinner table while Dad helped the boys with their homework. I'd finished it when Amber burst through the kitchen door after 9, letting in the damp air from the fall night, with Gram and Coral coming in behind her.

She bounced up to me and hugged me. "Dad talked to me! He's really groggy, but it was wonderful to hear his voice. He talked to Coral through a video call."

"It didn't sound like him." Coral slouched against the stove.

"Yes, it did." Amber spun to her. "He's just on a lot of pain killer."

"He didn't sound the same at all." She jammed her hands in the pockets of her jeans.

"Yes, he did." Amber's voice went shrill. "It sounded like him, and he's getting better."

"How do you know he's getting better?"

"Girls." Gram untied the leather cord that held her braid together. "You're both tired, and you have school tomorrow. Get ready for bed."

Dad gave Gram a hug. "Come downstairs with me a minute. You too, Rae."

Once the three of us gathered around the wooden table heaped with clean clothes, Dad said, "Ma, did Coral act any less ... well, less frozen after she talked to Hank?"

"She showed a little emotion on the call with him." Gram fingered the beaded bracelet on her left wrist. "She kept asking if he was really going to be all right. Hank started running a fever today. They're running tests and putting off his first operation until Friday. On the ride home, Coral hardly spoke."

Dad scratched his eyebrow. "It may just be shock that's affecting Coral. Being alone with Hank until we came had to be horrible."

I clutched myself. I couldn't imagine. Or actually, I didn't want to imagine how my twelve-year-old cousin felt, freezing as the night grew darker, Knight struggling to breathe, her dad unconscious, her shoulders aching, hollering the Branson yodel over and over and having no clue if anyone could hear her.

Gram rubbed my back as Dad said, "But something else is bothering her, more than just wanting to be with people all the time. She always has to be with at least two people."

"Jeanine noticed that too," said Gram. "We talked a lot about Coral."

"On separate occasions yesterday," said Dad, "Carrie and I tried to get Coral to talk about her experience. But she just looked at us with that blank face of hers and shrugged and said she was okay."

"Y'all can't force Coral to talk about it." I crossed my arms. "Right after Mom died, I moved in with the assistant pastor and his wife. They were always hammering at me to express my grief. You can't rush something like this. Coral's gone numb. She'll have to thaw on her own."

"It'll take time." Dad blew out a frustrated sigh. "But if we can help her thaw, we should."

He went upstairs as Gram said, "Rae, thank you for discussing the lost treasure with Jeanine. She needs something to distract her while she sits in ICU besides her work. She found the poem online and is trying to solve the clues."

"I'm glad. I got so sick of people asking me how Mom and I were doing. Sometimes, I needed a break from all the cancer stuff."

Gram turned her bracelet again. "Now that's interesting. You learned people in tough situations need distractions from dealing with your mom's cancer, and Hank learned it from dealing with his mom's diabetes."

"I knew Uncle Hank's mom died from a diabetic stroke. Did she always have problems with diabetes?"

"Her diabetes was very difficult for her to manage. But if you went to visit Amy in the hospital, she'd give you about three minutes to sympathize with her, and then she wanted to talk about anything but herself. Hank did that with Mal."

"Was Dad in the hospital with a serious — oh, when he broke his leg playing college football."

"No, not then. It was when he was grieving for Em." She pressed her hand against her cheek. "For two years, when Mal got home from work, he wasn't much better than a zombie. It took every ounce of strength he had to do his job. I had to tell him to do everything — 'Mal, give the boys their baths. Mal, read to them. Mal, you have to smile at them.' He always did what I said, but the sweet boy I knew seemed dead."

Tears pooled in her eyes, but she smiled. "Except when Hank came over. He treated Mal as he always had. He just never mentioned Em. He'd taunt him and kid him, and Mal responded a bit like his old self. I think that saved Mal. He needed sympathy, but he also needed someone to distract him from all the pain he was in, to do something normal."

She took my face in her hands and kissed my forehead. "Thank you for Jeanine."

"That's what family's for." I hugged her.

"Absolutely."

Chapter Twenty-Five

The next day at the library, the chief topic of conversation had shifted from questions about Hank's health to speculation about Lyra's séance.

During a morning lull in patrons, Devon said, "Jason told me the girls are welcome to spend the night with his kids, so I'm going to the freak show. Rick said he could get me in for free." She wiped dirt off a returned picture book. "I'm so glad Hank's doing better. When do they think he'll come home?"

Stacking board books, I said, "If his surgeries and rehab go well, maybe Thanksgiving."

Devon put her hand on her hip. "That's incredibly lousy for someone who loves the outdoors and being active like Hank does."

"Dad and I are going to see him this evening." My stomach churned as I scanned a board book.

Devon bent down and lifted a thick roll of book tape. "Is there any way I can help? Make you a meal or something?"

"Are you comfortable taking care of horses? We need people morning and evening for the animals at both farms. Gram has volunteers scheduled until Friday."

"I love horses. The girls and I will do an evening shift." She ripped off a strip of tape. "Would Lydia let me take over scheduling? It sounds like the Norrises will need help for at least a month."

"That—that—that's so nice of you."

"Don't sound so shocked." But she grinned. "I don't have many talents, but organization is one of them. I'll need a list of names and numbers and the chores that have to be performed."

No patrons were in the lobby, so I texted Gram about Devon's offer. She wouldn't have been serving lunch yet at school. Gram texted back that Devon handling the animal schedule would lift a huge weight from her. She'd get her all the information this evening.

Chris was trying to get ahead on assignments, so I ate lunch alone again. Pulling out the notebook I used for research, I removed the newspaper articles from *The Marlin County Recorder* I'd tucked inside and read more about the attack on Cyrus. No new information here, except Sheriff O'Brien seemed to have worked hard at finding Cyrus's attackers. Then I reviewed my notes.

Marlin County was the perfect place for Cyrus to bury the

inheritance. His actions showed with crystal clarity the contempt he had for the people here. But the county was almost 300 square miles.

Christians and women, especially Christian women, were his favorite targets. Could he have buried the treasure on the property of a church? Even if I knew which one, how could I pinpoint the location of the treasure?

I wiped my fingers on my napkin. First things first. Identify the churches of the pastors who rescued Cyrus. And where the Armstrongs lived. Rebecca had clashed regularly with Cyrus, confronting him in the middle of Main Street with his latest outrage. I'd have to spend my next lunches combing local records.

An hour after I came back to the desk, Timothy Morley, The Book clutched in his wrinkled hand, headed straight for the local history room.

My breathing quickened. He couldn't have stumbled onto the church angle, could he?

During the afternoon, I found reasons to detour into the local history room, and both times, Timothy was scrolling through old editions of *The Marlin County Recorder* on the microfilm machine. He probably hadn't reached the same conclusion I had.

After school, accompanied by rolls of thunder, Liberty and Serenity trudged in, strands of sweaty dark hair clinging to their foreheads or cheeks.

After a Halloween preview with a touch of winter last week, the weather had decided a repeat performance of July was what we needed in October, complete with a brief thunderstorm.

The girls dumped their backpacks at a table, and Devon got Serenity busy with cutting out shapes for a storytime craft.

Shortly before 5, Devon took a cart of books to storage in the basement, and Liberty hurried to the desk with a folded sheet of paper. "I almost forgot to give this to you," she whispered. "It's for Hank. I drew an x-axis and a y-axis and used multiples of the numbers in his birthday to make the shapes."

A jumble of shapes, colored in shades of red, covered the outside surface.

"*We* made it for Hank." Serenity planted herself beside her older sister, hands on her waist. "I helped color it."

"No, you didn't. You don't color neatly, so I told you not to color on the card, and you did anyway." Liberty pointed to a triangle and a pentagon next to each other. "See, Rae, how messy they are? I tried to color over them, but I couldn't—"

"You colored over my coloring?" Serenity's chubby cheeks tightened.

"I had to. Hank should get a nice card."

"I made it nice!" Serenity looked this way and that and grabbed the stapler from beside the computer.

"Serenity!" I dove for it.

She hurled the stapler at Liberty, who ducked, and it flew toward the glass lobby doors as Dad entered and thudded into his face.

Covering his nose, Dad said, "Aaron!" His bellow ricocheted around the lobby.

"Are you bleeding?" I ran around the desk. "Why'd you yell 'Aaron'?"

He took his hand away. "Reflex."

A cut ran along the left side of his nose, and blood dripped from one nostril.

"Stay right there." I turned around, reaching for the tissues at the checkout desk.

Serenity had vanished.

Liberty crumpled against the desk, sobbing. "Don't arrest my sister. Don't take her to jail."

I gave Dad a wad of tissues and then crouched beside Liberty. What was Rusty's technique for calming himself?

"I don't arrest little girls," Dad said through the tissues.

"Mommy says cops hit people," Liberty said between gasps, "and throw people in jail for nothing."

"What?" Dad's question was only a breath.

I said, "Liberty, you have to slow your breathing."

"Liberty," Dad's powerful baritone was almost a whisper, "what are two things you hear?"

"Uh-uh—something humming and—and s-s-something squeaking."

"What are three blue things you see?"

That was Rusty's calming technique. Still talking softly, Dad led Liberty through her five senses twice, getting her to focus on a different sensation and not her panic. She was breathing normally when Devon entered from the hall under the balcony, dragging Serenity. The six-year-old kept locking her knees to stop her mom from moving her.

"I told you, Serenity," Devon said with a grunt. "Stay in the lobby while you wait for—" She looked from Dad to Liberty to me and then glared at Serenity. "You threw something, didn't you, and hit the sheriff?"

"I didn't mean to." Serenity leaned away from her mom, pulling on her arm. "I was trying to hit Liberty."

"Does that excuse it?" said Devon.

Liberty took a quivering breath. "He said he doesn't arrest little girls, and he didn't hit me or anything, Mommy."

Dad's eyes rounded as Devon froze. For the first time in the year and a half I'd known Devon, I saw a faint trace of a blush creep into my best friend's cheeks.

Without a word, Dad got to his feet and limped to the bathroom, his brace squeaking.

Devon hauled Serenity behind the counter. "Rae, what happened?"

Two patrons approached the desk, so I explained the incident after we checked out their materials.

"This is terrible." Devon delivered another blistering glare to Serenity. "You will apologize to the sheriff when he comes back."

Serenity stamped her foot. "I wasn't trying to hit him."

Dad limped back to the desk. The inside of his nose had stopped bleeding, and he only held a tissue against the cut on the outside. "Rae, where's the library's first aid kit? I need a Band-Aid."

"I have some in my backpack."

"I am so sorry about this, Mal." Devon hauled Serenity from behind the desk. "Apologize."

"She doesn't have to if she doesn't mean it," said Dad.

For some reason, Devon took offense at that and bristled.

Serenity stared, open-mouthed. "You don't want me to say I'm sorry?"

"Only if you really are."

Crossing her arms, Serenity frowned in the same thoughtful way her mom did. "Yeah, I really am, Big Guy. I didn't want to hit you."

"Serenity," Devon said in a tight voice, "you call him Mr. Malinowski."

"'Big Guy' is fine," said Dad. "She's probably heard Hank call me that a hundred times."

Timothy Morley, on the march again, entered the lobby.

Dad stepped in his path. "Mr. Morley, I've been trying to get ahold of you."

"What about?" The question came out dry and irritated. Then panic leaped into his dark eyes. "Ms. Vex isn't breaking a law by trying to contact my father, is she?"

"No, sir." Dad removed the tissue from his nose. "I'd like to speak to you privately about her. Do you have time tomorrow? I'll meet you wherever you want."

"Privately?" He studied Dad, adjusting his grip on The Book. "I will save us both time. You want to warn me about Ms. Vex. I've had her thoroughly researched, and she has no history of committing crimes."

"If you had her thoroughly researched, you know she didn't seem to exist until two years ago. She may have committed fraud under another name."

Timothy lifted his nose. "Ms. Vex has demonstrated her powers to me. It's none of your business."

"I consider it my duty to advise you to rethink working with Ms. Vex. I have no proof of fraud, but this situation resembles cases of fraud I've dealt with."

"I am duly warned. Your conscience is now clear, Sheriff." Timothy brushed by Dad and out the lobby doors.

Dad watched him, frowning.

"You can only warn him, Dad."

"Unfortunately, true."

We headed to the back staircase, passing by the table where Liberty and Serenity were packing up their books and papers.

Dad waved.

Liberty permitted herself a tiny wave in return while Serenity said, as if people on the balcony needed to hear, "Hope your nose gets better, Big Guy."

Chapter Twenty-Six

As soon as Dad drove the Beast out of the library parking lot, he said, "Do you have any idea what Liberty meant when she said Devon had told her officers hit people?"

"Yeah." I sighed. "Sadly." I described Devon's intolerance of cops. "She won't tell me why. She just says she has a good reason. It's so out of character. She's usually very practical."

Now Dad sighed. "Well, once she gets to know me and my other deputies better, maybe she'll realize how ridiculous making sweeping generalizations about a group of people is. Although we've chatted several times. I'm not a faceless uniform."

"I don't know what to tell you. But Devon does want to help us." I explained her offer to take over scheduling people to tend the animals at both farms.

"That will help a lot." Dad settled back in his bucket seat.

"I have an idea where the inheritance is hidden." I explained my theory of the site being a local church. "If I could be certain of the church, the poem should direct me to the exact spot." I frowned. "Unless Cyrus threw all the money and jewels in the ocean, and the clues mean nothing. That's Alex Morley's theory. The more I read about Cyrus, the more I think that's a real possibility."

"Too bad Morley Sr. doesn't believe that."

When Dad and I entered the waiting room for ICU, Jeanine was sitting in a chair along one wall with Aunt Lily and Walter.

She popped up and hugged us as Walter eyed Dad's face. "What happened to you? Risk your life for another horse?"

"Long story, Walter." Dad put his arm around Jeanine's slender shoulders.

She said, "You and Rae can go back. Hank's woozy from all the pain killers, so he drops off at any moment. His fever's gone today, but the first surgery is still Friday." She lowered her voice. "I haven't told him about Knight. He doesn't remember the accident at all. That can happen after a traumatic event, even without a head injury. I have to remind him why he's in the hospital."

Jeanine peeled off the sticker that allowed her in to see Hank, handed it to Dad, and then got another one for me.

Dad pressed the sticker above his shirt pocket. "You ready, kiddo?"

Nodding, I smoothed mine to my t-shirt. My stomach balled up, and I took a deep breath to loosen it.

Nothing happened.

We walked through a door opposite of the one we came in by, and it was like a time portal. The colors of the walls were different and the nurses' station had curved desks instead of rectangular ones, but the hushed, depressed atmosphere mirrored the ICU Mom had been in.

I drew air in my nose and out my mouth as we passed shadowy rooms.

I wasn't going to see Mom. Hank would be okay. Doctors had actually helped him. This wasn't the same.

As I pressed my locket between my fingers, my breathing grew faster, the sickly clean stench crawling in with it.

A warm hand wrapped around my free one.

Exhaling slowly, I squeezed Dad's hand as we reached Hank's room. The blinds were up, flooding the dead white room with watery evening light.

Hank lay against the upraised part of the bed, his head tilted to the side, eyes closed. His right leg was encased in bandages and tubes.

"Loafing as usual," Dad said, louder than normal.

Hank's eyelids fluttered. "Oh, hey, Big Guy. Jeanine says I broke my leg. Fell off Knight."

Tears backed up in my eyes like a spring thaw behind a dam, and my stomach relaxed. Despite his slow, slurred speech, hearing him speak at all sent my relief into the stratosphere.

I took several big sniffs, attaching Liberty's card to a dry erase board already covered with cards.

"So how long do you think you can get away with lying around here?" said Dad.

"I think a while." Hank shifted in the bed, and his jaw clenched.

"Don't start ramming around." Dad's order was sharp.

"Okay," Hank murmured, his eyelids drooping.

We kept talking, but Hank wasn't up to sustained conversation.

Dad said, "I'll stay here, and you can go talk to Jeanine."

"Works for me." I hugged Hank, who thanked me in a whisper, and returned to the waiting room.

Walter's words came in a snarl. "So what if Jack gets mean. That ain't new. That's all he is."

Walter, Aunt Lily, and Jeanine had gathered to one side of the exit. Aunt Lily's posture was tight—legs together, arms held close against her sides, her fingers twisted in the strap of her worn purse.

"Walter," said Jeanine, "it's always hard on Aunt Lily when one of her kids is mad at her." She gripped Aunt Lily's other hand. "Jack should realize it's not your fault Mal wants to keep your mom's book."

"Why can't you toughen up and tell Jack where he can go?" Walter growled. "I done it to my kids all the time."

Of course he had. Which explained Aunt Lily's trouble standing up to men.

"Having The Book won't do Jack any good." I explained how Dad and the boys and I had worked on the clues Friday night.

Aunt Lily's forehead wrinkled. "Why're you all trying to solve the clues? You can't inherit the treasure."

"If I solve it, I'll call you or Claire, and either of you can touch the treasure and claim it."

"That's real nice of you." Her lips trembled. "I've never tried to solve it 'cause I'm too dumb."

"Don't say that." Jeanine squeezed her hand.

"So what if you're dumb?" Walter glared at his oldest daughter. "Troy's smart and look at all the trouble he makes. You're a hard worker, Lily. You work harder than anybody I ever met. Hard work takes care of you better than brains could."

Aunt Lily blinked, her fingers touching her lips. She looked as conflicted as I felt. Walter had complimented her, right?

"Well—" Aunt Lily's lips steadied into a smile "—I guess you taught me real well, Walter."

"Wouldn't matter what I taught if you didn't want to learn."

The elevator doors slid open, and the four of us got in.

As the elevator started its descent, I said, "Don't get your hopes up about the treasure, Aunt Lily. I think there might not be one. Alex Morley thinks there isn't." I explained his theory.

"I met Alex." Her tired face brightened. "He seems real nice."

"You can't tell that from talking to him once, Lily," said Walter. "And don't blab to Jack that Rae's workin' on the clues."

The bright light in her expression died out. "Oh, no. I won't."

I told Jeanine I'd read the entire section on Cyrus Morley in *In His Service*. "Those four people could have killed him if they'd left him up there long enough. I wonder if that was their plan or if they were just scaring him."

"Impossible to know now," said Jeanine.

On the ground floor, we left the elevator and headed for the glass doors to the parking lot.

With a shiver, Aunt Lily tugged on the strap of her purse. "Was my great-grandfather so terrible that people wanted to kill him?"

"He was terrible," said Jeanine. "But he should have been arrested and tried for the crimes he'd committed. Vigilante justice isn't justice at all."

"It is when it's all you can get." Walter mumbled it, like his mind was somewhere else.

The sun had slipped behind the hospital, spraying the hazy sky and remnants of storm clouds with bars of fuzzy rose. An evening breeze rustled the soggy golden leaves of the short, ornamental trees marooned between the sea of vehicles.

"Thank you for coming." Jeanine hugged Aunt Lily, who held on for a moment.

Arms outstretched, Jeanine moved to Walter, but he rubbed the gray stubble on his square jaw. "Rae, d'you think knowin' more about the bunch that strung up Cyrus could help you crack that code?"

Jeanine's arms dropped, Aunt Lily's forehead furrowed, and my eyes tried to grow out on stalks.

"I—I don't know." I hated to say it, but I had to be honest. "I doubt it, but—uh—I'd really like to know what you know."

"You want me to get the treasure, Walter?" Aunt Lily sounded stunned.

"That surprise you?" His question was so harsh that Aunt Lily cringed. He lowered his gaze to his boots bound in duct tape. "You'd do good for the whole family with it if you don't let your no-account kids talk you out of it."

A smile shimmered onto Aunt Lily's face.

Walter looked up. "Rae, give me a call when you ain't workin'. I got somethin' to show you." He stomped into the parking lot.

I called after him, "I can stop by tomorrow morning. I'm working late."

He waved a hand to show he heard me.

Aunt Lily hugged us and trotted after her father.

Jeanine turned to me, her enormous eyes bulging. "You have to tell me what he says."

I watched my great-grandfather's massive figure disappearing into the lot. "For sure."

Chapter Twenty-Seven

The next morning, as I drove the Rust Bucket to Walter's, my mind flitted from one scenario to another, like it had most of the night. What could Walter know about the attack on Cyrus?

He couldn't have taken part, being barely old enough for school. But he'd lived in Marlin County his whole life. Had someone confessed the crime to him years ago? Or had Walter figured it out somehow himself? Although Gram's side of my family was loaded with brains, I knew we also got a huge dose of intelligence from Walter.

My truck rocked as it rode the ruts up Walter's drive. The maples in the woods on either side of it showed sparse patches of vivid orange, like they were too shy yet to discard their somber green clothes for their flamboyant fall costumes. The haze from yesterday still hung in the air, mellowing the sun's white fire.

Walter's small beige house came into view, appearing younger and in better shape, since Dad, Carrie, Jeanine, and I, along with any other relatives we could convince, had painted it over the past summer. After a long, entrenched battle with Walter to let us help him. A dark blue van, scarred with rusty holes, sat in front of the garage.

I stomped on the brakes.

Aunt Lily's kids drove that van to The Haunting. Were Jack and Jesse here? Claire would be home with her kids. No other vehicles were visible. A good sign that the two cousins who lived with Walter, Egypt and China, weren't home. Dealing with Jack was bad enough, but adding Egypt and China to the mix would make the visit so hostile that I should have borrowed Dad's body armor. Besides, Walter couldn't tell me anything concerning the treasure if Jack could overhear us.

As I yanked up on my emergency brake, Walter came out onto the front porch, wearing a gray plaid shirt and jeans that were probably older than I was.

I hiked up the short slope to the house. "Morning, Walter. Is Jack or Jesse here?"

"Jack is. He came in drunk last night. He's sleeping it off. You want coffee?" said Walter.

"No. I'm fine."

He glanced at the house. "We can talk out here." But instead of taking a seat, he went inside, the screen door smacking the sill behind him.

I took a seat in a dark green plastic chair on the porch, assuming he'd be back.

The flowerbeds lining the porch were a battlefield with several clumps of orange mums and asters struggling against an invasion of Queen Anne's lace—or as Gram called it, wild carrot—and vines with red berries that I believed were bittersweet nightshade. The berries looked similar to honeysuckle, but that grew as a bush.

Walter returned with a mug and a photo album and sat in another chair beside me, setting the mug on the plank floor. He flipped open the album. All the pages he turned had black and white photos. He dropped the album in my lap and pointed to a photo about three inches square.

Three men and a woman, in their late teens or early twenties, posed around the kind of truck used in Depression-era movies. The men wore suspenders with their pants and hats—two with caps and one with what I thought was called a fedora. The woman wore a floral print dress, her hair loose on her shoulders.

I bent closer. Gasping, I pointed to the man in the fedora. "He looks like Uncle Troy."

"That's my dad."

I gasped again. I'd wondered what Walter Sr. was like. All I knew was that he'd left Walter, his mother, and sisters when Walter was twelve and was never in contact with them again.

"Who are the other—" My eyes swelled, and I whipped my head to Walter. "There's four of them."

Walter growled in satisfaction as the right side of his mouth pulled back. Then he pointed at each person. "The guy who's thin like Dad was Uncle Vince. Dad was the oldest, then Vince. Then Aunt Tess. The youngest was Uncle Stan."

Now I knew where Walter got his lineman build. Walter Sr., Vince, and Tess all appeared taller than average, compared to the truck, but Stan looked like he could lift the front end of the truck with one hand.

"When was this taken?" I said.

"1939. Dad would've been twenty-five."

"What did Cyrus Morley do to them?"

"He didn't do nothin' to Dad or my uncles. But he done somethin' to Aunt Tess."

I studied her. Pretty in a hard-boned way, she had a narrow face with sharp cheekbones and chin. But her light eyes would make any guy think twice before making a move. They seemed to blaze through celluloid and eighty years of history.

Walter gulped coffee. "I don't know if Cyrus sweet-talked Aunt Tess and dumped her or cheated on her or somethin' worse. Dad didn't say. But when Cyrus come back—he disappeared for a few years—Aunt Tess wanted revenge. And if Aunt Tess wanted to get you, you might as well give yourself up."

He pointed at the relatives in the photo again. "Dad and Uncle Stan were dumb and cowards. Uncle Vince was smart and a coward. But Aunt Tess was smart, had guts, and was so mean that if they'd drafted her, there wasn't no need for the landing at Normandy. She'd've wiped the Nazis off the map by herself. If she got to hating them."

I stared into those burning eyes. "So she wanted Cyrus dead."

"Dad said they was just gonna scare him. Aunt Tess told 'em to all wear black and wear masks and not say a word so Cyrus couldn't recognize them. That fits with lettin' him live. It also fits with Aunt Tess. She'd love watchin' Cyrus lookin' over his shoulder and jumpin' at every noise 'cause he wouldn't know if the people that got him once wouldn't do it again. I bet she was mad when he left Marlin County for good."

"Did your dad give you the details of what happened?"

Walter leaned back in his chair. "More'n that. When we was driving by the Morley place, he'd reenact the whole thing. 'Course, he was always drunk when he told me and acted like he was the brains behind the whole thing, but I figure the basics are true." He took another swig of coffee and launched into his tale.

Once Tess decided on their outfits and the method of terrifying Cyrus, the four siblings waited for an opportunity to set the revenge in motion. One night, Vince learned Cyrus was visiting a local woman. The four of them went to the valley he owned to wait for him.

Stan picked a skinny tree by the side of the road leading to the mansion and chopped it almost through. When Tess signaled Cyrus was close, Stan felled the tree across the road. As soon as Cyrus got out to see what was blocking the road, the Malinowskis grabbed him.

"Dad said it went better than even Aunt Tess expected. Cyrus began bawlin' and beggin' that they let him go, thinkin' they was demons. He said he hadn't thought they existed. He just liked foolin' around with ghosts and seances and all that s-s-stuff."

His stutter signaled that "stuff" wasn't his first choice.

"When they strung him up, he went wild, screamin' like a banshee and beggin' for mercy. They'd almost got him tied up when Uncle Vince saw lights out by the road. Aunt Tess—Dad said it was him but that'd take guts—she got close enough to see that it was the sheriff with a group of men. So Dad and them took off. Aunt Tess was so happy with how it came off that she thanked her brothers. Dad said that was the only nice thing she ever done to him."

Shoot fires. What a story. And they were my relatives.

I touched the photo. "From all the research Jeanine has collected, nobody ever suspected your dad and his siblings. The sheriff got nowhere with his investigation."

"That's a miracle, knowing Dad and my uncles never met a booze they didn't like. But they was so scared of Aunt Tess, they kept their mouths shut. I reckon Dad figured I was safe. But he made me promise I'd never breathe a word of this or Aunt Tess would get him. I haven't. Til today." He eyed me. "Does this give you any ideas? It never did me. I was hopin' maybe you bein' fresh to the hunt, you could crack the code."

"You tried to find the treasure?"

"Off and on, over the years, after Lily's mom showed me her book. Never got nowheres."

I pulled on my earlobe. "I don't think it helps, but I'll have to think it over. What happened to your aunt and uncles?"

"Stan got killed in a fight in prison, doin' time for manslaughter. Uncle Vince was found dead in an alley in Dallas. Heart attack. Aunt Tess just stopped comin' around. Last time I saw her, Lily was a baby. I figure she finally ticked off somebody she couldn't out-mean and ended up dead in a ditch somewheres." Walter dropped his cellar voice even lower. "You don't tell nobody what I told you."

"Aunt Jeanine wants to know, and I'd like to tell Dad."

Walter rubbed his jaw. "Them's okay. Nobody else. Especially not Lily. Her kids — the mean ones — can get anything out of her." He closed the album and got up with a grunt or a suppressed groan.

I looked at my phone. Plenty of time. "Walter, can I weed your flowerbeds?"

He glanced over his shoulder at the untamed plants. "China's real good about keepin' them cleaned up, but she got busy with homework and her job the past few weeks." He opened the screen door, set the album inside, and then stomped to the end of the porch near the drive and garage. "I'll get some gloves. There's poison ivy in there."

I might need them for the bittersweet nightshade too. Eating parts of the plant could make you sick, but I wasn't sure about touching them.

In a few minutes, Walter knelt beside me, cracking in several places, and handed me a pair of frayed gloves.

As I slipped them on, I swallowed the urge to tell Walter that he didn't need to help me. After his resistance to us painting his house, I knew it would do no good. He'd probably tell me to leave.

We'd cleared one bed when the noise of someone walking around in the house reached us.

Walter sat back on his heels and shouted, "Coffee's made."

I gave a wild carrot a powerful yank.

If Jack was up, I should leave, but I didn't want to run away, like I was scared of him. On guard, yes. But not scared.

My lungs constricted.

Okay. Maybe a little scared.

A few minutes later, Jack staggered onto the porch, carrying a mug. "Man, this stuff's like drinking dirt."

"Then don't drink it." Walter threw a vine of nightshade, choked with small red berries, behind him.

"Aww, I should take a picture." Jack's mocking voice went high. "It's so-o-o-o cute, the great-grandpa and great-granddaughter working together."

"You could help us if you wasn't bone-lazy." Walter patted dirt around a mum.

Jack's sharp face went rigid. "I got a job. I told you about it."

Walter sat back again. "Yeah, but I bet you're lookin' for that treasure instead of doin' your job."

Jack threw the mug into the yard, hot coffee missing our heads by inches.

I scrambled to my feet as Jack jumped off the porch.

Walter was creaking upright.

"I'm doing my job. Stop riding me!" Jack's light green eyes blazed as he drew back a fist.

Although Jack and I were the same height, I wasn't strong enough to fight him. And Walter wasn't fast enough.

Father, protect us.

My muscles coiling, I said, "You touch him, and I'm calling Dad."

Jack glanced at me, his fist in firing position.

"No, you ain't, Rae," Walter growled. "I can take care of myself." He straightened. "Don't start something you can't finish, Jack."

With his back to me, I couldn't see Walter's expression, but it froze my cousin.

Then Jack broke into a leer that Cyrus Morley would have been proud of, lowering his arm. "Someday, old man, you won't be able to count on your sheriff grandson to bail you out."

"You see me counting on him now?"

Jack kept leering, making my fingers itch to remove it, and sauntered toward his van.

Walter said, "You pick up that cup now or you will when you come back."

Jack's steps stuttered, then continued to the van.

As he backed down the drive, I went to the cup and bent over.

Walter said, "Didn't you hear me? Jack's gonna pick it up. And I don't need my great-granddaughter tryin' to protect me. Or my grandson." Walter stormed into the house, the screen door banging behind him.

I bit my lip, glancing from the house to my truck. Shrugging, I kneeled by the flowerbed.

I'd offered to help. No reason to quit.

By the time I had to leave, the mums were once again the stars of the beds. I drove away without seeing Walter.

Chapter Twenty-Eight

Liberty made a beeline for the checkout desk as soon as she and Serenity entered the library after school that afternoon. She whispered, "When's your dad's birthday?"

I smiled. "February 16. And his favorite color is blue."

During my supper break, I researched the churches represented by the pastors and priest who had rescued Cyrus. Of the six churches, all but one remained in the same building since 1951. If Cyrus hid his treasure where the Lutheran church had stood back then, no one could find it. The Wellesville fire station had been built on top of the site thirty years ago.

When I got home that night, my cousins and brothers crowded the bar, devouring a plate of butterscotch brownies with, to my surprise, Jeanine.

I rested my backpack on the counter. "I wasn't expecting you to be home."

"Luke and Carrie convinced me that I should come home for at least one night," she said. "Hank was doing really well today." She put her arm around Coral and kissed her head.

The affection didn't touch Coral's blank face.

"Won't Mr. Norris start harvesting soon?" I snagged a brownie.

"When he gets a couple dry days in a row, he'll start on the beans." Jeanine drank a cup of milk.

Gram put a baking pan in the sink. "Rae, Mal wants to talk to you. He's in his room."

Since my mouth was full of brownie, I gave her a thumbs up, trotted downstairs, turned right, and knocked on Dad's door.

"Who is it?"

Odd. He usually said either, "Come on in" or "Give me a minute."

"It's Rae."

"Oh. Come on in."

Despite two windows and sandy paint, Dad's finished bedroom always reminded me of a cave. With only his desk lamp switched on, his room held more gloom than usual.

He scooted back in the desk chair. "I borrowed Jeanine's research. Your timeline is helpful."

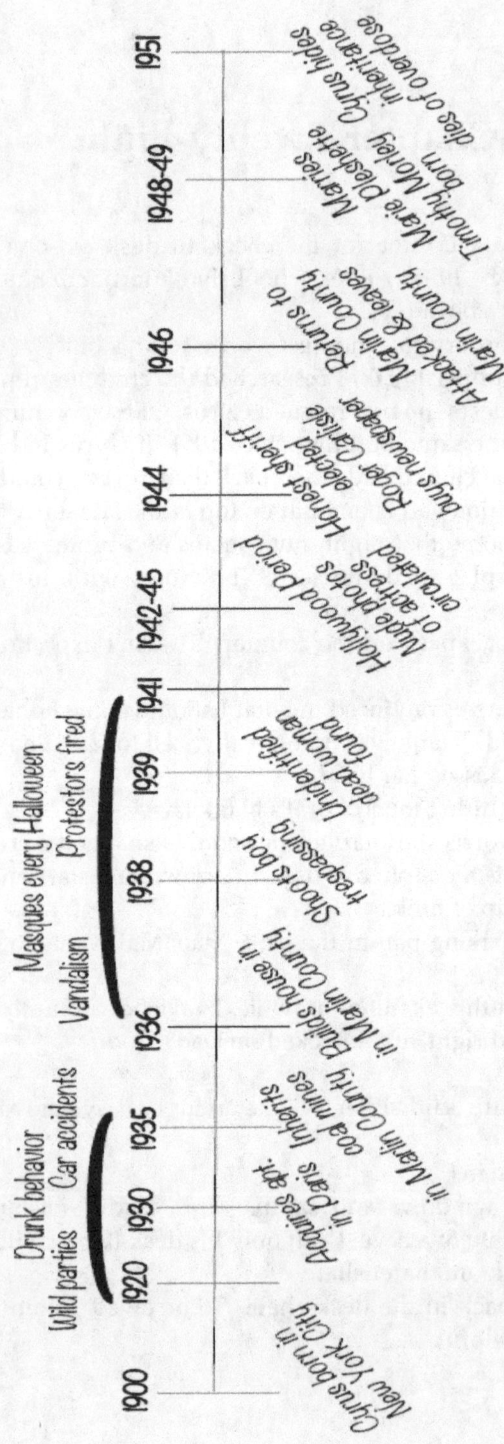
1900
1920
1930
1935
1936
1938
1939
1941
1942-45
1944
1946
1948-49
1951
Wild parties
Drunk behavior
Car accidents
Vandalism
Masques every Halloween
Protestors fired
Cyrus born in New York City
Acquires art in Paris
Inherits coal mines in Marlin County
Builds house in Marlin County
Shoots boy trespassing
Unidentified dead woman found
Hollywood period
Nude photos of actress circulated
Honest sheriff Roger Carlisle elected buys newspaper
Attacked & leaves Marlin County
Returns to Marlin County
Marries Marie Pleshette
Timothy Morley born
Cyrus hides inheritance
dies of overdose

The gloom in the room was nothing compared to Dad's depressed tone. His back seemed hunched under an invisible weight that also pulled his face into sags.

"I'm not done with it. Are you all right?"

He shifted some of the copied articles around the blotter on his desk. "Tomorrow's the anniversary of Dad's death."

I lowered myself onto his double bed. "Oh."

Gram had seemed her usual self, but maybe staying busy was how she handled the anniversary. And Jeanine was probably so relieved with Hank's recovery that the date wasn't hitting her as hard. I'd learned, through experience I wish I hadn't had, that people processed grief very differently.

I sat still. "Are we going to the cemetery tomorrow?"

He shook his head. "Jeanine said her nerves aren't up to visiting the graves. I'm not sure Carrie's up for it either." He huffed a sigh. "I'm not all that certain about myself."

As hard as it was to watch Mom die by inches from cancer, Grandpa Reuel throwing himself in front of a bullet meant for Walter was way worse, dying in the space of a few minutes. While Dad, Gram, and my aunts talked about how wonderful Reuel had been, they had only given me basic information about his death. And I hadn't researched it. It seemed a violation of their trust. From various comments, I'd learned that Walter thought he knew who the killer was, but no one had been convicted of the crime.

Dad said, "We'll wait until — well, maybe until Hank can come with us."

I nodded. "It wouldn't seem right to have a family event without him."

His swift glance showed he agreed.

Then he said, "What do you need to add to the timeline?"

I rolled out the tale of The Wronged Woman's Revenge.

Dad hung his left arm over the back of his chair, and a bit of his normal good humor lifted the droops in his expression. "I should have known. Anything outrageous or illegal in this county usually involves a Malinowski somewhere. Even going back seventy-five years."

"I'm only telling you and Aunt Jeanine. Walter didn't want me to tell anyone at first. He thought the story might help locate the treasure. I can't see how, though. Cyrus certainly had contempt for his attackers, but he had no clue who they were." I scooted to the edge of the bed. "Can I do something to help you or — or anyone else get through tomorrow?"

His enormous hand cupped my face. "Just you being home, kiddo, makes tomorrow better."

My brain tipped and spun. I'd forgotten that *I* was one of the people he'd mourned for years since he'd assumed I'd died in a fire when my mom was pregnant with me.

Hot tingles warmed my face. It was dizzying, and humbling, to realize that just showing up made someone's life better.

I hugged him. "I'm glad I'm home too."

~~~~~

Before Jeanine and my cousins left for their farm, I maneuvered her into my bedroom without Amber, Coral, or the boys noticing and repeated Walter's tale.

She listened with a mouth that gaped to the limit, but when I finished, it snapped shut. "After all these years ... I've wondered, since I read Rebecca's story, about the identity of those people."

She looked to the floor, her gaze turning inward, her right hand clutching her bangs.

I'd been in the family long enough to recognize the signs. "You've got an idea for a story."

"Possibly." Then she returned fully to reality. "Do you have paper at your desk?"

Jotting down her ideas delayed Jeanine and my cousins a half hour before going home.

So everyone was in their right beds when the call shot us out of them at 1:30 a.m. Gram and I floundered through the living-dining room to the landline in the kitchen.

I snatched up the phone. "Aunt Jeanine? What's wrong?"

"I need to talk to Mal." Every word shook.

My brothers tumbled out of the darkness and into the weak light coming from under the microwave.

"Is it Uncle Hank?" Rusty said in a strangled whisper.

I shook my head, and Dad's voice came over the line from his phone in the basement. "I got it, Rae."

I hesitated, then hung up. "Aunt Jeanine wanted to talk to Dad." But about what?

My bare feet shifted on the cold linoleum, and all of us stared at the basement door.

In a few minutes, Dad thumped up the stairs and into the kitchen.

We asked more or less at once, "What's wrong?"

He said, "Jeanine saw somebody sneaking around the farm. She went to the kitchen to get allergy medicine, looked out the window over the sink, and saw a silhouette turning the corner of the stable. Since Carrie isn't there, and her nerves aren't the best right now, Jeanine wants me to escort her and the girls back here."

"Maybe it was the black bear." Aaron spoke with the alertness of someone who'd woken up hours ago. "They can walk on two legs."
~~~~~

"Jeanine wouldn't mistake a bear for a man." Dad said through his teeth, "It'd better not be that bigfoot hunter."

Gram turned to me. "Rae, would you mind —"

But I'd already started for the stairs. "I'll get the inflatable mattress."

Chapter Twenty-Nine

"Where did Mal learn that exercise to calm Liberty?" Joining me at the checkout desk the next morning, Devon scooted book repair supplies aside on a shelf under the counter and placed her cloth purse in the space.

"From Rusty's therapist." I snapped a roll of paper in the printer for the due dates slips. "Rusty was traumatized after his mom died, so he saw a therapist for a few years. That's a technique he follows when he gets super anxious." I looked to my friend, whose mouth was hanging open. "What?"

"Mal took one of his kids to a therapist? I figured an alpha guy like him would tell his kids to suck it up if they had emotional problems."

Gritting my teeth, I turned my attention back to the small printer. "No, my dad actually likes his kids."

"I didn't say he didn't." Devon whirled around to the drop box.

At noon, I paced in front of the deli, waiting for Chris to meet me for lunch. If he had Monday off, I had the perfect date for us. As soon as Chris pulled into a parking place by the newspaper office, I hurried to his SUV and knocked on the window.

He rolled it down.

I said, "I need to talk to you in private before we get lunch."

His thick, black eyebrows tightened a moment, and then he opened the passenger door.

I settled in the seat. "It's about the treasure. I don't want anyone overhearing my theory."

His right eyebrow elevated a fraction. "And that is?"

I explained what I'd concluded about Cyrus's character and why I thought he might have buried the treasure at a church. "I think the most probable place to hide $400,000 in cash and jewels is a cemetery. Burying the treasure above an occupied grave would make it unlikely it'd be disturbed. I'm off on Monday. If you are too, I'd like to go on a ... treasure hunting date." My voice sounded goofy even to me. But I loved the idea of solving the riddle with Chris.

He smoothed his moustache with his thumb and first finger. "It'll be a first for me." He slid me his quick grin.

"Once we decide which churches are near geographic features that match 'Mountains of the Moon' and 'Valley of the Shadow,' we should look for clues that have something to do with 'knight,' 'pilgrim,' 'shade,' 'shadow,' or 'ride boldly.' Those are the words of the poem that stand out to me."

He stared out the front window. "You think you might find the treasure buried near a headstone for someone named Knight, for example."

"Or someone whose last name is Pilgrim. Or a grave with the picture of a knight."

"Have you checked a site that catalogs headstones?"

"I—uh—no. I was going to check county records."

Chris opened his phone. "Since I like local history, I've done some investigating and found a couple of sites that have photos of headstones." He texted me the links. "Because the sites are crowdsourced, I can't guarantee how complete they are, but you might find some matches to your criteria quickly."

"This could save me a ton of time."

"But this might all be moot." Chris closed his phone. "If Lyra Vex finds the treasure Friday night." His face was as serious as ever, but humor flashed in his eyes.

I grinned. "Whatever Lyra finds, it won't be the treasure."

We got out and went into the deli. After getting our food, we took the same table in the corner.

While ransacking my brain to find a way to lead up to an invitation to church, I told him about Jeanine's midnight visitor. "Dad didn't want to hunt for someone in the dark, so he went back over this morning and found fresh footprints by the corral. They're large enough to be a man's, but they could belong to whoever had evening duty with the animals last night."

"I'd like to catch that bigfoot hunter doing something illegal," said Chris. "Houston had a call two nights ago about a prowler at the McKissick's farm. As he was driving there, he saw Garrison walking along the road, very close to the farm. He found no one. But then he remembered what Mal had said about the guy and wondered if the prowler was Garrison." He drained his cup. "Rae, I've researched several community colleges that are within an hour's drive and offer digital design majors. Digital design is the best major for you if you want to include photography with more marketable skills. All of these colleges partner with OU. If you take the courses OU requires at the community college for two years, you can finish your degree at the university."

Good thing Dan Cervelli was running his air conditioner because I might have melted into a mound of happy goo. Chris cared so much.

"Rae? What do you think?"

"Oh—uh..." I sat up but couldn't erase what had to be a dopey expression off my face. "That's so nice of you." I couldn't tell him it was all wasted effort.

"I like to help you." His strong hand covered mine. "I think it'd be a mistake if you didn't go to college."

If he cared that much about me, he'd want to know more about something so important to me.

I cleared my throat. "Did you like your boarding school?" Since it was Catholic, it wouldn't take long to steer the conversation naturally to an invite.

A guarded look rose in his eyes, like a drawbridge going up, and his body recoiled an inch from mine. "Yes."

And ... nothing else.

I hooked hair behind my ear. "Going to a school that wasn't afraid to mention God must have been really different."

He took a big bite of his club sandwich. "Yes."

As my stomach tightened to close for business, I pushed away my BLT.

This wasn't working.

Chris glanced at me and bit a chip. "We could go over the college information at my house one evening this week."

He'd retreated to safer ground.

If I crossed his "no trespassing" tape to invite him to church, he'd never go. And he'd never go on our treasure-hunting date.

I leaned back in my seat. I'd wait for a better opportunity.

But as we talked about possible colleges and degrees for me, something ground in my gut, like two gears out of sync, and the need to issue an invitation made it difficult for me to follow our conversation.

What was wrong with waiting? The left side of my face contracted, and I placed my hand against it.

"When could you come over this week?" said Chris.

"I'll let you know," I said with an overdose of fake enthusiasm.

He smiled and finished his sandwich.

I got a container for my half-eaten sandwich and parted from Chris with a kiss at the library doors.

The grinding intensified, and a slow afternoon gave me hours to analyze it.

At 5, when I headed to the employees' kitchen to get my backpack, I'd figured it out, and that only worsened the grated feeling. I'd put my desire to have fun with Chris ahead of talking about what was much more important.

And God was letting me know I disobeyed.

I trudged out the basement door to the parking lot.

I'm sorry I bailed, Father. Now what do I do?

Chapter Thirty

My prayer never left my mind the whole long evening, even though I was busy helping my brothers with their homework while Dad and Gram spent time at Aunt Lily's. Two of my late grandfather's brothers also came to visit, but not Walter. Dad said Walter always disappeared for a few days around the anniversary of his oldest son's death.

And my prayer hung on as Devon and I checked in materials from the drop box the next morning.

My phone rang with a call from Dad. "I wanted to tell you we should ride together to the Halloween show tonight. Parking will be at a premium. I'm helping with crowd control."

I said, "So many people are coming that Dani needed to hire extra security?"

Dad barked a laugh. "You're right about the ticket sales, but Ms. Li refuses to spend money on extra security, although Carrie told her she should. So Carrie called me. She thinks it'll be a zoo. Ms. Li's opening an hour earlier and crammed more people into each timed entry. And almost everyone who's bought a ticket ponied up the extra money for watching the—the—I don't know what you call Ms. Vex's act."

"I'm going with séance. Devon calls it a freak show."

"Both work for me. I don't have the staff to assign an on-duty deputy to the event, although I told the night shift to park in the area when they're available. So Ms. Li gets the sheriff for free."

~~~~~

As patrons circulated through the library, they only talked about the séance. Everyone was going, either ditching the home football game or coming afterwards. A few people asked about Hank, and I told them his first surgery was this morning.

By lunch, I hadn't experienced any nudges or insights from my Father, so I forced myself to focus on checking the sites for finding headstones. Of the six remaining churches represented by the pastors and the priest, only four seemed to fit the description in the poem—sitting in some kind of a valley with hills nearby. None of them had cemeteries with graves that had the name Knight or Pilgrim. I even tried Shade, Shadow, and Ryder. Nothing.

As I returned to the checkout desk, Jeanine texted Hank was in recovery and the surgery had gone well. I passed that good news on to
~~~~~

anyone who asked until we closed.

At supper, Dad fueled up on pizza and large quantities of caffeine. I tried to, but the awful feeling I'd disobeyed my Father made food unappealing.

I really am sorry, Father. You've forgiven me, right?

Arriving at the former Morley property at 7, we found the makings of a zoo. Vehicles already packed the parking area across the road. Three times as many food trucks formed a semi-circle, and enough costumed people milled about them to start a parade.

Dad parked to the side of the drive, near the entrance. "At least Ms. Li invested in some more barriers."

A lot more. Plastic fencing flowed up the hill to the old home, making a broad U. A tent and a couple of trailers had been moved from in front of the home.

I pointed to it. "I guess that's where Lyra is going to contact him."

"Where else?"

Carrie dodged a zombie, a vampire, and someone in a costume so gross that I turned my head as Dad and I got out of the SUV.

She adjusted her black baseball hat that said "Security." "This is a good place to park, Mal, if you need to get out fast. You can take my Jeep home, Rae." She handed me her keys. "I'll go home with Mal. I have no idea how long we'll be here tonight. My Jeep's parked along the road, on the west side of the property. It should give you a quick exit." Carrie tilted her head toward the food trucks. "Lyra knows how to hold court."

The fake medium worked her way through the lines, chatting, posing for photos, and reading palms, leaving each person laughing.

Dad said, "Find anything suspicious on the property?"

"No. But Lyra could have planted a fake clue anywhere on the twenty acres here."

"Where do you need me?"

Placing her hand over heart, Carrie staggered. "My big brother is letting me give orders?"

"It's your zoo." A scream from the food truck lines made Dad frown. "Let's pray it doesn't turn into mine."

I headed to the booth. So many customers meant we'd be busy, and hopefully, I'd stop worrying about the mess I'd made with Chris yesterday.

The sunset had slipped from under mountains of charcoal clouds and barred the west with bands of peach and pale gold. The rusty red of the oaks, fiery orange of the maples, and the aged yellow of the sycamores dotted the darkening hills.

Once the attraction opened at 8, Claire, Nora, and I barely had time to breathe. After the tenth person, I had my spiel down. "Did you buy tickets online? Do you want to add the Raven's Riddle Escape Room? Do you want to add the séance in which so-called medium Lyra Vex will attempt to contact Cyrus Morley and discover the hiding place of the Morley family treasure? Food trucks are to the left, bathrooms are in the parking lot and between The Cask of Amontillado and The Masque of the Red Death. Please stay on the trails. You can wait for the séance in the field here at the front."

I didn't know how many times I'd repeated that when Alex stormed in.

"Claire," his voice was more nasal than ever, "did you take the Edgar Allan Poe book that I lent to Dani?"

"Uh-uh—" Claire swiped a credit card.

"Did you or didn't you?"

"She didn't go near Dani's trailer today." I ripped wristbands. "I got the tablets and walkie-talkie."

He spun to me. "Did you take it?"

"No." I punched out my reply, giving a couple dressed as skeletons the bands.

"Claire?" His glare locked onto her wide, pale eyes.

She shook her head.

Drawing back, Alex averted his gaze. "Dani says someone took it from her trailer sometime today. Are your brothers working tonight?" Accusation had left his tone.

I said, "But anyone who wants to steal the treasure might have stolen the book. It doesn't have to be Jack or Jesse."

He stroked his upper lip. "I'm sorry if I came on too strong." He hurried out.

"If he came on too strong?" said Nora. "He accused you two of being thieves. I'd say there isn't any doubt about too strong."

"At least he apologized," I said.

Minutes or hours passed—too busy to tell—but the dark was almost complete when Lyra made her way along the lines to the ticket booth, like a celebrity at a movie premier. And the crowd acted like star-struck movie-goers, working their phones hard enough to drain their batteries.

Shadowing her every step was Kyle Garrison. At first, I thought he was just being creepy, sticking to her, but when she kept turning to him with comments, it appeared they were friends, maybe even partners.

Lyra's cat face was more sleek and satisfied than ever. She still wore skinny jeans. Beads glinted and rattled on her sandals and headband. A cloak of sheer black material with silver threads woven into it hooded her head. In his scruffy camos and beard, Kyle looked like a beggar trying to gain favor with a queen.

"Lyra."

Claire and I froze, exchanging glances. We knew that voice.

Jack came around the ticket booth, carrying a cup. He held it out to Lyra. "Good luck."

"Oh, thank you." She took the cup in one hand and slid her arm through the crook in Kyle's elbow. "Isn't that nice, Kyle?" She sipped, cuddling up to his arm.

Jack went rigid. Then he lunged at her.

Kyle swung out a long arm, throwing Jack off balance, forcing him to windmill his arms as he fell into a crouch.

I grabbed the walkie-talkie from the table.

Kyle said, "Don't push it, kid."

His legs tucked under him, Jack shot forward.

I pressed the transmitter button.

"Jack, back off."

The bellow froze Jack in mid-pounce, as if a giant, invisible hand had grabbed him. It also brought the chatter of the crowd to a murmur, and most impressively, startled Lyra's sleek cat expression off her face. For once, she didn't look like she was sizing up everyone.

Dad strode into view.

"What're you doing here, Mal?" Jack assumed his leer. "Arresting ghosts?"

"If they break the law, sure. You've got a job, Jack. Go do it."

"Yes, sir." Jack saluted him. "Whatever you say, sir." He glared past Dad to Lyra and Kyle and then stalked by the booth.

The noise in the crowd increased as Dad stepped close to Kyle and Lyra. Waiting on customers, I couldn't catch the conversation.

Dad came into the booth, removing his broad, flat-brimmed hat. He hated it, but he wanted to stand out tonight among the vampires, Goths, and creeps. "Any trouble like that, ladies, I want to know about. I've got a walkie-talkie."

Counting wristbands, I said, "I had it in my hand when you yelled."

"Claire, congratulations on your new job," said Dad. "Aunt Lily told me you started yesterday."

Looking over her shoulder, Claire reddened and lifted her head an inch. "Thanks."

As Dad ducked out the door, I said, "You got a job at the lodge?"

She nodded. "As a waitress. They'll work around my hours here until I'm done."

"That's great."

The flood of customers never let up. Dani popped in twice to resupply our cash, the first time firing questions about the missing book, but she got the same answers as Alex.

The customers waiting for the séance meandered among the food trucks and the booth, seeping into every unoccupied space, making it hard to tell the people in line from the people killing time.

At some point, Dad and the others on the security team called directions over battery-powered megaphones, and the massive horde oozed toward the house.

Carrie entered the booth. "It's 1. Dani said to close shop."

Nora blew a springy curl from her lip. "We still have customers."

Another fifteen minutes of fast work got all the ticket buyers through, and we rolled down the metal blinds on our windows and locked them.

Carrie shut the cash box and tucked it under her arm. "Dani wanted me to bring her the money."

"I'll go with you." I pulled on my backpack and placed the last tablet in the bin. "Claire, we can watch the séance together, and then I can drive you home."

Claire sank onto the little table by the back wall. "I'm pretty tired." She wiped a few sticky strands of blonde hair from her flushed forehead. "I worked at the lodge last night. If you don't mind me waiting in your car, I'm going to try to sleep."

"Rae's driving my Jeep," said Carrie.

She told Claire where she could find it, and I gave our cousin the keys. Then Carrie and I toted our loads toward the trailer and the home.

The almost full moon beamed down from the top of the sky, gilding the hills in a ghostly light. Its rays would have gilded the customers too, if fifty-seven million phone flashlights hadn't dissipated them. Those lights from the crowd resembled the shining eyes of a seething blob.

A filtered spotlight on the house shone down on the crumbling steps that led to the empty front door. Timothy stood on the remaining part of the stoop, holding his copy of The Book. Lyra and Kyle lit dozens and dozens of candles set around the door and steps.

The atmosphere was tense enough to pluck like a guitar string. I would have loved to capture it in photos, but I hadn't brought my camera. It wasn't powerful enough to work in such low light.

As we approached Dani's trailer, I noticed three people, illuminated from their phone lights, standing on what looked like a platform made of packing crates, which raised them about four feet above the crowd. When the tallest person turned toward us, I recognized the thin man.

"It's Rick Carlisle," I said. "That must be Barb and Devon with him."

"Perks of the press, I guess." Carrie squinted. "It is Barb. Glad they're back together."

"You are?"

Dani flung open the door to her trailer. "What took you so long? I have to get out to the customer." She snatched the bin, then the cash box, shutting the door in our faces.

Carrie whispered, "Why wouldn't I be glad Rick and Barb are a couple again?"

"Well ... you seemed kinda interested in him over the summer." I matched her volume.

"Correction. He seemed interested in me. I was curious more than anything else. A Carlisle dating a Malinowski may be one sign of the Apocalypse."

The trailer door smacked back. Dani locked it and rocketed into the crowd, the beam of her flashlight bouncing.

"Gotta go, Rae." Carrie jogged toward the black mass of people.

I went to the "press box." "Any room for one more?"

Rick turned from his tripod. "Plenty for you and your setup." He lowered a thin but strong hand.

I didn't need it but took it to be polite, explaining why I hadn't brought my camera.

"You can take some shots from mine." Rick pressed buttons on the back of his camera.

Devon said, "Rick told Dani he wanted an elevated view, and she said he could do whatever he wanted to as long as he didn't go into the house. So we built this platform from some boxes we found stored in a tent."

Rags of mist hovered inches above the damp weeds of the lawn, snaking through the ankles of the blob. The chattering voices and pulses of movement conveyed the mounting tension

Rick and I discussed exposure and ISO until Dad's voice boomed over his megaphone. "Ms. Vex is about ready."

Chapter Thirty-One

Dad wheeled inside the empty U formed by the temporary fences. "Public, you must stand behind the plastic barriers. If anyone wants to leave during the performance, be polite and allow those people out as quietly as possible. No pressing forward. Or I will end this performance for safety reasons."

He crossed to one side of the U, opposite of Carrie. The remaining security members must have positioned themselves inside or along the edge of the blob. How many people were here? Despite the moonlight and the phone lights, it was impossible to count.

Dani spoke into a megaphone of her own. "Lyra asks that you turn off your phone lights."

Strained murmurs rippled through the blob.

"Or she can't make contact."

The blob's eyes winked off in groups, and the silver light traced its contours, as if it was outlining the muscles of a monster.

I took a few photos, then Rick lengthened the exposure as Dani told a very lurid biography of Cyrus Morley, which was lurid enough without the horror movie embellishments, along with the history of the missing inheritance.

Then Dani introduced Timothy and Alex Morley. Timothy nodded from the doorway at the smattering of applause. Stationed at the bottom of the U, Alex gave a weak wave.

"Silence, please," said Dani. "Lyra requires absolute silence, so she can concentrate her psychic powers. Any sudden noise or bright light could ruin her attempt. You are witnessing the potential solution to a mystery that has plagued this family and this county for seventy years."

"I've never felt plagued since I moved here," whispered Devon. "Barb, Rick, you grew up here. Have you felt plagued?"

Barb shook her head as Rick chuckled.

I said, "Nobody in my family has mentioned it. Must be a very light plague."

Dani retreated to the plastic fence as Lyra strode into the center of the cleared space, moonbeams glinting off the silver threads in her cloak as it flared around her. She could have been an enchantress with magic encircling her.

I clicked a picture. Rick and I studied the view screen and decided the current settings were the best for now.

Raising her hands and face to the moon and slivers of stars, Lyra began swaying. And humming an odd little melody, about four lines, in a minor key.

She called in her accented voice, "Cy-rus Mor-ley."

Shredded clouds glided across the moon.

"Cy-rus Mor-ley." The call was a bit deeper and rang like a lone bell in a wrecked steeple.

She lowered her arms. "Cy-rus Mor-ley." Deeper and harsher. Her shoulders rounded, hunching her back.

Humming again, she stutter-stepped to one side of the U, then the other. She called Cyrus's name over and over, each one growing deeper and more grating.

The blob shifted and muttered, uneasiness thrumming through it.

Devon whispered, "If she freaks out too many people, we'll have a stampede."

Lyra drifted around the clearing. The candlelight caught facets of her beads in flashing gleams. She was heading for the side we overlooked when she lurched to a stop, as if something seized her. Her body shuddered. Then she released a cavernous laugh.

Several shrieks pierced the silence.

"Stay calm." Dad's voice pretty much shattered what silence was left. "If you need to leave, tell the people around you to let you out."

A few people near us detached themselves from the blob.

If Lyra was possessed by Cyrus, he demonstrated more manners as a ghost than he ever had as a person. Lyra waited in her suspended position until everyone who wanted to leave hurried away.

Then, still crouched over, Lyra staggered toward one of the plastic barriers and pressed against it as if she thought it would give under her weight.

Dad raced to her and shouted, "Public, back up. Let her through."

Carrie ran to join him, carrying her own megaphone. Then Timothy trotted over to the group.

With the vague movements of a sleepwalker, Lyra stumbled into the crowd.

"Make way," said Dad.

He held out his arms to restrain one side of the blob while Carrie mirrored him on the other side. Noise must not have been the problem Dani had claimed because Lyra showed no reaction to Dad's shouts.

She careened to a stop by a tent positioned at a front corner of the house.

Rick swiveled the camera and took a photo.

Hurling off her hood, Lyra threw back her head and howled like a werewolf transformation was about to kick off.

More shrieks from the blob, and both Dad and Carrie overpowered them with commands to stay calm and leave if necessary.

More black figures broke off from the dark mass.

Lyra dropped to her knees by the tent.

"What's going on?" said Devon.

My height gave me a better view, but all I could see was an opening in the blob by the tent, Dad's hat, and Carrie's long, white-blonde hair.

"Lyra's digging by a tent stake." Rick looked at his camera's screen.

Shouts of "She's found it!" shot through the blob. As if it was now consumed with curiosity, it surged around the tent.

Dad was on the megaphone. "Public, stay where you are, or people will get hurt. I'll tell you what's happening. Right now, Ms. Vex and Mr. Morley have dug a tent stake out of the ground and lifted a box out of the hole. It's made of metal, and it's rusty. About twelve by eighteen inches. Mr. Morley is opening it. It's not locked."

Barb, Devon, and I stood on tiptoe.

The blob strained forward. The mist climbed higher, gliding in and out of the mass and encircling the "press box."

A man's voice, shrill, said, "It's the second volume."

"It's a book," Dad said. "Just a book, public. No money or jewels."

The blob deflated, pulling back from the tent with sighs, loosening its hold as people spilled away from it.

"Another clue!" the shrill voice said. It had to be Timothy Morley.

Devon touched my arm. "You said the clue to the treasure was in a book of Edgar Allan Poe. Was that book part of a set?"

"A two-volume set."

"It appears to be a second clue," Dad announced.

Claps and whoops mingled with sighs and groans as if the blob was having a schizophrenic episode, and the disappointed half of it broke off and rolled down the hill toward the road.

"Rae, would you keep taking pictures?" said Rick.

"For sure." I stepped over to the tripod.

Rick jumped off the platform.

Through the viewfinder, I saw Lyra cling to Kyle as if the contact had stolen all her strength, and Timothy danced from foot to foot, flipping pages in a book that appeared identical to the one tucked under his arm.

Carrie and Dad planted themselves on either side of the excavation area as members of the blob pressed toward them. I guessed those people considered another book a significant find.

"Back up!" Dad shouted. "You touch myself, a security member, or Ms. Vex, her boyfriend, or Mr. Morley, and you will be ejected."

The remnants of the blob stilled, some sounding very snarky.

Timothy spoke to Lyra, who nodded weakly. Then they both talked to Dad for a minute.

He announced, "Ms. Li, meet us at your trailer."

With Dad and Carrie acting as human barriers, Kyle practically carried Lyra past the tents and trailers and our platform, stopping at Dani's trailer, where she was waiting for them. Dad had a word with Dani, who unlocked the trailer and went in. Kyle and Lyra followed.

A protest rose from the small chunk of blob that remained.

Dad said, "Ms. Vex says she needs rest." He didn't quite keep the sarcasm from his sentence. "If anyone wants to ask her about her experience tonight, she will open her shop in Wellesville at noon tomorrow. Ms. Li said The Haunting in the Hollow will be open until 2:30 for people with a 1 a.m. entry."

Many people shouted, demanding more details about the book.

Dad glanced about and found Timothy standing on the steps to the trailer behind him. He held out the mike to him.

Timothy took it. "My father left me the first volume of a two-volume set of the collected writings of Edgar Allan Poe. In the first volume, he left a handwritten note. The book Ms. Vex found tonight is the second volume, and it also has a handwritten note, in the same handwriting as the first."

"Lyra Vex planted it." Alex's nasal voice was distinct as he pushed through the crowd. He emerged from it by Dad. "She's made a fool of you, Father."

"You think so?" Timothy's clipped tone turned smug. "The note in the second book was written on a page torn from the first book—my book. I've always wondered why that page was missing."

I fell back from my camera.

"It's not fake?" Devon stared up at me.

"Lyra couldn't have solved it," I said. "She solved in a week a riddle that no one has cracked in seventy years?"

"She must have." Barb removed her glasses. "Sometimes, when someone comes to a problem with a fresh perspective, they see things others have missed."

Timothy handed Dad the mike, opened the door, and went inside the trailer.

Alex darted after him, but Dad and Carrie blocked him.

"I'm going in, Sheriff," Alex said.

"I'll ask." Dad used his best cop tone.

Rick crossed to them from the other side of the trailer. "Ask if Ms. Vex is up for an interview."

"I can guarantee you that," said Carrie as Dad opened the door and relayed the requests to Dani.

Then Alex, Dad, and Rick went inside.

Carrie said into her megaphone, "Show's over, everyone. Go home or go to the other attractions."

A few people approached Carrie and another security guy as they flanked the trailer steps, but most of the blob melted into the night or gathered around the hole Lyra and Timothy had made.

Barb and Devon climbed off the platform, and using the lights on their phones, highlighted the hole so I could get a few shots. Then Barb and I packed up the camera and tripod.

"Aunt Carrie, do you think it's the real deal?" I zipped the tripod into its bag.

"I didn't get a good look at the book or the note." She had remained by the entrance to the trailer. "As soon as Old Mr. Morley saw the clue and compared it to his first book, he held onto both books like a kid with his blankie."

"It seems awfully convenient," said Devon, "that the box was buried under a spot that already had loose dirt around it."

"I'm sure Mal's bringing that up to Old Mr. Morley right now."

Since Devon would have to wait until Rick was done with his interview to ride back to town with him and Barb, I offered to drive her home.

"We'll have to drop off my cousin Claire first." I swung on my backpack.

"Fine with me."

Devon and I followed the edge of the woods until we reached the road. We walked along it until I spotted Carrie's Jeep parked at the overgrown entrance of what appeared to be a narrow trail that came out of the woods to meet the road.

I knocked on the window several times before Claire unearthed herself from under a blanket in the backseat and unlocked the doors.

"What happened?" She yawned. "The medium didn't find anything, did she?"

"She found a second clue." I slid into the driver's bucket seat and introduced my cousin and my friend.

"A second clue?" Claire smothered another yawn. "Then the treasure's still out there."

"Yes." I pressed the ignition button. "If there is a treasure."

Chapter Thirty-Two

When I got home at 3 a.m., Dad still hadn't arrived. I was alert enough to remember Aaron was beta testing his bear alarm and disarmed it so Dad wouldn't become an unwilling test subject. Again.

My guilt from not asking Chris to church interfered with falling asleep. Four hours wasn't enough while working two jobs, but I shored myself up with enough caffeine to function at the library branch in Barton.

I texted Chris about the results of the séance and that we didn't seem to have anything to investigate on Monday. So bailing when I should have invited Chris to church hadn't even gotten me the date I wanted.

I think my Father had a lesson there.

Chris: We could go to Great Seal State Park. It has some great views.

The grinding increased, and I winced. I wanted so much to spend time with Chris. But I had to invite him to church, and to do that, I'd have to break through his barriers.

I blew out my cheeks.

I didn't have the guts. I knew that after Thursday.

The pain grated on, even after I got home and changed into jeans and my military blouse.

Entering the kitchen, I said, "Gram, where's Dad?"

The aroma of bacon-flavored green beans cooking on the stove made my mouth water.

She adjusted a knob for a burner. "Down at the creek. He went fishing with the boys."

Rain had poured all day, but now as I headed down the hill to the woods, a few feeble rays of sunlight warmed the wet grass and the autumn fire accumulating on the branches of the sycamore and tulip trees.

Not far from our entrance to the creek and riding trails, Dad cast his line into a deep stretch of water. My brothers' voices floated to us from further downstream.

"Everyone give up but you?" I peered in the direction of the boys' conversation.

"Aaron wanted to build a dam. Since we weren't catching anything, that seemed a whole lot more fun to the boys."

"When did you get home last night?"

"Around 3:30." He reeled in his line.

"Dad, I—I have a problem." I zipped my sweat jacket to my throat, like I needed the coverage.

He turned to me. "I'm listening. And thank you for coming to me."

A smile came and went, then I said, "It's—it's—" My face burned so fiercely that I was afraid my hair would ignite. I threw up my hands. "I'm a coward."

In spurts, Dad learned of my failure with Chris. But through the whole miserable story, he didn't look disappointed or mad. Just thoughtful. And very kind.

I sunk my hands into the pockets of my sweat jacket. "Do you think God's forgiven me? I haven't felt like it."

"Of course, kiddo. He forgave you as soon as you were sorry. You don't have to beg. He *wants* to forgive His children."

The grinding ebbed, and relief made me so light-headed that I lowered myself onto a stump.

"But why hasn't He given me any ideas about how to invite Chris to church?"

"Because you know what you have to do." His gaze was steady. "You don't need any special instructions."

"Yes, I do. Chris is so closed off."

"Just because it's difficult doesn't mean you shouldn't do it." His voice became quiet. "His behavior in itself is a kind of answer."

My guilt was gone, but an ache replaced it, leaving me more tired than my lack of sleep.

I watched Dad cast a couple times, then shook back my hair, and said, "Do you think Cyrus Morley buried that book?"

"Yes but no." Dad hurled his line, and the bobber plunked on the surface of the creek. "It has to be genuine, but I don't see how Lyra cracked the code to locate it. I told Morley Sr. that her finding the box under a stake recently dug into place was highly suspicious. There's no way to tell if someone moved the dirt a second time to bury the box. That book looked in pretty good shape for being buried for seventy years."

"Lyra wouldn't have any trouble finding a copy of the second volume." I repeated what Dani had told me about Alex buying his own set.

"That looks suspicious too. But the clincher is the note. It's written on a page torn from Morley Sr.'s book. The edge matches perfectly with the ragged bit of the last page left in the binding of the first volume. He showed me. I don't see how Lyra could fake that. She needed to replicate the torn edge left in the first book exactly and then somehow switch books."

"She couldn't." I told him how Timothy had reacted when Serenity grabbed The Book at the library. "He looked ready to murder a six-year-old. Old Mr. Morley always carries The Book in his hand. Lyra couldn't have gotten it away from him." I had to ask, "Did you see what was written on the note?"

"Yes. When he showed me that the torn edges matched." Dad impaled a fake worm on his hook. "It said 'Above my pride.'" I didn't see which story or poem it'd been placed next to." He hurled out the line again.

What did "Above my pride" mean? And was there any way to learn where the note had been left in the second book?

The Branson yodel rang out from the house.

Dad reeled in his line, picked up his tackle box, and yelled, "Boys, supper."

After eating, Amber and I were heading for the kitchen door to go to The Haunting when Jeanine called from the hospital with news that Hank had finally been moved from ICU to a regular room. Gram said we'd all come to see him after church.

Buckling her seatbelt, Amber said, "If there's time before we open, can you show me where Lyra found the second clue?" Her voice held a lightness it hadn't had since the accident.

"We'll have time." I cranked the key, making my truck cough. "It's very close to Dani's trailer, and we have to get the tablets and cash box unless Claire gets there first."

But Amber and I arrived ahead of her, so we hiked up the hill toward the house, trailers, and tents. The damp air from the day's rain hung heavy, like we were moving through thick, soaked curtains. Clouds had sealed off the sunset, shrouding the valley in a twilight that seemed sinister because it was too early in the evening for so much murk.

The front of the house was still exposed, the trailers and tent moved away from it remaining in their new positions. The empty door appeared black in the gloom. Security hadn't switched on the spotlight to illuminate the interior yet.

I pointed at the hole where Lyra had found the box. Someone had replanted the stake.

Amber crouched by it. "So that stake was on top of the box?"

"Yeah. Lyra and Old Mr. Morley began digging around it with their hands. The dirt must have been loose enough for them to pull the stake out."

Amber moved to the front door and then walked back to the hole, counting. Then she did it again from the corner of the house nearest the hole. "It's twelve steps from the front door—twelve of my steps. And seven from the corner." She tilted her head to one side. "Maybe that's what Lyra found in the poem?"

"Okay, but how? What's the key to the code?" I looked to the hills, lumbering around the darkening valley. "I think the poem helps point to the general location. 'The Mountains of the Moon' might describe how the hills here form a crescent around the valley. I guess the valley could fit the line ' Valley of the Shadow'. But how did she solve the rest of it?"

Amber tossed a clod of dirt. "We've got another mystery."

At Dani's trailer, she gave Amber the bin with the tablets, walkie-talkie, and charger. I waited inside while she counted out the bills for the cash box. When I stepped down to the spongy ground, Amber wasn't in view.

Odd. It was a straight shot down the open hill to the ticket booth.

I'd only taken a couple steps when Jack's nasty voice came to me from the woods behind Dani's trailer.

"You're gonna hafta have more than your opinion of us to get St. Mal to arrest us."

I ran to the voice, clutching the box under one arm and pushing through tangles of berry-heavy branches of honeysuckle. My left foot rolled over a fallen osage orange, or monkey brains, as my brothers called them. Dodging more of the bumpy, lime green fruit, I peered through twisted branches of honeysuckle.

In a small clearing, Jack had backed Alex Morley against a broad tree trunk.

Jesse stood several feet off, sideways, his wiry body tense, like he wanted to break into a sprint. Brushing his thick, curly bangs under his baseball hat, he said in a high, begging tone, "C'mon, Jack. Mr. Morley's mad his phone's missing, and he shot his mouth off. Anybody can do that."

Alex's lean body was as taut as Jesse's, cords standing out on his neck. "Don't threaten me. I'll have you fired."

Jack broke up in a grating laugh, transferring a trail cam to his left hand that already held a severed arm, and placed his right one on the trunk next to Alex's head.

Alex sidestepped away from it, but Jack crowded him. "Maybe I'll just lay down and bawl if I lose this great job here. I figured I was gonna make my first million working here."

Jack might not get violent. Lots of people were within calling distance. But any word or motion from Alex might ignite Jack's temper. Without a walkie-talkie to call security, I had to improvise on my own.

"C'mon, Jack," Jesse said. "We gotta get set up."

Stepping clear of red-berried nightshade vines lining the edge of the clearing, I said, "Alex, your phone's missing?"

The three men jerked to me.

Hopefully, being the sheriff's daughter and pretending that I hadn't noticed how alarming the confrontation was getting would give Alex the exit he needed.

I rattled on. "Have you checked around the ticket booth? I'm heading that way."

Alex glanced at my two cousins. Actually, his two cousins — no, really actually — our two cousins and then jogged past me and into the woods.

Keeping up the clueless, cheerful tone, I said, "Don't want to keep y'all from your jobs. If we find the phone, I'll let you know." I spun around and ran back through the honeysuckle, rolling on monkey brains a few more times, until I emerged on the hill.

Alex disappeared into Dani's trailer.

I entered it and found him alone, shoving papers off the couch.

I said, "Do you remember where you last saw your phone?"

"Of course not. I'm a moron like my degenerate cousins." He slapped the table beside the couch. "My phone was dying last night, right before that ridiculous performance, so I asked Dani if I could charge it here with the trailer locked. I didn't want it to disappear like my book. She said only during opening and closing do people use the trailer. There's so much traffic that anyone could have stolen the book right out from under Dani's nose. If I got my phone before closing, she thought it would be safe. I plugged it in, locked the door, and watched the show. I didn't remember to get it until I was back at my cabin at the state park. When I returned this afternoon, it was gone."

"Who has keys besides you and Dani?"

"No one."

"A lot of people were in here with Lyra last night. Did Jack or Jesse come in?"

Squatting, Alex opened the cupboard under the sink. "I don't know. I wasn't in here long. First, my book is stolen, so it appears someone is looking for the treasure. Now my phone is missing. That same person might think I have information pertaining to the treasure on it."

I looked down at the cash box so I could roll my eyes in private. This guy was one lame detective. "Alex, anyone who wants to find the treasure could have taken the book, not just an heir. Anyone with access to the trailer could have taken your phone. It doesn't have to be someone interested in the treasure."

Alex shot me an irritated glower. "Shouldn't you be opening now?"

"Yes, sir." I left him to his search.

With darkness closing in, the humid air had grown chilly. As I descended the hill, I met Claire coming up it.

"Sorry I'm late," I said.

"Do you need me to get the tablets and other stuff?" Claire zipped her sweat jacket higher, turning around to accompany me.

"Amber will have that set up already."

"No, nothing's in the booth. I was coming to get all the stuff."

I stopped on the damp grass. "Amber's not in the booth?"

"No."

"But she left Dani's trailer a while ago."

Members of the crew and actors in nauseating make-up blended into the darkness of the wet woods.

I handed Claire the box. "I'll try to find her."

Following the trail that led to the grisly scenes from Edgar Allan Poe's stories seemed a good place to start. I'd asked two crew members and an actress who appeared to be bleeding from a thousand wounds if they'd seen a pretty girl with waist-length red hair when I came across Jesse testing the pendulum over the pit.

"Hey, Rae." He gave me his sweet, sad smile that pulled down the corners of his eyes. "I'm glad you stopped by when you did. Mr. Morley was getting real insulting, and Jack was getting mad."

I squinted down both directions of the darkening trail. "Have you seen—"

A scream ripped from the woods behind me.

"Amber!" I shouted and plunged into the pawpaw bushes bordering the trail.

The screams repeated like rapid fire shots.

Father, keep her safe.

I zigzagged through trees and around fallen trunks, trying to home in on the screams.

A figure pounded toward me, her red hair flying behind her, barely discernible in the faint light.

I held out my arms, Amber fell into them, and we tumbled to our knees.

"What's going on?" Jesse asked in a terrified whisper, scanning the woods.

"A monster." Amber gasped, clutching my arms. "A monster's eating somebody!"

Chapter Thirty-Three

Backing away from us, Jesse held up his phone and swept the woods with its light. "Where is it?"

I hauled Amber to her feet. "Let's go."

"It's not behind me?" She whipped her head around to check over her shoulder.

"What's wrong?" Carrie hurdled a log and sent up a spray of dead leaves as she braked beside us.

Actors in different versions of gross make-up and black-clothed crew appeared from between every tree and bush

"Amber ran into a mon—" I lowered my head to catch her gaze. "You mean, a black bear, right?"

She shook her head. "I just saw a black hairy thing—" she gulped "— eating a person."

Shrieks from the employees split the air behind us as Carrie said, "You've got to be—where?"

Amber trembled against me. "I—I don't remember. I got lost when I—the creek!" she shouted. "The monster ..." she closed her eyes and inhaled "... the thing was pulling a body out of the creek."

"It's got to be a bear." Carrie flicked on a heavy flashlight and said to the muscular, young guy who ran up beside her, "Gibbs, we approach this like a hostage with an armed suspect."

"With only tasers?" said Gibbs.

"Amber's screams probably scared the bear away. We can't wait for more firepower." Carrie lifted her walkie-talkie from her belt and said, "Dani? Call 911. A bear's attacked a person. Yes, a bear. Have Franklin meet us at the creek. He should follow it until he finds us." She snapped it off. "Spread out and move."

She and Gibbs ran into the woods, their flashlights forming a wall of illumination ahead of them.

"C'mon, Amber." My right arm hugging her, I turned us toward the trail, and the woods behind us were deserted. News of the attack had cleared away anyone who was curious, including Jesse.

I took a step, but Amber didn't move with me. "I have to find the bin with the tablets. I dropped it when I—" her lips quivered, and she pressed them together—"when I ran."

"Carrie will find it." I pulled at her, but my cousin remained planted.

"She's not looking for it. We have to find it. Dani will make me pay for replacements, and you know we don't have that kind of money. Because Dad can't harvest, we won't make much money this fall." She tugged me toward the woods. "Please help me find it. I can't let my cowardice hurt my family."

"Cowardice? There's nothing cowardly about running from a bear."

"I left that person to die." Her whole body shook like she'd spiked a high fever. "Can we find the bin? Please?"

At this point, reason would have slid off Amber.

I surveyed the woods with my phone's light. Only half-naked trees and enough dead leaves on the ground to make piles for an entire elementary school to jump into. My phone gave off a lot of light, but the things outside the comforting beam were what concerned me.

I turned in the direction Carrie and the security guy had gone. "If the bear is ahead of us, Carrie will run into it first. We'll walk slow and shine our lights ahead so we aren't surprised. Do you remember the path you took from the creek?"

"Not really." She swung her light in an arc. "I—I was so scared, I just ran." Her voice dropped to a whisper. "My cowardice has cost someone their life."

Gripping her arm, I turned her to me. "You are not a coward. The only thing you could do for that person was get help." I took hold of her hand and moved ahead. "What were you doing out here, anyway?"

"I saw Kyle Garrison sneak into the woods. I thought that was weird. Maybe he was getting a camera he had set up without permission. So I followed him. But in the dark, I lost track of him. And—and I sort of lost my way, and when I heard some noise, like someone shuffling through the leaves, I followed—"

"You don't have to go on." I blew out an aggravated sigh. "Were you following Kyle to prove your courage again?"

"Yes," she said in a small voice like a three-year-old.

"Amber, you've got to stop this. You're going to get yourself hurt or killed. You can't follow a stranger like Kyle into a lonely place. That guy or the bear could've attacked you."

"If it was a bear."

I stared at my cousin in the beam of the flashlight as a distant shout reached us. Maybe Carrie had found the victim.

Please let that person be all right, Father.

I swept the beam over the slope. "There it is," I said too loudly.

Down a slope, to the right, sat the bin next to a black walnut tree. Amber must have dropped it straight down because nothing had spilled from it.

We hurried through the layers of dead leaves.

Amber picked up the bin. "We'll have to make sure everything works."

I swung my light around us as voices drifted to us through the bushes. Near the beam's edge, I spotted a colorful lump where the slope pitched down at a much steeper angle. Not an animal, not vegetation. Something man-made.

"Stay here," I said to Amber.

The incline was so steep I had to hike sideways down it, slipping every few steps in rotten leaves.

A knitted purple and green purse lay open, some of its contents spilled into the leaves.

"It's Lyra Vex's purse," I called up to my cousin.

"What's it do—" Amber ended in a staccato shriek. "She dropped it when the monster attacked her!"

"Possibly." I crouched and set the purse upright, retrieving the items from the leaves, including a half sheet of copier paper. Dropping a compact, keys, and a phone in the purse, I glanced at the paper. I froze, except for my eyes bolting wide open.

Gaily bedight,
A gallant knight,
In sunshine and in shadow,
Had journeyed long,
Singing a song,
In search of Eldorado.

But he grew old—
This knight so bold—
And o'er his heart a shadow
Fell as he found
No spot of ground
That looked like Eldorado.

And as his strength
Failed him at length
He met a pilgrim shadow—
"Shadow," said he
"Where can it be—
This land of Eldorado?"

"Over the Mountains
Of the Moon,
Down the Valley of the Shadow,
Ride, boldly, ride"
The shade replied,--
"If you seek for Eldorado?"

"What're you two doing here?" Yards above me, Carrie appeared on the gentler slope of the huge hillside.

Amber shuffled to our aunt through the sea of leaves. "We had to get the bin I dropped. Did the monster attack Lyra Vex? Is she okay?"

"How did you know it was Lyra Vex?"

I held up the purse. "We found this."

"Is she all right?" Amber repeated, her question piercing.

"She's dead, but the bear didn't kill her. It didn't eat her either. Leave the purse where you found it, Rae."

"Why?" said Amber.

My mouth hung open, knowing what Carrie would say next. There was only one reason to leave a dead person's belongings where you found them.

"It's evidence," said Carrie. "It looks like Lyra Vex has been murdered."

Chapter Thirty-Four

Now Amber gaped as I hiked up the slope toward Carrie and said, "How do you know it's murder?"

But Carrie was telling Dani on the walkie-talkie to call Dispatch again and give them the updated information on the death. Returning the radio to her belt, she said, "Rae, go over to Amber. I'm standing in the spot where Lyra was probably killed, so we shouldn't disturb it." Her tone soured. "Disturb it anymore." Carrie directed her flashlight at small piles of churned leaves. "We found Lyra lying half in the creek. Your screams, Amber, very likely scared off the bear. It tore her clothes in a few places as it dragged her. From the rigidity of the body, she's been dead at least twelve hours. The right side of her head is damaged, like she was hit, and a possible stab wound is visible on her back."

Amber coughed as if she was too stunned to scream.

"How did you find where she was killed so—the bear." I joined Amber. "You followed the trail the bear made when it dragged her body."

"Bingo." Carrie squatted. "Decent amount of blood here. With the purse found downhill from this site, it either fell down the slope when the killer attacked her or the bear dislodged it when it dragged the body."

"I saw Kyle Garrison here in the woods." Amber blurted it out. "Just before I saw the—the thing."

"You can tell Mal everything when he comes." Carrie's walkie-talkie came to life, and she lifted it to her ear.

Retracing our steps, Amber and I hurried through the woods with my cousin carrying the bin, the electronics rattling with every step.

"Do you think it was Jack?" Amber said between breaths as we ran onto the hill where the house sat.

"Maybe. But that poem with the slash marks opens up a lot of possibilities."

~~~~~

"Where have you been with my equipment?" Dani yelled as Amber and I entered the ticket booth. "Staring at Lyra?"

The booth couldn't accommodate five people, even if one was Dani's size. Claire and Jesse pressed against the left wall as Amber and I squeezed past Dani to the right.

Jesse said, "Is Lyra the dead body?"

"Yes." I unpacked the bin.
~~~~~

"I bet you two have been texting like crazy," said Dani, "about the bear attack and scaring off customers and employees."

"We can't text anybody from here." I plugged in the charger for the walkie-talkie. "Have many employees left?"

"Only about a quarter had the guts to stay on the job." Dani's voice vibrated. "I get a signal by the house, so I'll text employees to see if they'll come back since Carrie said Lyra's crazy ex-boyfriend killed her and not a bear."

Claire's hand flew to her face, and Jesse let out a yelp, going rigid.

I said through my teeth, "Carrie only said it looks like Lyra was murdered. I heard her talk to you on the walkie-talkie. All she knows for certain is that it wasn't the bear."

"Who else would kill Lyra but that redneck who kept threatening her?"

Three other people leaped to mind, and Dani was one of them, but I said, "That's for the cops to figure out." I looked to Claire and Jesse. "Carrie's found no proof pointing to Jack."

"The cops will." Dani swept a glare from Claire to Amber and me. "You three—tell customers we have a staffing problem, but we'll open in an hour. You." She aimed that at Jesse, and it seemed to pin him to the wall. "Stay here so I know where to find you."

Scrolling on a tablet, Amber said, "Dani, if we close, how do we give customers a refund?"

"Refund?" Dani bristled to her full five feet. "I don't give refunds. For any reason. I say so on the page where you purchase tickets. If we close, none of you had better mention a refund or raincheck. Got it?"

Before we could respond, she barreled out of the booth.

"This'll be fun." I set my tablet in an open window. "Telling all these people the place is closed, and that they can't get their money back." I swiped to the correct screen. "Claire, Jesse, do you know if Jack left?"

"Oh, yeah." Hurt softened Jesse's voice as he whipped off his navy-blue baseball cap. "When I heard Amber say a monster was eating somebody, I came here to get Claire, but Jack took off in the van without us." He rubbed his right arm. "Jack's mean, but I don't think he's mean enough to kill a woman, do you, Claire?"

His half-sister patted his shoulder, smiling weakly, and turned to wait on a vampire and his bride.

Without a word, Claire confirmed my suspicions of Jack.

<div style="text-align:center">~~~~~</div>

We only had to tell a few customers about the hour delay. The fleeing actors and crew must have texted the news of the bear attack, and now the whole state knew to stay clear of The Haunting in the Hollow.

When three patrol SUVs swung onto the drive, I let out a long breath, easing stiffness in my muscles, and Amber held her forehead, tears glistening in her eyes. Dad was in the lead with Houston and Chris following.

All the remaining tension in me melted. Chris had finished his shift at 7. He'd come solely to check on me.

Stopping on the drive, Dad rolled down his window. "Are you and Amber okay? You do know a body's been found on the property?"

"Amber found it," I said.

Dad catapulted out of his SUV, ran around the booth and threw open the door. "Amber, how are you?"

Amber shrugged, then lunged at Dad, and grabbed him.

He wrapped his arms around his niece. Looking over his shoulder and finding Houston and Chris had joined him, he said, "Houston, we'll go to a trailer and get her statement. Kincaid, I can't order you to do anything on your own time."

"I'll take the equipment to the crime scene," said Chris.

"I can show you where it is," I said. "Claire, can you handle the customers?"

Her pained look revealed she didn't think so, but she said, "Maybe Jesse and I can handle them together." She looked to her half-brother, who'd huddled against a side wall since Dani left. "The app for taking tickets is real easy."

Dad, Houston, and Amber walked toward the trailers while I got in Chris's SUV and directed him to the head of the trail. He parked and lifted a large duffel bag from the back.

As we entered the woods, he gripped my hand. "Are you all right?"

"Now that you're here." The strength of his muscular hand was very reassuring.

I took him along the trail as far as The Pit and the Pendulum, then veered into the woods, plunging through the breaks in the pawpaws that the panicky staff had made.

We stopped on the hillside where Amber and I had found the bin, and someone blinded us with a beam.

"Oh, hey, Chris." The beam moved out of our eyes, revealing Gibbs guarding the patch of ground where Lyra had probably met her killer. "Glad you're not the bear."

Chris said, "But the bear hasn't killed anyone."

"Yet." Gibbs turned full circle with his flashlight. "Carrie said the girl who found the body only said she saw a black hairy thing."

Murmured voices mingled with a scatter of droplets as the wind sailed through water-logged leaves.

"Where's the body?" said Chris.

Gibbs aimed his beam at the ground. "Follow the drag marks, and you'll find Carrie with the body in the creek."

Chris turned to me. "Can you use your phone's light to get back, Rae?"

"Yes." I gave his hand a firm squeeze. "Be careful." I walked back the way we'd come, every sense on high alert for anything like a bear. Or a monster. Or a murderer.

~~~~~

Houston stepped out of the make-up trailer as I reached it.

He turned his good ol' boy grin on me. "I'll make sure a terrible beast doesn't savage your sweetheart."

I smiled. "I know y'all have each other's backs."

As I entered the trailer cluttered with wigs, bottles, brushes, and jars of make-up, Dad swiveled a barber chair to face Amber, who sat in an identical one. "Amber, you've got to get over this idea of proving yourself. Only you think you're a coward. Nobody else in the family does."

My cousin fiddled with a tear in the upholstery on the arm. "Dad might, once he learns what happened."

Seeming to grow, Dad released a roar. "Your father will not—"

We both jumped.

Dad closed his eyes. "Your father won't think anything like that," he said at inside volume. "Look. If you had seen Garrison getting a camera, what would you have done? Confronted him in the woods alone?"

Amber smoothed the torn fabric into place. "You don't have to worry, Uncle Mal. It won't happen again. I know I'm a coward. I'm no Eowyn."

Dad looked Heavenward for help. "No, you're not. You're not a warrior princess. Your uncle is a sheriff in Ohio, not a king in Middle Earth. But you're not a coward. Panicking when your dad might be dead is not cowardly. Neither is running from a dangerous animal. God gave us flight-or-fight responses for a reason."

Amber chanced a peek at Dad, then went back to studying the fabric on the chair's arm. "You didn't run when we needed someone to hold Knight's head out of the water, and you're scared of horses."

"They make me ner—" Dad took a deep breath. "Yes, I'm scared of horses. So does that make me a coward?"

Amber went still and then said in a gasp, "Of course not, Uncle Mal. Even though you're scared of horses, you overcame that and helped Knight."

"And even though you were freaking out, you still pulled your dad free of Knight."

"But you'd wanted me to leverage Knight off Dad, and I couldn't do that. Gram had to, and she hurt herself."

"If Ma hadn't had the strength to work the lever, I'm confident you would've stepped in and gotten the job done." He touched her hand.
~~~~~

She lifted her eyes a fraction.

"Amber, when you really have to be courageous, you will be. God will give you what you need when you need it. All you have to do is obey. He gave Coral what she needed because she was the only one who could save Hank."

Barely nodding, Amber looked to her lap.

Frowning, Dad turned his chair to me. "Rae, have you seen anything last night or tonight that might have something to do with Lyra's death?"

I replayed events and conversations from those two days. "Alex loaned Dani his copy of The Book, the first volume, and it turned up missing yesterday. Then tonight Alex said his phone was stolen." I told him what Alex had said to me in Dani's trailer and about his confrontation with Jack and Jesse.

As Dad took notes, Amber said, "The hairy thing could have been someone in costume. Maybe the killer disguised himself to move the body."

Dad looked up. "Don't think about what you saw, or you'll imagine things that weren't there. Just ignore it, and maybe a detail will come back to you that points to either a bear or a person dressed up."

I said, "Did you smell anything, Amber? Coral and I both smelled something pretty rank by the creek."

Amber sat still, her lips protruding. "No, I don't remember smelling anything."

"It could still be a bear." Dad tucked his pad into the back pocket of his jeans. "You might have been upwind of it, and the breeze carried the smell away from you." He stepped out of the chair. "I'll tell Ms. Li she has to close for tonight. I can't have hundreds of people trying to gawk at the crime scene. You girls can go home." He scratched his eyebrow. "The media will have a party with this, so leave now. I'll tell Rick to keep Amber's name out of the paper until she can tell Jeanine."

"We can't leave now," I said. "Claire and Jesse need a ride home, so we should wait until you get done questioning them. Did Amber tell you Jack left them when they heard about the monster?"

Dad nodded. "I'll send Houston back from the crime scene so he can question them next." Cupping the side of Amber's head in his broad hand, he caught her gaze. "You did the right thing, running away to get help."

She shrugged and slid out of the chair.

As we descended the few steps from the trailer, Dani rushed out of a tent, and Dad called to her. She stopped, and he strode over to her. Amber and I walked down the hill.

After we told Claire and Jesse to meet Houston at the make-up trailer, Dani arrived at the booth. "Your father is costing me a fortune." She slammed down the metal blind that closed off a window.

Amber and I helped her lock the other blinds and tape signs to them, saying The Haunting was closed.

Dani placed the equipment bin and cash box on the ground and locked the door to the booth. Then she struggled to pick up the two containers. "If he keeps me closed for tomorrow..."

I reached for the bin that was sliding off the box. "I can help you carry—"

"No one is getting in my trailer." Dani wrapped her arm around the bin, backing away. "I'll bring the box and the electronics to the booth tomorrow." She headed up the hill, muttering, "Bunch of redneck psychos."

Amber and I turned to the road.

Amber said, "Did she forget she's related to the redneck psychos?"

"I'll run back and remind her."

A tiny giggle might have escaped from Amber's lips.

Chapter Thirty-Five

When I pulled in beside the battered white sedan parked in front of Aunt Lily's double-wide, my great-aunt stepped onto the concrete blocks that formed the steps to her front door. "What're all of you doing home so early?" She tied the belt of a faded pink bathrobe. "Did you get fired?"

Jesse jumped from the bed of my truck and ran up to his mom. "That woman Jack left the county with last year — she's been murdered."

Aunt Lily released a short scream, staggering against the door frame. The weak light from the lamp in the picture window revealed the blood fleeing her face.

"Dad doesn't consider him a suspect." I hurried out of the cab with Amber and Claire. "He's interviewing everyone who was working at The Haunting tonight. Did Jack stop by here?"

"Oh. Uh — no." Her fingers shielded her mouth. "I haven't seen Jack since he left for work tonight."

That could have been the truth. But Malinowskis had a code of covering for each other, even the law-abiding members like Aunt Lily and Claire. Walter drilled that into everyone — if there was trouble, family backed family. If that meant lying to the police, you did it.

"Dad's at The Haunting now, so he can't receive calls unless he's on the hill by the home." I stepped closer, skirting a tricycle that showed more bare metal than paint. "But if you could call Jack and tell him Dad needs to talk to him, he can leave a message at our house about when he's available."

"Oh, okay." Aunt Lily lowered her hand, her lips trembling.

Fifteen minutes later, Amber and I straggled into the kitchen at home. Silence reigned except for the hum of the dishwasher, a creak from the recliner where Gram sat knitting, and a snap from the fire in the fireplace. My brothers and Coral had to be in bed.

"Are you all right?" Gram set aside her needles. "Mal called and said — "

Amber raced to Gram, dropped to her knees, threw her arms around her, and sobbed.

I thought she'd gotten out most of her emotions with Dad, but that was dumb. My cousin had stumbled across a murder victim.

I went to the easy chair near the recliner and explained to Gram everything that had happened since we stepped onto the old Morley property tonight.

Gram held Amber against her chest.

Eventually, Amber pulled back on her knees and coughed. "I have to call Mom."

She started to stand, but Gram took her hand. "Amber, I have to ask something very important of you."

My cousin lowered herself, her pale face blotchy.

"I talked a long time with your mom tonight. Nothing's wrong with your dad. The fact that they moved him out of ICU shows that. But you need to be calmer before you tell her about this." Gram twisted her beaded bracelet. "Hank's so worried about not being able to work during the harvest. He's going on and on about it — how he's letting his family down, Luke will kill himself trying to do the work of two men, about all the money they'll lose. Jeanine's never seen him like this. Since he doesn't remember anything about the accident, she hasn't told him yet that Knight died or Coral's having problems because she rescued him. Hank only knows he fell off Knight. Jeanine's afraid he can't handle anything else right now."

Amber went still. "I'll pull myself together." She sighed. "At least I can do something right for my family. I'm glad Dad doesn't remember the accident. I think memories of something that traumatic would give you PTSD. And he won't know what a coward I was, either."

"Your dad would never think you acted cowardly. Mal's right, Amber. You risked yourself for no good reason." Gram sat back in the recliner. "That poor woman. The killer is probably a boyfriend — either Jack or that new one you saw her with. Although ..." she turned the bracelet on her thin wrist "... Lyra's injuries don't sound like Jack. The murder was too well planned."

"You don't think Jack's smart enough to plan a murder?" said Amber.

"I don't know if it takes all that much intelligence. But Jack's bursts of temper are always sudden. If she'd only been hit or only stabbed, I'd be more suspicious of Jack."

"But luring someone to a lonely spot to kill them is sneaky," I said, "and that's what Jack is. Along with being mean."

"Yes, but Jack's sneaky because he has no confidence. He's been arrested for shoplifting items he can fit in his pocket. If he does anything bold, it's when he's so angry that he reacts without thinking. Or he's drunk."

Gram had known Jack his whole life. Her analysis made sense, but she hadn't seen how furious Lyra made him.

I put another log on the fire.

Gram said, "May I see the solution to the riddle you found in Lyra's purse?"

I fished my phone out of my backpack.

"What does it say?" Amber scooted over to my chair.

I pulled up the photo, but the screen wasn't big enough for the three of us to see it well. I went to the desk by the front door and connected my phone to the desk-top computer.

We studied the poem on the larger screen.

I wrote the letters that had been slashed through as Amber read them. "Ten ... steps ... from ... door."

Gram peered at the poem, touching her chin. "It doesn't say which door."

I said, "Carrie didn't find any disturbed dirt around the house, so Lyra couldn't have dug in several places until she found the box."

"The box was made of metal, wasn't it?" said Amber. "Lyra had to've used a metal detector and got lucky that Cyrus used a metal box."

"The code for finding these words must be very complicated." Gram pointed at the screen. "The letters for 'd' and 'o' in 'door' are right beside each other. But there's a big gap between 's' and 't' in 'steps' and between 'o' and 'm' in 'from.'"

I'd noticed that too. No consistent spacing between any of the letters existed, like you'd think would be the case for a pattern.

"I could take this to my pre-calc teacher," said Amber. "She might—"

"We can't show this to anybody." I took a quick breath. "It could be related to the murder."

Amber's forehead furrowed. "But how? If she faked a clue, I could see Old Mr. Morley might kill her in anger because she cheated him. Although ... it'd be easier to have her arrested. But the second clue is real."

"It looks like it is. Let me check with Dad first. We'll keep this confidential."

Amber crossed both her hands over her heart, her voice deepening as it became solemn. "I promise I won't tell anyone." Then it rose, pleading, "But it's okay if we try to figure it out ourselves?"

"Just work on it here. Don't take it to school or anywhere else." I clicked the print button to get a hard copy of the photo. "Gram, are we skipping church to see Uncle Hank? If we wait until after church, I can't come with y'all because I have to work tomorrow evening. If The Haunting isn't still closed."

"Oh, I forgot," said Gram. "Jeanine thinks it'd be better if someone drove just Amber and Coral to see Hank with the mood he's in. I think the four of them need some time together. If Hank feels like it, either you or I will drive the boys into town to get reception and do a video call with him."

"I can take Amber and Coral," I said. "We'll leave early enough so that we get to the hospital right when visiting hours start. I can hang out at

Aunt Marti's, to give them space."

"That'll work. I should stay with the boys because I know Mal will be busy all day tomorrow with this murder case." Gram moved toward the kitchen. "I'll tell Marti to expect you."

Amber straightened from studying the monitor. "Can I call Mom first?" She relaxed her shoulders, taking a deep breath. "I'm calm now."

Gram picked up the landline. "We'll both talk to her."

Amber kept her emotions under such tight control you wouldn't have thought she was capable of hysterics. She and Gram repeated over and over to Jeanine that she was fine. At one point, Amber started to protest something, but Gram narrowed her gaze in warning, and Amber swallowed and said, "Okay, Mom."

As Amber hung up, I said, "See? You came through for your family when they needed you to."

"Not bawling like a baby isn't brave," she said. "It's just mature. Mom wants to keep this from Dad for now." She sighed. "I can't work at The Haunting anymore. I know it's not much money, but I'd like to contribute something since Dad can't work the harvest."

I stared at her. "Dad may not want me to work there either."

"But Uncle Mal can't stop you." Amber trudged toward Gram's room.

After Amber and Gram had gone to bed, I sat on the couch, staring into the fire. Was there any way to persuade Timothy to tell Dad where he'd found the note with "Above my pride" on it in the second book? If Dad could prove it was related to his murder investigation, maybe he could get a warrant. But was it related?

I finally crawled into bed. If the riddle became even more puzzling, I might start leaking brain fluid.

Chapter Thirty-Six

With only four hours sleep last night, I hit the inflatable mattress and dropped off. In my dreams, fiery letters danced around the hillside where we found Lyra's purse. But I kept waking up, and so did Amber, getting out of my bed, which she shared with Coral, at least three times. Despite all the wakefulness, I didn't hear Dad come in.

When my cousins and I got up the next morning, Micah was already digging into a bowl of cereal at the bar and showed us a note from Dad. It said not to wake him, and he was sorry he couldn't visit Hank. He also wrote that Carrie was sleeping in at the Norris's farmhouse and not to disturb her.

Amber, Coral, and I headed west under a sky so dark the only reason we knew it was morning was because we'd recently gotten out of bed. As we climbed a ridge, both Amber's and my phones hit a patch of reception and went crazy with pinging.

Amber got them both out and gasped.

I shoved my hand through my hair. "What now?" Could I take any more shocks?

"People are asking ..." Amber glanced from phone to phone "... if we know why Alex Morley was arrested. Although some people think he was just questioned and released."

"Tell them they should ask Dad."

Coral said in her flat voice, "That'll stop their questions quick."

Amber also reported Chris asked how we were, and I told her to text we were good.

At the hospital, we got lost by taking the wrong elevator, and I had to ask for directions from two staff members, ignoring the icky, clean stench that wanted to gag me. Finally, we walked onto the right floor as visiting hours started. At the far end of the hall, collapsed against a wall, Jeanine covered her face with her hands.

My stomach churned the pickles I'd had for breakfast as Amber whispered, "Oh, no."

Coral raced down the hall, yelling, "He's dead, isn't he?"

"No!" Jeanine shrieked, throwing out her hands. "Just because I'm upset doesn't mean your dad is dead. You're as bad as your grandfather."

Amber put her arm around her mom. "What's wrong?"

"I had to tell Hank about Knight. Just now." Jeanine sniffed. "And he's got another fever, so they've delayed his second operation until that goes away." She sank against the wall. "I tried to avoid telling him about Knight, I really tried, but since the meds aren't making him as sleepy, he wanted more details about the accident. He can't remember anything after riding into the woods." Looking toward the ceiling, she wiped her cheeks. "Maybe you should give your dad a—Coral!"

My cousin raced down the hall, glancing into each room. Then she darted into one.

Jeanine broke into a run, and Amber and I followed her.

Coral leaped onto the edge of Hank's bed. Tubes and bandages still cocooned his right leg. But the top part of his bed was tilted more upright, and his extra big brown eyes weren't groggy anymore. They were damp and feverish.

"You're really going to be okay?" Coral peered at her dad as if she could see inside him for confirmation.

"I guess."

I lurched to a halt in the doorway.

That hopeless voice couldn't have come from my easy-going uncle.

"You're not going to die?" Coral inched closer on the bed. "You know that?"

Hank stared at his daughter as if he'd noticed something new about her, like a haircut or an outfit. "Yeah. Mom says this fever might not mean nothing. Just my body reacting to my leg getting all busted."

A tremor shook Coral from her head to her feet. Then she fell on Hank, sobbing. "I've been praying and praying you wouldn't die. I thought you were dead at the creek, and then I thought maybe you'd die here. Everybody keeps saying I was brave. But I wasn't. I've been scared since you fell into the creek with Knight." She pressed her face into her father's chest.

Hank held her, the whites of his eyes standing out as he threw a bewildered look to Jeanine.

She lowered herself into a chair like all her strength was draining away. "I haven't told you everything that happened at the creek, Hank. If Coral hadn't held your head above the water while your leg was pinned under Knight, you would've drowned."

Coral lifted her head, boring her gaze into Hank's. "Knight reared when that thing made noises in the bushes, and then he slipped off the trail and hit the water. And you were yelling and screaming and trying to get out from under Knight, and he was trying to get up. And then Knight moved in a really bad way, and you screamed—and—and I guess you passed out." Tears poured down her freckled cheeks. "I thought you were dead. Your head went under the water. I had to get you up 'cause you might be alive. So I got under your arms and held you. But I couldn't pull you free. I pulled as hard as I could, but I couldn't do it. And I couldn't check if you were breathing or had a pulse because I had to hold you. So I just stood there. I got so scared. 'Cause the monster might get us, or we'd freeze to death, and you were getting heavy, really, really heavy, and if I couldn't hold you up, you'd drown." A torrent of sobs shook her whole body.

"Oh, punkin." Still wide-eyed, Hank stroked his younger daughter's copper hair. "It'll be all right. I'm so sorry."

Amber's beautiful face was as shocked as her dad's, and Jeanine slumped in her chair. But relief rushed over me. Maybe giving air to all that fear would free Coral now.

"You didn't feel brave at all?" said Amber.

Coral shook her head against Hank's shoulder.

"It's your actions that counted, Coral," I said. "Not what you felt. You were still brave."

Hank's gown muffled Coral's voice. "I'll never let it happen again. We'll never go riding again, just the two of us."

"You always want to be with two other people." Jeanine's voice creaked with exhaustion. "And they have to be two older people."

Coral nodded, strands of hair clinging to her wet cheeks. "If anything goes wrong, one of them has to fix it. Not me. Because I'm younger than they are."

"But Coral." Amber blinked, her only movement. "Since you did it once, you know you can do it again."

"No!" her sister screamed, then she buried her face against Hank's chest again.

A nurse darted in. "What's going on in here?"

"Just some therapy." I backed to the door. "I'll be back at 4:30."

~~~~~

After I let myself into the palatial home of Gram's sister and brother-in-law, I trawled local social sites until they came home from church. So many rumors were flying around about Alex Morley and the murder that I couldn't tell what was the truth. I'd have to wait to ask Dad or Carrie.

I enjoyed visiting with Aunt Marti and Uncle Robert but left early, so I'd have time to make a call before picking up my cousins.

Once I parked in the hospital garage, I pressed Gram's number.

When Rusty answered, he said, "Does Uncle Hank want to do a video call?"

I softened my voice. "I don't think he feels like it today. But he's improved a lot since you saw him when..." shoot fires, how long had it been? "... when the ambulance took him."

My reassurance produced a thoughtful silence.

I said, "Is Dad home?"
~~~~~

"No, he went back to work while we were at church. He doesn't know when he'll be home today. He's got to investigate the murder at the Halloween place."

I told Rusty to pass on what I'd said about Hank to Gram. Then I called Carrie.

She picked up on the first ring, and I said, "Can you tell me what's going on with Alex Morley?"

"That didn't take long to hit the grapevine." Carrie yawned, despite it being 4 p.m. "Since Lyra's body was found lying half in the creek, Mal had Chris and Houston search it for evidence. Eventually, Houston found a phone, which Alex identified without hesitation. Mal brought him in for questioning and then released him. His story holds together." She repeated Alex's statement, which was the same as the story he'd told me in Dani's trailer last night.

Carrie went on, "Mal's testing the phone for blood, but it was located a good distance from the body and had been submerged in running water so long that the water might have washed away any evidence to tie it to the crime scene."

I tugged on my earlobe. "Finding the phone in the creek could mean Alex dropped it when he murdered Lyra. When he couldn't find it, he thought it might be with her body, but he couldn't risk going back there. So he made up the story of charging his phone in Dani's trailer and somebody stealing it. Or it could mean somebody's framing Alex."

"Or someone stole Alex's phone, got scared they'd get caught, or couldn't open it, and dumped it far from where they took it, and it has nothing to do with the murder. I gave Mal a list of everybody I saw in the trailer the night of Lyra's performance. When all the visitors cleared out, Lyra said she was still too weak to leave. Dani said she could stay. That was about 2 a.m. Dani said she returned to her trailer at 2:45, and Lyra was still there. Dani asked her to leave, and she did."

"So there's forty-five minutes when you don't know whether somebody came to the trailer."

"Right," said Carrie. "And we only have Dani's word that Lyra stayed in the trailer until 2:45."

I mulled that over. "I guess Dani could have the same motive as Alex, if the second clue was fake. Either of them could have hired Lyra to cook up that clue and then killed her to keep her from revealing that fact to Old Mr. Morley. That'd buy either of them time to find the treasure for themselves. But the clue is genuine."

"There goes the motive."

"Do you know if The Haunting will open tonight?"

Carrie said, "Mal released the crime scene this morning."

"What about the monster?" I sat up straighter in the bucket seat. The murder had pushed the threat of the bear out of my mind. "Did the warden find proof it was a bear?"

"He found bear prints around the creek, and then they head into the woods. It never came near while Mal and his officers investigated the crime scene. The warden said that was a good sign the bear still feared humans. The real problem is when bears get comfortable around us." She paused. "What else could Amber have seen but a bear?"

"She said it might have been someone in a costume."

"The bear prints rule that out, unless they were made earlier in the day. I don't think Mal found any shoe tracks he couldn't account for."

"Has Dad questioned Kyle Garrison? Or Jack?"

"Not by the time we left the crime scene last night." Carrie added, "By the way, Mr. Norris talked to me this afternoon. He says it looks like the weather will be dry enough Tuesday to start harvesting beans, and Jeanine told him I might be available to help. I said I'd be there any time he wanted and volunteered you too. I figured that was okay."

"I'll help any way I can. What do I have to do?"

"Drive the semi from the field to the grain bins on either Mr. Norris's farm or Hank's. Since you can drive a stick, it'll be easy." Pause. "Is Hank any better? I mean, in his mind. I've known him my entire life, and never heard him so depressed and — and — and overwhelmed like he did on the phone yesterday. I didn't think his brain actually contained worry cells."

"He doesn't seem to be." I explained how Jeanine had to tell him about Knight's death and then Coral's breakdown. Or, as I preferred to think of it, breakthrough. "I think Coral can be herself now. She knows her dad is going to live."

"I hope you're right. Tell Hank you and I are helping Mr. Norris with the harvest. Maybe that'll reassure him."

We hung up.

I slipped my phone in the back pocket of my jeans.

This was all so weird, having to reassure Hank. I'd never expected I'd have to do that.

Chapter Thirty-Seven

When I walked into Hank's hospital room, Coral was still sitting beside her dad on the bed. Had she moved at any point in the last seven hours?

"Maybe I should stay too." Amber had pulled a chair right up to Hank's bed.

"'Too'?" I said. "Coral's staying?"

Coral threw me a furious glare and gripped Hank's rough hand as if she dared me to drag her from her dad.

"She wants to stay." Jeanine seemed smaller, huddled in her chair, like all the worry over the past week and a half had ground her down. "Luke can drive her home tomorrow."

"Dad's gonna work himself to death." Hank's face was still flushed, so he hadn't gotten rid of the fever.

"Carrie and I are going to help with the harvest," I said. "Carrie's going to show me how to drive the semi."

"But you two can't work all day. You got regular jobs."

Jeanine said, "Carrie's only job right now is running security at The Haunting on the weekends."

"I can take some vacation days." I glanced at my phone. "I hate to bring it up, but if you're coming with me, Amber, we should leave now. I have to work at The Haunting."

Amber bit her lip, clutching her dad's hand.

"I am real, real sorry about this whole mess." Hank sighed, his whole body deflating. "I shouldn't have taken that trail. I should've known it was too slippery for Knight. One stupid mistake, and my horse is dead, and I could lose my leg." He rubbed his forehead. "I'm letting the whole family down."

"No, you're not. Nobody thinks you're letting us down." Jeanine spoke words she seemed to hate. "I've told you that. God will get us through."

"But if I lose my leg ..." Hank stared past me, as if into a bleak future.

"That's a possibility, not a certainty." Jeanine massaged her temples.

I clamped my jaw to keep from gaping. That hopeless talk couldn't have come from my uncle, who always saw the cup half full and the joke in any situation. Without a hint of his usual relaxed grin on his extra-wide mouth, Hank didn't look like the same person.

His huge brown eyes wavered to mine. "Rae, Jeanine and Amber were pretty sure Knight wasn't left alone until ... Doc Volmer came. Do you know for certain?"

"Either Dad or Chris was with him the whole time."

His Adam's apple bobbed. "Th-that's good to know. Can't believe the Big Guy got close enough to a horse — " He clenched his sheet.

Both Amber and Coral hugged him. I wanted to hug him too, but there wasn't room for the three of us, and my cousins seemed to have no intention of letting go. Ever.

Sniffing, Amber finally broke her hold. "I'll be back as soon as I can."

"Okay." His calloused hand patted Coral's arm as his gaze drifted to the large window smeared with rain.

I gave him a quick hug, then Amber and I left with Jeanine.

My cousin and aunt walked to the elevator like it was the last mile of a marathon they hadn't trained for.

Scavenging for something positive, I said, "I think Coral will act like herself again. She's spent time with her dad and knows he's going to be all right."

"'This isn't like Dad at all." Amber rested her head on her mom's shoulder. "He always thinks everything will work out for the best. It's got to be Knight's death. That makes everything else look hopeless."

Jeanine shook her head. "No. Yesterday, he blamed himself for the accident and told me how sorry he was about letting the family down at harvest time. That was before he knew about Knight."

"Mom, you're right not to tell him about what happened to me at The Haunting." Amber added in a careful tone, "I'd still like to work there."

Jeanine's hand rubbed her throat. "For the sake of my nerves, I can't let you."

The elevator doors slid open, and I said, "I don't know if this helps, but the pain meds could depress him, at least partially. Mom only took them when she was desperate. She hated the side effects. He might be depressed too from all the abuse his body's taken. Mom was always really jittery after a surgery or bad round of chemo."

Jeanine gave me a long look and then wrapped me in a tight hug. "I needed to hear that."

She hugged Amber again and then turned in the direction of Hank's room.

Neither of us spoke as Amber and I rode the elevator down to the second floor and then followed the correct lines to the parking garage. Amber kept squinting as if struggling to focus on something that slipped in and out of view.

"I'm so confused." She stopped at the top of the stairs in the garage. "I thought succeeding at something difficult or beating something that terrifies you would give you a lot of confidence. You know you can handle tough situations like that." She fingered a few strands of her red-gold hair. "But it seems like the opposite has happened to Coral. She's doing everything she can to avoid another scary situation." She looked to me. "After what you went through with those cases—do you feel the way Coral does?"

Gazing at the cold concrete floor, I rolled the hem of my t-shirt. "Well, even though I came out okay, I'd be fine if I never dealt with something like that again."

Amber's eyes widened. "But you won. You triumphed."

The confrontations I'd survived in the past few months scrolled through my mind. "I ... I don't know if *I* triumphed. I was almost scared to death. But I prayed and God sent me what I needed. I assume He'd do that again. I hope it doesn't come to that." I rubbed my locket. "I think that's what Dad meant last night. Pray God gives you courage when you need it." I added quickly, "But I'm not saying you were a coward at the creek."

As we headed home in Gram's SUV, the cover of bloated clouds fragmented. Diluted sunshine filtered through the cracks. My cousin was silent, playing with the ends of her hair and staring out the windows.

About halfway home, she said, "Uncle Mal also said when God gives you what you need, you have to obey. Do you think God wanted me to be brave at the creek and I rejected it?"

A burn crept up my neck. "You'd know it if God wanted you to do something and you refused." My memory replayed my lunch with Chris, and the grating pain returned.

The sun broke free of a dusty blue bank of clouds, shooting blinding light into my face. I flipped down the visor.

It might help her, Father, if I told her how I chickened on Thursday. But ... I really don't want her to think less of me. But it is the truth, and it might help her. Something good could come out of my cowardice.

Staring straight ahead, and with the burn growing red hot, I told Amber of how I couldn't bring myself to ask Chris to church, even though I knew it was something I had to do, because I didn't want to hurt our relationship.

Silence.

I gulped. I'd obliterated my following of one.

"Rae, that's not cowardly." Her voice wasn't just soft but warm. "He's putting up all this—this resistance, making you nervous about getting more personal. That's understandable."

I shook my head. "I knew what God wanted me to do, and I didn't do it." I shoved hair behind my ear. "I should invite him tomorrow, and I'm afraid I'll chicken again."

Silence again. "Why don't you pray God gives you courage like He did in those fights? You obeyed then. You can obey when you're with Chris tomorrow. Would it help to know I'll be praying for you all day? You're not in this alone." Her tone held a determination I hadn't heard before.

I tore my gaze from the windshield.

Amber seemed to have ... matured. Her gorgeous face reflected an encouragement that seemed beyond her age. And held Gram's quiet assurance.

I grinned. "That's a huge help."

Amber broke into a glowing smile that lasted the rest of the drive.

~~~~~

Dad wasn't home when we got there, and Gram said she didn't know when he would be. Carrie had come for supper and informed me that Dani had called, telling her ticket sales were so bad that she'd be the only person working security tonight.

I kept expecting Dani to call me and say I wasn't needed, but the call never came.

When I arrived at the booth, Dani had set up the gear. For one cashier.

"If you get swamped, call me." She pointed to the walkie-talkie. "But I doubt it. Only two-thirds of the staff returned, so I've had to close a few scenes. When that gets around, even fewer people will come."

The amount of customers was pathetic compared to Friday night, but people wandering out of their groups kept Carrie busy. Most of them claimed they'd gotten lost in the dark, but I suspected they were hunting for the crime scene. Three mediums, a ghost hunting team, and three bigfoot hunters asked about access, and I referred them to Dani so she could handle any drama when she refused their requests.

Dani closed the attraction at midnight, so I got home an hour earlier than I expected. That was a pleasant surprise, but it cost me an hour's pay.

Another surprise was finding Amber, peering with bleary eyes at sheets of paper spread over the couch.

"What're you doing up?" I said.

She yawned, her pale face exhausted. "Every time I close my eyes, I see that creature and get panicky. So I tried to work on the code." She sighed. "Uncle Mal told me not to think about it, but I keep trying to remember something that would tell us if it was a bear or a person. Do you think the murderer could have worn a costume because he ..." she sucked in a breath "...wanted to find his phone?"

"I guess that's a possibility. But then why did he drag the body?" I lifted a few of the papers. "And I guess you haven't had any luck with the code."

"No." She rested her head in her hands. "I'm so tired, but I don't want to go to bed."
~~~~~

"It takes time for an awful experience like that to wear off." I gathered the sheets. "But it will. I promise. But since you're up, will you pray with me about talking to Chris tomorrow?"

The weariness fled her expression. "I'll help any way I can."

We gripped hands, and I prayed for courage.

Chapter Thirty-Eight

"Your mind doesn't seem to be on your photos," said Chris the next afternoon.

I straightened from peering through my viewfinder. "Why do you say that?"

"That's the third time you've started to take photos, and you've forgotten to turn the camera on."

"Oh—uh, yeah." I bent back to the viewfinder. "I guess I'm a little preoccupied."

That was an understatement. I couldn't enjoy spending time with Chris, doing what I loved on the kind of fall day that made Ohio the best place to enjoy this season. From the overlook Chris and I had hiked to at Great Seal State Park, the patchwork of red, orange, gold, and lemon leaves rolled to the horizon like a cozy quilt. The clean, crisp air tasted like fresh apple cider. The clear sun had burned away all moisture that had waterlogged the atmosphere for over a week.

But inviting Chris to church and Lyra's copy of the poem consumed every gram of my attention.

"You didn't eat much lunch either. Anything you want to tell me?" He turned his head, and the sunlight delineated chocolate strands in his black hair.

"Well—uh, yes." I stepped back, taking a deep breath.

Start small.

"Have you seen the poem from Lyra's purse?" I said.

"I only glanced at it when Houston went through the items in her purse at the crime scene."

"I took a photo before I knew it was part of a murder investigation. It looks like she solved the code, but I don't see how." I sat on a fallen tree and showed him the photo. "Do you see a pattern?"

Chris took a seat beside me, his muscular arm pressing against mine. After a few minutes, he said, "Nothing leaps out at me. Why are you so interested? Do you think it's related to her murder?"

"I don't know. But it doesn't make sense. How did a grifter crack a seventy-year-old puzzle in a week?"

"You have a point."

Okay, I'd gotten the conversation rolling.

"Chris, there's something else I want to tell you."

He swiveled on the log, bending his left knee, and gave me his full attention.

My lungs withered to the size of raisins.

Father, give me courage. Give me Your courage.

"Will you come to church with me?" I blurted it into his face, making him rear back.

"Uh — why?" He shifted away from me.

My lungs remained shriveled, but I forged ahead. "Well, nothing's more important to me than my faith. It's a good way for you to understand what I believe, and you can see how it compares to what you believe."

The attention drained from his face, leaving his intense features blank. "I don't have to understand what you believe," he said. "I should just respect it."

Now my heart stopped. "So you won't come to church with me?"

He shrugged. "I don't see the need. We don't have to do everything together."

"Chris." I leaned toward him, touching his knee. "I'm not asking you to go on something like a hike, and that's not your thing. My faith makes me who I am. Don't you want to know me better?"

"I can do that without going to church with you." He stood and then put a container that had held pepperoni rolls in his backpack.

My heart sunk like a foundering ship. Since I'd come this far, I might as well say it. "I'd like to know what you believe about God and compare it to what I know." I turned my head to the view. I was pretty certain of the answer I'd get.

"That's rather personal."

I said to the hills rolling below us, "I thought we were in a personal relationship."

The breeze brushed strands of my hair across my cheek.

"It doesn't require us to know everything about each other."

"We should know something as basic as what we believe. I wouldn't be the same person without my relationship with God."

The sun was still an enthusiastic white, the air still dry and lively, but I was drowning in a whirlpool of depression.

"Would you like to visit some of the community colleges with me?" He spoke like I had said nothing since I'd mentioned my frustrations over Lyra's poem.

Something in my chest ignited, and I pivoted to him. "No. No, you aren't changing the subject again because you're uncomfortable. I'm tired of running into roadblock after roadblock with you. I know I shouldn't bring up your family, but you won't even talk about something as non-threatening as going to a Catholic boarding school."

Catholic ... Old news stories unwound through my mind, and I gasped. "You weren't—I mean, if something bad happened there, I understand why—"

Chris muttered something I didn't catch. "The priests at my school were some of the finest men I've ever known. You're too intelligent to make the ridiculous assumption that every priest is a pedophile." He glared straight at me.

Which I met, full blast. "Sorry for the ridiculous assumption, but since you won't tell me anything, I guess I'll make them despite my intelligence." I swallowed, trying to stamp out the fire inside. "Look, Chris. Why is it okay for you to encourage me to go to college, but it's not for me to encourage you to attend church with me?"

He smoothed his moustache with his thumb and first finger. "Those are two very different things."

"Not really. You think going to college would be good for me, and I think going to church would be good for you. Or at least, it'd help you understand me. We both want to help each other."

"You need to respect my decision. I'll respect yours about college."

"But you're still encouraging me to make the decision you want, like offering to look at schools with me. Why don't you come once? Then we could talk about—"

Chris rounded on me. "Drop it."

I jerked back, and an inferno burst inside me, shooting flames through every nerve. "I'm not a perp you can scare into doing what you want."

"Then stop committing assault with your mouth."

Chris thought I was verbally assaulting him? I'd gotten mad, but I hadn't been insulting.

Snatching up his backpack, Chris said, "It's a long hike back to my truck." He slung it over his shoulders and stormed down the trail.

I couldn't move. For the longest time, I sat motionless as a pressure crushed my chest. Finally, like each movement was agony, I packed away my camera and tripod. For two hours, I stumbled along the trail, fighting tears, replaying the conversation over and over until losing my mind seemed better than recalling it.

Father, what did I do wrong?

Chris was waiting in his pickup when I reached it. I stashed my backpack behind my seat.

Without a trace of feeling, Chris said, "I'll take you home."

He'd said this morning that he'd found a diner he wanted to take me to for supper before he drove me home in time for Carrie's driving lesson on a semi.

Choking on tears rising like a tsunami, I said, "If you want."

"I assumed that's what you want," he said to the windshield.

"You know what I want, Chris. So I guess the only logical thing to do is go home."

Chris turned the key of his pickup and roared out of the parking lot, hurling gravel.

Chapter Thirty-Nine

During the hour and a half drive, neither of us said a word. When Chris reached the dead-end road, I asked him to stop.

He shifted into neutral. "Why?"

I opened my door. "I'm walking home from here." I got out and tilted my seat forward.

"Rae, I can drive you to your door." Chris's deep voice was flat.

"I need time to think." Wiping my wet cheeks with one hand, I removed my camera backpack. "I'll get the food containers from you later." I shut the door and plunged into the woods.

My backpack thumping my back, my tripod rattling, I ran, putting as much distance between me and Chris as I could, until my sobs cut my air so much that I had to sit on a stump.

Father, how could being brave go so badly? You gave me what I needed when I needed it, and this is the result?

Praying, crying, I waited for a nudge or insight from my Father, but nausea at the thought of Chris was all I got. Brushing tears from my nose, I checked the time on my phone. Supper was over, nearly time for my driving lesson. The hike to the Norris's farm would take at least twenty minutes. Enough time to appear normal.

Twilight bathed the woods in a tired gold as I tromped through lakes of fiery leaves.

I found Carrie and Mr. Norris outside a faded red barn at his farm, hitching a trailer to a tractor.

"I'm here for my lesson." I put my backpack on a hay bale.

"Good. I don't think—" She straightened, studied me, and said in a rush, "Are you all right?"

So twenty minutes hadn't been enough to hide my destroyed spirit.

"Yeah," I lied and hurried toward the semi parked beside the barn.

Carrie side-eyed me through the entire lesson, but she didn't ask again how I was.

"You caught on quickly," Carrie said as I parked the big, blue cab and trailer. "You're a natural."

"I'm glad I can help." I climbed down from the seat.

Carrie said she would help Mr. Norris all day tomorrow, once the dew dried off by noon. Amber and Coral were getting out of school early to help.

"Jeanine's still trying to find somebody to drive the second combine.

She can, but she doesn't want to leave Hank. If we can get six people — two on combines, two on tractors with carts driving beside the combines, and two driving semis — we'll make real progress tomorrow."

Carrie offered to take me home, but I said no. Maybe another walk would give me time to pull myself together better. I really, **really** wanted to avoid questions about my day, and my brothers and cousins didn't have as many manners as Carrie.

Layers of fuchsia and straw striped the western horizon above the hills when I reached the garage.

Still wearing his uniform, Dad hurried out of the breezeway.

"Rae?" He stopped on the gravel drive. "Why're you ..." He zeroed in on my face.

My teeth dug into my lip. Then I broke for him, grabbing him in a hug.

He wrapped his arms around me. "You had a fight with Chris." Not a question. "You can tell me about it when I get back. If you want."

Stepping back, I wiped my cheeks. "Where are you going?"

"Ed Hawthorne called with the autopsy results for Ms. Vex. I'm meeting him."

I drew in a big breath. "Did he find anything that can ... I guess you can't tell me that." I wanted to talk about anything but Chris.

"Sorry, I can't."

"Well, can you tell me if Lyra died before 7 a.m.? Carrie thought she'd been dead around twelve hours."

"I'll say that, so far, it appears she died between 2 and 7 a.m."

"Will the meeting take very long? You looked dead tired."

He gave a weak chuckle. "It might, but I'll be fine. Then I'm going to see Walter to ask if he's heard from Jack."

My eyes widened. "You haven't found him?"

"Nope. The last report I can trust on his movements is yours — you saw him intimidating Alex Morley about 7:15 Saturday evening. Aunt Lily, Claire, Jesse, and everybody on that side of the family says they haven't had a word from him."

"Would Aunt Lily lie for Jack? I can't see Claire doing that. She doesn't like him at all." I paused. "But she's scared of him."

Dad sighed. "I'm sure that'll keep her mouth shut. That and Walter's rule that Malinowskis don't rat on Malinowskis. If Aunt Lily knows anything, she won't tell me because she wants to protect Jack and please Walter."

"Did you find Kyle Garrison?"

"Yes, at the site where he's been tent camping at the state park. He says he returned to his camp right after he left Lyra in Dani's trailer at 2 a.m. He offered to wait to drive her home, but Lyra said Morley Sr. had driven her to the séance, and she'd get a ride with him. Morley Sr. says Lyra told him she had another ride." He broke into a grim smile. "I also asked Morley Sr. for the details of the second clue because it might be involved in the murder. When I told him Lyra might have faked it, he almost shook apart with indignation and refused to tell me."

"That's how he acted when Serenity grabbed The Book. You can't get a warrant for the second book and the note inside?"

"Not unless I can show it's attached to the murder. I hoped Morley Sr. would volunteer the information as his civic duty. As far as Garrison is concerned, I can't find a witness placing him at the park until after 9 a.m. Saturday morning, when he ran into people in the bathhouse. He says Lyra told him to meet her at her shop at noon, but she never showed and didn't answer his texts. So he went to The Haunting to find her."

My eyebrows tightened. "That's why he was in the woods Saturday night? But she wouldn't have been there. She'd have been at the entrance, working the crowd."

"I'm only telling you what he told me. He stumbled over his words when he got to that part, so I'm pretty sure he's either lying or holding something back." He said in quieter voice, "If you want to talk, I can wake you when I get in tonight. Or if it's easier to talk to a woman, Ma and your aunts are always available."

"Thanks. You don't have to wake me." He needed sleep a ton more than me bawling all over him.

I hugged him again, and he kissed me on the top of my head.

Then I trudged across the front porch to the end where Dad had built my new bedroom to attach to it. Once inside, I dumped my backpack on my bed. I went into Gram's room and stood in her doorway to the living-dining room.

Amber and Rusty wrote in binders at the dinner table, while Gram sat beside Coral as she typed on the desktop computer.

"Gram, I'm home," I said. "I'm taking a shower."

"Rae, what's—"

I shut the door on Gram's question.

Where the tears came from, I didn't know because I should have run out of raw material by now, but I bawled all over again in the shower. I dried, dressed, locked my bedroom door, and threw myself on my bed.

A few minutes later came some very delicate knocks.

I pressed my face into my quilt.

Amber said through the door, "Would you like to work on the code?"

Swallowing a lump of tears, I hauled myself to my feet and opened the door. "I'd love to. It didn't go well."

Amber nodded solemnly. "I thought so. Say no more." She gathered sheets of paper from the top right drawer of my desk, and we sat on the wood laminate floor. "Dad's fever broke, so he's going into surgery tomorrow."

I took pencils from the desk. "Glad to hear some good news."

"I keep looking for a pattern. Like every fifth letter or every eleventh word. But nothing fits."

We tried different approaches, adding to the list of the ones Amber had already attempted. Eventually, my cousin uncrossed her legs and rested back against my desk. "This is perfect for crowdsourcing, but—"

"It's also part of a murder, and we don't want someone to beat us to the treasure."

"Do you think Cyrus used the same code for both clues? Of course, we'll never see the second clue. Old Mr. Morley is probably guarding it with an AK-47."

I sat up straight. "I forgot to tell you. Dad saw part of the clue. The note. It said 'Above my pride.' But he couldn't see what story or poem it was placed next to."

"Half a clue is as bad as no clue."

We studied "Eldorado" again until Amber said she should try going to bed. She was so tired that she didn't think the memory of the monster would get her heart racing even one extra beat.

I didn't lie down on the air mattress until well after the house had gone quiet. Amber and Coral's even breathing as they slept in my double bed was the only sound.

As soon as I pulled the covers over my shoulder, tears stung my eyes. *Father, I did what You want. Why did it go so badly?*

The tears became a torrent.

Maybe because we weren't meant to be partners.

Chapter Forty

The next day, my shift felt like eight and a half decades instead of eight and a half hours. My attention barely registered the work I was doing.

Now that he'd had time to cool off, what did Chris think of me?

By the time I headed down the back staircase at 5, I'd checked my phone so many times for a text from Chris that I couldn't stand to look at the thing anymore. Jeanine had texted. Hank had woken from his second surgery. Maybe putting another operation behind him would lift his mood.

Gram also sent a message, telling me I needed to change into work clothes fast because Dad and I were taking supper to the harvest crew and replacing Amber and Coral for the night.

Twisting the key in the lock for my truck, I stared at my phone.

"For the night"? How long were we harvesting?

I set a speed record for changing into jeans, t-shirt, and hiking boots, and then I hurried to the drive, the loose laces of my boots trailing through the grass.

Dad hoisted a cooler into the back seat of the Beast. "Anything you want to talk about on the drive?"

I slid a collapsible table that was leaning against the truck behind my seat. " How about the case?"

He gave me an understanding smile as I took my seat.

At the end of our drive, Dad turned left. "I'm letting Houston take the lead in the investigation since he took the call and needs the experience. But I'm working closely with him and with agents from the Bureau of Criminal Investigation. Did you hear about Alex Morley's phone?"

I bent over to tie my left boot. "Devon and a ton of other people texted me about it on Sunday."

"We found no blood on it. It had been in the creek for hours with water rushing over it. So if it was with the body, we can't prove it."

"Have you talked to Jack?" I said.

"Nope. The family still claims they've had no contact with him and no idea where he is. He's got to know he's our prime suspect with the way he acted toward Lyra. But I have no evidence connecting him to her death. I told Aunt Lily and Walter that I just want to talk to him."

"Gram doesn't think he did it." I switched to my right boot. "Not his style. Do you?"

"Honestly, no." Dad scratched an eyebrow. "This case runs in circles. Jack and Morley Sr. have the attitude to kill—Morley Sr. seems wound so tight he could lose control at the right provocation. But they would only do it in hot blood—Jack, because Lyra enraged him somehow, and Morley Sr., if Lyra had misled him with a fake clue. But this crime was carefully planned. That leads me to suspect Morley Jr. and Dani Li. Either of them could have bribed Lyra to fake that clue once they learned Morley Sr. was so desperate to find the treasure that he'd hire a medium. But that clue wasn't fake. So that removes both Morleys and Ms. Li as suspects."

"Do any of them have alibis for the time of death?"

"No. If any of them did, I'd be suspicious. No innocent person should have an alibi between 2 and 7 a.m."

"That leaves Garrison," I said.

"He doesn't have a motive I can find. He has several trespassing convictions, but nothing violent. The killer could be someone from Lyra's past, someone we know nothing about. Houston hasn't found a thing about her beyond two years ago." Dad growled, feeding gas. "We've got to find Jack."

"Could the poem we found in Lyra's purse be connected with her death?" I explained that I'd taken a photo of it, and Amber and I had been trying to crack the code.

"Since the clue was genuine, I don't see how. I appreciate that you and Amber and Ma have kept it to yourselves. My agency hasn't made that fact public either. If a suspect reveals knowledge about it, that might be the break we need."

We twisted through the hills as the sun's aging rays brightened the topmost leaves. I'd learned enough about farming to know that the field we worked in might be nowhere close to either Hank's or Mr. Norris's farms.

Around another bend and I spotted Carrie bouncing along on a tractor as a combine shot soybeans into the cart she pulled. Dad pulled off the road across from the field.

Two combines harvested beans. Coral drove a tractor next to the bigger one. Sunlight slanting off the windows of the combines shielded the drivers from view.

Dad carried the cooler, and I hauled a bin of food and paper products.

Amber climbed down from the cab of a semi parked at a tilt beside the road. "Great. I'm starved. I'll get the table."

I raised an eyebrow. Since Amber knew we had the table, it must have been standard operating procedure when bringing supper to the harvest crew.

As we set out bags of chips and a bowl of grapes on the table, the combines and tractors stopped. Mr. Norris climbed down from the bigger combine that Coral had been driving beside. The smaller combine's door opened and...

The bun I'd been ready to place on a plate remained suspended.

Walter dropped to the ground, skipping the steps that descended from the door of his combine.

I said, "I didn't know Walter could drive a combine."

Dad placed a bag of napkins on the table. "Why did you — " He spun around.

Carrie and Walter trudged behind Mr. Norris and Coral through the muddy field.

Amber took the bag of buns from me. "Mom was pretty sure Walter had run a combine at some point. She asked him if he could harvest today, so she wouldn't have to leave Dad." My cousin lowered her voice. "It's been pretty tense whenever Grandpa and Walter are within speaking distance."

"No surprise there." I placed the bun where it belonged.

Mr. Norris had to hate that the most notorious citizen of our county was helping him harvest and would have no trouble displaying his dislike. And Walter would have no trouble responding to it.

Another semi pulled off the road, and Jason Carlisle swung the door open.

I'd meant to stick a plastic fork in the bowl of shredded chicken and missed.

"Holy smoke, Carlisle," Dad called down the road to him, "I didn't know you'd been drafted."

Jason broke into a low-powered version of his million-watt smile. With his sunglasses on and dark brown hair sculpted with gel, he looked like a movie star approaching the lowly crew of his current production. Not that he'd ever treat anyone lowly, not even a checkout clerk at the library where he was on the board.

"Devon told me last night about Luke needing people for the harvest." He removed his sunglasses, revealing his warm, brown eyes. "She'd called to remind me of the evenings the kids and I are taking care of the animals. I freed up my schedule for the next two days, so I could come."

Dad cocked his head to one side. "This wasn't a last-minute decision? Then why didn't you wear old clothes?"

Jason glanced at his neat, dark jeans and red polo shirt tucked in with a narrow canvas belt that looked like he'd removed the price tag a moment before. "These *are* old clothes."

The rest of us stopped loading our plates and stared. Everyone wore jeans that were frayed or ragged or punctured by a few holes, and many of our t-shirts and plaid shirts were just as worn.

Carrie broke the spell. "We certainly need you." She piled chips on a plate. "With you and Walter, we're doubling our progress." She gave Walter a grin. "I didn't know you could operate a combine until you showed up today."

He plopped a healthy portion of chicken on his bun. "If a job takes sweat and grunts, I done it." He eyed Jason, his jaw jutting, like a challenge.

Oh, no.

"Surprised you could help, Carlisle," said Walter. "Wouldn't think no Carlisle could do more 'n read papers."

My grape got hung up halfway down my throat, Dad and Carrie stiffened, disapproval radiated from Mr. Norris's entire rigid frame, and Amber and Coral studied their food.

Jason broke into his dazzling grin. "It's true I only know a little about farming, but I can at least drive a stick."

"You don't got no chauffeurs to do that for you?"

"If you're going to pick a fight, Walter—" Mr. Norris set down his plate "—you ain't doing it while you're working for me."

My great-grandfather swallowed a huge bite of his sandwich. "How you figurin' on stoppin' me?"

Dad dropped his can of soda to the edge of the table with a crack, but Carrie spoke first. "Walter, we should focus on our jobs, not needling each other. We're all here to help Jeanine and Hank and the girls. If you had any doubts about Jason's ability to work, his performance today should have killed them. He's worked non-stop since noon, and he's prepared to stay until we finish this field."

Seizing an opportunity to change subjects, I said, "How long do you think that'll take?"

"If we don't get equipment stuck in the mud," said Carrie, "and that's happened twice now, Mr. Norris said 10:30 or 11. Then we drive the equipment to the next field to be ready in the morning."

My eyebrows wanted to climb, but I didn't want Walter to think I couldn't work that long, so I nodded quickly and loaded grapes and chips onto my plate.

"Jason, if you need to leave to be with your kids," said Amber, "I can stay."

"No," said Jason. "Rick's on uncle duty tonight."

We finished our meal in silence. Walter must have decided he wanted to help Jeanine more than antagonize people. He and Dad finished eating first and crossed the field to the smaller combine and tractor.

As Mr. Norris polished off his sandwich—nice to see him eating a full meal—Amber and Coral talked to him while Carrie chatted with Jason.

My aunt didn't just listen. She watched Jason when he spoke with the focus you give something you admire, like a hot car or a beautiful horse galloping gracefully.

As he finished a story about his youngest daughter Sylvie, Carrie threw back her head and laughed, her voice ringing out over the field.

I tore my gaze from my aunt and ate my last grape. She was so interested in Jason that she probably hadn't noticed me staring.

She was definitely attracted to him. But Carrie's comment about a Carlisle and a Malinowski dating being a sign of the Apocalypse seemed to show she thought he was out of her league.

I took a casual glance in their direction.

Jason's smile was now at maximum wattage as Carrie spoke.

Carrie might have thought Jason was out of her league, but I wasn't sure he thought she was out of his.

Once Mr. Norris, Carrie, and Jason had left for their vehicles, I helped my cousins clean up the food and trash.

As I toted the folding table to Mr. Norris's truck, Coral carried a bag with leftover food. "Rae, are you driving me and Amber to your house?"

"No," said Amber, holding a bag of trash. "I'm going to drive us in Grandpa's truck."

Freezing beside the tan pickup, Coral clutched the bag to her chest.

Amber bent down to her sister's level. "Phones get a signal here. If we don't call Rae in a half hour, she'll alert the whole family, and they'll find us." She told me the route she was taking, and I nodded.

Coral remained motionless, then lowered the bag. "I think—" she released a long breath "—I think that'll be okay." She got in the cab.

I hoisted the table into the bed and said in a low voice, "Nicely done, big sis."

"You really think so?" Her question combined a whisper with a squeal.

Shoot fires, one compliment and my faithful following was even more devoted. "Yeah, I do."

Beaming, Amber got behind the wheel and drove away.

Chapter Forty-One

At midnight, using what little energy I had left, I guided the Beast onto the drive to Mr. Norris's farm. I fell out of the cab as a yawn tried to pop my jaw. Good thing my shift at the library didn't start until noon.

Jason and I had made trip after trip with our semis, loaded with soybeans, to the grain bins on Mr. Norris's farm. I'd discovered two positive things about harvesting: I could support my new family through a crisis, and I had to concentrate so hard on my driving that I couldn't think about Chris. Much.

Walter, Mr. Norris, and Carrie took their time getting out of the cab, as if they were pacing their last ounces of strength. Dad and Jason dropped out of the bed.

Mr. Norris said, "Who's available to come back at noon? I know you said you could, Caroline."

Jason and Walter said they could return.

As Mr. Norris headed to his home, Carrie crossed the road to go to Jeanine's house, and Jason got in his Land Rover.

Dropping his thick arms on the hood of the Beast, Walter said, "Claire and Carrie told me that psychic woman found another clue, Rae. Anything in your research tell you there are more clues?"

"No." I covered a yawn.

Walter rubbed his jaw. "Maybe he hid a bunch of clues that don't lead to nothin'."

"I think it's a definite possibility. Cyrus had contempt for every person he met. And he liked to get revenge, in sneaky ways." As I told him about the nude photos of the actress and the vandalism at the Armstrongs' home and the newspaper office, it hit me I could also be describing actions Jack would take.

"But if there's a treasure," Walter said, "you can't do nothin' without the second clue. That old man's got it."

Standing behind Walter, Dad raised his eyebrows at me in warning.

He didn't need to. I wouldn't tell Walter that Dad had seen the second note.

"Morley Sr. probably sleeps with both books now." Dad pressed the heels of his hands against his eyes, then lowered them.

Walter stalked off to his pickup. "I bet he's rollin' in it. He don't need the money like Lily does."

~~~~~

After sleeping like the dead, I was glad to return at noon to the undemanding job of working at the checkout desk. Except when I thought of Chris. Which was all the time.

Could I text him something simple, like "how are you"? Did he need more time to cool off? If I didn't send something, maybe he'd think I didn't care. But he hadn't contacted me, so maybe *he* didn't care.

I still hadn't texted Chris when Gram called right before closing at 8. Dad was working late. She, along with a retired man from our church, was helping Mr. Norris so I could go home and supervise my brothers and cousins about getting their homework done.

I let myself in the outside door to my bedroom to give myself time to switch gears from work to homework patrol. All I wanted to do was crawl into bed and forget Chris for a while. But after I changed into sweats, I had to settle a fight between Coral and Aaron, check Rusty's English essay for typos, and read off Spanish vocab words for Amber. So I crawled onto my air mattress much later.

The next morning I got up to a drizzle. No harvesting today. Maybe that was for the best because Mr. Norris seemed set on proving Hank's prediction that he'd work himself to death.

After logging on the computers at the checkout desk, I called on all the courage God could give me and texted Chris.

Me: How are you?

In a couple minutes, he responded: Fine
Nothing more. My heart slithered to my ankles. Well ... at least he answered.
Ten more minutes passed.

Chris: How's Hank?

I reported what Jeanine had texted that morning: Hank appeared to be recovering well from the last surgery. I didn't add that he was sunk in depression, going hours without talking except to ask how the harvest was going and apologize for failing his family. This rain wouldn't make him feel any better.

Chris: Glad to hear that. How are you?

I stared at the phone. So much was going on that I didn't honestly know how I was except not happy. Should I text that?
I debated for almost a half hour before I answered.
~~~~~

Me: Overwhelmed.

An hour later, Chris hadn't texted back, but I really hadn't expected him to.

When lunch came, I asked Dad if I could eat with him in his office, and he said I could come over now.

I walked down Main Street under iron-colored clouds that appeared to hold more drizzle.

When I entered the reception area of the historic building that had been converted into offices for the sheriff's department, Dad and the chief of the Wellesville police department, Eric Simcox, were alone in the room. The admins must have been at lunch.

Dad looked past Simcox, aiming his lit-from-within grin at me, as the Chief gave me a curt nod.

Then Simcox said in his crisp voice, "I thought you should know that your cousin being the prime suspect in a murder impacts public perception of your handling of the case."

"I appreciate your concern," said Dad. "Houston's leading the investigation, and we have agents from BCI helping. It's not like I'm investigating myself and keeping other officers out. Besides, voters know I don't play favorites. I put two of my cousins away for assaulting me."

"But this murder isn't personal like that case was."

My eyebrows achieved lift off.

Once again, Simcox had twisted a conversation into an indictment of Dad's fitness for his job.

Dad seemed to turn to granite, his posture and expression solidifying. "After working with me for two years, you should know I put the welfare of the public above my own."

"I know that. But will voters?"

Dad's rock-solid face was turning crimson, but he kept his response at an inside volume. "If they have doubts, they can tell me or the county commissioners."

Simcox snapped a shrug. "As an officer with more experience than you, I thought it was my duty to give you my opinion. You always say our agencies should cooperate." He performed an about-face and strode outside.

Dad said through his teeth, "I expected him to be over losing the election to me by now."

I said, "I don't think he'll ever be over it."

"I need a walk, Rae. We'll do lunch another — "

"Can I walk with you?"

The blood in Dad's face diffused as a grin struggled into place. "If you like."

Once Liz, one of the admins, returned from lunch a few minutes later, we set out at a pace that forced me to jog now and then to keep up. The rain hadn't returned, although clouds piling into each other in the west promised wet weather at any moment.

After ten minutes of striding up and down Wellesville's hilly streets, Dad said, "Did Jeanine tell you that Hank doesn't want any visitors, including us? I can't believe it. Having visitors is the one sure way to improve Hank's mood, and he doesn't seem to realize it. He says he's not up to small talk." He stopped at an intersection.

A drop fell on my hand as I stood still. "B-b-but Uncle Hank always wants to talk with people. Even strangers he bumps into."

"I know." Dad glared at the houses, as if they were angering him too. "I've got an idea that might help Hank. I tried to talk to Jeanine about it, but she's determined to protect Hank against anything stressful. So unless someone confesses to Lyra's murder, I'm going to Columbus this evening to convince her to let me try it."

"But aren't you tired? You haven't had a real break since Saturday night."

"I'll be fine."

"Let me drive you."

He began walking. "That's not necessary."

I trotted beside him. "You might feel fine now, but later tonight you might appreciate someone taking over at the wheel."

He glanced down at me, sighing. "Okay. I know it'd make Ma feel better."

Light rain spotted our clothes. As we hurried back to the sheriff's office, Dad outlined his plan. I didn't share his confidence in it, but he assured me it was a guy thing and a parent thing.

At 4:30, Gram came to the library with her SUV and exchanged it for the Rust Bucket, so Dad and I didn't have to depend on my wreck to make a three-hour round trip.

When I returned to the lobby after delivering repaired books to the children's room, Dad was by the checkout desk with Devon and Serenity.

The six-year-old stared up and up at him. "Your nose looks pretty good, Big Guy."

"I guess I have a talent for healing," he said with a smile.

Liberty raced over to me, thrust into my hand a folded sheet of paper divided into a wild conglomeration of shapes in all shades of blue, and whispered, "Give this to your dad." She darted back to her table, behind a stack of books.

Devon said, "Rae told me Rusty had a therapist to help him with anxiety, and I'm looking for a new one for Liberty. She has the same problem. Would you recommend the one Rusty used?"

"Uh—yes." Dad's deep voice sounded uncertain but friendly, like he was glad to have a polite conversation with Devon but puzzled by it. He removed his phone from a pocket. "Rusty hasn't seen her in years, but I assume she's still practicing."

I held out the sheet to Dad. "This is for you."

"It was Liberty's idea, but we both made it for you." Serenity stood on tiptoes and pointed at the sheet. "I colored that square, and that triangle, and ..."

"He gets the point, Serene," said Devon.

Dad opened the paper. Inside, Liberty had printed: "We're really, really, really, really, really sorry about your nose." She, Serenity, and Devon had signed it.

Creasing it closed again, Dad said, "Thank you." He looked over to Liberty, hiding behind a tall book on wild cats. "Very thoughtful of you. You're a very talented artist."

Liberty peeked over the top of her book. She nodded and hunkered down behind it.

"It's the least we can do after Serenity clocked you one," said Devon. "Rae said you're going to see Hank. Please let him and Jeanine know the girls and I are pulling for him. Let me know if I can help any other way."

Dad said, "Taking over the care of the animals is enough."

Devon waved his gratitude away. "That's not much. I could run the state from a scheduling app if I had a complete list of names and numbers."

When my shift ended, Dad and I bought sandwiches at Cervelli's Deli and then drove out of town. We made good time until we hit the rush hour traffic crawling around Columbus.

Crumpling the paper my sandwich had been wrapped in, I said, "No new leads in the murder?"

"Nope," Dad said. "Jack is still missing. Everyone in his family still says they don't know where he is, including Walter. I can't find any motive for Lyra's murder except Jack's jealousy. Houston's tracking down people posted on her socials, but most of them are clients. They say they know nothing personal about Lyra, and that's probably true. The lab hasn't turned up any evidence that points to anybody yet. So we're in exactly the same place we were when we walked onto the crime scene Saturday night."

"Amber and I haven't discovered anything about the poem from Lyra's purse, although I don't think it has anything to do with her death. I'm more curious than anything else. How did she solve it?"

"You and Amber should still keep that information to yourselves."

At the hospital, as we neared Hank's room, voices reached us.

Mr. Norris said in a gentle tone, "It's going slow, but I have a lot of help. Even if they don't got experience, they're all working real hard."

Dad whispered, "See if Jeanine's in there."

I nodded and sauntered into the room.

"I'm real, real sorry, Dad," Hank said.

That hopeless tone sounded like someone had stolen Hank's real voice. A mesh of worry lines pulled his face out of familiarity.

"Henry." Mr. Norris awkwardly patted his son's shoulder. "Don't keep saying that."

Jeanine glanced toward the door where I stood, then popped out of her chair. "What are you doing here? Didn't Mal or Ma tell you that Hank's not feeling well enough for visitors?"

"Dad's out in the hall," I said, like our appearance was natural. "He wants to talk to you."

A fierce glare leaped into Jeanine's huge blue eyes, and I prayed Dad knew what he was doing.

"And I want to talk to him." She marched out the door like she was prepared to engage in mortal combat.

Disapproval tightened Mr. Norris's mouth beneath his bushy moustache. "If Jeanine told Walter not to come, then he should have listened." Nothing gentle about his tone now.

"Dad," said Hank, "Mal's here, not his grandpa. Oh, wait." He rubbed his forehead. "You meant Mal. I'm not thinking straight."

I looked to Mr. Norris. "Dad prefers Mal."

"Walter is his proper name." Mr. Norris turned to his son. "You need to focus on getting better, Henry. I'll take care of the harvest. If it turns out bad — well, that's what we have crop insurance for."

"I can't believe how stupid I was," said Hank. "I've put my whole family at risk because of one dumb mistake."

"If that were true — " Dad strode up to the foot of Hank's bed " — I'd have to arrest you for cruelty to animals."

Mr. Norris spun to Dad. He didn't bother with his usual disapproval. He skipped that and went straight for an outraged glare.

Hank closed his eyes. "Not up to it today, Mal."

Jeanine slipped into the room behind Dad and laid a slender hand on the sleeve of Mr. Norris's denim shirt.

"Good. I'll get to complete a sentence for once." Dad shifted his weight to his good leg. "This whole blame game is ridiculous, Hank. All you have to do is the job God's given to you. Right now, that's healing. Which is lousy. I think God would tell you that Himself. But He'll help you do it." He shook his head. "Now I know where Amber gets it."

"What d'you mean?"

"Jeanine didn't want to heap extra stress on you. But I've persuaded her that Amber needs you. Right now."

Hank raised himself off the mattress. "What's wrong with Amber?"

"Rae's been trying to help her," Dad said. "Tell him, Rae, about how Amber thinks she's a coward."

"What?" Hank's extra-big brown eyes swelled.

My stomach knotting, I told Hank what happened at the creek and how disappointed Amber was in herself for letting him and the family down. I also explained the risks she'd taken to prove that she was brave. That was when I had to bring up her discovery of Lyra's body.

Mr. Norris tried to interrupt a few times, and Jeanine's hand turned into a vise.

When I was done, Hank's jaw hung like it was broken.

Mr. Norris jerked his arm from his daughter-in-law's grip. "You said you weren't telling him about this mess, Jeanine."

"Why not?" Hank said. "I'd recovered from the first surgery by Sunday."

"No, you hadn't." Jeanine rubbed her thumb against her wedding band. "Hank, you've been so depressed that I didn't want to make it worse." She met her father-in-law's withering stare. "But Mal thinks Amber needs to talk to Hank. Today."

Dad said, "You have to tell her she didn't let you down, Hank. You're not angry or disappointed in her. I don't know if that'll convince her she's actually brave, but at least she won't be keeping a secret she's scared to death you'll find out."

Elevating the top portion of his bed, Hank set his mouth in a grim line. "Jeanine, where's a phone?"

Dad moved toward the door. "We'll give you some privacy."

Mr. Norris followed us into the hall. "You shouldn't have interfered, Walter. Henry doesn't need any more stress." His words were one long hiss.

"He needs to know he can still support his family," said Dad. "He can't farm, but he can still be a dad." He leaned into the room. "Hank, I know you're worn out, but my boys need to talk to you on a video call. I think Rusty suspects you died and we've been lying to him."

Dad turned back to Mr. Norris, whose narrow shoulders heaved with suppressed rage.

"If Henry gets sicker," he said, "it's your fault." Mr. Norris stormed away from us on his skinny bow legs.

Chapter Forty-Two

Dad and I waited without talking. He kept glancing down the hall where Mr. Norris had gone, a frown coming and going.

When we heard Hank chatting with my brothers, Dad and I reentered his room.

Aaron said over the call, "I think I've got the alarm worked out. I'm gonna do a few more tests before I set one up at your house."

"Please ask me first, Aaron." Jeanine sounded tired but not annoyed.

She'd placed her arm across Hank's shoulders, so they'd be close enough to appear onscreen together.

A warm rush welled in my chest.

Seeing Hank and Jeanine so close looked right—their natural position.

I glanced at Dad. A sadness weighed down every muscle in his weary face. Why? He'd accomplished what he'd set out to do—lift Hank from his depression enough to help Amber.

Hank and Jeanine spoke for a few more minutes, and then she swiped off. Hank fell back on the bed, like the conversation had taken his last scraps of strength.

I said, "Any progress with Amber?"

Hank rubbed his forehead. "I ain't sure. I mean, she got all choked up 'cause I ain't disappointed or mad or anything." He looked to Jeanine. "Why would she think that?"

Dad said, "Kids get worried about what their parents think of them. It happens to most kids at some point. No reflection on you or Jeanine."

Hank lowered his hand. "I don't know if I've convinced her she's brave."

Jeanine said, "Let's give her some time to consider what you told her." She kissed him on the cheek. "You were magnificent." She rested her forehead against his.

Dad's sadness seemed heavier—his shoulders slumped.

Relief flooded Hank's face, so intense that it would have been funny, except I knew it was sincere. He kissed Jeanine on the nose.

I was too stupid. Dad was probably sad because Jeanine's support for Hank reminded him of what he'd lost.

October really was a horrible month.

I slipped myself under Dad's right arm and squeezed him around the waist. His arm tightened around me in return.

Jeanine said, "Amber desperately wants to work at The Haunting. I think we can trust her not to put herself in danger again, but, Mal, do you think it's safe? Are you comfortable with Rae continuing to work there?"

The left side of Dad's face bunched, signaling a conflict about how he should answer. "No, I'm not, but I don't have a good reason. It's just me being protective. The game warden walks the property every day and hasn't seen a sign of the bear since Saturday night. I'm sure that's what Amber saw next to the body. Rae and Amber's chances of bumping into the murderer at The Haunting aren't greater than any other place in the county. It's up to you two."

I said, "We're only in the booth or the porta potties by the food trucks. There's always lots of people around. Amber would feel like she's helping y'all with a little extra money."

Hank mumbled, "Me 'n' Jeanine'll talk about it."

Since he appeared ready to drop off, the three of us went into the hall.

Jeanine hugged me and Dad but held onto her younger brother longer. "Thank you so much for coming. I was convinced Amber's problem would make Hank more depressed."

Dad said, "You know him better than anyone. But I know how I'd feel if I couldn't support my family. Contributing somehow would make me feel better." He looked at his shoes. "I'm sorry if I've caused a problem for you with Mr. Norris."

"When he sees Hank is better, he'll get over it." She hugged him again.

~~~~~

Dad and I were hanging our coats in the closet by the stairs when Amber launched out of the bathroom.

"Dad isn't mad at me." She beamed. "He doesn't care that I was a coward at the creek."

"Uncle Hank didn't say that." I hooked my hanger in the closet. "He said you weren't a coward."

"I know, but—well, he's too nice to tell me that." Amber's smile faded. "I thought we weren't telling Dad that I found Lyra's body."

"Change in tactics." Dad looked to the ceiling as if calling for divine strength. "Amber, you have a genius for extracting the wrong lesson from a situation." He bent to her eye level and clipped each word. "You are not a coward. Your dad does not think you're a coward."

"Well ... even if I am, he isn't upset with me at all." Her smile returned.

Sighing, I shut the closet door. At least she wasn't keeping a terrible secret from her dad. That was progress. Sort of.

~~~~~

The next afternoon, my phone pinged with a text.

Chris: Can I meet you at your truck at 4:15?

My heart contracted so strong that I pressed my hand against my sternum. My fingers trembled as I typed.

Me: For sure.

For the next twenty minutes, as I closed the library with Devon, I prayed for the right words. As employee after employee pulled out of the lot at 4, my heart hammered harder and harder, making praying difficult.

A stiff wind blew my hair everywhere I didn't want it to go, while denim blue clouds raced white ones east.

On the dot, Chris's patrol SUV rolled into the empty lot.

Leaving the motor running, Chris stepped out of his vehicle.

I tried to swallow. He wasn't planning on staying long—but he was on patrol. That didn't mean anything.

He took a grocery bag out of the back. "I needed to return these to you." He held out the bag, filled with the plastic containers we'd used for our lunch on Monday.

Monday ... that was only a few years ago.

"I also want to apologize." His black coffee eyes held mine without blinking. "I had no reason to speak so harshly to you."

The pressure in my chest easing, I said, "Thanks. I'm sorry if my invitation—"

"You owe me no apology." Studying the asphalt, Chris said, "I've been thinking ... about us."

"So have I." I let the bag dangle at my side.

"I—I think we want different things in a relationship."

Stinging prickles, like when my foot went to sleep, invaded my face. "Chris, I'm sorry if my invitation put too much pressure on you."

"It didn't. You wanted to share with me something important to you. There's nothing wrong with that." He squinted at the street. "I'm just not the right person for it."

The numbness traveled down my neck, like my blood was leaking away. "Why?" My voice was hollow.

He turned to me, and a muscle twitched in his sharp jaw. "Are you going to faint? You're very pale."

Maybe. So what? "Why aren't you the right person? What's stopping you from going to church with me?"

He smoothed his moustache again and again. "You'll have to take my word for it." He turned to his SUV.

Why was he being so secretive ... so mysterious? It was like talking to a living riddle.

The tingling stopped, and an energy surged through me as if my blood had returned in a raging flood. "Chris, there's a lot more to this than you thinking we're not right for each other. If you disagreed with my faith, you'd tell me, and that'd be it. So it's something else. I'd like to know."

He glanced over his shoulder with a look of—if I hadn't known better, I'd have said "fear." No, more like apprehension. Like when you hear footsteps behind you in the dark and aren't sure if they belong to a friend or foe.

The muscle in his jaw trembled. "We won't work." He slammed into his SUV, backed onto the street, and drove away.

Chapter Forty-Three

As the sun bobbed above the bonfires glowing in the maples and tulip trees, my mind spun and twisted, like a leaf caught in an updraft.

A fight with Chris had sunk me into a hole that seemed bottomless, but breaking up with him had given me so much energy that I felt I could run home faster than I could drive. Why the weird reaction?

I couldn't come up with an answer until I missed the dead-end road.

I backed up and made the turn.

The energy seemed to stem from the fact that, in this case, I wasn't to blame. I hadn't screwed up our relationship. Something else was eating Chris.

If I could encourage him to share it, we still had a hope of being together.

That was where my energy came from. Hope.

I slowed to a crawl on the dead-end road.

The Secret of the Bashful Boyfriend wasn't a mystery I could solve like The Riddle of the Lost Inheritance or The Murder of the Meddling Medium. Hands off was probably the best approach. I had to give Chris time and pray he'd trust me with what he was hiding.

But if he didn't ... the crushing pressure returned to my chest.

I took deep breaths against it, turning onto our drive and taking it up to the garage.

If he kept his secret, then all hope was dead.

Since the family was getting ready to go to a home football game to watch Amber march, I kept the latest development in my relationship with Chris to myself. It was too important, and I was still too uncertain about what it all meant, to announce it when my relatives were running in twelve directions.

As soon as the Marlin County Marching Marauders filed off the field after their half-time show, I left for The Haunting.

At the field across the road from the booth and food trucks, I locked the Rust Bucket, the greasy aroma of fried food drifting to me. Crossing the road, I noticed, half hidden in the shadow of the taco truck, Kyle speaking to Claire.

Business must have picked up since Dani had both me and Claire working.

I stopped on the old, broken-up drive.

Why was Kyle talking to Claire? Were they friends?

They stood in profile to me. Lights from the top of the taco truck highlighted half of Kyle and his fixed grin. The shadows wrapped Claire more thickly, obscuring her expression, but she was clutching herself, focused on the ground.

Was Kyle upsetting Claire? Or was she just uncomfortable talking to a man?

Customers milled around the trucks, moving in and out of glaring light and deep shadows.

Her head down, Claire hurried away from Kyle and almost ran into me.

"Sorry, Rae." She went right past me.

I trotted a few steps to fall in beside her. "Was Kyle bothering you?" She shook her head.

That was a dumb question. I could see she was bothered. "Anything I can do to help?"

She shook her head again, and we entered the ticket booth.

Dani looked up from a tablet she was holding. "Okay. I've added some services." She pointed to the screen. "Mediums can pay for one or two hours of access, starting at 11 p.m. Same for ghost hunters and bigfoot hunters. Or, if those groups only want to set up cameras or whatever kind of equipment they have, it's $25 per setup per day."

Claire and I traded surprised glances.

"What?" Dani turned to the cash box. "Sales are down, and all these loons are begging to conduct their investigations or contacts or whatever they call it here. A killer animal and a murderer don't seem to worry them like it has my typical customers. I turned away a ton of money last Sunday because I didn't expect this interest in contacting Lyra's spirit or tracking down the bigfoot that attacked her body."

Taking money so people could try to contact the spirit of a recently murdered woman seemed beyond exploitative.

"It wasn't a bigfoot," I said. "My cousin saw—"

"You're allowing bigfoot hunters to place cameras now?" Kyle had come up to a ticket window. His grin had vanished, and he glared at Dani from his towering height like the news was a personal insult. "Why didn't you let us do that a few weeks ago?"

"Because my head of security thought news of a bigfoot on the property would scare away customers. Well, now, they're already scared. But the bad publicity attracts you and ghost hunters and mediums. Which turns it into good publicity."

Kyle moved his glare to Claire, then stomped off.

Dani leaned out the window. "You're welcome to buy permission to install your cameras now." She darted outside.

Kyle disappeared into the dark outside the lights shining from the top of the booth.

I said, "Why is he so mad? Is he too broke to pay the price?"

Claire shrugged, her buttery blonde hair falling by her pretty Victorian face.

The customers came in spurts, so Claire had no problem covering for me when I wanted to refill my water bottle at a food truck. I'd just passed between the taco truck and one serving every kind of hotdog when I heard a very disgusted and nasal voice say, "Thanks so much for the advice."

I peered into the darkness behind the trucks.

Dim light revealed Timothy and Alex confronting each other.

I pressed against the hotdog truck.

"You have no reason to remain." Timothy's voice was as dry as ever.

"You should join your group, or security will eject you," said Alex.

"I didn't pay for a tour. A ticket isn't required to enter the food truck area. I wanted to speak to you."

"Why are you so concerned about me? It's the first time in thirty-nine years."

"I don't trust the police here." Timothy dropped his volume, sounding confidential, and I strained my ears. "I understand that the prime suspect is a cousin of the sheriff. What kind of police officer has a relative as a murder suspect?"

I stiffened. Sounded like Timothy had been talking to Chief Simcox.

"Unfortunately," said Alex, "the prime suspect is also my cousin, Father. And your great-nephew. The sheriff asked me not to leave, and he's been perfectly professional with me. If he wasn't, I'd be under arrest right now because of where my phone was found." His voice hardened. "Someone tried to frame me."

"But if the sheriff finds more evidence," said Timothy, "pointing to you—"

"He can't since I didn't kill—" pause "—do you think I killed Ms. Vex?" Alex's question turned hoarse.

"That's ridiculous." Timothy's objection was so weak my brothers could have figured out he was lying. "I'm afraid you'll be unjustly accused."

Alex snarled. "No. You think I did it and want me to leave so I don't embarrass you." Then he laughed, brief and nasty. "I'll be honest, Father. You were right."

I froze by the corner of the truck. Was he about to confess and I didn't have my phone to record it?

"I did suggest to Dani that she hold her Halloween attraction here to keep you from hunting for the treasure." Alex spoke with savage satisfaction. "But not because I wanted to search for it. It doesn't exist. One bad turn deserves another.

"Wh-what do you mean?"

"You showed interest in me for the first time in my life when we worked on the code together. Then, when your paranoia consumed you, you cut me off." Another ugly laugh. "Payback."

"I knew it, I knew it," said Timothy. "You're no good, just like your mother. But I still say leave, if you value your freedom."

Timothy strode past the hotdog truck on its other side.

I peeked out from between the trucks.

As Timothy reappeared in my view, he collided with a hulking man who loomed out of the shadows. Timothy bounced off him, falling onto his butt. The Book, under his arm, hit the ground.

Scooping up The Book, the huge man moved into the light shining through the window of the hotdog truck.

Walter?

My jaw hoped to hit my knees.

"I'm real sorry." Walter let The Book fall open in his enormous hands, glancing at the pages. "Should've watched where I was going."

Timothy struggled to his feet, swinging his satchel to his side. "Yes, you should have."

Walter clunked The Book closed and held it out to the much smaller man.

Timothy grabbed it and resumed his march, heading toward the road.

Walter watched him, then stalked in the direction of the ticket booth.

"Your age is catching up to you, Walter." I jogged up beside him. "Stumbling into people."

Walter stopped. "I thought you was takin' tickets."

"I'm taking a short break." That had grown so long Claire had to wonder what had happened to me. "Wait for me while I get some water."

I refilled my bottle at the taco truck and then walked with Walter toward the booth.

When we were alone on the drive that separated the admission line from the food truck area, I whispered, "Was it the second book? Did you see what you wanted?"

He gave a satisfied growl. "That note said 'above my pride.' And it was sittin' beside somethin' called 'The Pur-loined Letter.' That mean anything to you?"

"No. But it gives me a place to start."

Walter chuckled deep in his throat and turned down the drive toward the road.

Chapter Forty-Four

I apologized to Claire when I finally returned to the booth.

I was grateful to Walter. His information could occupy my mind instead of Chris. I wanted to leave that minute and read "The Purloined Letter"—I was pretty sure we had a book containing some of Poe's short stories sitting on the bookshelves beside the fireplace. With the customers trickling in, I had time to mull over what I'd observed.

Did Timothy actually think his son was guilty of murder? Or was his only concern that Alex would be unjustly accused? Or was the whole protective dad bit a charade?

Walter's act proved Lyra could have gotten the first book away from Timothy. But she couldn't have switched books without an accomplice. Walter had only a minute with The Book. And Lyra still needed to fake a tear in the back of the fake book that matched the real one.

The more I replayed the scene, the more surprised I was at how calm Timothy remained. Walter had touched his precious second clue. But maybe Timothy was wise enough to realize that he couldn't intimidate a man who was a foot taller than he was in the same way he had a first grader.

When I got home after midnight, I tiptoed past Dad, who snored gently on the couch, and scanned the shelves that flanked the empty fireplace. On a bottom shelf, I found the book of short stories by Poe and flipped to the table of contents. It contained "The Purloined Letter."

I dropped into the recliner.

Reading was a chore. The story was more interesting than "The Gold Bug," and it turned out to be a mystery, instead of a horror story. Sleepiness made the words smear into each other, and my conversation with Chris blew my concentration again and again, like a giant fish bursting through the surface of calm waters.

But I struggled to the end, and leaning back my head, groaned inside.

If the second clue was genuine, my treasure hunt was over. A reasonable assumption was that the short story pointed to the general location of the next clue or treasure in the same way that "Eldorado" had pointed to Marlin County as the general location of the first one.

"The Purloined Letter" was set entirely in Paris, France.

~~~~~

In the morning, as I mixed pancake batter, I told Dad the latest
~~~~~

developments at The Haunting as he sat on a stool at the bar.

Rubbing his crewcut, Dad yawned. "I should've known Walter would pull something like that. He's determined to get the inheritance for Aunt Lily."

"The clue being in Paris makes it more likely Lyra didn't fake it. Cyrus owned an apartment there. I assume that's how he met Old Mr. Morley's mother."

"But if you knew about the Paris apartment, Lyra could have discovered that fact and chosen that short story to give her fake clue some authenticity." Dad sighed, lifting his mug of coffee. "Although I don't see how she could have faked it." He took a sip, watching me as I cracked an egg on the rim of the mixing bowl. "Do you mind if I ask you how're you doing since your fight with Chris?"

"Uh—well ..." I hit the second egg on the rim too hard and slivers of shell sprinkled into the batter.

"I guess not."

I pinched out the pieces of shell. "No. With the boys down at the barn, now's a good time. I—I—it's kinda complicated."

I explained what had happened yesterday and what conclusions I'd drawn from it. "Should I just wait and see if Chris will tell me what his real issue is?"

"I don't think you have any other choice." Dad was quiet. "Even if he does, that doesn't guarantee he'll want to get back together with you. Or that you should be together."

"True." I clenched my teeth against the pain in my chest. A thought burst through. "But I want to help him with whatever's bothering him. If he's got a problem with his faith, helping him with that is ..." I shoved it into the air, though it hurt "... way, way more important than whether we end up together."

Dad's expression turned kind. "Then pray for patience and wait. Let him come to you." Then he cleared his throat, sitting up. "Since life is calmer, at least this morning, will you look at the materials I collected on those community colleges?"

My shoulders drooped. "Dad, you have to accept that I'm not made for college. If it's a mistake, I'll have to live with it."

"Kiddo, I don't want you to."

Micah banged in the back door. "It's getting warm, Dad. Can we go fishing today?"

Dad gave me a long look, then drained his mug. "We'll have to go now. The weather's supposed to be good for the next few days, so that means harvesting."

For the next four days, soybeans dominated our lives. Cutting them down, driving them, depositing them into grain bins. Carrie and I helped from the time the dew dried until we were too exhausted to drive straight. I used two vacation days, so I could keep harvesting after the weekend was over. Amber and Coral missed school, and Dad and Gram helped when they could. Jeanine finally felt confident enough in Hank's recovery to leave him for a few days and drive the second combine.

As hard as I worked, Chris never left my mind. I ran through a million scenarios of what he was hiding. And they could all be wrong. If Chris didn't haunt my thoughts, I analyzed the two clues and traded ideas with Amber, but we didn't have time to make any real progress.

Neither had Dad's investigation. I gave him the names of a couple of mediums who bought access to the property at The Haunting, hoping they might know more of Lyra's backstory. One didn't know her, and the other said most of the psychic community in Ohio considered her a fraud.

Still no motive for Lyra's murder except a jealous ex-boyfriend. And no sign of Jack. His disappearance made him look more guilty by the day.

The rain returned on Wednesday, halting the harvest. Not bad timing because it freed Jeanine and Mr. Norris to be in Columbus for another surgery. But the rain lingered, like a bad cold, into Saturday when Hank was transferred to a nursing home and rehab facility in Zanesville.

"Hank's so relieved that this last surgery went so well, and he can be closer to home now." Jeanine carried her dishes into the kitchen after a late supper with Amber and Coral at our house on Saturday. "He worried about all the driving the family had to do." She looked out the windows behind the dinner table as rain deepened all the colors of the fields and woods. "He's worried about this rain too."

I scrubbed a big pot in the kitchen sink. "Do you think Uncle Hank will feel like visitors tomorrow?"

"Probably. He was just exhausted today from riding in the ambulance and getting settled in his room. And from the last surgery." A puff of breath ruffled her bangs. "He's just exhausted. Period."

Amber set her dishes in the dishwasher and picked up a dish cloth. "He's also bummed he's missing trick or treat."

"But y'all don't get trick-or-treaters way out here." I glanced up from my work. "Oh, do you come into Wellesville and have kids trick or treat from your car?"

I'd noticed last year a lot of people handing out candy from their vehicles as they lined Main Street. Devon explained that many people who lived too far out in the country for kids to walk to their homes came into Wellesville to take part in trick or treat. Some people showed serious enthusiasm, decorating the back of their SUVs or trucks, wearing costumes, or providing games for the kids to play.

Aaron said, "We could trick or treat Uncle Hank." Wearing an old lab coat that was part of his scientist costume, he stood in front of Gram.

Leaning forward from her seat on the couch, Gram rolled up a sleeve of the coat. "I'm sure we could call other people, like Jason Carlisle, and ask if they'd come to the rehab place to trick or treat Hank. Jeanine, you'd have to clear it with the director or whoever runs the place, though."

"Since it's also a nursing home," said Jeanine, "they might already have arranged for a group of kids to trick or treat the residents."

"You know." Dad wandered into the kitchen with Micah on his back. "We could ask a lot of people to come and organize them in shifts, so Hank doesn't get worn out. Rae, do you think Devon could pull it together on such short notice?"

I handed Amber the pot to dry. "I'm sure she'd like to try."

The landline rang, and I picked it up.

It was Claire. Dani had asked her to work at The Haunting tonight, but a waitress had called off at the lodge restaurant and Claire wanted to cover her shift. Nora had quit when Lyra's body was found, so Amber was the only ticket taker left. Could Amber fill in for her?

I relayed the question to my aunt..

Amber set aside her towel, clasped her hands together, and put on a pleading expression.

Tensing, Jeanine pulled away from the bar she'd been leaning against, her posture telling me this was the last thing she wanted to decide. She looked to Dad. "Mal, do you still think it's okay?"

The left side of Dad's face contracted. "I don't like it, but I don't have any facts to back up my concern."

Jeanine took hold of Amber's hands. "Do you swear you will only do your job? You'll either be in the booth or at the restrooms."

Amber over-nodded, her eyes wide. "I swear. I won't let you and Dad down."

"I know you won't." Jeanine swallowed. "Rae, tell Claire Amber can fill in for her."

Amber threw her arms around her mom, who gave the embrace a feeble pat.

Chapter Forty-Five

When Amber and I reached the ticket booth, Dani whirled around to us from plugging in a charge cord. "Did one of you return my book?"

"It's back?" I swung my backpack off my shoulder and hit the little table. "When did that happen?"

"About a half hour ago. Somebody put it on the steps of my trailer. I guess since Lyra found the second clue, the thief didn't need it anymore. Nice of them to return it."

I stared at my backpack hanging on my hand. "Dani, could I look at the back page?"

She pushed up her black glasses. "Why?"

"I want to see if it's there."

Amber pressed a side button on a tablet. "You think the page for the second note came from Dani's book? But whoever stole it wouldn't return it if that was true."

"Maybe somebody other than the thief brought it back."

We'd seen Jesse walking ahead of us as we left the parking lot. He might have returned it to protect Jack, if Jack had stolen it, and followed the Code of the Malinowskis by not involving the cops.

Dani bustled out the door. "Come on."

I waited outside her trailer while Dani retrieved The Book. Flipping to the back, I saw the last page was intact.

Thanking her, I gave her The Book and had started down the hill when I saw the security guy Gibbs set up a ladder at the entrance of the trail that wound through the woods to all the gory scenes.

"Need any help?" I trotted over to him as a mist wetted my face.

He shrugged. "You can hold the ladder for me. Carrie wanted me to check the camera here. We aren't receiving a signal on the monitor in the security trailer."

I steadied the ladder as he climbed up to a small sphere with one side flattened to accommodate the lens.

As he examined the wire running from the back of the sphere, a memory from two weeks ago poked me. "Where do you have trail cams set up?"

Gibbs wiggled a wire. "You mean like the kind hunters use with a motion sensor? We don't use those. We need live feeds."

Jack carried one when he threatened Alex the night Lyra's body was discovered. A scene must have required it.

Gibbs finished a few minutes later, climbed down, and carried the ladder away while I stared into the dark woods that were turning black.

I felt uncomfortable, like a pebble, a very tiny pebble, was stuck under my big toe in my tennis shoe.

Why did the fact that security didn't use trail cams bother me?

My phone said I still had ten minutes until opening. I jogged down the trail and asked actors and crew at three different scenes if a trail cam was part of their staging. All of them said no.

At The Pit and the Pendulum, Jesse dabbed fake blood on the blade of the pendulum.

"Jesse," I said, "do you use a trail cam for your scene here?"

"Trail cam?" He brushed damp bangs from his forehead. "No. Why would we have one of those?"

"Do you know of a scene that uses one? Jack had a trail cam when he harassed Alex."

Jesse opened the battery compartment of the little remote he held. "I—I guess one of them does. That—that has to be the reason Jack had one." He took out a battery, studying it in the low light that illuminated the scene, as if fascinated to learn whether it was double or triple A.

I was making Jesse uncomfortable. Why?

"Oh—uh—Jesse, isn't it?" Alex walked out of the dark and into the filtered spotlights. "I never thanked you for trying to keep your brother from—well, I think he was prepared to beat me up."

"Maybe not." Jesse snapped a battery into its compartment. "I mean, if you yelled, ten people would've come running."

"Still, you attempted to diffuse the situation." He held out a bronzed hand. "I'm sorry I didn't thank you earlier."

Jesse shook it with energy. "No problem. Lot's been going on around here."

Alex's thin face clouded. "That's an understatement." He drew a finger across his upper lip. "You don't seem afraid of me like some of the staff."

"They're scared of you?" Jesse blinked twice. "How come?"

I said, "Because a deputy found Alex's phone near where the bear left Lyra's body."

"Not near at all," said Alex. "From what I understand, the officer found it halfway down that stream."

Jesse twisted his mouth to one side. "You didn't get riled up when Jack went after you. You don't act like the guys I know who hurt women."

Alex's head strained forward. "Who do you know that hurts—oh, your sister, Claire. She had abusive boyfriends."

Jesse's posture wilted as he pressed shut the lid for the battery compartment.

Alex waited a moment, then moved back down the trail.

I said, "Jesse, if you know anything that might help Dad with his investigation, please tell him. You don't have to cover for Jack, even if Walter wants you to."

An actor, covered in fake blood, stepped into the scene, and Jesse turned his back on me, helping him into the pit.

The mist had grown to a drizzle by the time I returned to the ticket booth. My first customers, a couple dressed in black and green camo, told me they were members of a bigfoot association and wanted to install trail cams on the property.

Although I expected Dani to pounce on me out of the dark, I had to tell them the game warden had found bear prints at the place where my cousin found the body. But they still wanted to buy access because of all the "reports" of bigfoot activity in the county.

As the drizzle gathered strength, drumming on the metal roof like it was practicing a song for a half-time show, the trail cam and Jack circled around each other in my mind.

The flow of customers dwindled in direct opposition to the flow of rain.

When we had a break, I picked up the walkie-talkie, and after a minute, Dani answered. "What's wrong?"

"Nothing. Had a quick question. Do you use a trail cam — a camera with a motion sensor to turn it on — for any reason?"

"I don't. We have a bunch placed in the woods now by bigfoot hunters. If you find one, don't touch it."

"For sure." I clicked off and turned to Amber, raising my voice over the beat above us as tingles scattered down from my scalp. "I think I've got a clue, but I need to talk it out."

"A clue about the murder?" Amber's voice became more breathless than usual.

"I don't know." I explained I'd seen Jack with a trail cam two weeks ago. "There's no reason for him to've been carrying one. Security doesn't use it. None of the scenes use it. But Kyle's hung around The Haunting since the opening night. What if he snuck a camera onto the property and Jack found it? He'd think it was fine to steal it."

"Sounds like classic Jack," said Amber.

"And I think Kyle knows Jack stole it. Last weekend, I saw Kyle talking to Claire. Since he can't talk to Jack, he might approach relatives to pass on the message that he wants his camera back. Claire looked very uncomfortable while Kyle talked to her." I held up a palm. "But she looks uncomfortable talking to any guy. Kyle could've just been flirting with her." Tugging on my earlobe, I looked to my damp tennis shoes. "Or Kyle might want his camera because it has proof that he killed Lyra."

"Or Jack took the camera because it shows he killed Lyra."

"Or Jack stole the camera to pawn it, found a photo with the murderer, and is blackmailing him or her."

"And that's why he's staying out of sight?" said Amber. "So the murderer won't get him?"

"Possibly." I looked into the pouring rain and the night. "But any way you figure it, a camera might have been running the night of the murder. It's gone, and so is Jack. If Dad can recover the camera, he'll want to look at the card."

Amber beamed at me. "Brilliant." Her beam fizzled. "If Jack's the killer, he'd get rid of the camera card."

"Dad still needs to know." I removed my phone from my backpack. "Dani said she can get a signal somewhere up by the house. I'm going to call Dad. Don't leave the booth."

Amber slumped against a metal wall. "I told you I'm no hero, and I promised Mom that I'd only be in the booth or the porta potties."

It took about two minutes for the rain to soak me as I ran up the hill to the house. Then I got more drenched as I wandered around the tents and trailers, holding my phone out to snag a signal. Beside the tent next to the hole where the second clue was found, I picked up two bars, swiped the number for our landline, and told Gram I had to talk to Dad.

"He's not here right now. He went out on a call with Chris.[1] A vacation home's been broken into, and the man renting it is very touchy. Mal thought he should go with Chris to smooth any ruffled feathers."

"I'll call back in an hour."

I swiped off and started to run back to the booth when the sign "SECURITY" on a gray trailer caught my eye. I veered toward it and knocked on the door. Carrie told me to come in.

"Good grief, Rae. You look like a drowned rat." Alone, my aunt swiveled in a chair beside a row of monitors.

Shaking off shivers, I wriggled out of my soaked jean jacket. "I've got a theory about the murder." I reported what I'd noticed, and what it might mean.

Carrie whistled. "Nice job, Sherlock. You're right. If a camera was activated that night, Mal needs to view the card. Only Amber knows this, right?"

"Yes."

"Could anyone have overheard you when you two were talking in

---

[1] If you want to read about Dad and Chris's call, check out the short story "Bovine" in the book *Ohio Trail Mix: Adventures and Inspiration Along the Ohio Literary Trail*

the ticket booth?"

My eyes stretched open. "No, I don't think so. There weren't any customers. But it was raining pretty hard. Someone could've eavesdropped, and we wouldn't have noticed.

She pulled her hand over the top of her head. "I'm probably being overly cautious, but ... I'll hang out at the booth with you and Amber until you go home. But I have to wait until Gibbs gets back from the john." She lifted her security windbreaker from another swivel chair. "Wear this. It should warm you up a little."

A few minutes later, Carrie and I headed down the hill, and I spent an uncomfortable hour and a half in wet clothes with the windbreaker only helping me feel slightly less than freezing. Dani told Amber and me to go home at midnight. I'd called at 11, but Dad had still been out.

I dropped Amber off at her house. Life was getting back to normal. Jeanine was now back home since Hank was in Zanesville, so my cousins didn't have to spend nights at our house anymore. When Amber got out, she gazed over the small blue ranch house and released a contented sigh.

I couldn't use the outside door to my bedroom because of Aaron's latest prototype of a bear alarm. I went through the garage to reach the screened porch. Besides, there was no point using my private door when I knew Dad would be waiting up since Gram must have told him I'd called twice.

There he was, on the couch, reading a magazine.

He flipped a page and looked up. "Rae, Ma said—how'd you get soaked?"

"Trying to get ahold of you. I'll be back in a minute."

After I'd changed out of my wet clothes and bundled myself in my winter bathrobe, I returned to the living room and sat on the end of the couch by the fire.

Dad took notes as I explained the theory Amber and I had worked out. When I finished, he said. "I'll contact Houston in the morning, since it's his case, and see how he wants to handle it." He grinned at me. "Good work, kiddo. It's unlikely the card has any evidence connected to the murder. The property's huge. If Jack's innocent of Lyra's death and not engaged in blackmail, he has no reason not to tell us how he acquired the camera and where it is now. Houston and I can tell Walter and Aunt Lily and Jesse to pass that along to Jack. It's likely at least one of them has been in contact with him."

The phone rang.

We both jumped, and then Dad shook his head. "It can't be about Hank anymore."

I smiled. He'd read my mind.

The caller was a farmer, who'd rather talk to the sheriff than bother

Dispatch. He'd fired at something near his chicken coop but didn't know if it was a bear or a man. Dad said he'd tell Dispatch to send an officer over.

As soon as my head touched my pillow, I dropped into a heavy sleep. When deafening music blared into my bedroom, I didn't even twitch, only peeking from beneath lead-lined lids.

Something had triggered Aaron's bear alarm.

Heaving myself out of bed, I fell to my knees.

"It worked!" Aaron yelled from somewhere in the house. "It worked!"

"Aaron, don't go outside." That was Gram.

I stumbled to my outside door. Opening it, I saw the floodlight at the entrance to the breezeway shining over the garage, half of the porch, and onto the hill that rolled down to the alpaca pastures.

Aaron ran to the edge of the porch, and Gram, pulling on her teal bathrobe, came up behind him.

Pointing into the yard, he said, "She's not a bear." Aaron sounded equal parts puzzled and disappointed.

Shielding her eyes from the searing light, Claire trembled from head to foot.

Chapter Forty-Six

"Claire?" Gram hurried off the porch. "What's wrong?"

My cousin turned her back to the light.

Gram put her arm around Claire's shoulders. Their voices were murmurs beneath the blast of music from the old phone.

"Aaron," I said, hugging myself, "turn that stupid phone off."

My brother dashed off the porch as Dad stepped onto it. "What's going on?"

The music quit blaring, leaving only the sound of pattering rain on leaves.

Pulling Claire a little as she walked to the porch, Gram said, "Mal, Claire has something she wants to tell you about Jack."

Although Claire had worn a windbreaker, she was drenched to the skin. After she'd dried off and borrowed a pair of my pajamas and bathrobe, she took a seat at the dinner table where Dad waited with an open notepad.

My brothers and I surrounded the table.

"If you wanted to talk to Dad," said Aaron, "why didn't you just call him?"

"P-p-people can check your phone if they really want to," Claire whispered, her green eyes wide and darting.

Had Claire experienced that with her boyfriends? Sympathy welled in me, and I pulled out a chair and sat beside her.

"Where'd you park your car?" said Dad.

"I didn't. I walked."

As my eyebrows rose, Gram stopped in mid-stride, carrying a steaming cup of tea, and Dad said, his voice going high with surprise, "From your house?"

A quick nod. "What time is it?" she said.

"About 4."

"Can someone drop me off close to my house?" She took the mug from Gram. "I don't think anyone'll be up before 5:30."

"I can. Okay, boys, Rae." Dad swept us with a glance. "Back to bed. Claire and I need to talk."

Whines came from Aaron and Micah, while Rusty's face pinched with annoyance.

I started to leave my seat, but Claire dropped her hand over mine.

"Can Rae stay, Mal?"

A sad smile softened Dad's expression. "If she makes you more comfortable, of course."

Claire released a long breath and took a sip of tea.

As I resumed my seat, a few tears jockeyed for release. Claire had known Dad her whole life, but because he was a man, he made her nervous.

"C'mon, boys." Gram herded my brothers away from the table.

Aaron spun around and dashed back to us. "Claire, since you set off my bear alarm, and I can't talk to a bear that could do that, can you rate my alarm? On a scale of one to ten, and ten being you were so scared you thought you'd die, how much did my alarm scare you?"

Claire broke into a fond smile, not at all timid. "Nine. I was so scared, I tried to run away."

Aaron jotted down the info on a sticky note he got from the bar. "Thanks."

Once we heard both bedroom doors shut, Dad said, "Claire, I'm glad you didn't run away. Rae, I expect you to keep anything you hear to yourself. I know you don't want to harm the investigation."

Claire said, "Do you mean the murder investigation? I don't think this has anything to do with that."

Dad stared. "Then why did you come sneaking here in the middle of the night?"

"I don't want Walter to know I talked to you. Mama and Jesse wouldn't never go along with this. But somebody's gotta stop that whacko. Mama thinks Walter could scare him into leaving us alone, but I think only a cop can do that. I want him stopped. Permanently." Heat simmered in her words, the first sign of anger I'd ever noticed in my cousin.

Dad lifted his pen. "Start at the beginning and take your time. I'll get you home before 5:30."

Bit by bit, her soft voice gaining confidence, Claire told us her story.

Two days after Amber found Lyra's body, Kyle Garrison stopped by the restaurant at the lodge and asked Claire to give Jack a message. Claire told him she had no idea how to contact her half-brother since he wasn't answering his phone. Kyle just grinned and said Jack had something of his that he wanted back.

Kyle appeared every night she worked at The Haunting or the lodge with the same message. He approached Jesse too, even following him to the warehouse in Lancaster where Jesse had his full-time job.

"I asked Jesse if he knew what Kyle was talking about," Claire said. "Jesse said no, but he wouldn't look at me, so I was pretty sure he was hiding something." Her round face hardened, as if steel had slipped under her pearly pale complexion. "Then after Kyle talked to Oak today, I made Jesse tell me what's going on."

Dad glanced up from his notes.

I shifted to the edge of my chair. "Kyle talked to Oak? Your son's only six. He couldn't know anything."

Claire said, "When I got home from the lodge this evening, Mama said Kyle had been hanging around our road most of the afternoon. When Oak went outside to play, Kyle came into our yard and started talking to him. Mama came out of the house and asked him what he wanted. Kyle said I knew what he wanted and said I had a real nice little boy." Her knuckles turned white on the handle of her mug. "Kyle hadn't come to the house before. He can creep me out all he wants, but he ain't doing that to my kids." Her gaze met Dad's, blazing. "So I figured you could stop him, Mal, especially after I found out what Jesse's been hiding."

"What's that?"

Claire explained Jack had been texting or calling Jesse and Walter since he left the county the night Lyra's body was discovered, insisting he hadn't killed her. Walter told Jack if he was innocent of the murder, he should just lie low until the real killer was caught.

Dad made a low growl. "Did Jack tell Jesse what he took of Kyle's?"

Claire nodded, then took a long sip of tea.

At The Haunting, opening weekend, Jack had heard Dani refuse Kyle's request to set up his trail cams. So Jack offered to sneak them onto the property for a hundred bucks. Kyle agreed. After a week, Jack was supposed to bring the photo cards to Kyle, who would give him new ones to install.

Claire said, "But then Kyle got all cozy with Lyra and made Jack look stupid that night Lyra did her — her thing. So Jack decided to get back at Kyle and steal his cameras. There were three. Jack was gonna pawn them and then tell Kyle that Carrie found them and he couldn't get them back."

Dad said, "Did he pawn them?"

"Yeah. The night he left Jesse and me, he drove straight to Columbus and pawned them. He was at a bar there when he heard about Lyra getting killed. He knew you'd suspect him, so he hid out."

Dad flipped through his notes, then looked to Claire. "Do you think Jack's innocent of the murder?"

Claire stared at him, like his question contained foreign words. "You want my opinion? How come?"

"You've known Jack his whole life, and you're observant."

A pleased blush washed over her cheeks. "Okay." She took a deep breath. "I could be wrong, but I don't think Jack did it. He wouldn't have the guts to trick Lyra into going to that lonely spot and killing her. He'd be too scared he'd get caught. If he was guilty, he wouldn't try to wait you out, either. He'd call Jesse and ask him to give him all the money he could get so he could escape."

She leaned toward Dad. "Mal, can you talk to this Kyle guy? I know he's not breaking the law, talking to me or Oak. Mama said he left the property as soon as she asked him to. But if he knew my first half-cousin is the sheriff, maybe he'd forget about his cameras."

Sitting back in his rail chair, Dad said, "You don't see the significance of the cameras, do you? Apparently Jack and Jesse don't either. And they must not've told Walter about them because if he knew about the cameras, Walter would know their importance and want Jack to produce them."

Claire looked from me to Dad. "What're you talking about?"

Dad said, "Rae, tell her what you figured out."

So I explained the theory I'd worked out tonight—last night— because I remembered seeing Jack with a trail cam.

Claire listened with complete concentration, her eyes slits as she watched me. When I finished, she gave me an approving nod. "Walter said you were smart."

That warmed me, although I wasn't sure why. Did I want the good opinion of a mean, violent-tempered old man? Even when he was my great-grandfather?

I said, "If Kyle wants his cameras back so badly, he could be the killer. Maybe he knows it shows him killing Lyra."

"Or he's a guy who just wants his property back," Dad said. "Garrison's behavior fits either scenario."

"Kyle was seriously ticked when he heard Dani's allowing cameras at The Haunting." I smothered a yawn. "It's the only time I've seen him lose his grin. Those three cameras must be the only ones he owns."

Dad tapped his notes. "I'll have to tell Walter about the cameras and that their cards could prove Jack's innocence."

Claire paled to sheet white. "You can't tell Walter what I've told you."

"Of course not." His voice grew strong. "I'll tell him how Rae figured it out. I don't need to bring up how you filled in the details or convinced me Jack didn't kill Lyra. Once Jack knows the cards could clear him, I think he'll give them to me, as long as the pawn shop owner hasn't done something to them." He dropped his volume. "Claire, I'll tell my boys not to mention your trip here, but I can't guarantee anything. I'll keep them away from Walter until this mess is cleared up."

Claire sighed. "That's the best you can do with kids." She wiped a drip of tea from the side of the mug. "What about Kyle?"

"Well, I don't want him to know that I know about the cameras in case he's the killer. You and your kids should stay in your house tomorrow—this morning—until you and Jesse leave for The Haunting. I'll meet you there, and you and I will put on a little performance for Mr.

Garrison."

Claire sagged back in her chair, releasing a long breath.

A thought popped up in my mind. "Claire, did you return Dani's book? Or Jesse?"

"Jesse did. He told me that tonight. Jack stole it so he could find the treasure. He asked Jesse to help him with the clues. Since Jack's gone, Jesse snuck it back to Dani." She looked to Dad. "What kind of performance, Mal?"

Getting to his feet, Dad broke into a fierce grin. "I can explain while I drive you home."

"Your clothes should be dry." I pushed back my chair.

Claire fixated on her hands curling into fists on the table.

Dad said, "Rae will be happy to come with us."

She released her fingers. "That'd be real nice."

"Glad to help," I said, a stab of sadness jabbing my chest.

With a small smile, Dad patted our cousin on the shoulder and headed to the coat closet.

Chapter Forty-Seven

We dropped Claire off on a road that ran behind the woods leading to her backyard. Later in the morning, Dad left for Walter's, then met us at church. He wouldn't discuss what happened, but his grim, flushed face told me something hadn't gone well.

Back home, I went with Dad to his bedroom.

Closing the door, he said, "All we can do now is wait. When I told Walter about the cameras, he cussed Jack so strong I'm sure Jack could feel it from wherever he's hiding. If it was up to Walter, I'd have those camera cards today. But he has to persuade Jack to bring them to me. I told Walter that I'd ask Post — he's the county prosecutor — not to bring charges against Jack for setting up the cameras and stealing them. Walter said Jack may think I'm trying to trick him so I can arrest him for Lyra's murder. But of course, Walter doesn't know what Jack's thinking because he hasn't talked to him in two weeks." Dad ended in a snarl. "I hate this charade. Walter knows full well I know he's helping Jack. But I can't admit I know without dragging in Claire."

Dad, Gram, Carrie, the boys, and I ate a hurried lunch so we could visit Hank at the rehab center. My brothers crowded him, like their favorite YouTuber. He seemed glad to see us, a faint smile ghosting by now and then. We didn't stay long so he could rest for trick-or-treat tomorrow evening. I maneuvered Amber into the hall and told her about Dad's conversation with Walter. I kept Claire's visit to myself. Although Claire liked Amber, I should honor her wish to limit who knew about her early morning hike.

When we got home, I puzzled over the poem and the other riddle — the one I'd been dating — and got nowhere, a location I was spending way too much time in.

I couldn't wait to get back to The Haunting.

~~~~~

People must have thought it was safe to enjoy fabricated horrors since nothing dangerous had occurred in two weeks. The parking field was much fuller as I pulled the Rust Bucket into a spot.

Dad parked the Beast beside me, and we headed to the booth. A blank layer of smooth platinum clouds, shading to black, hid the sunset.

Claire and Dani were setting up the equipment.

Dani cocked her head, warbler-like. "What are you doing here,
~~~~~

Sheriff? If you have to arrest somebody, don't do it here."

"Don't worry. I've just returned to the scene of the crime."

"Oh." Dani handed me a tablet. "I thought criminals were the ones who did that."

"Cops do, too. Girls, I'll be back." He moseyed out of the booth.

"You can both work tomorrow, can't you?" said Dani. "Your friend or sister or whoever she is—Amber—said she can work. Online sales have been building all week. I guess a murder can't keep the dedicated Halloween enthusiasts away on Halloween night." Her eyes glittered behind her glasses. "You should be here at 7:30."

Claire and I had barely gotten our agreement off our tongues when Dani flew out the door. It banged against the metal wall, and I reached for the handle.

Dani dodged in time to prevent from colliding with Alex.

"What are you doing here?" she said. "I told you last night that you didn't have to come back."

"Have you been talking to my father? You and he are determined to keep me away."

"Look, Alex." Dani patted his arm. "We're on track to make a choice profit tomorrow night. You wouldn't want to scare off customers because you make them nervous."

"I shouldn't make them any more nervous than you." Alex's nasal voice turned nasty. "You're an heir, you're interested in finding the treasure, and you had unrestricted access to my phone when it was charging in your trailer."

Dani's arms went stiff at her sides. "The cops didn't take me in for questioning, did they? If the sheriff ..." She angled at the waist to look around Alex.

I followed her gaze.

Dad strode toward the open door of the booth.

Alex and Dani separated, vanishing into the dark.

Dad filled the doorway. "Garrison's here."

"I know." Claire twisted her fingers together. "I saw him. Down by the road."

"You can do this, Claire. For your kids." Dad's voice softened. "I'll be watching the whole time, and as soon as he speaks to you, I'll be right there."

She caught a short breath, unknotting her fingers, and nodded in a jerk.

Dad said, "Wait two or three minutes after I leave and then go to the taco truck."

I timed three minutes on my phone, and then Claire shuffled outside. The plan was for Claire to hang around the line of customers at a food truck until Kyle approached her, but Claire hadn't even made it to the drive that lay between the booth and the food truck area when Kyle's gangly figure ambled up to her.

Despite waiting on some sort of ghoul and her date, I shifted most of my attention to the conversation to my left.

"Hey, Claire." I could hear Kyle speaking through his irritating grin. "Any word from Jack?"

I gave the ghoul her receipt, not catching Claire's response.

Kyle said, "Met your little boy yesterday. Cute kid. And real —"

"Claire." Dad's voice boomed over the chattering customers lined up at the booth. "Good to see you. Aunt Lily said you'd be working tonight."

I scanned a phone, then leaned out my window.

With an arm around Claire's shoulders, Dad walked with her toward the booth, Kyle in step beside them.

"Yeah, Claire's my cousin." Dad used a breezy tone. "I feel it's my job to look out for her and her kids. Her dad's dead, and she's a single mom."

Garrison said something with "Jesse" in it.

"Oh, you know Jesse? Yeah, I look out for him since his dad's dead too. We Malinowskis —" the breeze died in his voice " — know how to stick together."

Claire ducked into the booth, breathing fast, but mischief lit her pale eyes, making her look twenty-three for once.

Dad said, "Have you remembered anything that might help my investigation of Lyra's murder?"

"I only knew the woman a week, Sheriff." Kyle saluted Dad, touching the brim of his baseball cap, and turned toward the food trucks.

Dad reentered the booth, but several minutes passed before he could speak to Claire and me because of a fresh influx of customers.

"Unless he's a fool," said Dad when the flow of people broke off, "Garrison should leave your family alone, Claire."

"He could be a fool." Claire rested tight fists on the sill of the ticket window.

"I can stay longer, if you like. Up by the old home. I'll have a good view of the booth. If I see Garrison moving this way, I'll come down."

Her head lifting until her neck lost its usual arch, Claire glanced over her shoulder. "Thanks, Mal." She smiled so strong that dimples I'd never seen before appeared.

Dad winked at her and strolled outside.

The performance must have worked because when we left at 1, neither Claire nor I had seen Kyle again.

Chapter Forty-Eight

Halloween began like most days this October: raining.

I yanked on a book stuck in the slot to the drop box, a shower wetting my mass of hair, praying Mr. Norris and Hank weren't growing anxious since we hadn't harvested in almost a week.

"Rae."

My hands froze on the book as Chris approached me from where he'd parked his patrol SUV along Main Street.

"Oh—uh, hey." I tried to form a welcoming smile, but my face muscles had seized up like my hands.

"I heard your uncle has moved to a rehab facility. That means he should be home soon. Correct?"

Chris's deep voice sounded normal, like he hadn't dumped me ten days ago.

"Uh-uh—the doctors are still saying not until Thanksgiving." I took a deep breath. "How are you?"

"Oh, good." He looked at his shoes, smoothing his moustache. "I noticed something about that poem, the one found in Lyra's purse. Although I don't think it means anything."

I came to attention. "What?"

Chris pulled out his phone, and I stepped over to him.

"I noticed that each marked letter is the first one of that letter to occur in the message 'ten steps from door.'

No, his voice was different. It shook slightly.

I peered at his phone, brushing his arm.

He said, "The 't' in 'ten' is the first 't' in the poem. The 'e' is the first one after the 't'. The 'n' is the first one after the 'e'. It's like that throughout the poem. It's as if ..." he scratched the end of his moustache "... Cyrus knew what he wanted to say, found the letters he needed, and then created a code." He lifted his face from his phone, bringing it inches from mine.

Our gazes locked.

"B-b-b—" now my voice shook—from nerves. I swallowed. "But that doesn't make sense. You could never solve it, and I think Cyrus would want the heirs to solve it so they could find whatever nasty surprise he planned."

Some emotion rippled under his carved face. "I thought I should point it out."

"Oh, definitely. We should both think it over and see if anything comes to us." I couldn't move my eyes from his. "Chris, I'd like you to know—"

"I'd better go." He bolted for his SUV. "Got to get back on patrol."

As he pulled away from the curb, I sagged against the stone façade of the library, then inhaled deep to loosen the tightness in my chest.

I need patience now, Father, if I want to help Chris. But You already know that.

I fought my mind all day. It wanted to worry about Chris, while I wanted to focus on his observation about the poem. I confirmed it, studying the photo of the poem on my phone. But if it was the key to unlocking the code, I couldn't see it.

I covered for Devon at the desk later in the afternoon, so she and her girls could leave the library early and get to the rehab center in Zanesville before the first trick-or-treaters arrived. She'd done a fantastic job in twenty-four hours, scheduling two or three families to arrive every twenty minutes for two hours, so Hank would have plenty of time to visit. The kids could also trick or treat the nursing home residents.

When I pulled into the parking lot for the rehab place a little after 5:30, my brothers were playing tag with Liberty and Serenity, their costumes flapping as they ran on a strip of grass between the parking lot and the street. Dad, still in uniform, watched as a monitor.

I waved to him and then approached the broad walk leading to the front doors of the center. With a cast up to the middle of his thigh, Hank sat in a wheelchair with Jeanine, Amber, and Coral beside him in camp chairs. Gram spoke to Mr. Norris, who hung back on the sidewalk lining one wing of the building.

I gave Hank a hug. "You're looking great."

He gripped my arm. "Nice to be outside." The mask of worry lines had faded some from his face, and he rested against the back of the wheelchair.

We couldn't have ordered a better evening. A strong wind had blown away the last remnants of rain, and now brilliant sunlight smiled on the stunning leaves of the half-dressed trees surrounding the facility.

Devon hurried out of the center. "The staff said everybody's ready inside. So the kids can enter as soon as they're done out here."

Dad crossed the lot to Devon, glancing over his shoulder at the five kids chasing each other. "I can't thank you—the whole family can't thank you enough for all the help you've given us."

She punched something on her phone and looked up. "I'm very glad to help."

"Did you get ahold of that therapist?"

Devon smiled up at him. "Yes. I liked her from our phone call, so I've scheduled — "

"It's mine!" Clutching something in both hands, Serenity ran through the parking lot to the entrance, her witch's hat falling off.

Aaron and Micah charged after her.

She leaped into the flower beds that bordered the sidewalk, plunging through some shrubs.

"Uncle Hank gave Micah that candy bar," said Aaron, swishing back the open lab coat of his scientist costume.

Dressed as a cop, Micah pointed his foam dart gun at her. "I'll get my dad to arrest you."

"Mi-cah," Dad said with an eye roll.

"No, you won't." Serenity looked about, then snatched up a rock from under a shrub.

"Serenity Stone!" Devon's shout silenced everyone in view. "If you throw that rock, you will not trick-or-treat in town tonight."

A frown cutting through her chubby cheeks, Serenity glanced between the rock in her hand and her mother. She dropped the rock.

Devon nodded. "Wise choice, Serene."

Micah held out his hand for his candy bar.

Serenity slapped it into his palm and glared at the world.

As Devon rejoined Dad and me, Dad said, "That's an improvement."

Devon shrugged. "I guess Serenity wants to acquire candy more than she wants to inflict damage. But I can only use the trick-or-treat threat once a year."

Inflict damage. The phrase snagged my attention, and I tugged on my ear.

A small, dented white sedan chugged off the road and parked, and Aunt Lily, Claire, and Claire's two kids, Oak and Rose, climbed out of it with Walter.

Walter?

Oak, dressed as a ninja, raced straight for the Norrises as Walter stalked up to Dad.

He shoved his huge hand at him. "Here."

"What's this?" Dad's eyes rounded. "You got Jack's pawn tickets?" He took them. "Where's Jack?"

"Don't know. Found them in my mailbox before we left to come here." Walter's defiant tone seemed to dare Dad to challenge his statement.

Dad said, "I need Jack to go with my officer leading the murder investigation to identify the items and give a statement."

"That ain't gonna happen. Jack's too scared of being arrested. I'm guessin' that. I ain't seen him." Walter headed back to the white sedan.

Suppressing a growl, Dad tramped to the far end of the lot and pulled out his phone.

Carrying her one-year-old daughter Rose, dressed as a teddy bear, Claire asked if she could catch a ride with me to The Haunting after her kids finished trick-or-treating in the nursing home.

"For sure," I said. "I'm driving Amber too."

More families came, including Jason Carlisle and his three kids, and the Norrises chatted and handed out candy. Devon had to act as a traffic cop, moving families inside the center, because everyone wanted to talk to Hank, and Hank seemed to grow more talkative with each new group of people.

Dad strode from the far end of the building. "Never thought you'd be what I'd need, Hank, but I have no choice."

Vivid orange stripes lined the western horizon behind him, and the streetlamps winked on above us.

Hank shifted in his wheelchair, which wasn't easy because of the size of his cast. "What d'you mean?"

A lull had come in the flow of trick-or-treaters. Only my family and Devon's gathered around Hank.

Dad wore a savage grin that startled me. He looked more like Walter than I'd ever thought possible. He explained to Hank about Jack, Kyle and the three trail cams. "Someone has to verify that the pawned cameras were the ones placed at The Haunting. Since Jack's still hiding, I had Kincaid track down Garrison so he can identify them and give permission to check the camera cards. If the pawn shop owner hasn't removed them and lost them.

"I told Garrison I'd ask Post not to prosecute him for trespassing. But Garrison couldn't care less." Dad's voice grew louder as it grew disgusted. "He's been fined for trespassing before. He says the only way he'll help us is if he can interview my brother-in-law about his bigfoot encounter."

Half the family, including me, said, "What?"

Gram said, "Can't you get a warrant?"

Dad gave his head a quick shake. "I'd only need a warrant if Kyle refuses to give me permission to look at the cards. But I can't get one without confirmation that the cameras were running the night of the murder."

Hank leaned forward. "Is this bigfoot hunter the guy Jeanine thought was sneaking around our place?"

Dad nodded. "He's been harassing Claire, Jesse, and Oak, too."

"Oak? He's a little kid." Hank sat up in his wheelchair, his lips set in a tight line. "I'd like to help you and tell that guy where he can take all his bigfoot hunting. But I still don't remember nothing after Coral and me went into the woods."

"I know." Dad dropped those two words like stones in a still pond.

The ripples from those words hit me as the left corner of Hank's mouth shot upward. A grin flowed across his extra-wide mouth, clear to the right corner, forming the ornery grin all of us had missed.

Easing back in his chair, Hank held out his hand. "Give me the phone, Big Guy."

Dad punched in the number. "Kincaid'll pick up."

Mr. Norris left the shadow of the entrance where he'd been standing with Gram. "But, Henry, you ain't got nothing to tell this man."

Smiling with shining eyes, Jeanine left her chair beside Hank and patted Mr. Norris's arm. "Listen."

"Chris? This is Hank Norris." His grin dimmed, and he pressed his thumb and first finger against his eyes. "Hey, thanks again for everything you did for Knight." He lowered his hand. "Mal told me about this Garrison guy. Let me talk to him." The grin returned wider than before. "Hey, Hank Norris here. I'd be happy to give you an interview as long as you help the cops tonight with those cameras. Can you come to the rehab center where I am by ..." he looked to Jeanine "... 1 tomorrow afternoon?"

She nodded.

"No, not later tonight. I'll be too tired. I swear I'll tell you absolutely everything I remember about the accident."

Coral burst into giggles, and Amber shushed her and then drew in her cheeks, as if fighting her own laughter.

"All right." Hank gave Kyle the address. "See you tomorrow."

Dad took his phone and said into it, "Put my deputy on ... Kincaid, drive Garrison to the McDonald's on the west side of Zanesville by the interstate. I'll pick him up and take him to the pawn shop. Houston's meeting us there ... yeah, he was celebrating in Cincinnati."

He swiped off. "Boys, I can't go back to town with you to trick-or-treat. I'm sorry."

My three brothers frowned, but Rusty said, "When you get a break in a case, you have to work."

Dad rubbed Rusty on the black hood he was wearing as part of his costume as a character from his fantasy novel. "Hank, I expect you to give Garrison every detail of your accident."

Hank threw out a hand. "Hey, the man deserves a complete picture. I was gonna give him some background information too." He looked up at Dad, a glint in his eyes I hadn't seen in a month. "I was planning on starting at birth."

The whole family broke up, laughing.

Tears sprang out of nowhere, misting my vision, and a tightening throat cut off my laughter. I hurried to the corner of the building, dodging a new stream of pint-sized superheroes, monsters, and princesses, trying to pull myself together.

In a minute, Dad had his arm around me. "What's wrong?"

"Nothing." I wiped tears from my nose. "That's why I got choked up. I just realized Uncle Hank's going to be okay. If he loses his leg or not, if the harvest is bad or not, he's going to be okay. So our family's going to be okay."

Dad squeezed my shoulders, and I rested in his protective embrace. "God always has what we need. Sometimes, we have to wait and that makes it hard for us to believe, but He always delivers on time."

I stepped away, exhaling. "There's no danger driving Kyle to Columbus, is there? I mean, if he was the murderer, he wouldn't agree to identify the cameras."

"Got that right. If he wouldn't help us, I would have put him under surveillance."

"Walter, may I speak to you?"

The quiet question made Dad and me glance about, but when I saw Mr. Norris, I realized he was talking to Dad.

"Walter, I—uh—I ..." His feet shifting, Mr. Norris twisted the right end of his moustache. "I don't get how you and Henry get along—Amy tried explaining it to me time and again, but I don't get it." He cleared his throat. "I thought you were real out of line at the hospital, but it seems like it helped Henry and ... Knight!" Mr. Norris actually got loud, and he lifted his gaze for the first time to meet Dad's. "I forgot to ...if you hadn't stepped in to hold Knight's head out of the water, I wouldn't have been able to go to the hospital right away."

"Mr. Norris, none of us would have left you with Knight. Rae was ready to take over when I did."

The old man looked at his mud-streaked boots. "Well ... for that and— and what you did ..." more throat clearing " ... right now, which I don't really get either, but—"

Dad stuck out his hand. "You're welcome, Mr. Norris."

He looked up again, his moustache shading a faint smile, then shook Dad's hand. "Thank you, Walter." He ambled back to his family at the entrance as the little kids crowded Hank, Jeanine, Amber, and Coral.

I glanced at my phone. "I'd better head out. It's kind of shocking, Mr. Norris actually approving something we've done."

"Halloween's a time of shocks." Dad watched the older man as he spoke to Gram. "If he ever calls me Mal, I may keel over."

Amber joined me at the Rust Bucket as we waited for Claire to finish trick-or-treating with her kids.

"Oh, Chris told me something he noticed about the poem," I said.

"You talked to Chris today?" Amber's question was eager.

"Just about the poem." I explained his discovery.

Amber fished out her phone and studied the screen. "It must be a coincidence. Like you said, Rae, nobody could solve a code someone invented to fit the clue, instead of the other way around."

Claire kissed her kids by the sedan and then crossed the lot to us. Amber volunteered to endure the hour ride in the cramped back seat. I'd tell her later that proved her courage.

I steered my truck south under a sky that had faded to pumpkin orange. A half-moon rode high above stooped hills.

An unsolvable code someone solved.

My hand wanted to tug on my ear, but I shifted into higher gear and drove into the Halloween twilight.

Chapter Forty-Nine

"Hon, you owe me three dollars." A grouchy zombie frowned at the two bills I gave her.

"Oh. Uh—sorry." I pulled an extra bill from the cash box and handed it to her.

"Anything wrong, Rae?" Amber tore paper wristbands apart.

"I guess I'm distracted." I took a phone from a ... werewolf?... and scanned it.

Since we'd arrived at The Haunting, my mind had bounced between Serenity's violent fit and Chris's observation about the code. Both jumped up and down in my mind, like little kids acting out to get attention.

"Miss," said the werewolf, "you didn't give us our wristbands."

I ripped three apart and gave them to him. "Amber, Claire, could you cover for me for a few minutes? I need some time to clear my head."

Claire's eyes widened in alarm.

The crowds were as thick as the night of the séance.

Amber said, "We'll handle it."

I stepped outside and rested my back against the cool metal wall of the booth.

A constant wave of voices rolled over the field, like an incessant surf. The clear sky sharpened the pricks of starlight.

Why was I so obsessed with Serenity's habit of wanting to damage things when she was mad? What she'd done at the center wasn't anything different from her two fits at the library.

The library.

Tonight, Devon said Serenity wanted to inflict damage, and when she examined Timothy's book after Serenity grabbed it, she said, "It's not damaged."

If that were true ...

I launched off the wall.

... then Lyra's copy of the poem actually was unsolvable.

I stuck my head back in the booth. "I'll be up on the hill, making a call."

I ran up to the line of tents and trailers, then paced in front of them, hoping to catch a couple bars.

Below, the wildly costumed customers milled in and out of harsh spotlights and shadows like heaped leaves stirred by a weak breeze.

Two bars. I swiped Devon's number.

"Oh, hey, Rae," she said. "What's up?"

"This is critically important. Remember when Serenity tried to hit that kid with Old Mr. Morley's book?"

"Of course, I couldn't—"

"You took The Book from Serenity, looked it over, and told Old Mr. Morley 'it's not damaged.'"

"Ye-es. Are you okay? You sound like you've been running."

Ignoring the question, I said, "You opened The Book and looked at the front and back, right?"

"Yeah, I was looking for damage and saw that it wasn't a library book."

I sucked in a breath. "So you saw the last page in The Book?"

"The last few pages, yeah."

"Nothing had been ripped out? No pages missing?"

"Rae." Her tone soured. "If a page had been ripped out, I would have said something and looked for it on the floor."

"That's what I thought. Devon, call one of Dad's deputies—actually, I'll text you Chris's number. Tell him what you know. It's evidence in the murder investigation."

Not much, though. It'd be Devon's word against Timothy's, and anyone but Dad would be more likely to believe Devon had made a mistake than the owner of The Book.

"But how can I have evidence? Wait. Wasn't the second note written on a sheet of paper ripped from the first book? You mean it was the last page? But how can that be?"

"I'll explain later."

I swiped off, texted Chris's number to Devon, and then stared at the horizon above the blackening trees.

Dad needed evidence. The only way to prove the second clue was fake was to find the treasure based on the first clue alone.

I turned almost a full circle at the top of the hill. The higher hills did ring the valley like a crescent, fitting the lines of the poem, "Mountains of the Moon" and "Valley of the Shadow." Cyrus seemed to have more contempt for the people of Marlin County than anyone else, especially after my relatives strung him up near the old church somewhere on his ...

Every nerve stilled, leaving only my mind in motion.

Then I whipped out my phone.

"Yeah?" Walter's basement voice growled in my ear.

"Walter, can you meet me at The Haunting? And bring anything you need for digging."

Long pause. "You think you know where the treasure is?"

I took a deep breath. "For the first time, I've got a serious shot at it."

~~~~~

Walter said it would take him forty-five minutes to collect the equipment we needed and get to The Haunting.

I went back to the ticket booth. When we had a break in customers, I whispered to Claire and Amber they'd have to cover for me when I left with Walter.

Amber said in a squeaking whisper, "I knew you'd figure this out."

"We did. With Chris's help." The left side of my face scrunched up. "I'm sorry you can't go with me, Amber, but Claire can't handle the customers on her own, and I don't think your parents—"

"—would ever trust me again if I did anything but work in the booth." Her face fell. "No, they wouldn't. And I don't want to let them down." She looked up, smiling. "Tonight was the best Dad's been since the accident."

A rush of monsters kept us busy for several minutes.

Then I said, "Claire, if Water and I find something valuable, I'll come get you so you can touch it. But I'm sure Cyrus left nothing except a note saying that he dumped the money and jewels out of a plane or boat or something. But if we find it, I can solve Lyra's murder and prove Jack's innocence."

Amber gasped. "How?"

But more customers made it impossible to explain my conclusions, and it wasn't smart to discuss it in such a public location, anyway.

Walter's battered red truck crept under the light of the temporary streetlamp positioned at the bottom of the drive, stopping and starting for herds of customers crossing the road.

"Gotta go." I grabbed my backpack. "Amber, call Carrie and tell her Walter and I will be at the abandoned church. If Dani has a fit—" I rolled my eyes "—I'll pay for a ticket for Walter."

I ran through huddles and lines of people to the road.

As I opened the door, Walter said, "What's goin' on, Rae?"

I slid onto the bench seat. "Did the church on the Morley property have a cemetery?"

He shifted, and the gears whined. "Yeah. You think the treasure's buried there?"

"It's the easiest place to start. And if we find it, we can prove Jack's innocence."

Walter drove past the parking area and around a bend, then pulled off the road where Carrie had parked her Jeep the night of the séance.

I got out. Using a flashlight Walter brought, I played it over the gap in the trees that the Jeep had sat in front of. "It doesn't look like anyone's used this path in a long time."

Two maples crowded so close together that even a compact car couldn't get through.
~~~~~

"It's gotta be a couple months. Either the township or the church in town the cemetery belongs to takes care of it." Walter lifted a pick and shovel from the bed of his truck. "Probably the township. I reckon church people would come more regular to mow in a cemetery full of their family and keep this path from getting choked up."

I shouldered another shovel, Walter took a second flashlight from the cab, and we entered the woods.

Despite almost bare branches vaulting over the path, their dense webbing still blocked most of the light from the high half-moon.

Walter led the way, and the trail quickly descended with banks growing taller on each side.

"'Valley of the Shadow,'" I murmured, and a tingle of excitement quickened my steps.

"What makes you think the treasure's in the cemetery?" said Walter.

"Well, it was an easy place for Cyrus to bury it. No one comes here except to take care of the graves." I described the contempt Cyrus had had for Christians and that he might have buried the treasure in a spot connected to the words "knight," "pilgrim," "shadow," "shade," or "ride boldly." Maybe even "gallant."

"How come finding the treasure is gonna prove Jack didn't kill that woman?"

"Because it'll prove Old Mr. Morley had a motive to kill Lyra." I pushed monkey brains—they really did look like decaying brains rather than an orange, even if you put "osage" with it—out of our path with the shovel. "I assumed, along with everybody else, that if Lyra faked the second clue, somebody had hired her to trick Old Mr. Morley. One of the heirs wanted to send him on a wild goose chase while they searched here. But it works the other way too. Old Mr. Morley hired Lyra to fool the other heirs. When he was in the trailer with Lyra after the séance, he let the second book with the second clue fall open, and Dad saw the note. When you picked up his book after you ran into him, Old Mr. Morley didn't go psycho like he did when Serenity Stone grabbed the first book." I told him about the incident at the library.

"My friend Devon swears none of the last pages were missing from the first book as of the first Friday in October. So Old Mr. Morley tore it out. He must have been confident no one, including his son, had handled The Book enough to notice whether the last page was missing. He wrote the second note and bought the second volume to the set. He and Lyra buried it. She pretended to discover it, and then he killed her so she couldn't tell anybody the clue was fake."

Walter stomped along beside me. "So he hired that psychic woman to kill her."

My stomach clenched. "I think that was his plan all along. Old Mr.

Morley is so obsessed with finding the treasure that he had to keep Lyra from telling about the fake clue."

A thick carpet of wet leaves muffled our steps as we pushed deeper into the black woods.

I said, "Then Old Mr. Morley stole Alex's phone and placed it by the body. But the bear dislodged it, ruining that frame. He also planted a copy of the poem in Lyra's purse with letters marked off." I told Walter how Amber, Chris, and I tried to crack the code. "Chris noticed the letters were slashed like Cyrus had just picked the letters that would spell out his clue. When I knew the ripped page was fake, then the poem in the purse had to be too. Old Mr. Morley put it there so if people didn't believe Lyra had contacted his father, they'd think she cracked the code by herself, found the second clue, and did the séance to take advantage of him.

"If we find the treasure based on the first clue, that will prove the second one is fake and prove, I hope, Timothy Morley is the killer."

Walter gave a snarl of satisfaction. "With your friend bein' a witness, and if we find the treasure, no slick lawyer can get around it. Jack'll be safe."

Not a breath of wind stirred the few leaves overhead or on the honeysuckle and spice bushes that clung to the steep sides of the banks. Faint screams from The Haunting wafted to us through the mostly bare branches. Vines of crimson berries insinuated themselves along the edges of the path.

The land leveled out as the beam of my light revealed a crumbling stone chimney encircled in maple trees.

"The cemetery's to the left." Walter swung his light that way.

I screamed.

A rust-encrusted fence with a much newer metal gate couldn't hide that someone had been digging in the graveyard.

Chapter Fifty

I spun my back to the horror, my stomach lurching. "Walter, are some coffins open?" I whispered, holding the sides of my head.

"Looks like a couple of them are. What's the matter with you?" He stalked up behind me. "Nobody in there cares. Only their families would."

"I—I know." I took a quivering breath. "I—I just wasn't expecting it, but it makes sense." I turned to Walter, locking my gaze on his cinder block face. "This is why Old Mr. Morley was so angry over The Haunting. He suspected the treasure was here and wanted to look for it without any interference."

"Wonder why he didn't wait." He looked back toward the cemetery. "Everybody'll be gone by tomorrow."

"Either he did this before Dani and Alex moved in, or—" I gulped "—he's so crazy for the treasure he couldn't wait until tomorrow."

Walter moved toward the gate, leaves squishing under his heavy steps. "If he's that crazy, then he probably found the treasure already."

"If it's here."

The gate creaked, and Walter said, "You mean you ain't sure?"

"No. I said this was the easiest place to look. There's a better place, but I don't know how easy it'll be to locate."

Walter stomped around the cemetery, muttering. Taking deep breaths, I focused on the quiet black of the sky. The half-moon peeked through the spidery fingers of the trees like a sly eye.

Walter's heavy steps returned to me.

"There are two coffins he busted into. The names on the graves are Goldie Hall and Dirk Poels. I reckon he picked Goldie 'cause he's looking for treasure. Don't get the other."

"Did you say Poe?"

"No, Poels." He spelled it.

"I bet it was so close to Poe that he dug it up." I moved back up the trail. "We'll check the most likely place for Cyrus to have buried the treasure before we hunt any more in—in there."

"Where's that?"

"Where your dad and his siblings strung him up."

The flashlight caught a malicious glitter in his deep-set eyes. "How you figure that?"

We squished back up the path.

"For his whole life, Cyrus took revenge on people who crossed him. In a cowardly way, so no one could prove he was behind it. But he couldn't get revenge on your family—our family. Your dad and uncles and aunt did the one thing the police and the press and the government and even the power brokers in Hollywood couldn't do—they stopped Cyrus Morley. They exposed him for the chicken and fraud he was to the people he seriously wanted to fear him. I'm sure he loathed your dad and his siblings for it. So he showed his contempt in a spoiled brat way by burying the treasure near the trees where they hoisted him up." I looked up at him. "Do you think you can find the trees?"

Walter swung the beam of his flashlight around the banks and woods crowding the path. "We'll go back to the head of the trail and walk it like I did when I come with my dad. I'll find 'em. They was two oaks, and one's got a big burl on it."

We went back to the gap that led to the road, and then, walking slowly, retraced our steps.

Walter's grizzled head swiveled back and forth with his flashlight. "It was on the left."

The banks grew taller again. I studied every tree on the left, but I could only identify trees if they still held leaves.

The air was too still. No voices reached us, not even a murmur. Halloween itself seemed to hold its breath to see what Walter and I would find.

Walter gave a satisfied growl and hiked up a bank. "That's them." He slipped back down to the path, and cussing, struggled up to level ground.

I climbed ahead of him and held out my hand, but he ignored it.

Reaching the top of the bank, he panted and pointed. "See the burl?"

Two gigantic trees, one with an enormous bulge several feet above the ground, stood half a dozen yards from us. Their canopies must have been thick because the ground beneath them, about twelve feet from trunk to trunk, was free of any understory shrubs or bushes.

"If it's buried here," I said, "Cyrus had to leave some kind of sign tied to the poem."

Walter wandered around the area, poking the ground with his shovel. "You said it'd have something to do with a knight or a pilgrim?"

"Or 'shade,' 'shadow,' 'gallant,' or 'riding boldly.'" I studied the smeared colors of the fallen leaves on the muddy ground. "After seventy years, it probably isn't here. I guess we have to dig up all the ground between the trees."

"Maybe not." Walter aimed his flashlight at a tree beyond the oaks. "There's that."

I followed the light. "The maple tree?"

"What's growing on it." Walter crossed the open ground and lifted a vine with one spike of his pick. "Bittersweet nightshade."

I mouthed the last word, staring at the scarlet berries. "But we can't know if it was here seventy years ago."

"Why wouldn't it be?"

Scarlet berries ... "Walter! Does nightshade go by another name around here? Like osage oranges are also called monkey brains."

"I heard my dad call it scarletberry."

I bounced on my toes. "The priest who tried to rescue Cyrus broke his ankle getting tangled up in vines of scarletberry. So it was growing here seventy years ago. Maybe Cyrus planted it over the spot where he buried the treasure."

"If he wanted it to stay where he planted it, he had to put up a stake. If it's made of metal, and nobody moved it, it might have lasted." Walter poked the ground in the center between the two oaks with the tip of his shovel, then dug into the leaves and dirt.

We hadn't dug more than a couple inches when my shovel uncovered a brittle, metal trellis about three feet high and a foot wide.

Walter and I exchanged triumphant grins.

I tried to lift the trellis, but the metal crumbled to pieces. We cleared it away and dug with fresh energy.

Clods of mud flew out of the sheet of light laid by our two flashlights. The illumination highlighted the lower edges of Walter's face, making it look sinister. If anyone stumbled across us, they'd think we were grave robbers, lost from another century.

We removed a few more inches of dirt, and I leaned on my shovel, catching my breath.

Twigs snapped to my right.

"Who's there?" I snatched up a flashlight.

Walter turned around. "You better come out."

My beam swept the woods, revealing only thick tree trunks and thickets of honeysuckle with vines of nightshade snaking through them.

We returned to our work, and in a few minutes, Walter's shovel clunked against something metallic.

He gave me another fierce grin.

Using the tips of our shovels, we scraped away dirt.

An old-fashioned metal lunch box with a crack in it stared at light for the first time in seventy years.

Kneeling, I lifted it with both hands in case the metal was fragile.

"There's another one underneath it," said Walter.

Carefully, I laid the first one aside and reached in for the second. My fingers brushed against cold metal. "There's another box, buried right next to this one."

"We'll have to make the hole bigger and see how many there are."

Walter pushed on the shovel with his cracked boot. "You go get Claire."

I lifted out the second box. "Let's see what's in—"

A figure burst out of a honeysuckle thicket, swinging something long.

Wielding his shovel like a sword, Walter blocked the long thing. The flashlight revealed it was pruning shears and lit up the rage on Jack's sharp face.

I held my shovel across my body as Jack skidded in the slick leaves.

Walter said, "How'd you get here? Did you follow me? You had to still be at the house—"

Jack swung the shears at Walter. He blocked them again, but the impact threw my great-grandfather off balance, and he went down on one knee.

Releasing an ugly chuckle, Jack flung the shears at Walter's head.

I threw out my shovel, catching the shears inches from Walter's ear.

Snarling, Jack lowered his shoulder and slammed into me, knocking the shovel out of my hands and the air out of me as I landed on a lunch box, which burst.

Straddling me, Jack raised the shears.

Digging in with my heels, I sucked in what air I could, pivoted my hips, and hurled him off.

I rolled away from Jack, expecting a stab of pain any second. Twisting onto the balls of my feet, I scanned the area for the next attack.

Jack lunged for the shears he'd dropped by the hole, but Walter stomped on them.

Jack rocked back in a crouch.

"You're an idiot," Walter said between pants. "Us finding this treasure proves you didn't kill that woman. Then you gotta assault Mal's daughter. You didn't clear out of my place like I told you to after you gave me them tickets."

"I was hungry." Jack placed his hands on the ground, his gaze never leaving Walter.

I picked up my shovel.

Walter went on, "You saw me get the shovels and picks and then you went to wherever you hid your van and followed me."

"Good guess, huh?" Jack looked ready to pounce.

Walter kicked the shears away. "Don't you try nothin', boy."

"Don't any of you try anything," said a brittle voice.

I whirled around.

Timothy Morley stood down on the path with a gun trained on us.

Chapter Fifty-One

"Good job, Jack." Walter turned around, stepping forward. "If you hadn't attacked us, we'd've heard this guy."

"I said don't move." Grabbing a handful of honeysuckle branches, Timothy pulled himself up to the flat ground where we'd been digging.

"You two, get behind me." Walter took another step toward Timothy. "You fire that gun, pal, and you'll have security back here in no time. And my granddaughter's in charge of it."

On all fours, Jack inched back from the hole.

What was Walter planning to do? My palms wetted the handle of my shovel. Too much was happening too fast.

"Your granddaughter's head of security?" Timothy's shriveled lips puckered. "She's the sister of the sheriff."

"That's right. And this here's his daughter. And I'm his grandpa. You tangle with us, and you'll have every county cop raining down on you." Walter moved forward again.

Timothy backed up. "I will shoot. Drop the shovel."

"Better think that over. Morleys are oh and three going up against Malinowskis."

Timothy's eyes narrowed. "What does that mean?"

Walter released a muted snarl. "I got a look at that book of yours. We found the treasure. And my dad strung up your dad."

"What?" Timothy gasped, his gun lowering.

"Run!" Walter swung his shovel.

Jack shot into the woods as I lurched forward.

Timothy leaped clear of the shovel.

And into Carrie's open arms. She flung one around his scrawny neck while yanking the gun from his hand.

"No!" Timothy screamed, twisting against the arm around his throat. "It's mine! The treasure's mine!"

Carrie released him. "Stay right there, Mr. Morley. I'm placing you under citizen's arrest for threatening these people with a gun until the police come."

I released an explosive breath, dropping my shovel. Dad would have to arrest him for more than that, but I didn't want to share my proof in front of Timothy.

Raising on her toes, Carrie looked behind us. "I heard Jack's voice.

Where is he?"

"He took off." I lifted a runaway hank of hair from my forehead. "He attacked Walter and me. To get the treasure."

"Why am I not surprised?"

"But it's mine." Timothy trembled like seizures gripped him. "No one has worked harder than I have to find the treasure."

"But you didn't find it," said Walter. "We did. Rae, open that first box and see if there's—"

"No!" Timothy lunged forward and fell on top of the hole. "It's mine. All of it!"

Carrie came over to me. "He's nuts. I have his gun, and he couldn't be sure I wouldn't use it. Walter, you're nuts too, attacking an armed man with a shovel."

"He moved faster'n I counted on."

As Timothy scrabbled in the hole, I crouched beside the broken lunch box. Dark grains, fine like sugar, coated the corroded metal.

"Dust," whispered Timothy, staring at the contents of the second box.

I rubbed the dust between my fingers. "It feels more like sand."

"This can't be right." Timothy flung away the box he'd opened.

A glint of shiny metal caught my attention. I brushed the sooty grains from it and lifted a silver earring. "The jewels have been removed from the settings." My fingers froze. I knew exactly what the grains were.

"That's my mother's." Timothy stared at the earring dangling from my fingers. He charged me.

Carrie pushed him back with her foot, toppling him backward. She took the earring from me and tossed it to him. "Here."

I picked up the lid of the broken box to look for more jewelry and noticed white paint on the inside surface. "There's writing on the lid."

I got to my feet, and Walter, Carrie, and I peered at the faded words.

I read out loud, "'For dust thou art, and unto dust shalt thou return,'" I looked to my relatives. "Cyrus ground up the jewels. He stripped the jewels from their settings and probably used the cash he had with him to buy more jewels."

"Ground them up?" Timothy watched the earring turn in his hand like he was hypnotized.

"Why didn't he grind up the earring?" said Walter.

"Well," I said, "since it's in the top box, I think Cyrus left it so any heir wouldn't doubt what the dust is. And they wouldn't doubt how much he hated them."

For a moment, no one spoke, staring at the dust, as Timothy dug in the hole with his hands. This was all crazy. The amount of effort Cyrus exerted to exact his revenge—I brushed my fingers together to clean them of the dust. They suddenly felt filthy.

Walter said, "Why'd you come back here, Carrie?"

"Amber notified me." Carrie's gaze never moved from Timothy. "Sometime after you left, Rae, Amber saw the dark blue van that Claire and the guys own drive by on the road. She assumed Jesse had come to work late. When they got a break in the customers, Amber asked Claire why Jesse hadn't arrived at opening. When Claire said he had, as far as she knew, Amber told her she'd seen the van. Claire said Jack took the van the night Amber found Lyra's body and has had it ever since. Amber called me, explained where you and Walter had gone, and said Jack's presence might be connected to it. So I came here as fast as I could."

"Amber and you saved the day," I said.

Carrie grinned. "You'll have to tell her that."

"Nothing but dust." Timothy let the grains fall from his spreading fingers into a third lunch box he had unearthed from the hole.

"Rae, go call Mal," said Carrie.

Walter looked down at me. "I reckon you think you have to press charges against Jack."

"Walter, he's dangerous. He didn't care if he stabbed you or me," I said.

"Jack tried to stab you?" Carrie's voice rose, but her attention never left Timothy.

"He didn't have much time, but he might have." My strength seemed to vanish, and my voice sounded elderly. "Be careful with Old Mr. Morley, Carrie. I can't tell you the details, but—"

"Nothing but dust," Timothy said in a sing-song that set my nerves on guard. He tossed two handfuls of dust into the air. "Nothing but dust. All my years and years and years of work. All my planning. Hiring that woman, doing the séance, killing that woman, framing Alex—"

Walter sucked in a breath as my jaw fell, and Carrie said, "What?"

"He's the killer." I watched Timothy throw more dust in the air.

Thrusting the gun into Walter's hand, Carrie whipped out her phone and squatted by the hole. "What woman did you kill, Mr. Morley?"

With wide eyes I wasn't sure could perceive much reality, Timothy looked straight at Carrie's phone. "That stupid woman who said she could contact my father. She knew I fabricated the second clue, so I had to kill her. No one could know. No one. I had to have time, time to find the treasure. And I did. But it isn't a treasure. But it is. But it isn't."

He laughed, high and scratchy, rocking where he sat in the dirt.

Her phone still recording, Carrie said, "Tell me about the fake clue, Mr. Morley."

But Timothy didn't seem to hear her, rocking and laughing and tossing dust.

Carrie said quietly, "Go, Rae."

Walter handed me his keys, watching Timothy through a squint.

I fumbled for them, unable to tear my gaze from the man in the hole. Then I hiked down the bank to the path and followed it toward the road, listening to a madman laugh at the hooded moon.

Chapter Fifty-Two

When I came out of the woods, a compact BMW glinted in the moonlight next to Walter's heap. Timothy must have noticed Walter's truck while driving by, and being paranoid because someone parked by the path to the cemetery, stopped to investigate.

I shuddered, squishing through the moist grass.

His laughter skittered up to the black sky.

I followed the road back to The Haunting. I didn't pass Jack's van, so maybe he'd parked somewhere more secluded. As I turned onto the drive, Cyrus Morley leered down on me from the banner, and a horrible weight draped over me like a lead shroud.

He'd won. Even though we found the inheritance, his game had led his family to fighting and murder. He'd be delighted a great-grandson had attempted assault to get his hands on the treasure. And his son had committed murder, tried to frame his grandson, and gone mad..

Marie and Rebecca had both been right. It was a fool's game, and Cyrus was a fiend.

I glanced at the lines winding to the ticket booth. Amber and Claire had to be dying to know what had happened, but I had to call Dad first.

I parked by the biggest tent and dragged my feet to the home. The shell of the stone house perched like an evil creature. The spotlight inside made the empty windows blaze like evil eyes watching the people below. Now that I knew the depths of depravity of the man who'd built it, I couldn't ever feel the same about the place where Dad and I had found each other

Dad answered after one ring. "Anything wrong, Rae?"

"Yes and no." I explained what I'd figured out about the torn page and Lyra's copy of the poem. When I got to uncovering the treasure, I said quickly, "Jack attacked me and Walter, but we're good."

"What do you mean?" Dad's voice rose to ear-splitting decibels. "How did Jack attack you and Walter?"

I described the fight and hurried on to Timothy's confession. "Dad, he went crazy. Right in front of us."

On the dark field below, the costumed customers drifted up the road. Toward the path to the church. Had word spread already?

I said, "Carrie got his confession on her phone. Is that admissible?"

"If it's obvious the man has lost his mind, a clever lawyer might get it thrown out. But with the clues you pieced together, and Devon's testimony, and the proof I got on the camera card, we'll have a strong case without it."

Before I could ask, Dad said, "One of the cards has one photo of Morley Sr. carrying a satchel, which must have held the knife and the weapon he hit Ms. Vex with. The time on it is 3:11 a.m. the morning of the murder. He told me when he left Lyra in the trailer at 2, he went straight to the lodge. So he lied, and he's in the right place at the right time. I'd already issued a bulletin for Morley Sr. to be picked up. I'll issue another one for Jack and tell—I'm assuming you're pressing charges against Jack."

"Walter doesn't want me to, but I am. Jack might have stopped at murder, but he definitely didn't care if he hurt us."

"I'm glad you're okay, kiddo," Dad said in a grave voice. "Dispatch will send an ambulance. I'll be there in eighteen minutes."

I swiped off and started back toward Walter's truck when Chris popped into my mind.

Would he worry when he heard over his radio about an ambulance being sent to The Haunting? He had to know I was working. He'd been concerned when he thought there'd been a bear attack. But we were still together then.

My fingers hovered over my phone. Then I typed, "No matter what you hear about The Haunting I'm fine."

The flap of the tent next to me slapped back, making me jump.

Alex emerged. "Don't worry. I won't murder you."

"Alex," I said with a strained sigh, "you'd better come with me."

~~~~~

"I can't believe it." Standing beside the oak tree with the burl, Alex stared down the path where the paramedics had taken Timothy. "My father planned to murder that woman so no one else could find the treasure." He looked at Dad with wide eyes. "It's murder one."

"That will be the charge," said Dad. "If your father's competent to stand trial." His voice grew quiet. "That's very much in doubt now."

"Fourteen." Walter handed me a lunch box from the hole. "That's the last one."

After the paramedics had removed Timothy, Walter and I had finished excavating the hole.

"Why lunch boxes?" said Alex.

"Cyrus was dying of cancer," I said. "Making a lot of trips with lightweight boxes had to be easier for him than carrying a few heavy ones."

"My own father framed me." Alex pushed both hands through his bronze hair.

"Maybe he thought he was stealing Dani's phone." I poured all the
~~~~~

kindness I could into my words. "A murder charge against her would have removed an heir and protected him."

"When he found out it was mine," Alex's voice turned bitter, "he kept quiet because it would accomplish the same purpose."

I said, "Dad, can I bring Claire, Jesse, and Amber back? They said they'd wait at the road until Old Mr. Morley was gone."

"Go ahead. Ask Carrie if she needs help with the crowd."

I walked to the head of the trail.

Carrie and her security team guarded the entrance from the massing horde of curiosity seekers. Under the half-moon light, vehicles glittered up and down both sides of the road. The amount of cars represented a gigantic crowd, and the area should have been as noisy as a football stadium on Friday night, but the crowd was subdued, talking in murmurs and whispers, like at viewing hours at a funeral home. Seeing the condition Timothy was in could sober anyone.

I said to Carrie, "Dad wants to know if you need help holding people back."

"Not yet." Carrie swept the crowd with a glare she must have perfected as a deputy marshal.

Spotting my cousins, I waved them over to me.

The crowd came to life, protesting, and Carrie picked up a battery-powered megaphone. "They're related to the Morleys," she barked into the mike. "Back down."

As we entered the tunnel-like trail, Claire, Jesse, and Amber stuck close to me, using their phones to light the way. No one said a word.

When we hiked up the bank to the oak trees, now bathed in bright lights Dad carried in his SUV, my cousins pulled away from me. The illumination seemed to dissolve some of their anxiety.

"None of the other boxes have anything but dust." Dad shut the lid to one of them.

"You wasn't expectin' nothin' different, was you?" Walter wiped grimy hands on his jeans.

The seven of us surrounded the hole, and Amber and Jesse squatted, pinching some grains.

"Grand-mere said Cyrus only hid the inheritance to drive his family mad." Alex looked down the trail again. "He succeeded."

Claire said in a hushed voice, "I'm real sorry about your dad." She raised her chin. "Mine wasn't no good, either. He was a grifter and cheated on my mom."

Jesse rubbed the grains between his fingers. "My dad hit my mom. He died before he got around to Jack and me."

"You all are better off without them." Walter scraped mud off a shovel with his boot.

His thin frame slumped, Alex said, "Sheriff, I need the address of the hospital."

"I still recommend someone driving you," said Dad. "And someone should stay with you here until you can go home. Even if you aren't close to your father, this must be a terrible shock."

"I told you." Alex bit off the words. "I only have two ex-wives, a law firm, and a business partner who is very likely, right now, hawking tickets so people can come down here and gawk, especially at the open graves." He trudged down the bank.

Dad turned to Claire and Jesse, raising his eyebrows.

Claire's small eyes leaped open. "Alex wouldn't want us to drive him."

"Why not?" said Dad. "You're family."

Getting to his feet, Jesse held out his sinewy arms. "He drives a Range Rover. He wouldn't want a dumb hick driving it."

Alex called from the trail, "I don't see any of those here." He broke into a brittle smile. "I could use the company."

Claire and Jesse exchanged looks, and Claire nodded. "I'll call Mama and tell her what we're doing."

Jesse started down the bank to Alex, then turned. "What do we do with the boxes?"

"Leave 'em." Walter lifted the pick. "They're nothin'."

"This isn't fair." The sentence burst from Alex. "You two girls solved the riddle. You should get something. You solved it for your cousins, and they should get something." He swallowed like it hurt. "I wish I wasn't a Morley."

Jesse and Dad picked up the lamps, and Amber and I gathered the shovels and flashlights.

I began to walk away from the hole, but Walter said, "I gotta talk to you, Rae."

"What about?" Dad had stopped on the trail with Amber as Alex, Jesse, and Claire moved ahead.

"Am I talkin' to you?" Walter said in a snarl.

"It's okay, Dad." I knew when I'd told Walter I was pressing charges against Jack that he'd bring up the subject again.

Walter stepped close, but not like he was trying to intimidate me. He lowered his head. "It'd hurt Lily, seein' Jack in jail. I can fix him."

Ouch. I hadn't expected that argument, but I went ahead with my planned response. "Walter, you want Malinowskis to look out for each other. Jack doesn't care about anybody but himself. He doesn't deserve your protection."

Walter opened his mouth, but I rushed on. "Aunt Lily will be upset, but she might be secretly relieved. I know Claire and Jesse would love living in a Jack-free home."

Our eyes met, Walter's scanning mine.

"Oh, shoot." I slapped my forehead. "I forgot to thank you for rescuing me from Jack. I don't know what he would have done to me if you hadn't stomped on those shears."

His block of a face didn't alter its searching expression. "You're welcome." He hiked down the bank.

With a shovel on my shoulder, I joined Dad and Amber on the path.

Walter turned to me. "Twenty years ago, you would've been good to have in a bar fight." He stalked up the trail.

I watched the night swallow him, blinking. "I think Walter just thanked me. For stopping Jack from hitting him with the shears." I blinked again. "I think."

Dad said, "That's an accurate translation."

Heading up the path, he transferred the lamp to his left hand and placed his right arm around Amber's shoulders. "You saved the day, kiddo. Contacting Carrie was way more effective than checking on Walter and Rae yourself."

"Thanks, Uncle Mal," Amber said with a tired smile. "I told you I've learned my lesson. I'm glad I finally did something right." Her forehead furrowed. "I guess I did see a bear dragging Lyra's body. Old Mr. Morley didn't have a reason to wear a costume and move the body."

"Thank the Lord, your screams scared it off," said Dad. "And scared it so much that it hasn't come back."

Someone with a bobbing flashlight ran down the trail, past Walter.

"Rae." Chris jogged up to us. "I got your text. A call kept me tied up until now."

"You helped crack the case." My grin grew for no good reason that I could think of.

As we walked beneath the lattice of black branches, I explained what I'd figured out from his observation. My fingers longed to lace with his.

Chris's eyes widened so much that I couldn't call them narrow for once. "You figured all that out, and you still think you can't succeed in college?"

"Doesn't make sense, does it?" said Dad.

As a blush warmed my cheeks, I muttered, "I don't need to be tag-teamed."

The four of us left the woods, entering the small half circle of grass kept clear of onlookers by Carrie and her security staff.

Blaring through the megaphone, she said, "Get back!"

Walter and Claire got into his truck while Jesse vaulted into the bed. Alex hesitated a couple seconds, then climbed into the cab of the heap.

Dad took the mike from his sister. "There's nothing to see, public.

Cyrus Morley left fourteen boxes of ground up jewels. There's no treasure. Please leave. Anyone found on this part of the property, especially in the graveyard, after fifteen minutes will be trespassing."

Grumbles rippled through the crowd, but it began to disperse.

Chris touched my arm and stepped back into the shelter of the trees. "I'm very glad you're safe."

I watched his face. "It's nice you came to check on me after ... after everything."

He bent his head, smoothing his moustache. "I've been thinking a lot. Especially today."

My heart pressed against my sternum, and I gritted my teeth.

Please, Father, let him tell me what he's hiding.

"Sheriff, you should do something," someone said out by the road.

Scowling, Chris said, "Excuse me."

He joined Dad where he stood planted with the security team, blocking access to the trail.

Amber appeared at my side. "I think Chris coming to see if you're okay is a good sign."

I shrugged, trying to squash the eagerness his words had stirred up.

The bigfoot hunter I'd waited on a few days ago said to Dad, "Somebody's down in the woods along this side of the road here, pretending to be bigfoot."

"We told him to come out," said the woman, still dressed in camo, who accompanied him before, "but he wouldn't, and now a bunch of teenagers are throwing rocks into the woods, and there'll probably be a fight."

"Show me," said Dad.

He and Chris wove through the thinning crowd with the man leading the way.

Amber whipped around to me. "Maybe I did see somebody in a costume, somebody pretending to be bigfoot. And he's pretending now. Maybe Kyle Garrison."

"But why would he do that if he didn't kill Lyra?"

Her lips protruded in thought. "He'd gotten to know her. Maybe there was something on her that pointed to him, and he thought the police would think he was her killer."

"I ... guess that's possible. But why would he come back tonight?"

The woman bigfoot hunter pulled her phone from her vest. "And, Sheriff, tell whoever it is they're overdoing the odor. Ohio bigfoots don't stink like skunk apes in the South."

Every cell in me turned to ice, and Amber sank her nails through my jean jacket.

We catapulted into a run.

"Dad, Chris, it's the bear!"

"Uncle Mal, don't get close!"

We dodged several bunches of people and saw in the beams of their flashlights Dad and Chris talking to four teens.

"It's the bear!" Amber and I shouted together.

Dad turned in our direction as one boy chucked a rock into the woods behind him.

A roar exploded the night, and something dark erupted from a pawpaw thicket.

Screams pierced the roar, and the crowd stampeded.

The bear swiped at Chris as he drew his gun.

"No!" I raced toward him.

He fell flat on the ground.

My heart thudding, I crashed into one fleeing person after another.

Dad fired two shots.

I dropped to my knees beside Chris.

The bear slammed Dad to the ground and smothered him.

Chapter Fifty-Three

"Dad!" I tried to leap to my feet, but an iron grip caught my arm.

"My gun." Chris squeezed the words out. "I dropped it. Get it."

I glanced about wildly. In the dark, with people racing by me, how could I find it?

Amber ran past me. Straight for the bear that covered Dad.

"Amber!" I screamed.

Braking at the bear, Amber brought both hands together in front of her in a gesture that only meant one thing.

BAM!

A gunshot rocked my cousin back on her heels and threw her clasped hands over her head.

"Help me over to her." Chris gripped my shoulder.

With my arm wrapped around his back, I half-pulled Chris toward Amber as she lined up a second shot.

BAM!

Amber reared back again.

The bear's head lay on Dad's chest as he struggled underneath the huge, black body. "Get-this-thing-off-**me**!"

Please don't let him die, Father.

Chris put his hand over Amber's wrists, making her yelp.

I dropped next to Dad.

Dad fought under the bear's bulk. "Get it off!"

Gripping Dad under his shoulders, I pulled.

Amber almost fell on top of me, crying, "Don't die, Uncle Mal. Don't die."

With his gun pointed at the bear, Chris pushed it with his foot, and his supporting knee buckled. "It's dead."

I released Dad, grabbed Amber by the hand, and pulled her to the bear's back. "We'll roll it off," I said between pants.

Carrie appeared out of nowhere, along with the two other security guys, and on our knees, the five of us pushed on the bear's broad back.

Let Dad live, Father. Let him live.

Groaning, grunting, we lifted the dead weight of the bear off Dad.

The second he was free, Dad scuttled away from the carcass, using his elbows and heels.

"What're you doing?" Carrie yelled. "You'll tear open your wounds."

We dropped the body on the ground.

Hot tears stinging my eyes, I fumbled for my phone and kneeled at Dad's shoulder. "Hold still until I get a light."

Blood streaked his black shirt.

Oh, Father, not Dad too. My throat sealed off.

"I don't think I'm hurt," Dad said in a dull voice. "Kincaid went down. Where is he?" He sat up, craning his neck.

"I'm fine, Mal," Chris said as Carrie yelled again, "Mal, quit moving."

Amber sobbed on Dad's other shoulder. "Don't die. Please don't die."

I glanced from Dad to Chris.

Alone, Chris sat on the ground with his left leg stretched out and his right bent under him. Blood glistened on his left thigh.

"It clawed you, Chris?" I didn't mean to, but it came out in a scream.

"Not badly." Chris's deep voice was steady. "It only stings slightly."

Dad started to rise. "Kincaid, are you sure you aren't—"

Carrie shoved her older brother back on his butt. "Let me check you out. Rae, take care of Chris.

"I-uh-okay." I kissed Dad on his temple and crawled to Chris.

My flashlight revealed five slashes in his left pant leg, blood oozing through them. I said, "I'll get the first-aid kit from your cruiser and drive you to the hospital."

"Um ... if you want to." Chris fished the keys from a pocket of his shirt.

"You're not hurt," Carrie said, her voice hushed.

She and Amber had helped Dad remove the black shirt of his uniform, and he sat in the phone's illumination in his white t-shirt, dribbled here and there with blood. Bear blood, apparently.

"There's not a mark on you, Mal." Carrie sat back on her heels, staring wide-eyed at her big brother. "How can that be?"

Dad held his head. "I hit it with the two shots I fired. It had to be dying when it hit me."

Amber said between bawls, "So you weren't in any danger?"

"Oh, no. I felt it breathe ..." Dad shuddered "... on me. If you hadn't run up, it might've ... done damage before it died." He dropped his hands. "Holy smoke, Hank and Jeanine are gonna kill me."

"Why?" Carrie said. "They're fans of the bear?"

"I told them it was safe for their daughter to work here." His eyes swung to Amber's tear-stained face, but it took them a moment to focus. "Why did you take on the bear?"

"I-I heard Chris say for somebody to get his gun, and—and I saw it, right by my feet, and—and—" fresh sobs burst from her as she threw her arms around him "—I couldn't let it get you like it did Dad!"

Dad patted her arm. "Y-y-you got some kind of guts, kiddo."

I hung my head, wiping back hair.

Thank You, thank You, thank — that really doesn't seem enough, Father.

I took the keys from Chris and climbed to my feet like I was climbing a mountain peak and ...

Dad, Chris, Carrie, Amber, the dead bear, and I were in the center of ring after ring of recording phones.

"Put those things away!" I roared, flinging out my arms.

A few people near me jumped back, but the rest just shifted their phones to me.

"I said git!" Another roar came from deep within the crowd.

Gawkers yelped and parted like something was plowing through them to the scene of the drama.

Walter emerged from between a cringing zombie and a skeleton. "Who fired them shots?" He looked over Chris, his grandchildren, and great-grandchildren. "Mal, you rescuin' bears now?"

Chapter Fifty-Four

Amber volunteered to get the first-aid kit from Chris's SUV, so I gave her the keys and stayed with him. Carrie used Dad's radio to ask Dispatch to send the game warden, and as we waited, Dad kept trying to help Carrie hold back the amateur influencers who ran their phones like this was their ticket to a viral video and fame. And she and Walter kept yelling at him to sit and rest.

I dabbed disinfectant on Chris's wounds, which didn't look deep, but I was no expert, and the light was lousy. I wrapped his thigh in long layers of bandages until blood was only seeping through the material instead of soaking it. Then Walter scared back the crowd so Amber and I could help Chris to his SUV.

Amber opened the passenger door.

Holding the top of it, Chris lowered himself into the seat.

"Stay with Dad, Amber. He's pretty shook up." I took the keys from her. "Don't you ever call yourself a coward again."

The left corner of her mouth rose. "It's funny, but I don't care. I think that's how Coral feels. Dad's okay, so she doesn't care what people say about her. Uncle Mal's okay and —" Amber gasped and ran her hands up the sides of her head, pressing her temples. "I saved my uncle from a fell beast."

"Are you all right?" I gripped my cousin's elbow. "I think it's 'fallen.' Not 'fell.'"

She clapped her forehead. "You know nothing about *The Lord of the Rings*." She clutched my arms. "Eowyn's uncle is badly injured by a Ringwraith. But she saves him from being devoured by the evil beast the Ringwraith rides on. Then she takes out the Ringwraith. Although he isn't eaten, her uncle still dies." She lowered her hands, a smile lifting her entire posture. "Mine won't."

My grin threatened to rupture cheek muscles. "No, he will not." I hurried around the hood.

Amber gasped again. "Rae," she whispered, "do you think God designed it this way?"

My hand on the latch for the driver's door, I paused. "Well ... He controls everything. He knew you needed to know what you're capable of. And you prevented the bear from hurting Dad or anybody else."

"I'm sorry for the bear. I think it was suffering. It has an awful cut on one of its rear legs."

"Maybe that's why it kept coming back here. For food. It's not nice to think about, but you probably gave it a quicker end than it would have had dying from an infection."

"God gave me what I needed when I needed it," Amber said in an awed voice.

"And you obeyed."

"I don't remember obeying. When I saw the gun, I knew I had to try to save Uncle Mal."

Tears surged again. "Thank you, Amber." I opened the driver's door.

"Mademoiselles!" Alex jogged toward us. "I'm glad I caught you." He stopped to inhale.

"I have to go." I slid behind the wheel.

"I just want to ask if you ladies think a thousand dollars is fair compensation for solving the riddle. You two deserve something."

I fell forward, against the horn, making Chris and Alex jump, and Amber planted her hands down on the hood, like she needed the support.

I stared. "Th-th-that's so nice of you. But we can't accept."

"We can't?" said Amber in a squeak.

"We're the daughter and niece of a sheriff. People in the county might think it was a bribe." Like Chief Simcox.

"Oh." Alex looked genuinely disappointed that he couldn't shell out two thousand bucks. "Does that rule apply to any member of your family?"

"I—I don't know," I said. "Who else do you want to give money to?"

"Claire and Jesse and their mother." Alex's thin lips pressed thinner. "You solved the riddle for them. They should get something. In the truck, I told them that although it wasn't much, I would give them my profits from The Haunting, around $7 to $8,000. They acted as if—"

I clutched the wheel to steady myself as Amber yelped.

Ales nodded. "Claire and Jesse acted like it was a significant amount too. Claire said it would pay for more than a year at a community college."

"Aunt Lily is the half-sister of my late grandfather," I said. "I can't see how that's a close relation. But check with my dad."

"That's very generous of you, Mr. Morley," said Chris.

My lips parted in a grin that I bet looked a whole lot like Walter's in a malicious mood. "Cyrus would hate this—his treasure hunt bringing his descendants together instead of tearing them apart. It's even better that the money's coming from exploiting his horrible reputation. He wanted people scared of him, not benefiting from him."

Alex stroked his upper lip, then his head snapped up, as if he'd made a decision. "Then The Haunting will return next year, and every year, as long as people buy tickets. I'll establish a fund for Claire and Jesse and their mother to get the profits." He broke into a fierce smile. "I'll milk Cyrus's reputation for every penny I can get out of it."

"You'll help the people of Marlin County too," I said. "It's the perfect revenge. Cyrus may come back to haunt you."

"Then you could hire him for next year." Amber broke into giggles, teetering on hysterics, and covered her mouth.

Alex said, "I'll talk to the sheriff." He bowed, in a sincere way, not like the mocking bow I'm sure Cyrus used when he introduced himself to Rebecca. "*Merci*, mademoiselles."

Amber followed him, and I put the key in the ignition. "How are you feeling?" I asked Chris.

"Still fine." He fumbled with his seat belt, trying to fasten it. "I think I just need stitches." His fingers shook as he clicked the buckle.

"Maybe a few days off, too?"

"Maybe." His smile flashed by. "You're right. From what you told me about Cyrus, benefiting his family and the people of Marlin County would be the last thing he'd want." He shifted his leg, tightening his jaw. "I hope I don't sound nosy, but do you mind telling me why Amber needed to know what she was capable of?"

Pulling onto the road, I began The Saga of the Counterfeit Coward.

~~~~~

I exceeded the speed limit when I thought I could get away with it, but I shouldn't have bothered.

The emergency room at the hospital in Zanesville overflowed with patients whose injuries were more urgent than wounds from a bear attack. At least, that was what the nurses told me. A few seemed to doubt the source of Chris's injuries until they saw his uniform and figured a cop wouldn't lie about it.

So Chris and I waited.

And waited.

While ignoring the hospital stench that hit me in waves, I had time to manage the six billion texts that had my phone pinging like Christmas bells.

> Amber: Gram and boys came. Aaron mad no bear to test alarm on. Mom and Coral here too. Mom did not kill Uncle Mal. Game warden says bear unusually large but thin. Would have died from infection in leg
>
> Devon: Are you okay? Mal says I can give him my statement tomorrow.
>
> Gram: How are you? How's Chris?
>
> Dad: What did the docs say about Chris?
>
> Amber: Coral impressed I killed bear. Very impressed.
~~~~~

Wish she had

After I asked for a third time how long we were supposed to wait, Chris said I didn't need to bother the nurses. But he mostly remained silent, shivering now and then, and smoothing his moustache.

Near midnight, a nurse pushed a wheelchair over to us.

As I helped Chris switch seats, he cocked an eyebrow at me. "Do you want to come back with me?"

"I do if you want me to."

He hesitated, then said, "I do. Very much."

As the nurse pushed him to a curtained area, my heart warmed me so much that I took off my jacket. After a nurse helped Chris onto the bed, the physician's assistant got to work.

When she snipped the thread on the last suture, she said, "That's thirty-eight. The wounds are long but not that deep. Have your primary care doctor remove these in ten days." She collected her tools and supplies. "We'll get a prescription for antibiotics and get you out of here soon." She pushed through the curtain around Chris's bed and left.

Chris pulled up his left knee, grimacing.

"Be careful," I said.

He straightened his knee. "I—I appreciate, very much, all the help you've given me tonight." He spoke to his lap. "I'm surprised after the way I've acted."

I hooked hair behind my ears. "Chris, I'll always be your friend, even if you're not ..." I brought my teeth together.

How exhausted was I to let that slip out?

Without lifting his head, Chris said, "I'm still your friend, Rae. You were right. I wasn't telling you everything, and I should have."

I remained still, not wanting to break whatever spell might be making Chris open up.

"I don't like talking about my high school years for two reasons. First, because I was abandoned there." His face betrayed a spasm of pain that didn't come from his wounds. "My family—the Moore side—got tired of dealing with me every time my mom was arrested for possession or ordered to do rehab. So they pooled their money and stuck me at St. Vincent's. It proved ideal for me, but they didn't care. They just wanted me out of their hair." Another spasm, and he rubbed his right hand on his leg. "It's embarrassing to admit."

Sparks flared in my chest. "Why? Your relatives are jerks, not you."

He slid me his smile. "The second reason..." He cleared his throat. "Your faith is vitally important to you, and I didn't know how you'd feel about a guy who—who lied about his in the past."

I didn't move a muscle.

Chris smoothed his moustache. "I told you I admired several of the priests who were my teachers. I knew it would please them if I joined the church. There were parts of church doctrine I had serious questions about, but I went ahead and became Catholic at fifteen. So I lied in church and feigned a devotion I didn't feel. I—I've always felt guilty about that. Once I graduated, I avoided church. I didn't want to perpetuate the dishonesty."

His eyes finally lifted to meet mine. "I thought you would break up with me once you knew. So I beat you to it. It was an act of cowar—"

"Don't say that word." I scooted my chair closer to his bed. "Chris, I don't care what your faith was like in the past. Since you have questions about God, church is the place to go."

His gaze bored into mine. "You're not disappointed in me?"

I suppressed a groan. Another person worried about letting others down. "No, Chris. Not at all. I appreciate you being transparent with me." I leaned toward him. "Nothing's more important than deciding what you believe about God."

The corner of his right eye crinkled. "Do you believe God tailored the encounter with the bear to meet Amber's needs?"

"Yes. A good earthly father wants to help his kids. Our Heavenly Father wouldn't do less."

"The priests at my school never talked about God like that."

I held onto the bed railing. "If you're interested, I'd like to help you figure this out. That's what a friend should do."

Chris's gaze pressed deeper. "Are we just friends?"

"Chris, you broke up with me."

He looked away.

Father, what can I say?

I needed to study the rule about Christians only marrying Christians to understand it on my own. But one thing I did know: I didn't want to disobey my Father again. I owed Him too much.

Chris said in a whisper, "That may be the biggest mistake of my life."

My heart attempted to soar to the ceiling, but I took a deep breath. "I want to be more than friends, but you need to decide what you believe first. So we can be friends, really good friends, working on an issue together. Once you've come to a decision, then we'll see what kind of a future we have together." I sat back, staring at my fingers gripping Chris's hand.

When had I taken hold of it?

I released it, but he grabbed it back, the lines of his taut face near snapping point. "One visit to your church won't do it."

"I know." I put my other hand over his. "My schedule's not exactly full. I'll wait."

His face relaxed, or as much as his fierce features ever did, but his grip strengthened.

"Back here?" Dad's powerful voice carried throughout the emergency room.

I leaped to my feet, pulled back the curtain, and found Dad and a nurse just outside it. I wrapped him in a hug as the nurse hurried away, waving a hand in front of her nose.

He stroked my hair. "I'm really okay, kiddo."

I nodded against his navy-blue thermal shirt, sniffed, and got a whiff of bear. Pulling away, I coughed.

He groaned. "I still stink, don't I? I spent a half hour scrubbing in the shower."

"I only smelled it because I'm so close." Returning to Chris's bedside, I took his hand. "Chris is coming to church with me. He's got a lot of questions about God, and I want to help him find the answers." And since he was taking my advice ... "It wouldn't hurt me to visit some of the community colleges around here, either."

Dad broke into his lit-from-within grin. "Glad to hear it for both of you. You're looking good, Kincaid, for getting mauled by a bear."

"So do you," said Chris. He looked up at me. "You won't regret your decision."

"Neither will you."

"You're both right," said Dad. "As I was parking, I got a call that highway patrol picked up Jack."

I blew out my cheeks. "That's great news. Dad, did Alex Morley talk to you about giving Aunt Lily the profits from The Haunting?"

"Yes. I told him he needs to keep me informed so I can be transparent about it. I also said he had to set up the money in a way that Aunt Lily's dishonest kids can't scare her or trick her out of it. He said Walter had already mentioned that, and he can have his lawyers set it up in several ways."

A grin spread all over my face.

You lose, Cyrus.

Dad said, "If it's okay with you, Kincaid, I'll go home with you tonight, so you can take it easy. I guess Rae will be coming too."

"For sure."

"Thanks, Mal," said Chris. "But don't you want to go home and take it easy yourself?"

"I have absolutely no intention of closing my eyes for a week." A shudder traveled from Dad's head to his heels. "So I might as well stay up and help you."

"Excuse me." The physician's assistant who'd stitched up Chris returned, holding her phone. "This is what happened to you, isn't it? When you said a bear clawed you, I didn't realize you meant ..."

She held out her phone, and I got up and stood by Dad to see it.

Despite the dark, the video clearly showed the bear bursting from the woods, clawing Chris, ramming into Dad, and —

I spun away.

"Oh, I'm sorry, honey." The PA slid her phone into a pocket.

Dad's mouth flopped open. "Did you see how many views it's had? It's only been a few hours. Did I read the hashtag right? 'Bear eats sheriff'?"

She peeked at her phone. "Yes. And that's not the only video. A ton have hit my phone and everybody else's here in Emergency, and they all have that hashtag."

Dad peered at the screen. A wide smile melted his shock, and his entire stance relaxed.

"What?" As much as I loathed that video, I had to know what had relieved Dad.

He pointed at the date at the top of the screen and said with a satisfaction that seemed to resonate from the depths of his soul, "November."

The End

DISCUSSION GUIDE

Here's a lively set of discussion questions for your book club's discussion of *A Riddle in the Lonesome October*!

The Mystery & Plot
1. **Clues and red herrings**: Which moments or details in the story made you suspect you'd cracked the treasure's location or the murderer's identity—only to be proven wrong?
2. **Book-within-a-book**: The Poe anthology plays a key role. If *you* were hiding a secret clue in a classic book, which one would you pick and why?
3. **The big switcheroo**: How did you react to the fake clue reveal? Were you surprised, or did you see it coming?

Characters & Relationships
1. **Rae's detective skills**: What's her most relatable (or most frustrating) trait as a sleuth?
2. **Unlikely allies**: Which side character (Devon, Mal, Amber, etc.) would you want as *your* partner in solving a mystery?
3. **Chris Kincaid's role**: Should Rae and Chris be partners or do you think their dynamic works better as friends?

Themes & Atmosphere
1. **Small-town spookiness**: How does the rural setting add to the story's mood? Would this mystery work in a big city?
2. **Courage**: Several characters faced different challenges in which they had to find courage. When did you face a situation that took courage? (Like overcoming a fear of heights or flying.)

Wild Cards & Personal Takes
1. **Crackpot theories**: What's your most outlandish guess about what "Beneath My Contempt" *really* meant?
2. **Poe's influence**: If you've read "The Gold Bug" or "The Purloined Letter," how do they compare to this mystery?
3. **Real-life treasure hunts**: Have you ever gone searching for something lost or legendary? (Bonus points if it ended badly!)

BONUS ACTIVITY:

- *Create your own cryptic clue* inspired by the book (e.g., hide a "treasure" in a household object and give the group a riddle to solve it).

Keep the conversation flowing with snacks themed around the book—maybe "Poe-tato chips" or "Marlin County cider"! Rae also likes Gram's pepperoni rolls and scones, honey from the family's hives, pickles, and tea, especially black tea.

Acknowledgements

Once again, I'm eager to thank all the people who helped turn an idea in my head into the book you're enjoying now. Huge thanks to —

My publisher and cover designer Tamera Kraft and my publisher and editor Michelle L. Levigne, for always having faith in my stories and encouraging me as a writer and a Christian.

Scott and Kathy Bauder, for educating me about farming in Ohio, which I find fascinating.

Laura Cobb, for informing me about how Rae could pursue a degree at a community college.

Dr. Jessica Barnett, for answering my medical questions.

Debra Guyette, for helping me name my obnoxious bigfoot hunter, Kyle Garrison.

My neighbor, Pat Getha, for answering my questions about horses.

Dave Butler, for always being willing to help me with questions about law enforcement.

Kellen Freeman and Alexis Singleton, at The Maker's Studio, for getting my graphics to look so sharp.

My sister, Ellyn Boynton, and my niece, Anna Boynton, for being my alpha readers and giving me such helpful, and sometimes, challenging feedback as I wrote the first draft. Your suggestions were inspiring.

M. Liz Boyle, Kip Kreager, Shelley Vanderzee, and Theresa Van Meter, for being my beta readers and providing the comments that gave my manuscript the polish it needed. Also, for pointing out logic problems. Like the fact I'd forgotten to mention what part of Hank's leg was broken. I saw it in my head and forgot readers can't read that.

My brother-in-law, Dr. Mark Boynton and my massage therapist Cheri Clem, for keeping my shoulder, neck, and back in writing shape.

To my husband Bill and boys, Will and Cole, and my extended family, for supporting me and inspiring me. These mysteries wouldn't be what they are without you.

To my Heavenly Father, for gracing me with a gift that is so enjoyable and leads me into a deeper relationship with Him.

I pray this book does the same for you.

Books Used for Research

Bushcraft First Aid: a Field Guide to Wilderness Emergency Care by Dave Canterbury and Jason A. Hunt, Ph. D.

Monster Trek: the Obsessive Search for Bigfoot by Joe Gisondi

Living Ready Pocket Manual: Fundamentals for Survival by James Hubbard

Abominable Science! Origins of Yeti, Nessie and Other Famous Cryptids by Daniel Loxton

Wildflowers of Ohio: Field Guide by Stan Tekiela

The Complete Stories and Poems of Edgar Allan Poe, editors Arthur Hobson Quinn and Edward Hayes O'Neil

Standing in the Shadows: Bigfoot Stories from Southeastern Ohio by Doug Waller

About the Author

JPC Allen started her writing career in second grade with an homage to Scooby Doo, and she's been tracking down mysteries ever since. The first novel in her Rae Riley Mysteries series, *A Shadow on the Snow*, won first place in the ACFW KidLit contest for YA fiction in 2024. *A Storm of Doubts*, her second novel, came in second for YA fiction at the Selah Awards in 2025. Online, she offers tips and prompts to ignite the creative spark in every kind of writer. She also leads workshops for tweens, teens, and adult, encouraging them to discover the adventure of writing. Coming from a long line of Mountaineers, she's a life-long Buckeye. Follow her to her next mystery at www.facebook.com/JPCAllenWrites/, www.instagram.com/jpcallenwrites/, www.bookbub.com/profile/jpc-allen, and www.goodreads.com/author/show/18623122.JPC_Allen.

THANK YOU!

Thank you for reading this book from Mt. Zion Ridge Press.

If you enjoyed the experience, learned something, gained a new perspective, or made new friends through story, could you do us a favor and write a review on Goodreads or wherever you bought the book?

Thanks! We and our authors appreciate it.

We invite you to visit our website, MtZionRidgePress.com, and explore other titles in fiction and non-fiction. We always have something coming up that's new and off the beaten path.

And please check out our podcast, **Books on the Ridge,** where we chat with our authors and give them a chance to share what was in their hearts while they wrote their book, as well as fun anecdotes and glimpses into their lives and experiences and the writing process. And we always discuss a very important topic: *Tea!*

You can listen to the podcast on our website or find it at most of the usual places where podcasts are available online. Please subscribe so you don't miss a single episode!

Thanks for reading. We hope you come back soon!